THE LIGHT BEARER

A Humorous Fantasy Novel

THE WESTERN LANDS AND ALL THAT REALLY MATTERS

BOOK III

ANDREW EINSPRUCH

Cover design by Maria Spada of Maria Spada Design.

Editing by Vanessa of Red Dot Scribble.

Proofreading by Abigail of Bothersome Words.

Layout by Andrew Einspruch of Wild Pure Heart.

ISBN: 978-0-980627-26-8

DEDICATION

To Billie and Tamsin

Everything of greatest value that I've learned, I've learned from you.

And to my parents, Norman and Edith Einspruch

For your love and support.

PROLOGUE

The horse lay on his side, eyes rolled back against the midday sun, tongue lolling on the ashen, snow-flecked ground near an active lava flow. He was Nergüi Unbenannt Nimetuseta, khan of the Central Ranges, and his legs twitched, hinting at the swirling sights, sounds, and signs of the Purity. His painted body's positioning carefully balanced all that was sacred to the Us—proximity to fire and earth, exposure to water and air.

At a respectful distance sat the dream wife, the only human permitted to live among the Us. She'd administered the mixture of vision herbs that connected the horse to the Purity. Now she held space, sitting cross-legged on a blanket, cradling a ready bowl of water.

Next to her, less still, was the new herd rememberer, who gave a small shake of his mane. "Dream Wife, how long until His Alacrity speaks?" he whispered.

The dream wife turned her head to face him as if roused from her own connection to the divine. "The Purity does not see time like the Us, Herd Rememberer. The khan will speak when the khan speaks."

Hours passed, marked by little. The khan panted and sweated, occasionally swallowing some of the ash, dirt, and snow sticking to his tongue.

Night crept in, and the snow began to settle. The herd rememberer shifted a few weak lengths closer to the warmth of the nearby lava flume, earning a disapproving glare from the dream wife.

The full moon reached the top of the sky and, as if on cue, the khan jolted upright with a loud "Huuuuh!"

Legs scrabbling, he stood, bad leg buckling, sweat dripping from his coat. The dream wife also stood. She walked forward in silence, offering the water bowl. The khan slurped, sluiced, and dribbled, clearing his mouth. She threw her rug over him, knowing the shivers would soon start.

The herd rememberer was unsure whether to stand or stay down, so he didn't quite do either. His forelegs stretched awkwardly forward, but he did not heave upward.

The khan, his voice thick from his connection to the Purity, said, "We must prepare to receive the Light Bearer."

"The Light Bearer?" asked the herd rememberer. "Khan Nergüi, I thought you gave no truck to myths." Too late, he realized his mistake. One never questioned the khan's pronouncements from the Purity. Plus, the herd rememberer's role was to remember, not comment. "My apologies, Your Alacrity. Forgive me."

The khan looked at him. On his forehead, a painted third eye incorporated the white splotch that passed for the khan's blaze. The fake third eye was supposed to open him up to the Purity, but right now, it seemed to bore into the herd rememberer.

"I do not forgive, Herd Rememberer," said the khan. "But you are new to your role. This time, and this time only, I will choose to forget."

"Thank you, Your Alacrity. Your words will be remembered for the Us."

The khan's teeth clacked as the shivers began. The dream wife took a cloth from a pocket and wiped away the ochre symbols from the khan's neck and body.

The khan had seen the light born, but not the Light Bearer. It was clear the bearer was coming. He prayed to all the equine deities that the bearer would be one of the Us. But he knew the ways of the gods, and it was just as likely the Light Bearer would be a horse of the Not Us or an armadillo or a stick insect of the savages. The gods were perverse in their humor—one of the many burdens the Us had to endure, along with harsh boiling lands and sparse grasses.

Then the khan was lost to the fevers that came from being in touch with the Purity.

❧ I ☙

SEVEN BEAN SOUP

Princess Eloise Hydra Gumball III, Future Ruler and Heir to the Western Lands and All That Really Matters, had spent way too much time over the past couple of days thinking about seven bean soup.

She didn't like seven bean soup. She was fine with pinto beans, adzuki beans, black beans, and guard's homage beans. But cannellini beans hit her stomach like they were taking revenge. She'd been forced to eat lima beans as a little girl, which ruined them forever, and eating Tears of Çalaht beans just seemed blasphemous.

Thinking about seven bean soup served several useful purposes. First, focusing her attention on an imaginary bowl of hot soup helped divert her attention from the horrific weather she and her companions were riding through. She tried to trick herself into drawing a sense of warmth from the picture in her mind. Second, it kept her from doing physical harm to her champion and best friend, Jerome Abernatheen de Chipmunk. Jerome sat in front of Eloise on her Equine Designate, Hector de Pferd, his claws wound into Hector's mane. Jerome also tried to distract himself from the miserable weather, but instead of thinking about soup like a normal person, he hummed "Three Bags of

Groats for my Sweetheart." The events of the previous days, including the death of her uncle, King Doncaster, and her sister Johanna's decision not to return home with Eloise, had chased the infernal song from her brain. Now Jerome, consciously or not, had planted it back in her mind.

Eloise pulled her travel cloak tighter, trying to keep the slashing winter rain from soaking her any more. She patted her pocket and felt the Çalahtist rosary beads given to her by her handmaid, Odmilla. She sometimes used them to keep the nudges and itches of her habits at bay, but there was enough going on that she didn't need them at the moment. Something to be grateful for.

Careful not to lose balance or "accidentally" knock her champion's bushy tail and groat-humming ways off his perch, she twisted her torso left, then right, easing the stiffness from spending days on horseback hunched against the elements.

It was only supposed to be a week's journey from Castle Blotch at Stained Rock along the main road through the Half Kingdom to the Adequate Wall of the Realms. Castle de Brague and her own warm bed were another six-ish days beyond, weather permitting.

The problem was, the weather was not permitting. Not at all.

The weather was, in fact, acting like a petulant child whose parents had forgotten its birthday, then produced a moldy kumquat as a gift. This moldy kumquat weather made Eloise wish she had a weak magic for staying warm. But that's not how weak magic worked—for starters, you didn't choose a weak magic. You either had it or you didn't. And in the great scheme of things, a weak magic for keeping warm might not be the best choice. Then again, neither was her own weak magic for throwing things.

Weak magic was stupid, Eloise thought, not for the first time.

Eloise, Jerome, Hector, her guard Lorch Lacksneck, and his Guard Horse, the Nameless One, had been on the road for almost four days, covering little more than two days' worth of the distance they would have in less kumquatty weather.

6

The person in highest spirits was Kïïit, the scullery mare they had brought along to haul the cart containing the sock. Kïïit was irrepressibly cheerful. She had never been more than a few hours' travel from Stained Rock, so every moment was a revelation. Normally chatty, Kïïit had been almost silent on the journey, overwhelmed by the newness of every tree, moss, rock formation, and bend in the road.

The "sock" that Kïïit carted was actually Turpentine Snotearrow McCcoonnch, late the jester of Castle Blotch and usurper of the Half Kingdom's throne. None of them spoke of Turpy by name, and "the sock" referred to the way he was tied up, chained, and had his movements restricted by a sack. Eloise suspected he was the most comfortable among them. Yes, he was shackled, which made it inconvenient when his bodily requirements had to be accommodated (thank Çalaht Lorch was willing to oversee all that). But Turpy was settled in a comfortable spot in the cart and wrapped snug against the crummy weather. That freed him up to focus all of his attention on sending out hateful glares, which he directed at anyone who strayed into his eyeline.

Eloise couldn't wait to deliver him into custody at home. Her mother, Queen Eloise Hydra Gumball II, could work out what justice needed to be meted out. There were plenty of transgressions to choose from: plying the late King Doncaster with prattleweed to make him suggestible, plotting to overthrow a realm, conspiracy to kidnap, forgery, inadequate personal hygiene, using weak magic to nefarious ends (Turpy, a longwalker, had used that weak magic to stay ahead of Eloise's search party and led them astray for weeks), false ascension to a throne, inadequate jestering—the list went on and on.

Eloise also hoped her mother would be able to tell her what to do with the Star of Whatever, the magical stone she'd recovered from deep within the Purple Haze. She'd ended the spell that the Star of Whatever amplified—the spell that sustained the lavender-colored, luminescent mist that sucked away all magic and life. But even with the spell ended, the Purple Haze remained, and its effects would be felt for centuries. Eloise suspected the stone in the sturdy little box strapped to her hip contained an incredible amount of magic and life force. And surely if she had to carry the most dangerous object in all the realms, the least the weather could do was cooperate.

The thing that bothered Eloise most about going home was the prospect of explaining to her mother why she had failed to bring her fraternal twin sister with her. They had sent messengers ahead to explain their circumstances and let their mother and father know that Doncaster was dead and buried. Johanna had stayed behind to help stabilize the running of the Half Kingdom, where there was no clear successor. She'd even confided that she might put her hand up to be queen. If anyone could pull that off, it was Johanna.

But Eloise had left Castle de Brague with her mother's last words echoing in her head: "Make sure you return with your sister, not without." That wasn't happening, and Eloise wasn't looking forward to the conversation. Perhaps the queen would understand.

Perhaps she wouldn't.

"Princess Eloise?" Lorch guided the Nameless One alongside Hector. "This weather is not letting up. I suggest we stop at an inn."

"What, and miss out on such slow, unpleasant going? I thought you guards were made of steel."

"There are conditions that induce even steel to rust."

Eloise smiled. "I have a hankering for soup. Let's find some."

"Gubhun Hungh," said Turpy through his gag. At a nod from Eloise, Jerome hopped from Hector's back to the cart and freed the prisoner's mouth. She had noticed Jerome could finally deal with Turpy without lapsing into a brainless frenzy. Perhaps he'd stopped thinking of Turpy as a jester, and instead considered him a usurper, pretender, schemer, or murderer. Whatever it was, it shifted Jerome enough that he could handle him without flying into a squealing, jester-phobic panic.

"Gutrot House. We're near Stoney Feld. Half a strong length off this road at the next crossing. Left. Gutrot House will have beds and food." He licked his lips and resumed his baleful stares.

Jerome nodded and replaced the gag. He looked at Eloise. "Gutrot House?"

"I guess," said Eloise.

Jerome looked at Lorch "Should we trust him?"

"Not at all," said the guard. "But I don't know of any alternative, and there aren't any on the map."

"Gutrot House it is." Eloise shrugged. "I hope seven bean soup is not all they have on the menu."

2

GUTROT HOUSE

They made it to Gutrot House following Turpy's directions, but what they found made them question their decision.

"What do you think, Elodrigo?" asked Jerome. "Would you call it 'stylishly dilapidated' or 'modishly disheveled'?"

Eloise feigned artistic consideration. "You have to admire the daring cants and angles of the structural supports, as well as the wavy, swooping slope of the roof."

"You always did have a soft spot for ramshackle neo-deconstructed cubby-inspired architecture."

"Oh, you're right about that. The more bedraggled and neo-deconstructed, the better."

The innkeeper was a rotted stump of a woman, whose clot of salt and pepper hair, dearth of teeth, and overall lemon-inspired demeanor all suited the rickety facility she ran. She wore an unflattering galley wench's outfit, complete with gathered skirt and poufy sleeves. Perhaps it had looked cute on her a few decades previously. She filled the lower half of the doorway, standing there rearranging the grease on her hands with a dishcloth that looked like it was about to start wiping itself free of her. "Yes?"

Lorch dismounted and bowed. "Good evening, Mistress. Have you accommodation this evening, as well as sustenance?"

"Youse want grub and a kip?"

"Yes, Mistress."

"Mistress, is it? Oh, very fancy. Just call me Old Yelper. Everyone does. Not fair, cause I only yelped that one time, but there you go. Rooms are up the top. I don't have no proper stables for youse three horses, but there's a lean-to out the back. Extra for that, but you can use it. Don't go eating my lawn. Find your own grass."

"Thank you, Mistress Yelper," said Lorch.

"Not Mistress. Old. Wasn't that clear?"

"Sorry. Thank you, Old Yelper."

"Youse go settle then come get your comestibles soon as you can in the salle à manger. I don't have all night. I got to be finishing early on account of the gout in my great left toe." She walked back into the falling-down building, leaving them to it.

Jerome looked at Eloise. "Comestibles? Salle à manger?"

"That's what she said."

"I'll get the sock settled in a room," said Lorch. "Then dinner."

"Once you unpack us, Kiïït, the Nameless One, and I will find the lean-to and whatever non-lawn grass might be about," said Hector. "Enjoy your dinner."

Eloise's room was easily half a step better than being outside, but not a full step. The nautical decor was odd, given how far from the sea they were. Perhaps it explained Old Yelper's galley wench get-up. The walls sported a ship's wheel, a ringed lifebuoy (which might have a splotch of dried blood on it), and three seascape paintings of surprising skill. Eloise glanced at the bed, flinched, then looked away leaving the horror of it for later contemplation. At least the roof did not leak, although it did seem warped into dangerous, unstable curves.

The "salle à manger" was half a dozen tables curtained off from the kitchen by what looked, at first glance, to be two bedsheets hung from the ceiling. When she got closer, Eloise saw they were sailcloth. Lorch and Jerome were already there, sitting at a table as far from the kitchen as possible. "You've left the sock alone?"

"Appropriately secured, Princess," said Lorch.

"To an oversized anchor," added Jerome. "That might or might not fall on him."

"I see."

Old Yelper pushed her way between the two sails, carrying a slab of flat wood and a piece of coal to write with. "What do youse want for your grub?"

"I have an inclination toward soup," said Eloise.

"This is a brothel," said Old Yelper.

"I beg your pardon?"

"A brothel. Brothel. Don't you know what a brothel is?"

"I, uh... Yes."

"So you know what you can order in a brothel, right?"

"I'm not sure..."

"Broths. I only serve broths. No soups. I got potato broth. Leek broth. Carrot broth. Potato and leek broth. Leek and potato broth. Potato and carrot broth. Carrot and potato broth. Leek and carrot broth. Carrot and leek broth. Potato, leek, and carrot broth. Leek, potato, and carrot broth. And carrot, leek, and potato broth. Broths. On account of this being a brothel."

"I see," said Eloise.

"In that case," said Jerome, "I'd like the carrot, potato, and leek broth."

"Sorry. Out of that one. But the carrot, leek, and potato broth is to be recommended. Youse might like it. Or not. All the same to me. Hurry up. My great left toe is a'gouting."

"I'll have the potato, leek, and carrot broth," said Eloise.

"Leek, potato and carrot for me," said Lorch.

"Carrot, potato, and leek," said Jerome.

"Out of that. I told youse that already. Youse ever been thrown out of a brothel before?"

"No," said Jerome.

"First time for everything, matey, you keep being cheeky with me. Now, youse gonna order or what?"

"Uh... Carrot and potato broth," said Jerome. "With a side of leek broth. And if you can pour the leek broth into the carrot and potato broth, that would be great."

"That would ruin the carrot and potato broth. Why would I do that?"

"I believe that was an attempt at a witticism, Mistress Old Yelper," said Eloise. "That will be the last one. He'll have what I'm having."

"Potato, leek, and carrot it is. Youse want hardtack with that? A coin extra all together."

"Sure," said Eloise. "Hardtack for all of us."

A few minutes later, they were slurping warmth and nourishment. Surprisingly, the leek, potato and carrot broth was distinct from the potato, leek, and carrot. Hungry from the day's riding, they all had second helpings, dunking the hardtack in the broth to render it edible.

When they were done, Jerome sat back, his tail curled around him, content. "I think I would have to leave a positive Yelper review. That was as good a broth as you'll find anywhere."

Old Yelper appeared again from the kitchen. "Youse all having dessert?"

Jerome perked up. "What do you have?"

"Sweet carrot broth."

His whiskers drooped. "Anything else?"

"Sweet leek broth. Sweet potato broth. To be clear with youse, that's not made from sweet potatoes or anything yam-like. Normal potatoes, but cooked into a sweet broth."

"Anything not in the broth department?"

"What did I tell youse earlier?"

"That this is a brothel."

"Too right. So, youse having dessert or not?"

"I'm sure it's delicious," said Eloise. "But I'm full."

"Me too, Mistress Old Yelper."

"Same."

"Youse can wash up your dishes in that pail. I've got to go elevate my gout toe." Then she turned and hobbled through a side door. She closed it behind her and a chair scuffed, then there was a grunt as she sat, and a loud sigh of relief. Then they heard, "For the love of Çalaht, I thought youse was gonna fall off."

Jerome wrinkled his nose, and whispered, "Did she just talk to her great left toe?"

"I'm not sure I need that much detail about our hostess's life," said Lorch.

"And we're supposed to wash our own dishes?" said Jerome. "What sort of inn is this?"

"It won't be hard, and I'm too tired to argue," said Eloise. "Let's get on with it."

3

INADEQUATELY SUSPICIOUS

Dishes done, they lit candles and found their way back to their rooms. "I'll take first shift outside the princess's door," Lorch said to Jerome.

"OK, but wake me so you can get some sleep as well."

"We'll see how I go."

"Then let me go first, and you can..."

They negotiated this every night. It was even more complicated when they slept rough, as Hector, the Nameless One, and Kïïït joined in the haggling. Eloise yawned a "good night" and closed the door, ready for a few hours' rest.

Eloise looked at the bed, a rickety shambles of slung rope and stained ticking. Her habits twitched and itched. If she wasn't so tired, there'd be no way she'd consider putting herself anywhere close to the thing. She rather sit on the floor and lean against a wall. Or sleep outside. Eloise flipped the mattress over, but the other side was worse. *Ugh*, she thought. *Just ugh*.

But she was exhausted. Despite the nagging of her habits, she resigned herself to a night on the thing.

She barely had her boots off when Jerome's squeal pierced the air. "You!" he screamed. "What are you doing? Get away from—"

Eloise grabbed her candle and ran for the door. She glimpsed Lorch's back as he dashed into the other room. "Stop!" he bellowed. There was a thud like a hockey-sacking girder landing a tackle. Eloise reached the doorway and her candle filled the room with flickering light. Half a dozen armed rats faced off against Jerome, swords drawn. Lorch lay across Turpy, who was almost out of his bag and thrashing with all his might.

Weaponless, Eloise reached for a dish full of decorative sand dollars on the dresser. Drawing on her weak magic for throwing, she flicked the dish, sending it and the flat shells flying toward the rats. Two found their targets, knocking them sprawling. They rolled and sprang up, ready again to fight. The dish and the other sand dollars grazed the rest, and the distraction gave Jerome time to charge in, his champion's sword slashing.

"Retreat!" called the biggest rat. "Run away!" The rats scattered, leaving Turpy behind snarling epithets through his gag.

"Rope!" called Lorch. Eloise tossed him the coil he kept tied to the outside of his pannier, and he re-wrapped the jester's restraints, then stood and left him to thrash.

"Well done, Jerome, Lorch," said Eloise. "That was close."

"Too close, Princess." Lorch took the candle from her and made sure no threats remained in the room.

"It appears we did not anticipate adequately," she said.

"Apologies, Princess," said Lorch. "I should have been more suspicious."

Jerome sheathed his sword. "If we'd had dessert, they would have succeeded. He'd have escaped."

"I would not have thought the sock had such allies. Who knows if there are more, or what they'll try next," said Eloise. "I think we're going to need a day-and-night watch."

"I do not know how we can guard both you and him at the same time," said Lorch.

"I don't need guarding."

"Princess Eloise, please. Have we not covered this—"

"Guard Lorch Lacksneck, I believe I can—"

"Stop it, both of you," said Jerome. "El, I'm with him. From Old Yelper on down, we don't know who has what loyalties. Both you and the sock need guarding."

"Fine. Just fine. But I don't like what it means."

"Means? What do you mean, 'means?'" asked Jerome

"It means we have to be in the same room. All of us."

There was an uncomfortable silence.

"You're right, Princess. It might be best," said Lorch.

"Please give me a few minutes to prepare myself for bed and then let's settle for the night. And make sure you wake me when it's my turn to stand watch."

"Princess, no," said Lorch.

"Watch takes a toll, and we don't want this jaunt home impeded by anyone's lack of sleep."

"Yes, Princess."

Eloise returned to her room, lamenting the lost privacy. As she finished preparing for bed, she wondered how Turpy had arranged the attempted rescue. Had he done it before they left Stained Rock? Did the rats here at Gutrot House recognize him and form a plan on their own? Was it just opportunistic, or did Turpy have Old Yelper and her resident rats as longtime conspirators? Had he guided them there knowing what lay ahead, or did he just seize the chance? If he'd arranged it once they'd arrived, he'd done it awfully fast.

Bringing Turpy to face justice in the Western Lands and All That Really Matters might not be as simple as she'd expected. The complications were the last thing she needed.

Eloise didn't sleep much. Turpy thrashed and grunted in his sleep, making noises through his gag. Jerome, as always, snored. Lorch had the practiced quiet of a guard on watch, but he sighed when his thoughts headed in vexing directions.

There were a lot of sighs.

Despite what she'd said, when Lorch tried again to dissuade her from taking a turn at watch, she acquiesced, managing a few hours of fitful rest between bouts of drowsy worry. One thing was clear—Turpy would not go easily to his fate.

Eloise woke at first light, having finally found some sleep. Jerome was on watch and wide awake.

He sat on Turpy's chest, staring at him.

"What's going on?" yawned Eloise.

Jerome did not look at her. "Master Turpentine Snotearrow McCcoonnch and I are having a little chat."

"Oh? What about?"

"It's been hard to understand what Master Snotearrow McCcoonnch's contributions have been. The gag is not helping his diction. From what I can tell, most of it has been language I would not use in front of my mother. For my side, I have been speculating on what justice might look like when we get to Castle de Brague. Did you know, Eloise, that I have some familiarity with the castle's dungeons?"

"No, I didn't. What sort?"

Jerome turned around to look at Eloise, pointing his back end at Turpy's face. Turpy jerked trying to shake Jerome off, but the chipmunk held on, ignoring him. "My mother, in her role as Court Seer, sometimes goes down there. One of the long-term residents—a deranged bilby—babbles in a way she finds useful for prognostication. I didn't like her going on her own, so I accompanied her. As such, I'm familiar with the opportunities that await Master Snotearrow McCcoonnch once he gets there. I wouldn't call any of them 'pleasant.' During our little chat, I shared this insider information. I'm hoping it gives him something to think about."

"I see."

"My first inclination was to compare and contrast them to the dungeon amenities one finds elsewhere, like the Sclerotic Wold in The South, as well as those of the Half Kingdom. Master Snotearrow McCcoonnch must have at least a passing knowledge of the Northo dungeons, having thrown people like me in there often enough."

"Jerome, don't do this."

He ignored her and turned back to Turpy. "In the dungeons of the Western Lands and All That Really Matters, Master Snotearrow McCcoonnch won't find jail chiggers like The South or taunters like here in the Half Kingdom. What he will find depends on the cell he's given. There's one that has a drip. It's almost impossible to find a spot in the cell where the drip does not land on you. Most annoying. There's another that has a horrific smell. Not a constant smell, but one that blasts the nostrils at unpredictable times so you can't grow used to it and ignore it."

"Jerome, seriously."

"But I have a problem, El."

"What?"

"There are a couple of cells that I'm not sure I could choose between. There's the Grit Cell (not to be confused with the Grits Cell), which has no bed. Just a thick layer of grit—sand, broken bits of shell, small pebbles, that sort of thing. If you're in there long enough, it gets into every corner of your clothes and body. That one's pretty good. Then there's the howler cell. I'm not sure what goes on there because I've been too afraid to look. I only know that anyone who's in there for more than three days starts howling."

"I mean it, Jerome. Don't."

"But I think my favorite is the jingle cell." He leaned in closer to Turpy's face. "The jingle cell employs a team of retired heralds. There's always one outside the dungeon door. They sing advertising jingles over and over and over. It's insidious. The jingles get lodged in your head. Your thoughts become dominated by inane slogans for Lurid Eddy's Carriages or Golden Brand Olives. 'Oy ye, oy ye, oy ye! Lurid Eddie Commands You to Have a Bargain' or 'Golden Brand Olives— they're olive-vacious!' The heralds only know about eight jingles each. They sing them over and over and over and over and over and over and over until they displace every other possible thought. I hope that's the one they give him."

"That will do, Jerome."

"Yes, Princess Eloise. I think it will." Jerome walked across Turpy's face, spat, and left the room.

❦ 4 ❦
GRASS STRUDEL

Breakfast was what Old Yelper called Morning Broth. It had a distinctly carroty, leeky, and potato-y taste. Neither Jerome nor Lorch felt like talking, so they ate in silence.

Lorch purchased stoppered gourds full of broth to take with them, as well as a sack of hardtack. As Eloise wished Old Yelper good luck with her gout-ridden toe, Lorch put the sock in Kïïït's cart, and minutes later, they were back on the road.

As they rode, Lorch gave the horses the full details of what had happened the night before.

"Goodness me," said Kïïït. "You were set upon by brigands! It's like a Biscuit Night campfire story. How exciting!"

"Exciting? Interesting choice of words," said Jerome. "And I'm not sure I'd call them brigands."

"Ruffians? Ne'er-do-wells? Goons? Hooligans? I've met plenty of those sorts at the Splintered Dray in Stained Rock. I'm used to that type being larger than rats, though. Usually they're drunk to their withers and brawling over their troughs of fermented hay. Could I call them brutes? Rowdies? Dirty bubbins?"

"Something like that will do," said Jerome.

"Well, this is much more exciting than a public inn brawl," she bubbled. "Maybe the most exciting thing I've ever been involved with. And I wasn't even there!"

They rode through a crisp, clear morning—a welcome relief after the day before—and made good time despite the badly maintained road. The cart and its contents had to be maneuvered around fallen trees and potholes and through muddy stretches, but it was much easier going compared to the previous days.

Jerome's needling of Turpy had put thoughts of jingles in the chipmunk's mind. A few times every hour, for no apparent reason, Jerome would exclaim, "I command you to have a bargain!" or "It's olive-vacious!" It made Eloise grit her teeth, but she decided it was better than random snatches of That Song. Besides, the weather was nice, so she just did her best to ignore him.

Of all of them, Kïïït was in the best mood. Her smile matched the glorious, blue sky. Kïïït seemed to have recovered from her initial stunned overwhelm, and now let flow a steady commentary on the wonder of everything around her. That is, when she wasn't chewing. Without slowing down, she ducked her head and nibbled each new grass, sedge, bush, and bracken. It was almost compulsive. Every fescue drew her eye, and every meadow-grass called her name. She'd chomp, taste, and comment on each plant she tried. "Oh! That one was a bit minty." "How can a grass taste like ginger?" "Bland." "Bold." "Boring." "Delectable."

Eloise found her delight and enthusiasm infectious. She noted that Kïïït had two main categories of superlatives. If she nibbled something she especially liked, she'd exclaim, "Ain't that the grass strudel!" If she really didn't care for a plant, she'd grouse, "That ain't fit for a turf war." Her knowledge of species was thin, but her ability to distinguish the taste of one tussock from another was keen.

Hector surprised Eloise with his encyclopedic knowledge of the different plants and their names. He contributed his thoughts on which were the tastiest, which best avoided, and why. "Don't eat that one," he said as Kiïit reached for a taste. "It's serrated tussock. It combines an unpleasant mouth feel with a bitter aftertaste."

Later, during a break, he showed her a grass growing near a tree. "Try two mouthfuls of squirrel-tail fescue and a nibble of spicy wattle."

Kiïit smiled and did as he suggested. Her eyes went wide. "Wow."

"It's a surprisingly flavorsome mix."

"That's the grass strudel! Nameless One, come try this!"

The Nameless One, ever wordless, joined their discussion. Using snorts, sniffs, sneezes, sighs, and foot movements, he made it clear that this time he agreed. He didn't always, but he often added nuance. Kiïit brought out a side of both Hector and the Nameless One that Eloise had not seen before.

Eloise sat with Jerome and Lorch, eating a snack of fruit and nuts from a muslin pouch. They watched the three equines turn to cropping grass three dozen lengths away. "What do you think of Kiïit?"

"Chats a bit," said Jerome, nibbling a prune half the size of his head.

"Pot, meet kettle," said Lorch.

"Oy," said Jerome.

"I think she's nice," said Eloise. "And I think they're both sweet on her."

"No, really?"

"Eat your prune, Jerro. What's interesting is there's no jealousy or tension between them. And she shows no favoritism."

Across the field, Kiïit bumped the Nameless One gently with her hip and laughed. Her "Ain't that the grass strudel!" was loud enough for Eloise to hear. It must have been the tenth time she'd said it since they'd wandered off.

Lorch picked a macadamia from the mix. "Perhaps, Princess, this is simply the way of herds."

"Perhaps."

"You don't see them like this when they're practicing on the parade grounds," he said. "They seem to want their herd hierarchies."

"Different context," said Jerome. "Or maybe on the parade ground our Hector is just a bossy boots who wants his way."

"Maybe," said Eloise. "But the interaction between the three of them fascinates me."

The day passed uneventfully. They rode hard and made good time. When they stopped for a late lunch, they supped on Old Yelper's broth. It proved surprisingly delicious, even when eaten cold from a hollowed gourd.

Back on the road, what they were doing struck Eloise as rather normal, despite all the not-so-normal that was going on—transporting a criminal, and carrying a massively powerful magical object. Even so, she'd almost had enough. Eloise was AWOL from her duties at Court and had been for weeks. She was grateful for this journey, its diversions, everything she had learned, and the people of all species she had met. But she was ready to get back to the castle, her room, her particular ways, and the simpler life of Court intrigue. This kind of travel covered her in a cloak of unreality. She felt like she was outside of time, because none of the things she normally relied on to mark time's passage—rituals and routines, the demands of Protocol and the rhythms of daily life—were there. It felt like a displacement.

They slept rough that night, not wanting to risk staying somewhere else where Turpy might have connections. The star-filled night threatened frost, but their fire warmed Eloise. She wrapped herself in blankets and her travel cloak against the chill, and watched the flames cast their hypnotic light. "One could get used to this," she thought. "Even if one would rather not."

RESULTS OF THE CLOUD REFERENDUM

The brief spell of cheerful winter weather petered out the next morning. Clouds gathered and let loose. It was like they held a referendum and resolved to maximize unpleasantness for all below. Eloise hunched inside her travel cloak, hood pulled down over her head, and did her best to ignore the cold slashing rain that hammered them.

Once again, the most comfortable person was Turpy. His sack was weatherproof and warm, and an overhang on the cart protected his head. Eloise glanced into the cart to find him dozing, upper lip curled in a snarl.

If the wind, wet, and cold had any upside, it was that it kept Jerome from haranguing Turpy—thin comfort, but Eloise would take it.

After several hours of fighting their way down the wretched, slippery road, Eloise leaned down toward Hector's ears. "Could you please catch up with Lorch and the Nameless One?"

"Yes, Princess."

They came level with the guard and horse. "I think I need a break from this weather," she yelled through the rain. "I'm guessing we all do."

"Yes, Princess, but it will be some time before we reach the next village. The comfort of an inn is not close at hand. Can you wait?"

She shook her head "Even if we just find an overhang for half an hour's lunch, that would help."

"Yes, Princess. We will see what can be found." Lorch and the Nameless One trotted ahead and were soon out of sight.

They were gone half an hour, but returned smiling. "We have something, Princess. The Nameless One found it. If you'll follow, please."

"Thank Çalaht for small mercies," muttered Jerome. Hector and Kïïït picked up their pace, the promise of rest and shelter putting a fresh spring in their hooves despite the rising wind, and rain that teetered on the edge of hail.

The spot the Nameless One had found was a hidden miracle. Jutting rock outcroppings formed a natural covered alcove. The faded footprints in the dry dirt testified that it had once been a popular stopping place, but they were old, and it had been a long time since anyone had rested there.

Eloise slid off Hector then helped Jerome down, and they sought cover under the rocky ledge. The relief was immediate, a welcome break from gusts and driven wet. The horses slid under as well, grateful to be out of the rain. They stood, dripping, not shaking dry like they normally would, to avoid showering everyone else.

Lorch heaved the sock out of the cart and set him in a far spot where he could lean against the back wall. The guard squatted and looked their prisoner in the eye. "I will relieve you of your gag if I can rely on you to hold your tongue." Turpy nodded once, and Lorch untied the strip of cloth. The jester opened his mouth and flexed his jaw, then made as exaggerated a bow as he could, given his restraints.

"I shall take that as a thank you," said Lorch.

Turpy shrugged. Maybe it was, maybe it wasn't.

The weather worsened. Lorch turned to the others. "I don't think we'll be going anywhere for a while." He got his flint and steel and lit a fire from a small stack of wood left behind by previous travelers.

"I reckon we have our accommodation for the night," said Eloise.

"Yes, Princess. If the wind does not change direction, it should be comfortable. I'll unpack."

"I'll help," said Jerome.

Fire lit and gear sheltered, the seven of them hunkered down. Eloise listened to the winter storm rage with renewed intensity. The space was tight, made tighter because no one wanted to settle next to the sock. Eloise wanted as little to do with him as possible.

An hour later, Eloise stood and took a couple of apples from one of the panniers. "What I wouldn't give for one of Chef's haggleberry teas right now."

"Oh, yes." Jerome got a dreamy look on his face. "She does that blend of Haggleberry Harpy Bud from the village of Persistent Mess in The South and Haggleberry Messiah from the hamlet of Towering Colossus in the Eastern Lands. But I'd settle for a cup of Happier Zappier from the Central Carbuncle. No one knows exactly where it's grown."

"No?" asked Lorch.

"Nope. It's one of the Five Great Haggleberry Mysteries."

"What, pray tell, are the other four great haggleberry mysteries?" asked Hector.

"That, Your Gracious Equitation, is one of them."

"Humph." The horse swatted the ground with his tail, but held his tongue.

Eloise was glad. She wasn't up for one of Jerome's ridiculous haggleberry tea ramblings.

She slipped her small knife from a hidden pocket in her travel cloak, cut the apples into exact quarters, then the quarters into eighths. She let Lorch give Turpy his, but passed around the rest herself. When she got to Kiiit, the mare hesitated. "Are you sure, Princess Eloise?

"I beg your pardon?"

"Are you sure it's OK for me to have some apple?"

"Of course."

"Really? Because..." Her nostrils flared a little, sniffing.

"Don't you want some apple?"

"Yes, please."

"Why wouldn't I offer you some?"

The mare shook her head slowly. "At Castle Blotch, the scullers—those of us who worked in the scullery and the kitchen—were not allowed to touch apples, except to serve them or prepare them for others."

"Really?"

"Oh, the thrashing Cook delivered if she saw someone with an apple. Others would sneak little bits of core or peel, but I never wanted to risk the bruises. The rule applied to all fresh fruits. Peaches, plums, berries, all of them." Kiiit drew a deep breath, remembering. "It's not like there were a lot of apples hanging around the Splintered Dray or any of the other equine establishments I went to. There, it was always 'Gimme some hay' and 'I'll take a bran mash.' I never figured that out. The horses seemed to think it unstalliony to want fruit. Stupid, if you ask me."

Eloise furrowed her brow. "Are you telling me you've never had an apple?"

Kiiit laughed. "Oh, Princess. Don't be daft. Of course I have. Five, maybe six, easy. Once, when I was a foal, my mother got me one. I remember it because it was a golden color. Then there were a couple of slightly sour green ones I found once. They must have bounced off a cart, but they were small and hard. And a stallion who tried to court me once gave me a red one. I didn't fancy him so much, but the apple was nice. So, yes, I've had apples."

"I see. Well then." Eloise gave the remaining eighths to Lorch, went to the pannier again and pulled out two more apples. She sat cross-legged in front of Kiiit, spread out a small, clean handkerchief from a pocket in her cloak, and cut each apple into four exact quarters. Then she stood and bowed to the mare. "Mistress Kiiit, may apples fill your world from this day forward. I hope you enjoy them all."

Kiiit's eyes widened. "Princess! Really? For me?"

"For you."

"Oh! My goodness! Thank you! All of it?"

"All of it."

Kiiit beamed one of her huge smiles and delicately picked up the first slice in her lips. What followed was the most intense, thorough, concentrated, and appreciative chewing that Eloise had ever seen. The mare lost herself in it, savoring every morsel, then repeated the process for each of the seven other quarters. Kiiit spread her enjoyment of the two apples across almost a half hour. At first, Eloise watched her, transfixed by her complete absorption. Then she looked away. It seemed a rude to watch, even if the horse was oblivious.

The others, too, busied themselves rather than watch Kiiit's rapturous eating. Everyone except Turpy, who stared right at her, making no effort to mask his disgust. Eloise decided she preferred it when he had the gag in. It helped hide his face.

Jerome saw him, too. He stood up, placed himself directly in front of Turpy, and stared at him. The jester shifted his gaze and locked eyes with Eloise's champion. They stayed that way for a long time, their mutual hatred palpable.

✖ 6 ✖

GRAPPLING AN EEL

Eloise's sleep was fitful. Turpy's hateful stare stole into her dreams. She spoke to a crowd at Court, and his eyes stared out at her from every face she saw. She woke unnerved, wanting more than ever to get this journey over with.

Overnight, the storm worsened. The wan morning light barely penetrated the thick cloud and constant rain. A damp chill pervaded their shelter.

"A warm breakfast will do us good," said Lorch. "I'll find some more wood."

"Let me help," said Eloise, standing.

"No need, Princess. I won't be long. Perhaps you could perk the fire with the remaining sticks."

"Sure."

Hector, the Nameless One, and Kïïït stood and stretched. "The three of us might brave the rain and have breakfast as well," said Hector. One by one, they hunched into the weather after Lorch.

Eloise fed dry twigs into the coals and blew them into flames. Then she busied herself tidying her blankets, rolling them into a cushion she could sit on. She did her best to ignore the sock, who'd stopped snoring and now followed her every movement with dull, glassy eyes. Jerome took out his champion's sword and sharpened it. The alcove filled with the soft *scritch, scritch, scritch* of his sharpening stone working the steel edge.

Lorch returned with a clutch of sodden sticks. He broke them into pieces, slicing away wet bark to expose a dry surface.

"I have a requirement." Turpy had kept his word and said nothing all night. His sudden utterance jarred the morning quiet.

Lorch stared at Turpy a moment, then lay the stick he held onto the fire. "Stand," he said, and went to the jester. Turpy wormed his way up onto his feet. Lorch untied the sack and slid it down, letting Turpy step out. His hands were bound in front of him, and shackles hobbled his shoeless feet. His broken thumb—the thumb Eloise had shattered —was splinted and bandaged. The healers had not given Turpy any hope for its repair, but he refused to let them take it off.

The jester waggled a foot. "It would be easier and less messy without these."

Again, Lorch stared at him, assessing the risk, then he nodded and retrieved a key from his pocket. He unlocked Turpy's left iron ankle cuff, leaving the right attached. "That should do." He pointed to the alcove's opening. "After you."

Jerome lifted his blade in the dim light, squinting at its edge. "See if there's a cliff nearby. Maybe you can push him over it."

Turpy turned on the chipmunk. "I've had enough of you, rat."

Jerome stood and took a couple of practice swings with his sword. He pointed it at Turpy, jabbing the air as he spoke. "Don't. Call. Me. Rat. I am a rodent, not a rat."

"Rat, bat, scat, I don't care what you are. I'm sick to the pupils of you. You and your alleged cleverness," Turpy spat. "You are a fly. A demented fly buzzing gibberish. You spew forth a vomit of nonsense. I would rather have you ram your knitting needle of a sword through my ear than listen to your gnat-brained soliloquy."

"Stop it," warned Eloise. "Stop it, both of you.

Jerome stepped closer to Turpy and poked his sword into Turpy's leg, not so hard that it cut or damaged his legging, but hard enough to be annoying. "I'm (poke) so (poke) sorry (poke) that (poke) you (poke) find (poke) me (poke) so (poke) unpleasant (poke). I (poke) don't (poke) exactly (poke) find (poke) you (poke) a (poke) delight, (poke) either (poke)."

"Champion Abernatheen de Chipmunk..." said Lorch.

"I said stop, you insignificant speck of mindless chatter." Turpy leaned down, his face menacing.

The chipmunk raised his sword until it pointed at the jester's nose. "Stop (poke) what (poke)?"

Turpy didn't flinch. "I said don't mess with me, rat."

Jerome moved his sword to the side so he could lean in as well. "Don't call me 'rat.'"

"You want a cliff?" growled Turpy. "I'll show you a cliff."

Turpy swung his bound hands down. Eloise thought he meant to smash Jerome, or maybe knock away the sword. Instead, he grabbed Jerome by the tail with his good hand and hauled him up. Jerome, dangling in front of him, swung his sword wildly, but Turpy held him out of reach.

"Put him down!" yelled Eloise.

Lorch threw himself at the jester, but Turpy anticipated it. He shifted his hips and stepped out of the way—a move worthy of a pro hockey sacking left flutter—letting Lorch crash past him. As he sidestepped, the jester swung Jerome and his sword in an arc that brought the blade slashing down at the guard. Lorch jerked aside to avoid the sword, but was not fast enough. The whistling steel nicked his forearm as it flew past, staining his sleeve with red. Lorch hissed in pain and fell, instinctively curling to protect the injury. Turpy leapt toward the alcove's opening.

Jerome swished his sword back and forth, wild cuts slicing the air. One caught Turpy on the wrist, cutting the back of his hand but also biting into the rope that bound him, fraying the hemp.

Eloise threw herself at Turpy's legs, aiming to trip him, or at least slow him. But it was like trying to grapple an eel. The jester slipped past her, dashing forward as she also hit the ground.

Something slithered beneath her, and Eloise instinctively threw herself off it. She realized too late that it was the chain and loose shackle that jerked along behind the jester. She scrabbled forward, trying to grab it, but it snaked just out of reach. Eloise lunged, and managed to grab the open cuff.

She held fast, but Turpy's stride pulled her forward across the dirt floor with an unnatural force. Eloise clung on as long as she could, but it was either let go or have her arm dislocated. She released her grip and the shackle flew forward as Eloise slid to a stop.

Turpy reached the mouth of the enclosure, moving impossibly fast, and deliberately clunked Jerome on the stone entryway as he went past. Eloise heard Jerome's groan and saw him go limp. The champion's sword hung loose, and Turpy snatched it before it clattered to the stony floor. Then the jester was out in the rain.

"Jerome!" Eloise screamed, getting up to give chase. Lorch was also back on his feet and running.

How could the jester move that fast? How could his stride have threatened to pull her arm from its socket?

Eloise gasped, remembering. "He's a longwalker! Lorch, we can't let him get away or we'll never see him again!"

"Yes, Princess." Lorch said it without looking back. At the entryway, he cupped his hands and called, "Nameless One! To me!" In a practiced motion, the horse charged over at a canter. As he passed Lorch, the guard grabbed a handful of mane and swung himself onto the horse's back. They sped off in pursuit.

Hector cantered over as soon as he saw what Lorch and the Nameless One were doing. It took Eloise much longer to mount up, and by the time they were charging away from the campsite, Lorch was easily 50 lengths ahead. Eloise rode low and close to Hector's neck, her hand wrapped in a knot of mane to steady herself as the stallion dodged branches and leapt fallen trees.

Kiïit, moved by simple herd instinct, chased after them. "What's happening?" she called.

Hector yelled back, "The sock escaped," and rushed ahead, leaving her to follow.

Eloise saw that Turpy still held the chipmunk by the tail, and Jerome was still limp to mind-numbness. That, or he was dead. No. Unacceptable. Eloise pushed the thought from her head and focused on staying atop her rushing horse.

Ahead of them, the jester zipped between trees and around stones. Where was he going? Was he simply running away, or did he know the area? Was he running toward something? Eloise guessed the latter, but had no idea where it might be.

Or was it as simple as he had said? Was he heading for a cliff? That thought made her hunch lower on Hector's back, urging him to go faster. "Hold on, Jerome!" murmured Eloise, more prayer than anything else.

Hector's hooves thudded across the rain-slick, rock-strewn ground. Turpy wove through narrow gaps in the terrain and stretched his lead by forcing his pursuers to take a less direct route. Could a longwalker outrun a galloping horse? Turpy's speed was incredible, his weak magic taking him away from them faster than seemed possible. No wonder he'd been able to stay ahead of them, spy on them, and plant false clues leading them toward The South.

Hector and Eloise burst through a stand of elms into a clearing, where she saw that Turpy's wrists were no longer bound. They used the open stretch to gain ground, and Lorch and the Nameless One came within 25 lengths, but then it was back to dodging boulders, skirting trees, and a lengthening gap.

Turpy flashed through the forest, a blur of black moving through the semi-darkness of the rain-soaked morning. Eloise struggled to keep him in sight.

They reached another clearing, and Turpy ran toward the steep face of a domed incline. The formation looked like someone had taken a giant's breakfast bowl, turned it to stone, and slammed it upside down into the landscape. It was not a cliff, but there was no way anyone could get up it—not in this weather.

We have him, thought Eloise.

7

STONE DOME

But they didn't have him.

Turpy barely broke stride when he reached the bottom of the dome. He shoved the sword in the back of his belt, bit the back of Jerome's tunic to hold him in his teeth, braced himself with his bandaged hand, and found a handhold with his good one. Ignoring the rain and slickness, the jester clambered up the dome's rocky face.

Less than a minute later, Lorch and the Nameless One clattered to a halt at the same spot. Lorch jumped off the horse and, despite his armored boot coverings, followed Turpy's path upward. The first ten lengths went smoothly, but as Eloise and Hector reached the wall, Eloise saw Lorch's foot slip out from under him, once, then again. Both times, he saved himself with sheer strength and a firm grip.

"Careful, Lorch!" Eloise yelled. Hector stopped next to the Nameless One, who looked up into the rain, pacing.

"Below!" Lorch called, and moments later, an armored boot cover dropped between them. "Below!" he shouted again, and the other cover clanked off the stone wall. Kïïït dodged it as she reached them.

Eloise slipped off Hector's back, retying the laces on her own boots.

"Princess, no," said Hector. "Please. You can't endanger yourself like this."

"He's got Jerome."

"We've got Lorch."

"I... I can't just stand here and hope that's enough. Lorch is injured. Nameless One, could you tell how badly?"

The guard horse shook his head.

Hector pressed his lips together and grimaced. "Go then."

Eloise stood, secured her travel cape so it wouldn't flap, and made sure the box holding the Star of Whatever was cinched to her hip. She reached to grab the first handhold, but she was too short. She tried a different spot, but slipped.

"Climb onto my back," said Hector, positioning himself. Eloise hauled herself onto his back, stood, then found purchase on the wall.

If it hadn't been windy and wet, it would have been an easy enough climb. It was certainly simple compared to the one she'd faced at the bottom of a sea-facing cliff shrouded in the Purple Haze. But the rain, cold, and wind turned what might have been a fun bouldering exercise into treachery. Eloise focused by counting her steps, diverting her mind from conjuring disaster scenarios. Hand reach, hand reach, foot lift, foot lift, pause, repeat—always keeping at least three points on the rock at any moment.

There was a definite slope to the dome, which made it feel like she was climbing "up and along," not just "up." It reminded her of something she and Jerome would have climbed on the Skills Course at home. But there, she would have ropes, proper handholds, and a safety net. At home, free-climbing in conditions like these would have earned her a scolding, a helping hand to get off, and a directive to go inside and warm up with haggleberry tea and soup.

No soup here. No helping hand. Even a scolding sounded nice at this point.

She moved upward, and soon the slope eased so she could see what was ahead. There was Lorch, struggling more than Eloise would have expected. Beyond him, Turpy favored his damaged hand, but still moved fast. He was far enough ahead that the slope fave him an advantage, and his motion was more walk than climb. The distance between them continued to grow.

Eloise caught up with Lorch, who was red-faced and puffing. "Apologies, Princess. I would be better barefoot. These boots are slipping too much, but I can't see how to remove them up here."

"Your arm!" His coat sleeve was soaked elbow to wrist with blood.

"It is also not helping."

"How can I help you?"

"Leave me and keep going, Princess. He can't escape."

"Right. I'll see you up there."

"I won't be too long behind you."

Eloise moved past him, and soon she was running instead of climbing.

Turpy glanced back, and picked up his pace, putting 75 lengths between them, then 100. Now that he was on a flat surface, he'd taken Jerome from his mouth. The chipmunk now dangled by the tail from his good hand again.

Eloise's lungs ached as she ran as fast as she could, determined to catch him. She was used to running, but she'd not yet recovered from her grueling trip into the Purple Haze. Her speed was slower than it should have been, and her stamina was a fraction of normal. She wondered if she would go faster without the Star of Whatever bobbing on her hip, but didn't think it made that much difference.

There was no way she would reach the jester. Not like this.

Suddenly, Turpy sprawled face-first onto the stone, yanking to a bone-jolting halt. Eloise heard him yell, then saw him roll over and sit up. Blood poured from his nose. He spat something out, and tucked his sore hand under the opposite arm, like he'd hurt it. The loose shackle dragging behind him was wedged into a crack. Eloise watched Turpy tugging it to pull it free, then he stood and tried to jerk it from the other direction. Turpy wrenched at it, pulling it in every direction he could, but it was stuck. He looked around at Eloise, saw her running toward him, and frantically hauled on the chain.

Nothing. He yelled in frustration and tried again and again.

Eloise closed the distance. When she was 40 lengths away, she saw Jerome lying flat and unmoving on the ground. Turpy grunted with the effort to free the chain, but nothing he tried worked. Eloise wondered what to do when she reached him. She needed to restrain him long enough for Lorch to catch up. Should she slam into him like she had his brother? Or should she keep her distance, since he seemed genuinely stuck? Maybe she should find something to hit him over the head with and render him as mind-numb, as he had rendered Jerome.

Thirty lengths.

Turpy spun and faced her, looking her straight in the eyes. "No!" he growled. He took a stance like a sprinter at the starting line. What did he think he was doing? He was stuck.

Twenty lengths.

The jester gritted his teeth, breathed three fast breaths through his nose like he was preparing to do something unpleasant, then shot forward.

The iron chain and cuff held fast in the crack. Turpy screamed as the bones in his shackled left foot cracked, then broke. Then he screamed more as he pulled his damaged foot through the cuff.

❧   *8*   ❧

MORTIMER FALLS

The shock of what he'd just done to himself pulled Eloise up short. He'd used his weak magic against his own body. Turpy had bought freedom from the shackle, but paid with damage and pain. What kind of mind would even think of that, let alone carry it out?

Somehow, he stayed upright, gingerly touching the foot to the ground to see if it would bear weight.

Eloise stood, watching him, then realized he wasn't just testing out his damaged foot. He was moving away from her again. Turpy limped to where Jerome lay and grabbed him by his tail. Eloise heard a small "Hmmmph" from the chipmunk. So he was still alive. She resumed running across the stony surface, determined to stop Turpy.

Even with a broken foot and a bad limp, his longwalking still worked. Turpy moved slower—how could he not—wincing with every step. But as hard as Eloise ran, he remained ahead.

She rounded a bend, and an unfamiliar sound pushed through the rasping noise of her breath. It was a rushing noise that got stronger as she ran. Turpy was definitely moving toward something.

Something loud.

He crested a rise and disappeared from her view. Eloise ran harder than ever, and when she reached the top, the rushing noise became a roar.

Turpy ran toward the largest, longest waterfall Eloise had ever seen. As if coordinated by a second-rate drama consultant, the moment it came into Eloise's view, sunlight cut through the cloudy sky, casting a blinding ray of light onto the falling water. Its mists shone a spectacular rainbow of drifting color.

This must be Mortimer Falls, thought Eloise.

Fed by the River Thurmond, the falls were named after the nominatively determinative Mortimer Stolpern Caer Tomber Rrëzohem Yıxılmaq Ahhhhhh! Falls. Not much was known about Mortimer Falls, except that he was the first recorded person to plunge to his death in the pool below. His last words were said to be, "Wouldn't it be funny if someone trip—"

The falls' unexpected natural beauty impressed Eloise, but she had scant attention for it as she pounded length after length, desperately trying to catch the hobbling escapee.

Turpy reached a cliff edge and Eloise panicked, thinking he meant to throw Jerome over. Instead, the jester followed the path to the right, limping along the cliff edge, drawing closer and closer to the waterfall.

Eloise followed, careful to leave enough room that if she tripped on the uneven ground or slipped on wet stone, she'd land in a safe spot and not imitate the falls' namesake.

Eloise felt her legs burning and her lungs straining. Turpy, too, must have been feeling the effects of pain and fatigue, because for the first time, she was gaining on him. She pushed harder—for Jerome, for Doncaster, and for all the wrongs Turpy needed to account for. As they neared the falls, Eloise narrowed the gap from 50 lengths to 40, then 30. The crashing roar of rushing water filled her ears, and mist soaked any patch of dry clothing that the rain and her own sweat had missed.

Eloise tried to figure out what Turpy meant to do. It looked like the jester was following the path toward an observation platform jutting out from the side of the cliff ahead. The platform was positioned so one could walk out onto it and see the falls, the pool below, and the opposite edge of the natural, U-shaped cliff formation. But that didn't make sense. Why let her corner him on the observation deck?

Turpy stopped when he drew even with the observation platform. He hunched over, hands on knees, chest heaving, Jerome dangling limp at his calf. Eloise didn't think much about why he'd give her a chance to catch up. Maybe pain and exhaustion had finally gotten the better of him, and he was ready to give in.

Jerome roused. He blinked, moaned, flexed his claws, and touched his head like he was making sure it was still attached. His eyes cleared, and he saw Eloise racing toward him. "Hey, El. Why are you upside down?" His voice slurred like he was just waking from a bender.

Twenty lengths narrowed to ten, then five.

Just as Eloise got close enough that she might grab Turpy, the jester looked directly at her, his face a mix of hatred and provocation. He turned toward the observation deck and ran. This time, he did not favor his damaged foot. He ran like it had been healed. Only a grunt each time the foot hit the ground betrayed his pain.

Jerome twisted left and right, wildly trying to figure out what was going on, and screaming in panic as the world rushed by.

Eloise knew that whatever this was, she had to stop it. She darted after the jester, and her feet hit the platform just four steps after him. Was he trying to kill himself? To kill Jerome? Both? Eloise could live with Turpy committing suicide, but there was no way he was taking Jerome along for the ride.

Her mind raced in strange directions in the seconds available to her. She considered that the observation platform was clearly a public health hazard. There was no guard rail, banister, or anything to hold on to. There wasn't even a piece of string letting you know you were getting close to the edge. No signs warned parents they'd better hold on to their children, or that the platform surface was slippery. As Eloise tried to reach Turpy, she wondered who in the Half Kingdom was responsible for such blatant violations of public safety. The king? Obviously not any more, being dead and all. But if you're going to make something like this, why not add a few safety measures? Then again, the Whacking Great Hole didn't have a railing either. Maybe it was a realms-wide issue.

The near-hysterical part of her mind wrestled with why anyone would hurtle toward something so dangerous. *No. No you don't*, she thought. *You're not going to hurt Jerome.*

Two steps from the edge she caught up with Turpy. Eloise couldn't quite grab his tunic with her fist, but she did manage to pinch it between her fingers. When he stopped, she'd have him.

Except, he didn't stop. With a final grunt of effort, Turpy planted his good foot at the edge of the platform and hurled himself up and off the observation deck. The full force of his longwalking took Eloise by surprise, and with a whoosh, it swept her along in its wake.

Turpy's leap tore him away from her, and he sailed up and away, his pedaling legs churning like he was running on air, striving to reach the far side.

His magnificently executed long jump was accompanied by Eloise's long, loud scream of "Nooooo!" as the jester carried her champion away.

Eloise didn't have enough momentum to follow his leap. Instead, she went over the edge of the observation deck and plummeted, following a very similar path to the one pioneered by the late Mortimer Stolpern Caer Tomber Rrëzohem Yıxılmaq Ahhhhhh! Falls.

9

IMITATING AN ARROW

*I*t really is a long, long way down, thought part of Eloise's brain. *Ahhhhhhh!* screamed the rest of it.

As she plummeted, her travel cloak flapping like it was being blown by a hurricane, her thoughts careened all over the place.

She contemplated how certain it was that she would die, and if there was anything she might do in the little time she had left to tip the scales in her favor. Certainly Mortimer Stolpern Caer Tomber Rrëzohem Yıxılmaq Ahhhhhh! Falls hadn't managed to do such a thing.

Ahhhhhh!

Eloise had heard of cliff divers who leapt down shockingly long drops and into water. If that was a real hobby, then it must be possible. So how did they do it?

The answer was in their name. They weren't cliff belly-floppers, cliff cannonballers, or cliff just-hope-you-get-it-righters. They were cliff *divers.*

They dove.

Aaahhhhhh!

Diving had to do with the shape of your body and the direction it was headed. Eloise guessed that a cliff diver wanted their body to be pointy. If you dropped a stone into a puddle, you got a very different effect than if you dropped a knife into it. Eloise reasoned she needed to be pointy so she'd hit the pool below like a knife, not a sack of aubergines.

Fine. Next, did she want to slice into the water head-first or feet-first? Logic said she should go feet first. That way, any underwater objects she encountered (say, boulders), would shatter her legs and not her arms and head.

Aaaaahhhhhhhh!

There was just one problem. That wasn't the way she was currently oriented.

Aaaaaaaahhhhhhhhhhh!

Not too late. Eloise swiveled her body so her head was up and her feet and legs were tight together and pointing downward.

In that moment, the spark of something in the Star of Whatever seemed to rouse from its slumber. It sent out one of its simple probes to her: "?"

"Not now," Eloise sent back.

"?" it insisted.

The scream blended with her "!!" response. *Aaaaaaaaaaaaahhhhhhhhhhhhhhhh!!*

"?!?" replied the spark of something. This was the most complex combination Eloise had ever received from it.

She really didn't have time for this. She was plummeting toward the bottom of a waterfall, and now the thing had decided it wanted to chat?

A split second before she hit the water, Eloise threw her arms over her head to protect her skull, took a deep breath, and hoped Çalaht wasn't in a grumpy mood.

There was a sudden glow from the Star. A flash of light flared just as Eloise hit the water.

Wet.

Wet, wet, wet.

And cold!

So very wet and cold.

The impact hadn't killed her. And she'd not impaled herself on, or dashed herself against, anything lurking beneath the surface.

Bonus.

As Eloise held her breath and tried to figure out what to do, the spark of something dropped back into silence. Eloise wasn't sure what to make of their interaction, nor its timing. That was something to think about later—when she wasn't busy trying not to drown.

The cascading waters of the River Thurmond were sourced high in the mountains. It was like diving into the liquid heart of winter. If she hadn't been underwater, the shock of the cold would have taken her breath away. Eloise knew the water was lethal, and she had to keep a clear head. Priorities: find the surface, get some air, and get to land without being swept downstream. Given that she wasn't yet sure which way was up, she didn't like her chances.

She twisted around, figured out which direction had more light, and swam toward it. Her sodden clothes slowed her down and her lungs screamed, but there was no way she was going to let herself drown. She'd survived where Mortimer Stolpern Caer Tomber Rrëzohem Yıxılmaq Ahhhhhh! Falls had not, and she would live to tell the tale even if it killed her.

Kicking with all her strength, she swam upward, the light getting brighter with each stroke. Just when she thought she'd have to suck in a lungful of water, she broke the surface and desperately gulped air.

She looked around and saw that she was close to the cascade. Much too close. If she didn't move away, she'd get sucked under again, maybe even caught behind it. That seemed just as fatal as the fall.

Eloise flailed left and right, trying to work out where to go. She pointed herself away from the downpour and swam several strokes. The tug of the current was palpable, and within moments, the pull became a drag, then turned into a rush, shoving her downstream.

Rocks were everywhere. Eloise bounced off a boulder, bruising a rib, then tried to grab onto another, only to have the water tear her away from it. Grappling rocks wasn't going to work.

Fighting the sweeping water and her wet clothes, Eloise flipped herself around so her legs aimed downstream. Once again, she decided it would be better for her feet to take a hit than her head. The river pushed her faster than she thought possible, and she bounced off one rock then another. A third spun her around, and the current pulled her under. She struggled back to the surface, coughed out freezing water, and battled to get back into the safer position.

The current was merciless, tossing her like a leaf. Eloise kept her head just above the surface to see where she was going and kicked away from rocks when she got too close. It took everything she had to avoid being trapped by underwater snares.

Somehow, she had to get to shore. Keeping her belly to the sky, she jounced along for a full strong length, exhaustion and cold sapping her strength. By the second strong length of the Thurmond's angry swell, she felt like a waterlogged rag doll.

Then came a moment of unexpected luck—a bend in the river slung her wide toward a tree branch wedged between two rocks. This was her chance. Eloise aimed herself for it, chanced a lunge when she got near, and managed to loop a leaden arm around it. Hugging the branch with everything she had left, Eloise prayed it would not break or dislodge and send her back into the rapids.

The branch creaked, bending against her weight.

But it held.

Eloise threw her other arm around it and allowed herself a few moments to catch her breath. With half-numb legs and bone-weary arms, she dragged herself along the branch and onto the bank, where she collapsed, teeth chattering, onto the muddy embankment.

10

IGNORING THE SMIRK

Lorch hadn't been thrilled with the idea of transporting the felon between the realms, even if he could appreciate the mercy the princesses had chosen to show.

But now this.

He'd been close to catching up with Princess Eloise and that Çalaht-cursed criminal Snotearrow McCcoonnch. But not close enough.

Now, the possibility that his princess and charge was dead was too high for him to consider directly. He could only contemplate the pieces that might go together to form that awful puzzle. Had she gotten out of the river? Had she sustained serious, even mortal, injury? Had the princess gone mind-numb, delirious, catatonic, or suffered some ravage of the soul?

Lorch swore at himself for failing. Why had he not climbed and run faster? Why had he allowed his arm to be cut? The princess had passed him up on the stone dome, and he'd never caught up. He'd come close, though—close enough to see her go over the edge. Close enough to see the longwalker's incredible leap and crash landing, and to hear Jerome scream in terror, then go silent. Close enough to see his princess plunge into the depths.

Even as he watched her fall, he imagined having to inform the queen that her daughter had smashed herself to bits in pursuit of a felon. Çalaht must have heard him scream, "No!" because, miraculously, Princess Eloise had entered the rocky pool perfectly, accompanied by some trick of green-tinged sunlight that flashed when she hit the water. More miraculously, she'd bobbed back up out of it, flailing and with no hint of trailing red. The last he saw of her was when she rounded a bend, the Thurmond's rapids washing her from view.

That last moment of her fall and its accompanying burst of light burned in his brain. How had she survived?

And did she still live?

Something else burned in Lorch's brain: Turpy's smirk. Lorch had glanced up to see Turpentine stand up after his jump, one leg steady and one damaged, then turned back to follow Eloise's fate. The jester saw the princess flailing in the outflow, and barked a laugh. Lorch's head jerked up in time to see Turpy—Çalaht take his soul and stretch his thumbs the length of the realms—smirking.

Smirking!

The jester's self-satisfied sneer had beamed across the Mortimer Falls spillway.

Snotearrow McCcoonnch had picked up Jerome, waggled his limp body as a taunt, and sauntered away with a leisurely, pained limp. There was no need to hurry. He knew Lorch would not pursue him. The guard would go after the girl.

Lorch swore that if he ever had the chance, he would wipe that smirk from Turpy's face. But for now, there was more important business to attend to.

The guard forced himself to work under the assumption that Princess Eloise was still alive. It was the only way he could function. He'd maintain that position until faced with incontrovertible evidence to the contrary.

It took him what felt like forever to get back to Hector, the Nameless One, and Kïïit. He was explaining the situation even as he finished climbing down the stone dome.

"Right," said Hector. The grim news brought out his practicality. "Do we search for the princess on this side of the Thurmond or the other?"

"We could do both if we split up," said Kïïit.

"I saw the Thurmond sweep her toward the far side. I say we head downstream and find a place to cross so we can search there."

Kïïit shook her head. "With respect, I think that's a mistake."

Lorch was already unhitching her from the cart. "Why?"

"I know the area. My herd used to come here to picnic every year. From what I remember, you won't find a reliable way across downriver. Not in this season. Not with the rain we've had."

"What do you suggest?" said Lorch.

"There is a reliable crossing upstream. It will be treacherous this time of year. and cold. But that is what I suggest."

"Going that way will add time," said Lorch.

"Yes, it will. But if you want to get to the other side that is how I would go."

Lorch looked at Hector and the Nameless One.

"We have to get to the princess," said Hector. "Whatever is fastest and will work."

The Nameless One gave a single nod.

"Agreed, then, Mistress Kïïit." Lorch finished unhitching the cart, secured a pannier with basic supplies to her back, topped up the bags carried by the others, then mounted the Nameless One, and let Kïïit lead the way.

It had taken time to make it back to the horses, decide what to do, and then work their way around the stone dome to the edge of the River Thurmond. More hours were taken by going upstream to find Kïïit's spot so they could ford the waters. They reached the spot at dusk.

"The rains have swollen the river here," said Kïïit. "I don't remember it being so violent."

"We're here now," said Lorch. "Do you think we can make it across?"

"We have to," said Hector. "Let's not spend too much time dallying. We should cross while there's still light."

"You can see the path on the other side where we're meant to come out. Aim for that. I'll go first," said Kïïit. Without waiting for their agreement, she stepped down from the bank and splashed into the water. "By Çalaht's chafed chilblains!"

"What?" said Hector.

"It's bloody cold!" The mare shivered, gritted her teeth, and strode into the torrent.

The Nameless One followed with Lorch, who laced the fingers of both hands tightly into his mane.

Hector went last, giving an involuntary "Oof" as he entered the freezing flow.

Lorch felt the Nameless One stepping carefully along the riverbed, sinking ever further into the icy water. He did his best to ignore the cold that swept up his calves to his thighs and hips. The river tugged at him, making it hard to stay on the horse's back, especially as the creeping numbness in his legs set in.

Ahead, Kïïit's back submerged and her movements changed—she swam instead of walked. Lorch saw her paddling through the water as she moved against the turbid current. Moments later, the Nameless One also launched himself forward, his legs churning below the surface in a mimicry of cantering.

The Thurmond pushed them, its debris-filled water shoving them along. The three horses struggled toward the other side, but were soon far downstream from where they meant to be.

The Nameless One barely kept his face above the surface and Lorch feared that his weight was the problem. "Should I get off and swim?" Lorch asked.

The Nameless One shook his head and kept going.

After what felt like an age, Lorch saw Kïïit's body moving differently, and moments later, the Nameless One's hooves touched the river bed again. Less than a minute later, they stood on the far bank, chests heaving, their clothes, hides, and panniers all dripping.

Hector moved a few steps away and shook. "That was a misery I hope never to repeat." Lorch slid off the Nameless One so he could also shake off.

"It was definitely not the grass strudel," agreed Kïïit. "What I would give for a nice, warm meadow to roll on."

Lorch felt the chill of wind bite through his clothes, but there was nothing to be done about it. Any clothes in the saddlebag would be just as wet. "Do you need me to build a fire so we can warm up and rest a while?"

Hector shook his head. "I'll be warm enough if we can just keep moving. Kïïit, any idea where your trail is from here?"

"Not really. It'll be somewhere around." Kïïit's teeth chattered, and she began shivering. "I agree with Hector—I'd rather keep moving."

"Let's go then," said Lorch. "I'll walk awhile so I can warm up as well."

They picked a path away from the river, and half a strong length later, stumbled across the trail. Turning to head downhill, they walked as fast as they could and, where possible, trotted. Eventually, Lorch dried off enough for him to ride the Nameless One through the more open stretches so they could go faster.

As evening became night, their trail took them toward the bottom of Mortimer Falls but skirted the top, so they did not come to where Turpy had landed with Jerome. With only the thin glow of a shrouded full moon to light their way, Kïïït picked her way down the escarpment, finding routes Lorch knew he would never have seen—paths more suited to goats than equines.

Concentrating on not falling wasn't enough to distract Lorch from silently cataloging worst-case scenarios. The princess might have broken bones. Damage to internal organs. Pieces missing or mangled. They might find her dead. Find her dying. Find her alive, but then have her die before they could do anything to help her. The might find her alive and physically whole, but mentally damaged.

As it neared dawn, the path emptied them out at a spot far enough away from Mortimer Falls that its roar was muffled and distant. "Hector and Kïïït, backtrack upstream to see if she's there," said Lorch. "The Nameless One and I will go downstream from here."

"Right," said Hector. "If you find her—"

"*When* we find her..."

"Of course. *When* we find her, we'll let you know."

"And we'll do the same."

Lorch took the stretch closest to the river, letting the Nameless One move along higher up the embankment. Behind him, Lorch heard Hector and Kïïït calling out for Eloise, and he did the same as he went, climbing over the long-fallen carcasses of trees and debris washed down by long forgotten floods.

The winter rains had eased overnight, replaced by fog that severely hampered visibility. "Princess! Princess are you there?" he yelled again and again, as he and the Nameless One searched in a carefully overlapping, zig-zag spiral to ensure they covered everywhere she might be.

The misty light yielded countless tricks to the eye—shapes that could possibly be the princess, but which resolved to be nothing up close. It reminded Lorch of the first (and only) time he'd had his heart broken.

Her name was Devorkah, and as a teen, he'd loved her with the heat of a million suns. When Devorkah looked at him with her crossed eyes—one mud brown and one the hazel of pond slime—or smiled at him with those too-small buck teeth, or held his hand (always his right in her left, because the oozing psoriasis of her right hand was bandaged), his heart swelled like it was blasted by a blacksmith's bellows. Once, she even let him kiss her cheek, which he did, careful to avoid the small weeping sores that gave her such a beautiful red flush. He'd have swallowed seas for her, picked a paddock of wildflowers, or searched every harvest bushel in Lower Glenth to find her the perfect radish.

She had said "yes" when he'd asked her to the Radish Fest's Radish Bash. He'd bought her a radish corsage, dressed in his best going-to-town tunic, and pinned a radish boutonniere to his chest. They had a wonderful time (or so he thought), dancing jigs and reels and learning the latest set dances called by the fiddler.

Midway through the evening, Lorch left Devorkah for a moment to fetch her a mug of sweet radish punch. When he returned, she wasn't at the table. Instead, she was dancing a slow hornpipe with Proctor Morton, the youngest of the village elders. Proctor had a better tunic, a larger radish boutonniere, and much sweeter words. Devorkah had taken Lorch's corsage off her hand and replaced it with one Proctor Morton had given her.

They were married a fortnight later.

Lorch was not invited.

It shattered him. For weeks, Lorch moped from one end of the day to the other, unable to look at a radish. The worst part was the way his mind played tricks on him. Every female shape with rat-brown hair seen from behind was her, if only for a moment. So was every bandaged hand (right or left). And the same for every pair of crossed eyes. Lorch saw Devorkah everywhere, in everything and everyone.

This torment went on for months, until an uncle, one of the prattle-weed users who usually didn't have much to say, told him to "Quit yer sulking and go get a job with the queen's guards. It's what your Da would have done." So Lorch packed up, went to Brague, and enlisted as a guard. Mercifully, the change of location, the distraction of soldier training, and the camaraderie of new friendships finally drove thoughts of Devorkah from his head.

But those thoughts came sneaking back as Lorch looked for Princess Eloise along the misted banks of the River Thurmond. He'd been such a fool, especially in the weeks after Devorkah and Proctor had gotten hitched. But here he was again, seeing a young woman's form everywhere. Every branch, mound, and dark hollow jolted his insides as possibly being the thing he sought.

Lorch just hoped this story would have a better ending.

"Princess! Princess Eloise! Are you there?" Lorch's voice rasped as he yelled above the Thurmond. "Princess! Can you hear me?"

As the searching stretched from a second hour to a third and his voice grew hoarse, Lorch became more and more scared that things would not end well.

And then a screaming neigh ripped through the air.

The Nameless One had broken his perpetual silence.

He'd found something.

Lorch prayed he'd found something alive.

SOLDIER'S COLD

Lorch ran to where the Nameless One stood by a mud-streaked, Eloise-colored mound. She was curled up on her side beneath an inadequate branch that provided only token cover. Her clothes were sodden, from the cuffs of her breeks to the hood of her travel cloak.

She did not move.

Lorch swallowed his apprehension and knelt down beside her. "Princess. Princess Eloise." His voice was gentle, but his tone commanding, like an officer expecting a report. When none came, he sat back on his heels to see if there was the movement of breath. None was obvious in the dense mist.

Lorch reached for her wrist to find a pulse. As he pinched it, he realized it was the first time he'd ever deliberately touched her. Out of respect, Lorch had always kept his distance. Sure, there had been the odd, accidental grazing of skin when a cup of tea or a loaf of bread had been passed between them. But this was deliberate, premeditated. It struck him, even in this dire situation, as somehow inappropriate. It was not his place.

Lorch tried to hide his discomfort from the Nameless One.

Feeling for her heartbeat, he held his breath and closed his eyes to focus. He couldn't feel anything, but his hands were half frozen, and he didn't trust his ability to detect the delicate movement at her wrist.

"I'm sorry, Princess," he said, more for himself than for her. Lorch wiped his hand on his breeks, trying in vain to dislodge some of the grime before he touched her again. Feeling even more self-conscious, he pinched the sides of her neck below the jaw, seeking her assassin's artery. Again he closed his eyes and slowed his breathing, searching for a sign of life.

Nothing.

Tears fought to escape the guard's eyes. "Princess," he whispered. "Come on, Princess."

And then, just as he was about to let go, he felt something. It was like an elderly butterfly's drunk hiccups. Her pulse fluttered once, then after way, way too much time, slowly tapped the side of his index finger again.

"She lives!" Lorch wiped an eye with the heel of his hand, then looked at the Nameless One. "Get the others. I'll try to revive her."

The Nameless One galloped off in the direction they'd come.

Lorch wanted to rush into action, administering every kind of treatment he could think of, including picking up the princess and sprinting for Brague and the healers he might find there.

But he had to be careful. He didn't know if she was injured, or if so, to what extent.

What was the acronym for soldier's first aid? The letters represented the steps one was supposed to take. F.L.A.B.B.E.R.G.A.S.T? F.I.L.B.E.R.T? F.L.U.M.M.O.X? F.A.B.U.L.I.S.T?

No, no. He remembered—it was F.A.D.O.O.D.L.E. "F" for "Figure out if anyone is about to explode, implode, or toss a caber at you." "A" for "Ascertain if the person's head is still fully attached." "D" for "Dash around in a panic for a while." "O" for "Originate a scream for help," and then another "O" for "Organize your emotions so you can face whatever it is that's probably disgusting and awaiting your attention." "D" for "Do whatever needs doing." "L" for "Live life to its fullest, especially if the disgusting thing in front of you has died and makes you question the meaning of your life." And "E" for "Extend a hand to the person you've just helped so they can either use it to stand up and get on with things or shake it farewell so they can go stand with Çalaht."

"Princess, can you hear me? Princess, are you there?" He repeated the phrases to give her something to hear. Lorch swallowed back his hesitations and gently squeezed down her arms, then her legs, feeling for fractures. He found nothing obvious.

Lorch took another moment to consider her. The princess's clothes were sodden, and her skin was cold and tinged blue. Yet, she was not shivering. In fact, it looked like she'd tried to take some of her clothing off. Strange. She was mind-numb, and did not speak or moan when touched. Her pulse was slow and possibly erratic. She'd been exposed to the elements all afternoon, all night, and all morning, and the weather had been misery itself. Her breathing was slow and shallow.

Lorch realized he'd seen this before.

That she'd tried to take off some of her clothes tipped him off. He'd seen it once on campaign. They had been trapped by a blizzard on a mountain crossing and forced to hunker down in the freezing cold. Everyone was cold and miserable, and several had lost digits to frostbite. But two of the soldiers had something worse. They went past feeling cold to the point where their minds fooled them into thinking they were too hot, and they began stripping away coats and tunics. Lorch's captain had called it "soldier's cold," where the body could not heat itself up.

The men had died.

Lorch looked up when he heard the thunder of horse hooves heading for him.

"We came as soon as we heard the scream," said Hector, sliding to a stop. "Is she still alive?"

"Only just. I think she suffers the soldier's cold," said Lorch.

"Oh. Not good. Not good at all," said Kiïit. "What can we do for her?"

"She needs warmth," said Lorch. "I should build a fire somehow."

"With all this wet? That will take too long, surely," said Hector.

Kiïit leaned town and touched the princess gently with her nose. "We need to get these wet things off her. They'll be making the cold worse."

"I'll start working on the fire."

"No, you have to tend her," said Hector.

Lorch's face reddened. "I would rather set the fire."

"I would do it," said Kiïit. "But it would take me forever."

"Lorch, what's the matter?" asked Hector.

"I... I cannot." The red in Lorch's face deepened.

"What? Why ever not?"

"It..." Lorch swallowed. "It would be improper for me to undress her. Just as it would be improper for me to see her undressed," he stammered. "It is simply wrong."

"Sweet," said Kiïit. "Sweet, if wrong-headed."

"Please don't mock me," said Lorch.

"It is improper to let her succumb to the soldier's cold," snapped Hector. "You were blessed with an opposable thumb. Stop dithering and use it."

"I—"

"Try treating her like a fallen comrade," said Kiïit. "That is what she is right now. She's not the princess. She's a fallen comrade who needs your help."

It was a line of thinking Lorch understood. On campaign, especially after an armed engagement, bodies stopped being things that were private and became things to tend, mend, and, if necessary, bury. If blood gushed, you staunched. If viscera were exposed, you bandaged. If bits were sliced, you tried to sew them together.

"Right. That..." Lorch straightened himself, face still flushed. "That I think I can do."

A snort came from up the embankment. The Nameless One motioned for them to come.

Hector trotted over. The two disappeared, then Hector came back alone. "Bring her up here. The Nameless One has found shelter, of sorts."

"Right. Good." Lorch moved to Eloise's other side so he could pick her up. "She's a soldier. Just a fallen soldier," he muttered as he gently lifted her. She was lighter than he'd expected.

Eloise roused from the depths of her mind-numbness and moaned. Her lips moved, and she seemed to be saying something.

"Princess?" said Lorch. "What was that?"

She coughed the barest of coughs. "Seven bean," she whispered, then dropped back to the La La Realms.

Lorch strode up the slope, hoping he wasn't causing internal damage by moving her. He found the Nameless One standing beneath a thick-needled conifer. It had a tangle of overlapping leaves forming an upward spiral that shed rain like a parasol.

"It's dry underneath," said Kïïït. "Ain't that the grass strudel."

"Amazing," said Lorch. He carefully laid the princess near the tree's trunk. "Our blankets will be wet from the rain and the river crossing. The needles will have to do for a bed."

He untied the princess's travel cloak and slid it out from under her, folding it carefully before placing it to the side. Next, he unlaced her boots and removed both them and her socks. Her feet were stiff with cold, and he made himself rub them, possibly as an excuse to put off what came next. "I'm sorry," he whispered, then closed both eyes and, doing what he could to avoid touching her, untied the laces of her tunic, and then her breeks. "She's a soldier. She's just a fallen soldier. A soldier."

But, of course, she wasn't. No amount of saying it would change the fact that he was doing something that only her handmaid should ever do. This went against every notion of propriety that he held dear. He just hoped he could finish the job without looking.

He felt more than heard one of the horses sitting down next to him. Opening one eye a crack, he saw that it was Kiïit. "Hang in there, mate. You'll be alright," she said.

Lorch wasn't sure if she meant him or the princess.

He untied the sash that held the box containing the Star of Whatever. Eloise reacted to that, moving her hand to the box, protecting it. That was a good sign, if odd. Lorch did not try to take it from her.

Carefully, he slid off her drenched tunic, leaving her in the undershirt she wore. He folded the tunic and then, shutting his eyes a little tighter, slid off her breeks. As he got her second leg free, he felt another horse sit down on his other side. A squint revealed it was the Nameless One who, like Kiïit, sat with his back to the princess. Lorch understood what they meant to do. They'd put Eloise between them, using their two bodies to warm hers. Smart. Being as big as they were, there was more of them to provide heat, certainly more than Lorch could have provided, assuming he could have brought himself to do so. Plus, a horse's body was normally warmer than a human's.

"Is she ready?" asked Kiïit.

"Yes. I think so."

"Roll her on her side, like she was giving me a hug."

"Right." Lorch walked around to kneel at her head. He slid a hand under her shoulder until he could feel her shoulder blade through her shirt, then rolled her against the mare. While he held her in place, the

Nameless One eased backwards until he pressed Eloise firmly against Kïïït. Lorch turned her head so her face was free and tucked her arm between them so it would be warmed as well.

"I'll light a fire now," said Lorch. He moved to gather twigs and tried not to dwell on what he may or may not have accidentally seen the few times he had briefly had to look at what he was doing.

He hoped the princess would forgive him.

He hoped she lived. If she survived the soldier's cold, he could survive his embarrassment.

12

NOT A CHOICE, REALLY

Eloise sat wrapped in five blankets, hugging a mug of something she wished was haggleberry tea, but which had the consistency of thin tar and tasted of peat, hickory, and malicious intent. Kïïït insisted it would help revive her, but Eloise would rather drink tea made from Gordon the Noisome's ear wax than finish the cup of evil in her hands.

She forced another sip, resisting the urge to fling the mug as far away as she could, and wondered if her clothes were dry enough to wear yet. Lorch had barely looked at her since she had woken up smooshed between two horses wearing just her undergarments.

Awkward.

Rain fell beyond the rim of the tree, and she sat near a small fire. It was far enough from the tree trunk to make sure the flames did not hurt it, and small enough not to threaten any of its branches. Eloise was grateful that Lorch had chosen to dry blankets first, since she needed the warmth. They all did, except Kïïït, who seemed impervious to the chill air. But Eloise was not really comfortable huddled barely dressed beneath the blankets.

"So, Princess," said Hector. "Can you tell us what you remember?"

The plunge from Mortimer Falls kept playing through her mind, every moment still vivid. "I almost caught him. I laid a hand on Turpy, but I think that was his intention. His longwalker magic sort of sucked me along behind him and over the edge. I remember Jerome's scream as he crossed the canyon above me. I think I screamed too." That was a lot of words for her at the moment. It was tiring to speak.

"You did, Princess, yes," said Lorch. "I heard you."

Eloise didn't want to talk about the strange interaction with the Star of Whatever. She suspected—no, she was certain—it had kept her from being smooshed flat or broken into a thousand pieces. But the back-and-forth with it had taken three heartbeats at most, and now the thing was as quiet as ever. One of these days, she was going to have to figure out what the deal was with the thing. For now, it would stay her secret.

Instead, she gave a quick recount of how she had dragged herself out of the river and failed to make a fire. "All the wood I found was wet, and I didn't have a flint. I tried rubbing sticks together, but that wasn't going to happen. I may as well have waved them in the air and made a wish." Eloise forced herself to swallow another sip of the restorative tea. "Ugh."

"Anything else happen?" asked Kiïit.

"There was lots of shivering. I thought I'd found a nice, cozy spot to curl up in, but from what Lorch said, I was completely exposed. I must have been delirious. I have a vague memory of feeling hot."

"That's part of the soldier's cold," said Lorch. "It plays tricks on the mind."

"Strange. Well, tricks or no tricks, I could do as little about feeling hot as I could about the cold I'd felt before. And then I just let go to mind-numbness, having worked out that I probably wasn't going to survive the night."

"But you did survive the night," said Hector.

"Apparently. Unless something happened to all of you as well and we're all chatting in the next world." Eloise pulled the blankets around her. "The next thing I remember is waking up pressed between the two of you. It took me a very long time to figure that one out, since I couldn't move or speak. How did I faceplant into a horse?"

Eloise sipped again. Hot malice in a mug. She wondered what Johanna was drinking at the moment. Probably not a cup of malevolence.

"How are you now?" asked Kïïït.

"I'm not staring at Her gap-toothed beneficence. That's a start. But I hurt everywhere. Every muscle and every joint. My fingers and toes, especially. This really is an amazing tree, the way it keeps the rain off." She paused. "It's possible I'm having attention issues." She took another sip of the heinousness in her mug and pulled the blankets tighter. "So. Any thoughts on what we do next?"

"Princess, let's not concern ourselves with that just yet," said Lorch, staring intently at the small branch he was feeding into the fire. "You need more time to recover."

"We can talk about it. I'm ready. Please."

"Yes, Princess."

"Tell me, does anyone have any idea why Turpy took Jerome with him? Why not just drop him when he first got clunked and went mind-numb?" asked Eloise. "Why not clunk him harder and end his life? Or chuck him into the falls and be done with him. With everything going on, why keep Jerome?"

"You know how Jerome can be," said Hector. "He was needling him. Constantly, it seemed. Perhaps the answer is simple—Turpentine wishes to exact blind revenge."

"It seems like a lot of effort for little return," said Lorch. "Even for someone as craven as Turpy, it's hard to see where there's value for him."

"Perhaps we need to look at it from another angle," said Eloise. She sipped again. The drink tasted worse as it cooled. She'd have to slug it down soon.

"What do you mean?" asked Hector.

"Let's think about what he did. He contrived a means of escape and executed it. When he ran away, the direction was conscious. Not random. I think his taking Jerome was the same. It may have been opportune, but it was not without reason."

"You're right that he's very deliberate in his ways," said Hector. "Look at everything he's orchestrated since he visited Castle Brague."

"Exactly," said Eloise. "A lot of planning, thinking, and manipulation went into all of it. So we know he's capable of all that. It's clear he knew where he was going. He probably chose the stone dome as a way to limit pursuit. I would guess that all along, he thought he might be able to jump Mortimer Falls. He'd make it or die trying. Either result would appeal more than facing the queen's justice at Brague."

Lorch stood and brushed conifer needles from his breeks. "He's met our queen. He'd have a keen sense of what awaited him in Brague."

"Going back to the princess's first question: why take Jerome?" asked Kïïït. "What's the point of keeping the princess's champion with him?"

"I think you have it there. He's my champion," said Eloise.

"With respect, Princess, so what?" said Kïïït. "It's not like Jerome presents a physical threat that Turpy has to neutralize."

"Maybe it's just his twisted way," said Lorch.

Hector tilted his head. "Possible, but not certain. He has four and a half realms to get lost in. He need never see us again. He need never see *anyone* again. Why not go somewhere and start over?"

"Possible, like you said. But Turpy's ambitious." Eloise paused, avoiding another sip of the swill. "He's ambitious, smart, persuasive, cunning, has longwalker weak magic, and wants his own way. Perhaps more than anyone else I've ever met. He isn't afraid to manipulate people, whether he's using coin or prattleweed. It doesn't matter if the person being manipulated is a drunkard like Lёёèstéёèr at Ye Olde Inn, his brother, or someone as noble as the late king himself, may he stand with Çalaht. No, Turpy wants something, and he wants it bad. Maybe it's being king, or king-like. Maybe he still wants this." Eloise patted the box containing the Star of Whatever. "It's what he wanted at Stained Rock. But who knows? He's like a good hockey sacking left flutter—always thinking down the field, always trying to be seven steps ahead of everyone else on the paddock, always adjusting his tactics and moves. If he has Jerome with him, there's a reason. Probably several. If nothing else, possessing Jerome gives him a bargaining chip."

"A bargaining chipmunk, more like," smirked Kїїït.

No one laughed.

"What would Turpy be expecting us to do, in this circumstance?" asked Lorch. "If he's thinking a few moves ahead, what would he want our next move to be?"

"Holding Jerome makes that clear, I think," said Eloise. "He wants us to follow. To come after him. Having Jerome makes it certain we'll pursue."

There was a silence while they all contemplated this.

"I think you could be right, Princess." Lorch was still not looking at her directly, but he at least glanced her way.

"I'm sorry, but I have to ask this," said Kїїït. "Do we really think Champion Abernatheen de Chipmunk is still alive?"

"We can't say, Mistress Kїїït," said Lorch. "I can say for certain he was alive when the felon landed, but then Jerome went suddenly quiet. I saw Turpy pick him up off the ground and take him as he limped off in the other direction. If Champion Abernatheen de Chipmunk was dead, I don't think the felon would have bothered to do that."

"I agree," said Hector.

"He has to be alive," said Eloise. "He just has to be. I say, there's absolutely no choice about what we do next. None, zero, zip, nada, nichts." She slugged down the rest of the vile sludge and thunked down the mug. "We do what the miscreant expects us to do. We go after him."

"Yes, Princess," said Lorch. "And then?"

"Then we find him, and we find Jerome," said Eloise. "Or we find him, find out what he's done with Jerome, and make him pay for it."

"And if we just find Jerome?" asked Hector.

"That'll be good enough."

❧

THE FIVE OF THEM PASSED ANOTHER COLD, RAINY NIGHT UNDER THE tree. Lorch insisted that Eloise have more time to recover before they resumed the rigors of travel.

The next morning was shrouded by another heavy fog, and they all felt its heavy hush.

Lorch walked over to where Eloise sat. He handed her a mug.

Eloise sniffed. "Oh, thank Çalaht, it's haggleberry tea." She took it from him and sipped. "It's excellent."

"Thank you, Princess." Lorch stood a few moments looking out beyond the edge of their shelter tree. "Fog this morning."

"Morning fog makes the promise of blue skies later on. Something to look forward to." Eloise wrapped her hands around the mug. Her fingers ached, and she hoped the warmth might help.

They stayed there several long moments, Lorch standing and Eloise relishing her tea.

"Are we really going to speak of the weather?" asked Eloise.

"I have concerns, Princess. I always seem to have concerns, don't I?" Lorch squatted so he was at her level. "Are you well, Princess Eloise?"

"Well? No, I don't think so."

"I feared not."

"Lorch, I think I just want to go home. I've had enough. I'm tired and I'm sore, and I could sleep for a month of months. And I'm worried sick about Jerome. What if we don't find him? What if I never see him again?"

Lorch met her eyes for a moment—the first time since she'd awakened—then he looked away again, still awkward. "Yes, Princess, I know. We will do this as quickly as we can. With any luck it won't be more than a few days extra."

Both of them knew that was probably a lie, but it was a comfortable one for the moment.

"And we will find Champion Abernatheen de Chipmunk. On my word, I will do everything I can to make that happen."

Eloise nodded. "And so will I." She turned toward him and gave a formal bow, or as formal as she could manage while sitting down holding tea. "Guard Lacksneck, thank you for everything. Thank you for coming after me. Thank you for saving my life."

Lorch returned the formal bow, as well as he could from a squat. "You're welcome, Princess. You cannot know how glad I am that that is our result. Your living was far from certain."

"Well, thank you again."

"Always, Princess," said Lorch. "Always."

Eloise paused. "There is a matter we have not discussed."

"Oh?" Lorch's face reddened. He guessed where she was headed.

"The very tiny matter of how I came to find myself squashed between two horses, clad in my smalls."

"I'm sorry, Princess. I truly—"

Eloise put up a hand to stop him. "Lorch, I cannot have things awkward between us. I cannot do this journey without you. Without any of you. What was done needed to be done for me to live. Please, it's fine."

"Yes, Princess." Lorch's face and neck reddened even more. "That's kind of you to say."

"I mean it. I do." Eloise took a long drink of her tea, trying to hide the pink that rose in her cheeks. "That said, I'm glad I wasn't really there to know what was going on."

Lorch rubbed the back of his neck and cleared his throat a little. "If it helps, one kept one's eyes closed the whole time. The others can confirm that. Anything that was a secret before remains a secret still."

Eloise nodded. They both knew that that, too, was probably a lie, but was also a comfortable one. It would do for now.

13

THE DRAGGED FOOT

The two humans and three horses picked their way through the thick woods and made it back to the top of Mortimer Falls by mid-morning, just shy of three days since Turpy's escape. The group emerged from the forest trail to bask in a bright winter sun. A light, favorable breeze blew the mist from the falls away from them, keeping them from getting soaked.

Eloise forced herself to look across the crevasse to the observation deck on the far side. Then, pushing aside queasiness, she forced herself to look down and see just how far she'd plunged. "Çalaht chucking chintzy cheroots at chastised cherubs," she swore under her breath. "That's a bit of a drop."

The others came and stood near her, also taking in the enormity of the distance. The crash of the falls squelched conversation, but Eloise was pretty sure she heard Kïïït say, "That ain't fit for a turf war," before shuddering and walking away.

The Nameless One nodded at Lorch to catch his attention, swept his head in the direction of the pool below, and snorted.

Lorch tilted his head and looked over the edge, calculating. "Hard to tell exactly," he yelled. "I'd put it at 120 lengths, maybe 150."

The Nameless One pawed the ground once in Eloise's direction.

"I don't know," he said, this time much quieter.

Eloise leaned in. "Don't know what?"

"The Nameless One has bad depth perception. So he was asking how far down I thought it was."

"I got that bit. I meant the other bit."

"Oh." Lorch lifted one shoulder, then the other. "The Nameless One asked how it was you are still alive. I truly don't know. Do you, Princess? Do you know how you survived?"

"I have a theory," she said. "But I'm not quite ready to share it."

Lorch widened his eyes a moment, then shrugged. "I look forward to hearing it. When you're ready."

"So where did Turpy land?"

Lorch looked across toward the observation platform, then back to their side of the falls, trying to recall the path Turpy had flown. He gestured for the others to follow, and walked upstream toward the falls.

Fifty lengths along, he stopped. "Somewhere around here," he yelled, motioning with his arm.

Eloise saw that the platform was now straight ahead on the other side. How could Turpy have possibly made it this far and survived? He was a longwalker, not a bird. Then again, essentially the same question had just been asked of her. But Turpy didn't have the Star of Whatever. How much weak magic would someone need to jump that far, especially with a mangled foot? Plus, he was running like his life depended on it, which it almost certainly did. Whatever he'd done, he'd done it successfully. Now he was gone, and with Jerome. Or so she assumed. For all Eloise knew, Turpy was sitting behind a rock or up a tree watching them, with Jerome stuffed in a sack or tied up and hanging upside down, gagged. These thoughts made her skin itch.

They spread out to see if they could identify the exact landing point, or find some clue as to what direction they needed to go. They all stepped carefully, searching for footprints, a clump of hair, or maybe a bit of torn clothing.

Lorch had been surprisingly accurate, because it was only a few minutes before Hector yelled, "Come here! Look!"

It was a small blade, half out of its scabbard. "It's Jerome's champion's sword." Eloise picked it up, wiped mud from it, and looked at it closely. "The buckle is damaged, and the strap's snapped."

"It must have broken when he hit the ground," said Lorch. "Champion Abernatheen de Chipmunk would never have left it deliberately."

"I agree."

"Unless he meant us to find it," said Hector.

"I agree with that, too. Although from what Lorch said, Jerome was limp when Turpy walked off with him. That suggests this was not deliberate. But either way, it's evidence of him."

"Look there," said Lorch. He pointed to a trail of steps leading away from the falls. They didn't look like normal footsteps, more like the trail of a one-legged man dragging a log. "Snotearrow McCcoonnch."

"He's clearly in pain," said Kïïit. It was the first time she'd made herself heard above the crashing water.

"How can you tell?" asked Eloise.

"His steps." She pointed with her nose, and led the others along the trail, stepping carefully to the side to avoid disturbing the footprints. "See how they are narrow. They are labored. He is lame, stepping hard with his right foot, and dragging the left one behind him. See how far into the ground the forward foot goes, especially the heel? He favors the right one almost completely. He cannot move fast. Or maybe he does not feel he needs to. Either way, his escape, the damage he did to himself with the iron cuff, and the jump, all look like they've taken their toll."

"He deserves every bit of it," muttered Eloise, quiet enough that the others wouldn't hear.

They continued following Turpy's tracks until they were far enough from the falls to be able to speak normally. Eloise was happy to leave Mortimer Falls behind. Despite its exquisite natural beauty, it was not a place she would remember fondly. She turned to Kiiit. "Can you tell where he's headed?"

"Not yet. We'd need to follow his path a while further. He might be going back to Stained Rock. That's where most people who come here would come from. But he might be going on to the Western Lands and All That Really Matters. He might be going..." She trailed off, like she was looking at a map in her mind.

"Really, he might be going anywhere."

"Yes, Princess," said Kiiit. "One might guess he'd go somewhere to find an apothecary or a healer."

"Wherever he's headed, he has three days' head start. I suggest we get moving. We'll follow his trail and see where it takes us. Even if he is a longwalker, we should be able to catch up if he's in as much pain as Kiiit suggests."

Eloise mounted Hector, Lorch got on the Nameless One, and they again let Kiiit lead the way. Turpy's trail led them through the bare trunks and branches of a deciduous forest, where the fallen leaves of oak, beech, hickory, and elm carpeted the ground. For the most part, the dragged foot was an easy thing to track. After two hours, they came to a place where Kiiit said Turpy had stopped and rested a while.

They paused so the mare could scout the area. While she did, Lorch and Eloise dismounted. The guard took a pouch from the Nameless One's pannier. It contained nuts, seeds, and dried fruit. "May I ask a question, Princess?"

Eloise cupped her hands so he could pour some of the mix into them. "Of course.

"What do we do when we find them, Princess?" asked Lorch.

"What do you mean?"

"Do we attempt to recapture the felon, or do we simply attempt to rescue the champion?"

"Both, if we can."

"I agree with that. But we might find ourselves having to choose one or the other?"

"Jerome is my friend and champion."

"Princess, I would suggest Snotearrow McCcoonnch is a genuine threat to the realms."

"Is he?" Hector joined them, but declined the offered food. "He no longer has King Doncaster as a sponsor, protector, or facilitator. He does not control the throne through the tool of prattleweed. He does not have the means or access that being court jester once gave him. He has no coin and no papers. Is he not just a man with longwalker weak magic, a broken foot, and a kidnapped and, one might guess, very angry chipmunk in his possession?"

"When you put it that way, he doesn't sound like a compelling threat."

"Princess, it would be a mistake to assume that he's given up all ambition. He has been enough trouble already—it would be wrong to underestimate him."

"When you put it that way, I agree he remains a threat." Eloise ate a walnut and thought. "We will recover Jerome and capture Turpy. And if we have to make a choice, we will make a choice based on what's before us. But there's no way I'm abandoning Jerome. None."

"Yes, Princess."

❦ 14 ❦

KÄÄÄCHÖÖÖ

After another two hours of tracking, Kïïit said, "I think I know where he's going."

"Oh?" said Eloise.

"Kääächööö."

"Çalaht bless you. Do you need a handkerchief?"

"No, no. Kääächööö. It's the 'healers' village. Everyone there is some sort of 'healer.'" Kïïit indicated the air quotes using her ears.

That Kääächööö was the "healers" village (as distinct from a healers village) was part accident, part commerce strategy, and part survival mechanism. For millennia before the village was founded, healers of various forms had practiced their arts peacefully to whatever degree of success they had. For years, it was very much live and let live (or die) when it came to healing modalities.

However, about four centuries before, some of the more successful forms of healing had started getting snooty, valuing a result where people healed over those where they did not. This prejudice toward efficacy created a huge stink, and caused the practitioners of the healing forms to band together. Organizations sprang up, like the Order of the Odors (aromatherapists), the Solidarity of Spinners (rotational therapists who worked with the healing properties of dizziness), and the Club Club (healers who used various hammers on their patients).

As the healers factionalized, tensions escalated across the realms, finally boiling over when the Herbalists Guild banded with the League of Bone Sawers and the militant Lodge of Leechers, and got out the muscle. They knocked heads with members of the Trepanationists Union and roughed up a meeting of the Society of Therapeutic Phlebotomists in what became known as the Blood Letting of the Bloodletters. This violence sparked the all-out Great Healers War, a hard-fought battle for the literal hearts, minds and bodies of the realms. It was a war waged with scalpels and scissors, poisons and pendulums, mortars and pestles, massage stones used as projectiles and healing cups heated to torturous levels. The strife lasted a full century, despite the occasional ineffective ceasefire. For decades, you were taking your life in your hands if you practiced a healing art in a manner that one of the more strident guilds looked down on.

Healers fell often and fatally. The conflict was barbaric, and whether the fighting was conducted as an open skirmish or with guerrilla tactics, the results were inevitably gruesome.

It was Gwendolyn the Irritable who staunched the bloodshed. She managed it just before she fell in love with King Brüüütus of the Northern Lands and the wheels fell off her reign. Gwendolyn decreed the foundation of a Consolidated Healers United Guild of the Generally Efficacious Remedy Systems (soon known as the "Chuggers Guild" and its members simply as "chuggers"). By Gwendolyn's design, this healers' guild would be a single, unifying body covering all accepted and acceptable healing practices. She then commanded that the warring parties put down their specula and singing bowls, their oil diffusers and healing needles, and petition for entry to the guild.

It worked.

The various healers were either allowed in the guild, in which case they promised to wear the guild's blood-red hoods and, and ply their arts side-by-side in peace, or they were rejected by the guild, and banished from practice. An armistice was signed, the guild flourished, and everyone was happy.

Well, not everyone.

Practitioners of non-chugger modalities, deprived of their livelihoods, fell on hard times, and suffered.

One such person was Wïïïlbüüür Pääätëëënt, a purveyor of serpentine-derived, oleaginous viscous solutions. Pääätëëënt had medicines, balms, salves, lotions, creams, and liniments full of exotic ingredients he claimed would cure all ills. There were nostrums for everything from colds and cankers to "the shakes" and "male complaints" (which could be pretty much anything).

Pääätëëënt applied to be a chugger, but was denied entry when, at his admittance hearing, one of the panel of evaluators died after trying a nostrum for hair regrowth. He was stripped of the privilege of plying his trade and was soon forced to declare himself bankrupt.

But Wïïïlbüüür Pääätëëënt was not one to suffer in silence. He moved to a remote location in an unincorporated section of the Northern Lands known, if at all, for its rutabaga farms, and set up shop out of reach of guild eyes and ears. There, he founded a village, and began attracting a steady clientele of those who had not found success with chugger-approved healing approaches. These patients were followed by other practitioners who had not found a place in the guild. The latter set up shop there as well, and it was not long before you had your choice of all manner of healing. There was fluttering, where the healer fluttered his or her hands around your body. There was staring, where the healer would simply gaze at an audience and induce a healing state. There was cabbage fasting, grapefruit fasting, the locally developed rutabaga fasting, as well as fasting from fasting. There were micro-poisoners, who administered tiny amounts of poisons, infectors who'd slice you open and shove something into the wound so infection could really set in, and ague spreaders, who would come and give you an ague so you could die of that instead of whatever else you were suffering from.

Someone eventually put up a sign at the town's entrance that read, "Welcome to the Healers Village."

A chance chugger traveler happened on the hamlet, saw the sign, assessed what was going on, and reported it to guild headquarters. The guild, based in the Western Lands and All That Really Matters, sent representatives to King Brüüütus' court at Stained Rock in the Northern Lands to get him to shut the rogue healers down. But by then he was getting over his fling with Queen Gwendolyn, and wasn't inclined charitably toward Westies. He ruled against them, saying they did not have standing to petition against a town in an unincorporated part of his realm.

So the Westie representatives hired advocates, who fashioned a petition to the king based on something akin to false advertising. As the people in Pääätëëënt's village were not healers, since the term could only legally apply to officially sanctioned chuggers, they could not advertise themselves as such.

King Brüüütus reluctantly ruled in their favor. A sneering delegation of chuggers journeyed to the remote Northo village and presented Wïïïlbüüür Pääätëëënt with the official king's judgment: the village sign had been ruled out of order. Pääätëëënt read the scroll, shrugged, got out some paint, and added some quotation marks around "Healers." "There you go. We're not healers. We're 'healers,'" he said, air quoting the word with his fingers.

He then formally named the village "Kääächööö," so everyone who heard of the village would know they could get cold remedies there and, by extension, other non-guild treatments.

When the advocates returned to Stained Rock and complained to Brüüütus, he simply laughed at Pääätëëënt's cleverness and waved the chuggers away, sending them back to the Western Lands and All That Really Matters. Queen Gwendolyn saw their treatment by Brüüütus as one of the final insults to her and her realm. Not long after, Gwendolyn the Irritable massed her armies at King Brüüütus' border, and Melveeta the Elusive cast her devastating Purple Haze spell.

At least Brüüütus got a good chuckle out of the whole thing before his kingdom's devastation.

❧

Eloise, Lorch, and the horses arrived at Kääächööö late afternoon, having followed Turpy's tracks to a main-ish road, where they stopped. Presumably, he got a ride on a cart.

The village was decorated in rutabagas—it was time for Kääächööö's annual Rutabaga Revelry. Rutabagas were everywhere: in shop windows, in the costumes people wore, especially their rutabaga hats, in the placards for Miss or Mister Regal Rutabaga, as well as for the Rutabaga Review, and the dance that night, the Rutabaga Do. There were rutabaga fritters and rutabaga cordial, rutabaga juggling, rutabaga stacking, and largest, sweetest, sourest, and funniest-shaped rutabagas. Somewhere in the village, there would be rutabaga decorating, speed rutabaga classifying, and feats of strength involving weights and strong weights of rutabagas. Eloise looked up. Yep, there it was—a rutabaga poked onto the spire of the local Çalahtist devotional house, which the House Minder would inevitably pretend to rail against, before taking bets on when it would come off due to decay.

Eloise teared up. She couldn't help it.

"What's the matter, Princess?" asked Lorch.

"It's this Rutabaga Revelry. Jerome would love this."

"Yes, he would."

"But he's not here to annoy us with his overly enthusiastic love of all things swede." She wiped her eyes.

"We'll get him back, Princess Eloise."

"We have to, Lorch. We just have to."

BONGOS DE BONGOS

All three inns in Kääächööö were, of course, fully booked out. There wasn't a spare broom closet nor stable stall anywhere. Hector pointed toward a field full of tents, conveniently located near the temporary stage where the festival's performances happened. At the moment, a bombard quintet stood in front of a banner that read "Midnight Oleaginous Liquid," which Eloise guessed was either a band name or a festival sponsor. The five bombardists (don't ever call them "bombardiers") played their hearts out which, given the nature of bombards, could easily have caused mass eardrum ruptures. The crowd, however, seemed to enjoy their rendition of "Beds Are Smoldering," and even sang along to the chorus of "How can we kip when our beds are smoldering a little?"

Eloise and the others gave the stage area a wide berth, and followed Hector to the packed rough-sleeping field, which was marked out into ten length by ten length sites. An attendant stood at the entrance. He took a coin from Lorch and told them to pick an empty square.

There weren't many. Clearly the festival had been going on for at least a couple of days. The few vacant squares they found were obviously vacant for a reason—one housed a big stump, another had rocks all through it, and another contained a sinkhole.

Finally, Hector found one. "Does this one work for you?" asked Hector. The square included a red cedar, which would provide shelter if the weather turned, and was as far from the performance area as they could get. Presumably that made it undesirable for people who wanted easy access to the shows, but it also had the benefit of preventing overexposure to further bombard assault. The unoccupied spot was bordered on all sides by other clusters of rough sleepers. Plus—and this was likely the reason it was still empty—it was half the size of all the others. It would be a tight squeeze for three horses and two humans.

"Of course. It'll be fine," said Eloise. She hoped that her habits would tolerate so much proximity to so many other people, and that she'd be able to sleep. It was not a sure thing. "Shall we settle in?"

"Pri—" Lorch looked around, realizing that calling her "princess" might be information others didn't need. "Mistress, with permission, I'd like to go scout out opportunities for provision while there's still light."

"Good idea. We'll set up."

Eloise took the panniers off the horses and set them at the base of the tree, then walked to the edge of a nearby woods to hunt up some firewood and kindling. She got back to her square with an armload of branches that would do if the night was not too cold, let the horses wander off to find some grass to crop, and began to set the wood for a fire.

"Excuse me, mistress," said a small voice. Eloise looked up to see a young mountain bongo, just old enough to start showing growth in her horn buds. She was brown with thin white stripes circling her body and stood at the border between Eloise's square and her own.

"Yes?"

"G'late afternoon, mistress. My mother and father asked me to come over here to invite you and your friends to join us at our campfire." The young bongo pointed with a horn bud. "We have plenty of space. Four squares."

Eloise looked over. A family of five other mountain bongos smiled at her. Three of the antelopes—a younger female and two older male children—were reading, possibly studying. They waved their hooves briefly, then went back to their scrolls. The father nodded a hello, giving his lyre-shaped horns a graceful wave, and returned to roasting his vegetable kebabs. The mother, busy mixing things in clay pots, also greeted her.

"That's most kind of you," said Eloise. "I really don't want to impose at all. But thank you."

"Father said you might say that. I was to respond with generalized words of encouragement, which he left to my discretion. Would you like to hear what I came up with?"

"Sure."

"Mistress, you have arrived late in the day, and I have observed that you are sharing your already limited space with three horses and another human. We have organized to occupy four squares of space, and as such, we have much more area per person than you do. Even if we add you and your friends, our area-to-person ratio would still be more favorable. As such, offering you hospitality does not impose an undue imposition on our space allocation. Moreover, by accepting our offer, you save yourself the need to use some of your limited space for a fire. Logic, therefore, would indicate that sharing our fire, and by extension, our company, is the best opportunity to maximize your position. Plus, we're fun. We play bongos."

"You're bongos who play bongos?"

"Yes. We're going to perform on the main stage later. We're..." She struck a dramatic pause that immediately reminded Eloise of their onetime companion Alejandro Diego Ferdinando Felipe Esteban Iglesias Desoto de Lugo. Then, as though she was introducing her family to a crowd, she said "We are Bongos de Bongo."

"You are a very well-spoken young lady," said Eloise. "And you have presented a most compelling argument. It will be my pleasure to accept on behalf of myself and my friends. May I ask your name?"

"I'm Áäànnáäàlîîisáäà. But everyone calls me Lîîiz."

"Pleased to meet you, Lîîiz, and may I say that Áäànnáäàlîîisáäà is a fine Southie name. I'm Eloise."

"What? Like the Westie queen? You'd better not let her find that out. She'll have your guts on a palette and paint a portrait of someone else's guts using them."

"So I've heard. I promise, I'll be careful."

"I'll introduce you to the others." She turned to her family. "Máäà, Dáäà, everyone! This is Eloise. Eloise, this is my máäà and dáäà, and this is Mîîisÿÿÿ, or Mîîiz, Dóöòúüùgláäàs, or Dîîiz, and Béëèáäàúüùréëègáäàrd, or Bîîiz."

The father bowed to her. "I am Fortitude de Bongo. And my wife is..."

"Préëècîîíóöòúüùs de Bongo née de Tragelaphus." The bongo matriarch smiled and added, "I'm so glad you decided to join us. The children love meeting new people."

"Pleased to meet you all. And thank you again for your kindness."

"Do you play bongos?" asked Mîîiz. She looked younger than her sister.

"I don't know," said Eloise. "I've never tried."

"We'll show you," said Lîîiz. "After dinner and before our show."

Eloise smiled. "That's kind of you."

Over the next hour, as sunset blushed the sky, the three horses and Lorch drifted back to their allotted square and, along with Eloise, threw in with the de Bongo family. Eloise was struck by how comfortable, warm, embracing and fun it was to be with them. The Bongos were close-knit, quick to laughter, worked together like the well-rehearsed travelers they were, and something musical was always just a moment away, whether a snatch of song or an improvised drum lick on an upturned bucket. Their camp life seemed to have a grace and smoothness to it. Whenever one of them was not needed for a task, whether child or adult, they sat down and practiced rhythms on their bongo drums, all except for Prééècîîíóöòúüùs, who played the zither. Every now and then, one of them would say, "But I don't want to dance," and another would answer, "But you have to dance," and they'd burst out in giggles. It didn't make sense, but was cute.

When dinner time came, they shared their veggie kebabs and salad with Eloise and Lorch, augmented by bread, fruit, and a sweet nut roll dessert that the guard had purchased.

Eloise thought how different this family's life was from her own. Hers was marked by obligation, formality, and Protocol, Protocol, Protocol. The royal responsibilities were huge, the resources commanded by her mother were massive, and the consequences of their decisions profound for many, many people.

The de Bongos, she learned, went from festival to festival, entertaining and seeing the realms, answerable only to themselves and the muses of travel and music. They most certainly did not chase criminal jesters or try to recover kidnapped champions. Eloise knew she'd never trade her life for the one these mountain bongos had, but she couldn't help feeling a little jealous. It seemed like a much simpler way to be.

"Do you have a favorite festival?" Eloise asked Lîîìz.

"I do! My favorite is Spoontastic!î! in Löööffeldell!î!. It's not just for spoons. It celebrates cutlery of all kinds. They have everything. Food-sticks. Sporks. Skewers. Pointy twigs. Splayds and sporfs and knorks and spifes. If you can use it to help put food in your face, they have it."

"I had no idea that existed," said Eloise.

"I like Plushiefest," said Mîîìz.

"What does that celebrate?"

"Plushies."

"Like, stuffed toys?"

Míîîz got a dreamy look in her eyes, like she was revisiting heaven in her mind. "Yes," she drawled. "Plushies. I like plushies."

Bíîz scratched his head, then got a similar faraway look. "My favorite is Lavapalooza. It's at an active volcano in the Central Ranges. We go every year."

"Also interesting. Díîîz, how about you?"

"Easy," he said. "Coachella. All those carriages and drays are incredible. We even met Lurid Eddie last time. He signed my buggy cushion."

"Díîîz has a buggy cushion he uses as an autograph scroll," said Líîîz.

"I see," said Eloise, although, really, she didn't.

Once the meal was cleared, Líîîz and Míîîz brought out two sets of bongos from their caravan, and offered one to Eloise and the other to Lorch. When Lorch tried to demur, they charmed and cajoled until he relented. The bongo girls sat, and using slow, careful hoof movements, instructed Eloise and Lorch, still reluctant, on the basic rhythms that all bongo players had to know. Once they'd grasped the basics, the two young antelope got them to keep a steady rhythm while they frilled and trilled around them.

Ten minutes later, Eloise looked at Lorch, expecting to see him wearing his usual determined, focused guard's expression. Instead, she saw something that she realized was a rare occurrence for him—a smile. Guard Lacksneck was having fun.

After 20 minutes, the bongos invited the two humans to start adding in variations of their own, and from then on, they took turns leading and supporting. When it was Eloise's turn to lead, she tended toward awkward, syncopated beats that jumped around the main beat like a drunkard. Lorch, on the other hand, favored speed, rapping and tapping in rapid patterns. Then the two bongo brothers sat down with them and added their own personalities to the mix. Bíîz showed what you could do with slow, unexpected, emphatic beats, while Dîîiz mirrored him with sharp regularity.

Eventually, they all sped up, faster and faster, until Lîîiz and Mîîiz let out five simultaneous whoops, and they all stopped at exactly the same time.

"Thank you," said Eloise, smiling. Her cheeks were flushed with the effort. "That was fun. And if that's what you can do when you're just messing around with a couple of people who have no concept of what you do, I can't wait to see the six of you on stage tonight."

"Thank you, Mistress Eloise. You and Master Lorch have a natural knack for the bongo drums. You should purchase a set, so you can always have this kind of fun when you travel."

"It would be different without you."

"It would be different even with us," said Lîîiz. "It's always different. That's part of what makes it exciting. It's never the same."

Eloise realized the same applied to what she was doing right now. Circumstances had brought her to this point where she was having a lovely afternoon and evening with a delightful family of bongos. If she ever came this way again, even if it was to another Rutabaga Revelry, things would inevitably be different.

Lîîiz walked over to her mother and father. "What do you think?"

"Sure. Go ahead."

"Really?"

"Really."

She came back to Eloise and Lorch with a shy smile. "Would you like to perform with us tonight?"

The thought of performing while Jerome was still unaccounted for felt strange. Eloise shook her head. "I couldn't possibly—"

Lîîiz didn't let her finish. "Sure you can. It'll be fun."

"Maybe Lorch can. But I'm..." She hesitated, not sure what to say. "I'm not nearly good enough."

"Mistress Eloise! How can you say that? We all just heard you. You're certainly good enough to at least sit on the stage and keep up a simple rhythm. Come on, it'll be fun."

Eloise looked at Lorch. To her surprise, he tilted his head once slowly to one side. He was up for it. This was not a Lorch she knew. Eloise turned back to Lîîîz. "Do I have to sing?"

"Máää does most of the singing. Sometimes we do harmonies. But mostly it's bongo playing. After all, we are..." The dramatic pause again. "Bongos de Bongo."

Once again, it was just like Alejandro. He would have encouraged her. She could almost hear him: "Señorita Princesa! You must grasp this opportunity!"

"OK, then," she said. "Let's bongo!" And in her head, she added, *Jerome, this one's for you.*

✿ 16 ✿

BUT I DON'T WANT TO DANCE

Eloise and Lorch stood to the side of the stage with the de Bongo family, waiting their turn to step up. Eloise's stomach butterflies fluttered in a way she wasn't used to. There was the nervousness she felt before standing up in front of a crowd at Court. There was the kind of terror she might experience if she was expected to sing in public. But this time, the butterflies were dancing a dance she recognized as not wanting to let down the family of bongos. To distract herself from her nerves, she counted people in the audience, organizing them into sets of five. In the torchlight, she made it to four hundred, but she was certain there were more. It was a decent crowd for a small festival in an out-of-the-way place.

Eloise nudged Líîíz and pointed at the performer on stage. From his songs and stories, it was clear he wasn't heading toward barddom, and from his jokes, jesterdom was a way off as well. "Who's this?"

"Jimmy the Knucklehead. He's very good."

Míîíz, who held a bongo that was almost as big as she was, echoed her sister. "Yes, Jimmy the Knucklehead. He's very good."

"You think so?"

Lîîz shook her head fervently, then repeated, "Jimmy the Knucklehead. He's very good."

"I don't get it."

"Máää and Dáää don't like it when we disparage our fellow performers," said Lîîz. "They say, 'There's always something good you can say about them. You just have to look for it.' So, Jimmy the Knucklehead is very good. That is, if you like stale jokes about errant body parts that weren't funny when Gwendolyn the Irritable first heard them. Or if you like songs sung with the grace and skill of a cross saw caressing a tin roof. In that way, Jimmy the Knucklehead is most excellent."

"Most excellent," agreed Mîîz. "Also, if you like garish clothing that is not washed well or often."

"What do you say if you actually like someone?"

"Depends."

"On what."

"On what they're doing. For example, two days ago on this very stage, there was a most peculiar performance."

"I know the one you mean," said Mîîz. "That funny act."

"He looked like such a sour thing. He was thin like his favorite food was watery gruel, and there was something going on with his foot. Like it hurt him."

"It did hurt him," said Mîîz. "It was bandaged, like one of the Kääächööö 'healers' had been paid overtime to do extra work on it. He used a cane."

Bells started going off in Eloise's head, her stomach clutched, and she looked at Lorch. He, too, was focused on the two bongo girls. "But he performed?" asked Eloise.

"He sure did," said Lîîz. "Hilarious. He had this sidekick with him, so it was a kind of double act. A squirrel."

"He was a chipmunk," corrected Mîîîz. "He had stripes on his face. Squirrels don't have face stripes."

"OK, chipmunk. Whatever," said Lîîîz. "The premise of the act was that his partner was reluctant. Didn't want to do it. The guy pulled him out of a pocket, took him out of a sack, put him on top of an upturned barrel, which was a most unusual way to make a stage entrance. Then he tried to get his sidekick to dance."

"He didn't want to dance," giggled Mîîîz. "The chipmunk kept saying..." She raised her voice to an exaggerated high pitch. "'No, no, no. I don't want to dance.' And the man said..." She dropped her voice unnaturally low. "'But you have to dance.' 'But I don't want to dance.' 'But you have to dance. Otherwise there will be no supper.' And the man poked the chipmunk with his cane."

"The next bit was the funniest," said Lîîîz.

Mîîîz jigged up and down. "Oh, let me tell it! Let me tell it!"

"OK. Go ahead."

"So the chipmunk was all 'But I don't want to dance,' and the man was all 'But you have to dance,' and then the chipmunk got all snooty and started pretending he was, like, a super important person from the Westie Court." She put on her chipmunk voice again, and Eloise could just hear Jerome in it. "'You can't do that to me. I'm a champion.' Everyone started laughing then, and that made the chipmunk even madder, and the man started mocking him. 'Oh, a champion! He's a champion, everyone! Like anyone would be stupid enough to pick a rat as champion,' and then the chipmunk was all, 'I'm a rodent, not a rat.' And he tried to bite the man."

"It was so convincing. He seemed really peeved," said Lîîîz. "He ran around trying to get close enough to the man, but the man used his cane to keep him at a distance. And somehow, and this was the clever bit, he manipulated the cane to move the chipmunk around in such a way that, even though he was pretending to be so mad, the chipmunk ended up jumping about, and suddenly, he was dancing! Like he didn't realize it."

"What happened then?" asked Eloise.

"Everyone clapped and cheered," said Lîîîz.

"And threw coins on the stage for them," said Mîîîz. "The man put his sidekick back in the sack, which was also pretty funny, and picked up a bunch of coins. Thirty. Maybe fifty."

"They deserved them, too. Their act cracked everybody up."

"We've all been saying, 'But I don't want to dance' and 'But you have to dance' for two days now. That one's going to stick for a while."

Lorch used his height to look around at the crowd. "I don't see them."

"Are they still here?" Eloise asked the bongos.

"I wish," said Lîîîz. "I wouldn't mind seeing them again. But no. We looked out for them the next day, and today as well. But from what I can see, they're gone."

Eloise waved Lorch closer so she could whisper in his ear. "We have to go after them. Like, right now."

"I understand that's what you want to do. But one question if I may. Where exactly would you go?"

"I don't know. We'd work that out."

"Pr— Mistress Eloise. The simple truth is that unless you are happy to choose a direction at random, we need to check around. We need to gather the facts and then make a decision."

"I suppose. I just can't stand the thought that Jerome was so close, and we're about to waste time playing bongos."

"Take heart in the fact that he is alive."

"At least, he was three nights ago."

"Yes, Pr— Mistress Eloise."

Giggling interrupted them.

"But I don't want to dance," said Mîîîz in her chipmunk voice.

"But you have to dance," said Lîîiz in a scarily close imitation of Turpy.

The two girls bubbled into laughter.

Jimmy the Knucklehead thought it was for him, and gave the girls an exaggerated bow. Then he turned back to the audience and delivered two more "jokes" about "healers" that got a couple of amused snorts, but not much more. At his "Thank you and g'night everyone," there was a smattering of clapping, most of which came from the very polite bongo family. A single coin, then another, clinked onto the stage. Jimmy the Knucklehead had trouble hiding his disappointment, but smiled, waved, and came off stage. "All yours," he said to the de Bongos. "I've warmed them up for you."

"Thank you, Master Jääämes," said Prééècîîíóöòúüùs. "Some good material you're working on. Keep at it."

"That's very kind of you, Mistress Prééècîîíóöòúüùs. I will."

The master of ceremonies was a deadpan marmoset with a megaphone. "Jimmy the Knucklehead, everyone. Let's give Jimmy another round of applause." His use of "another" was generous.

The de Bongos all applauded again, and a few more in the crowd joined in. Lîîiz leaned into Eloise. "Dáää always says, 'You have to give good audience to get good audience.' So we always make a point of being good audience members."

"Makes sense."

"The organizers have asked me to make a few public announcements," said the marmoset. "First of all, the sweets monger would like to apologize for the incorrectly labeled sweets. The candies labeled 'elderberry' were supposed have been labeled 'habanero.' The sweets monger apologizes for the error, and hopes there was no permanent damage caused." He droned on with more festival housekeeping.

Mîîiz nudged her sister with her flank. "Hey Lîîiz, do you know where we're from tonight?"

"No. Bîîiz got to pick today. It'll probably be somewhere stupid."

"Probably."

"What do you mean 'Where you're from?'" asked Eloise.

"It's a family joke. They always introduce us as, 'All the way from somewhere, it's Bongos de Bongo!' But the 'somewhere' is different every time. We take turns getting to choose."

"Right."

"Mîîz usually picks Fluffydale or Rainbow Run. I choose obscure villages we've traveled through that day, to give it a bit of local flavor. The boys usually try to get the MC to say something that might be taken as rude, although it got so bad that Máàà makes them tell her their choices in advance now."

The marmoset finished his public announcements, then said, "Next up, ladies and gentlemen, straight from Certain Desolate Emptiness of Existential Dread, uh..." He looked over at the bongos, confused, "Where is that, exactly?"

Bîîz took a step forward and put on a kind of extreme Southie accent. "Théëè Sóöòuth. Júüùst úüùpriver fróöòm Íïntolerable Éëènnui áäànd îïnland fróöòm Wháäàt's théëè Póöòint óöòf Góöòing Óöòn, Áäànyway?"

"I see," said the marmoset. "Is it nice there?"

"Véëèry, áäàlthough théëè péëèople áäàre áä bîît dóöòur."

"Right." He turned back to the crowd. "Ladies and gentlemen, boys and girls, bucks, does, kids, larvae, or whatever you happen to be, all the way from Certain Desolate Emptiness of Existential Dread, upriver from Intolerable Ennui and inland from What's the Point of Going on Anyway, it's the percussive stylings of Bongos de Bongo!"

The de Bongo family clattered onto the stage with tremendous enthusiasm and energy, Lorch and Eloise following at the back. They circled the stage twice before settling down and hammering out a complex set of rhythms on their bongos. Eloise kept her simple rhythms on the beat and was grateful she didn't have to join in any of the harmonies that blended with Préëëcîîíóöòúüùs de Bongo's lead vocals. Lorch bongoed away with an abandon she'd never seen before, but Eloise's heart just wasn't in it. Her mind was elsewhere, worrying though the problem of where Turpy had gone next. At least, thank Çalaht, it looked like Jerome was still probably alive.

❧   17   ❧

PODCASTER

Instead of breaking camp first thing the next morning, they shared breakfast with the de Bongos, then split up to scout for information. Lorch headed for the fair stalls in search of more provisions and gossip. Hector set out to see if Turpy had hired a transportation horse. Kïïït made her way to the inns, pretending to look for work so she could ask the maids and serving wenches if they'd seen or heard anything. The Nameless One went off to do whatever silent thing he had in mind. That left Eloise looking for the "healer" who had worked on Turpy.

Eloise strolled the streets of Kääächööö, which were packed with rutabaga revelers, some fresh from a night's sleep, others looking like they had enjoyed a bit too much of the rutabaga cider. The latter were well placed to avail themselves of one of the many "healers." The volume and variety of them struck Eloise as overwhelming. How would you ever choose? Would you want a beer spa or a mercurium blood cleanse? Someone who "healed" by blowing smoke or one who preferred blowing distilled potato liquids? A regimen involving members of the Loosely Affiliated Maggot Debridement Brigade or treatments that relied on things that clearly were very, very, very bad for you, like arsenic, Çalaht's cowl mushrooms, listening to the bombard up close, or raw haggleberries? At least Eloise could narrow her search to methods that involved bandages and foot bones.

Kääächööö in full mid-morning light was colorful and quaint. Beyond the rutabaga decorations was a riot of flags, awnings, stained glass, posters, and paint, all lifting the small wooden buildings out of drabness. Eloise guessed that the intuitive types attracted to "healing" would tend toward the artistic side of things.

As Eloise walked through the village, "healers" spruiked their offerings from doorways, stalls, and barrows.

"Leeches! Finest leech work in town!"

"Tooth extractions! Get that sore tooth yanked!"

"Phobias! Phobias engendered or dissipated! Your choice! Hundreds of phobias catered for!"

"Abrasions! Sandpaper abrasion therapy!"

"Ablations! Searing good healing!"

"Ablutions! Ablutions using the finest spring waters! Freshwater ablutions from River Thurman waters, or saltwater ablutions with unfiltered, unadulterated water all the way from the Gööödeling Sea!"

"Lucky dip potions! See what mystery awaits!"

A shop called Salvation sold unctions, creams, and liniments. A store called Potentate carried strongly healing spuds. At Impeachment you could take advantage of the healing power of stone fruit, and at Loquacious there were allegedly efficacious loquats. Lackadaisical promised to solve anything that was due to a deficit of daisies.

There was something for everyone, no matter your purse or proclivities. Eloise meandered through it all, not finding anything that might lead her to His Jesterness Turpentine. She wondered idly if he could still be called a jester if he no longer served a monarch. Probably. Jester was likely a state of being for him.

"Curative comestibles!"

"Spleen fleaming!" Eloise thought that one sounded particularly painful.

"Phlebotomy! Your humors are no humorous matter to us!" That sounded like a Lurid Eddie kind of slogan.

"Hot iron! Red-hot iron poker. I can burn off anything." The man caught Eloise's eye. "How about you, mistress? Got any bits you require burned off?"

"No, thank you," said Eloise. "That's very kind of you to offer. If I come across anyone with troubles that need the attention of red-hot iron, I'll be sure to send them to you."

The hot iron man doffed his hat. "Most appreciated, young mistress. Most appreciated, indeed."

She moved on to a side street where there were more "healing" shops and stalls.

"Ritual scarification! Make peace with your ancestors!"

"Necrosis Awareness Support Group!"

"Reflux suppression!"

"Aversion inducement!"

"Massively dilute tinctures!"

"Hardening measures for softening of the brain!"

"Vapors to cure the vapors!"

"Keys to unlock lockjaw!"

"Catharsis for the catarrhous!"

Eloise was about to cross the alleyway and head back to the main street when she heard an unusually musical voice from a nearby doorway. "Podcasting! Podcasting while you wait! Get your podcasting here!"

She stopped. Podcasting? That was a new one.

Curiosity got the better of her. The store was run by a man in a black coat, black breeks, and black tunic. These contrasted sharply with his ample silver hair, which was tied in a top-knot. His deep green eyes and clean-shaven face had a practiced expression, calculated to put a potential client at ease. The years had not been kind to him, but he bore this with dignity. The man would have looked dashing half a century before, but now, it looked more like life had dashed him against its shoals, and left him on the beach to desiccate.

"Excuse me, good sir," said Eloise. "Might I ask what kind of 'healer' you are?"

"I'm a podcaster."

"A podcaster? So, you hurl bean pods??"

The old man laughed. "You misunderstand."

"You have a group of whales, and they calculate on your behalf by means of astrology?"

"No, no, no. Much simpler than that. 'Pod' as in 'of or pertaining to the foot.'" The man pointed to a sign above the doorway to his shop. It was foot-shaped, but broken, mangled into an unnatural contortion. "I specialize in the fixing of broken feet using rigid plaster casings," he said. "I'm a podcaster."

"I see. Are there many of you podcasters in the village?"

"No, no. It takes a great deal of skill and training to be a podcaster. It's not like anyone can haul off and do a podcast on their own. This is a highly specialized business. I am the only fully qualified podcaster in Kääächööö. Nëëëville Täääradiddle, at your service, mistress."

Eloise wasn't sure if this was luck or fate. But this man had to have worked on Turpy. "May I come in?"

"You do not look like you are having pod-related discomfort, mistress. But, of course."

He moved aside and Eloise stepped into a darkened storefront jammed from floor to ceiling with splints, bandages, hammers, pliers, forceps, various grips and clamps, scary things with screws, scary things with hooks, scary things with points, bowls for draining blood, bowls for mixing plaster, sacks of plaster, bags of cotton, and a sign that read, "Our shoppe welcomes those who refrain from screaming and cursing, as it spooks the neighbors. Your cooperation is appreciated." A second sign read, "Please Abide Our List of Unacceptable Profanities," then gave a list of proscribed swears, which included but was not limited to "anything that starts with 'mother-,'" "most phrases that start with 'Çalaht-,'" "anything involving fruit," "all words starting with Q or X," "anything involving parts of the body that are normally covered in public and private during the day and night," "hurgle," "splink," and "otherwise anything you would not say in front of your grandmother or her likeness, whether she is still alive or stands with Çalaht."

That all seemed quite reasonable to Eloise.

Täääradiddle bowed to Eloise again like it was the first moment they'd met, and said, "G'mid-morning to you, mistress. How can I be of service?"

"I am visiting your fair village on my way to see an uncle who is in the region. I fear my Uncle Güüüstav may be in some kind of foot-related distress and I wish to make him aware of possible remedies. Your podcasting might be of use to him."

"Oh? What sort of distress?"

"It is not clear to me. My Aunt Ïïïsolde has a very flowery way with words when she writes, but poor quillmanship. Each additional syllable she scrawls takes her meaning further away. From what I can tell, poor Uncle Güüüstav is suffering quite an affliction caused either by teaching dancing to horses or from preaching against chancing to hippos. But he's the reticent type, and stoic. I do not think he will seek help on his own. Still, his foot is apparently quite a mess."

"Then this is the right place for him. You need simply to bring him here, or send him on his own. I will examine his foot, and if it can be saved, I'll help him out. And if not..." He nodded at a frightful display of deeply-stained saws along one wall.

"I don't know." Eloise shook her head. "I'll try, but they've not much coin. Still, I'll try to bring him, or at least send him along. He may not give his name, as he has had more than one run-in with, shall we say, 'persons of significance.' But my guess is you'll recognize him. Thin of face. About yay tall." Eloise held her hand to roughly Turpy's height and wondered if she was laying the story on too thick. "Wears clothes that look like they might have been found at a second-hand jesters' supply shop." She giggled for effect. "Dear Uncle Güüüstav always had terrible taste in clothes."

"Wait, wait, wait," said Täääradiddle. "Beanpole of a man? Not a lot of words. Voice like he's polishing stones in a rock tumbler? Travels with a companion in a sack?"

"I don't know about the companion in a sack, but the rest sounds about right."

"Why, he's already been here!"

"No!"

"Yes!"

"Really?"

"Yes, really. He was here just two days ago. I'm sure it was him. Now *that* was a foot worthy of a podcast."

"That bad?"

"That bad. I don't know what your uncle did to it, as he refused to say. But getting stepped on by a hippo might go some way toward explaining it. By Çalaht's elongated thumbs, I don't know how he was still walking around."

Täääradiddle picked up a very lifelike model of a foot. No, Eloise realized, not a model, an actual foot, stripped of its muscle and sinew, sawn off 40 weak lengths above the ankle. The podcaster began pointing at some of its two dozen bones, turning it over as he described the state of Turpy's foot. "Crushed. Broken. Smooshed. Fragmented. Cracked. Crushed. Crushed. Crushed. Broken. Broken. Fractured. Fractured. Fractured. And, somehow, missing."

"Ouch."

"Definitely ouch. I tried to get your uncle to let me just take it off, but he wouldn't have it."

"What did you do?"

Täääradiddle rubbed his face, patted his silver top-knot, and then smiled with professional pride. "I did the finest podcast I have ever done. I mean, his foot will never be what it once was. It's not like I've got a weak magic for podcasting, like Dorianna Gangle, the Step of the Steppe. She's a true foot hero. They say she performs miracles on the mangled. Anyway, if I may say so, I did a pretty reasonable job for your uncle."

"Uncle Güüüstav must have been pleased."

"If he was, he did not say so. And he certainly broke the house rules." He pointed to the two signs on the wall about swearing. "All things considered, that might be understandable. They're more guidelines than rules, really. Fortunately he passed out, leaving me to work in peace." Täääradiddle waggled the dismembered foot and set it back down on a table. "It will never be the same, of course. I suggested he buy one of my canes, and he did so reluctantly. Tight with his coin, he was."

"That's Uncle Güüüstav. Tight, tight, tight. I don't know how Aunt Ïïïsolde puts up with it. But the heart craves what the heart craves."

"So said blessed Çalaht. Anyway, I fixed your uncle up as best I could. I told him to rest his foot, but one got the impression your uncle is not one who will be told what to do."

"You and Aunt Ïïïsolde could have a long and very flowery correspondence about that, I'm sure. Did dear Uncle Güüüstav say where he was going? Back home, presumably."

"He didn't say, I'm sorry. I gave him some concoctions for the pain—he's going to feel a lot of it for a long time. He gave me the coins we'd agreed on, then he was gone without so much as a thank you."

"No hints of anything? No direction? No references? I just don't want to make the journey to Uncle Güüüstav and Aunt Ïïïsolde's homestead if they're not going to be there."

"Sorry, I can't help you there."

There didn't seem much else she would get from him, so she made to leave. "Well, Mr Täääradiddle, thank you so much for helping my uncle. I'm happy to say it, even if he's too much of an old stick to do so himself."

"That's most kind, mistress." He walked to the door and held it open for her.

Eloise bowed to him politely, smiled a final thank you, and headed for the door.

Täääradiddle frowned and looked down, then seemed to come to a decision. He held up a hand before she went past. "One other thing, mistress."

"Yes?"

"Your uncle's companion. The one in the sack."

Eloise waited, unsure what was coming.

"Such a tragic case," said the podcaster. "Your uncle is most kind to help out such an unfortunate soul. To be so afraid of the world around you that you have to travel in a sack. And even then, to scream and scream from terror and *Weltangst*. His cries of 'Help me! Help me!' were as heart-rending as your uncle's when I was working on his foot." Täääradiddle shook his head slowly. "Mistress, if you meet this companion, know there are many 'healers' here in Kääächööö who might help one suffering so profoundly. Do let your aunt and uncle know that."

Eloise's stomach felt like it dropped off a cliff and it was all she could do not to cry. "I'll do that. I'll tell them."

❦ 18 ❦

GESUNDHEIT

They met up at a packed, 'healing'-oriented public inn called Gesundheit that specialized in vegetable slurries, meals that featured yeast paste, and strictly uncooked food. The dishes all had overly perky names that didn't describe them at all, like Sunshine Explosion!, Earth Tone Jig!, and Thunderbox Whisperer! The inn also had a posted sign that read, "We cater to all species. Come one, come all, come large, come small." That meant the horses could enjoy an inn-prepared (but not cooked) meal as well. Eloise ordered something called Willingness Fable! that she hoped was mostly salad. Lorch got the Hearty Har Har Bar!, Hector the Greenlands Glade!, Kïïït the Sprouted Grain Rainbow!, and the Nameless One ordered Olfactory Ingenuity!

While they waited for their food, Eloise told the others about her conversation with Nëëëville Täääradiddle, which essentially confirmed the bandage and cane that Mîîz and Lîîz had mentioned, as well as Turpy's carrying Jerome around in a sack.

"I've had a most interesting morning," said Lorch. "I suspect Turpy knows we're coming after him, either because he has seen us or is working under the assumption that we're not far behind. He seems to be spreading the same conflicting information that he did when we were heading toward The South. Half a dozen people said they spoke with a man fitting his description, and hundreds saw him perform. But I got six different responses to my question, 'Where was he headed?'"

"So does he want us to find him or not? He has Jerome. If Jerome is the lure to us, what's his game? Why make it hard for us to come after him?"

"I can think of many reasons," said Hector. "The main one would be to keep us off balance and guessing, giving him the advantage of greater information. But it could also be to give him time to plan. Or heal. Or gather alliances. Maybe he has to get more money to do whatever he has in mind. If he's performing for coin, then he's not exactly flush."

"He'd find it demeaning," said Kiiit.

"How so?" asked Eloise.

"I mean, he was practically king there at the end. And for years, he had only the finest audiences—nobles, kings, queens, that sort of folk. The full grass strudel. Now he's here in the middle of nowhere forcing Jerome to dance for tossed coins, which probably physically hurt him to pick up. How would you feel?"

Eloise didn't respond. Given everything he'd done, she was disinclined to feel empathy toward Turpy.

"He would feel horrid," said Hector. "I think he'd feel deprived of what was 'rightly' his. He'd feel angry, which the pain would not help. He's not the type to curl up and die, or just say, 'Well, I gave it a go.' He'd want to do something about it."

The Nameless One nodded.

"Given what we know he's capable of, that 'something' would not be pleasant for others," said Lorch.

"But it would advance his cause," said Kiiit.

"He's doing things logically," said Eloise. "Orchestrating the rat attack at Gutrot House. Running to Mortimer Falls when he escaped. Coming here to get his foot worked on. Performing to gather needed coin. There's logic there. Planning and strategy."

"The obvious question is, 'What will he do next?'" said Lorch.

"I don't know if we can answer that one until we know what he wants," said Kiïit.

The Gesundheit serving wench arrived with their meals, plates piled high with leafy greens, grains, and seasonal raw vegetables. "I've thrown in a plate of yeast balls for you to share," she chirped. "And there are yeast flakes as a condiment."

The five of them ate in silence, thinking.

"I still don't get how Jerome fits into this whole thing," said Eloise. "He doesn't need Jerome to perform. He's perfectly capable of doing that himself."

"Spite?" suggested Hector.

"Spite might have been a possibility. At first," said Lorch. "But I don't think that covers it anymore. It takes energy and attention for Turpy to keep Jerome around. He has to keep him confined. He has to keep him fed. If it was mere spite, then he could have just done something horrible and left it at that. There's more to this."

"So what do we do next?" asked Eloise.

The Nameless One nodded at their food.

"He's right," said Lorch. "We eat our lunch, we gather more information if we can, and we bide our time just a little while longer."

"In the meantime, Turpy is probably putting strong length after strong length between him and us," said Eloise.

"It's what I would do if I was him," said Hector.

"I hate not knowing what to do," said Eloise. "I hate what he's doing to Jerome. I hate *him*."

They fell back into silence, eating their enthusiastically named meals with little gusto.

19

GLIMPSE

After a fruitless afternoon of information gathering, Eloise and Lorch again shared dinner with the de Bongo family. Eloise felt her mood lifted by their humor, banter, and their tendency to drop into song and rhythm.

"Will you be performing with us again tonight, Mistress Eloise?" asked Mîîîz.

"That's so kind of you, but my mind really is elsewhere," said Eloise.

"Oh, please, mistress," said Lîîîz. "Dáää always says there's no problem that can't be solved with a good, long bang on the bongos. Master Lorch said he would be joining us."

"Really?"

"Yes."

Eloise looked over at Lorch, who nodded and gave a little "why not?" shrug. "We are here," he said. "It was..." He swallowed. "Fun. It was fun. And it is not often the case that a guard gets to choose fun. Plus..."

"Yes."

Lorch lifted his shoulders. "It seemed churlish not to accede to such a simple request from our two young, extremely persistent hostesses."

Eloise smiled and turned back to Mîîiz and Lîîiz. "Then I shall join you, too."

An hour later, Eloise found herself waiting at the side of the stage holding a set of bongos.

The act on stage was a duo of bard wannabes called Mug Half Empty. One of the performers, Catatonic Harold, used grunts, throat noises, taps, and buzzes into a hollowed out rutabaga (clearly a sop to the festival crowd) to produce a variety of complex rhythmic sounds. His partner, who called himself SBOR (for Shannon's Blistering Open Rage), did not so much sing as rhythmically recite poem-like pieces about all manner of food. It was challenging listening, and not to Eloise's taste at all. Still, she took her cue from the de Bongos, who once again practiced good audience, and they all gave enthusiastic applause.

"That was a very good performance," said Mîîiz. "Especially if you like atonal, unsung pieces that aren't quite singing and aren't quite recitation."

"I agree. A very good performance," said Lîîiz. "I particularly appreciated the innovative use of the rutabaga. That's always a crowd-pleaser."

"So you didn't like them either," said Eloise.

The two bongos shook their heads. "They were very good," the pair said in unison.

Mug Half Empty finished their set and were rewarded with two dozen tossed coins. The marmoset who was again ushering the acts on and off the stage then introduced the family as, "All the way from Pretentiously Grandiose Bombast, it's a festival favorite and the most beloved bongo-playing bongo family in this and every realm! Put together your hands, your hooves, your paws, your claws, or whatever protrusions you happen to have, and raise a racket for Bongos de Bongo!" The crowd applauded enthusiastically.

Instead of bursting onto the stage in a rush of energy, the antelope family and the two humans walked onto the stage slowly, deliberately, accompanied by a single, thumped drumbeat from Bîîz. They spread themselves evenly across the stage, facing away from the audience, and one by one they joined in the sparse, single beats, until all of them were striking the note in unison. Finally, Prééècîîíóöòúüùs de Bongo moved in front of them, turned, and faced the audience. Her face was painted with white stripes to accentuate the natural patterning of her body, and she wore ribbons that Eloise had woven into her horns, accenting their sleek lyre shape. "I think this first song is one you might know. Feel free to join in if you like."

Fortitude de Bongo began a slow, simple rhythm. It was stark, forceful, and fit easily into the slow beat still held by the others. One by one, the de Bongo children, then Eloise and Lorch, shifted their drumming to match Fortitude's. At a wave of her hoof, Prééècîîíóöòúüùs encouraged the audience to join in with claps that matched the pattern. Next, she began humming, weaving a background line of music that both her family and the audience joined in with. The hummed line felt warm and soulful, grounded and earthy, and she let it fill the air for four, then another four, repetitions.

Then Prééècîîíóöòúüùs de Bongo hopped off the stage and waded into the crowd, encouraging all to hum the background line. When she was directly in the middle of the audience, she opened her mouth and let the song pour out of her.

"There's a lady who knows all that glitters is groats..."

Turpy's brother Gouache had sung "Three Bags of Groats For My Sweetheart" at Court, and his rendition of the tune had been playful and eye-winky. When they heard it sung by the song's writer, Jaminity Delgado Blister, it was rendered with the sound of an old friend brought to musical life. Later, Jaminity performed it with diva Lydia Thrind and his friend, the effervescent Alejandro Diego Ferdinando Felipe Esteban Iglesias Desoto de Lugo. Their version was anthemic and grand, wrought with rich, three-part harmonies. Eloise's performance at the Southie Çalahtist devotional house under the influence of prattleweed seeds was an atonal embarrassment, although The South's Queen Onomatopoeia assured her it was spectacular in its own way.

But this was different. Prééëcîííóöòúüùs de Bongo turned "Three Bags of Groats For My Sweetheart" into a slow, incredibly personal, and sad exploration of the lyrics. She tinkered with how long she held the notes, swapping majors and minors, giving the words unexpected shading and emphasis. The audience sat rapt, keeping up their humming, and absorbing every nuance as she sang her heart out. Prééëcîííóöòúüùs drifted back up and onto the stage as she sang, so that when she got to the end, where the singer in the song offers three bags of groats for true love's first kiss, she paused the song dramatically, leaned over, and shared a kiss with her husband. The crowd roared, caught in the moment. It was a performance that would have made Jaminity proud.

As the couple parted lips and Prééëcîííóöòúüùs finished the song, tears welled in Eloise's eyes. *Oh, Jerome*, she thought. *You would have loved this.* It seemed like a lifetime ago, but it had only been a matter of days since he'd been driving her spare with random snatches of "Three Bags of Groats For My Sweetheart," back when Turpy was just the Sock and their biggest concern had been kumquatty weather.

Back then, she could not have imagined she would think of those times fondly. Now, she felt distinctly nostalgic for the certainty and simplicity of the task of transporting a felon.

Prééëcîííóöòúüùs de Bongo brought the song to a close, and coins clinked to the stage. Bííîz gathered them up and popped them in a pouch. Prééëcîííóöòúüùs positioned herself on stage with her zither. There followed a set of classic songs, each arranged to emphasize the family's percussive talents. "Party in the Half Kingdom." "Born to Limp." "Dancing in the Dirt Path." "Son of a Devotional House Minder." "While My Bombard Gently Weeps." "Shine On You Crazy Compressed Lump of Coal." And lastly, "Brunchberry Fields Forever." It was a set designed to please a crowd, and from the shower of coins at the end, it succeeded.

Eloise stood at the end of the line next to Lorch and took a bow. The applause was even louder than the night before, and the coins rained down on the stage. She looked from one end of the torch-lit audience to the other, hands clapping and faces dancing in the flickering light, and allowed herself to feel the warmth of their appreciation.

Then she saw him. Or thought she did.

There, at the far side of the crowd toward the back, face in shadow. Was it him? She would have missed him altogether if it weren't for an enthusiastic listener waving his torch back and forth in appreciation. It certainly looked like him.

He was there. She was almost certain that she'd glimpsed him, or someone who looked a lot like him. He was visible for a fraction of a second in a sway of the torch, and then another. On the third wave of the light, he was gone.

It looked like Turpentine Snotearrow McCcoonnch was still in Kääächööö. And so was the pouch at his waist.

Eloise dropped her bongos and ran.

20

THE RUSTLING OF FURTIVE FEET

Eloise rushed off the stage and headed toward the place where she thought she'd seen Turpy, ignoring the stares and pointing from the audience. She reached the spot, grabbed the torch from the audience member, and waved it around, looking for the apparition.

Lorch caught up, peering into the darkness. "What is it, Princess?" he whispered. "What's the matter?"

"I thought I saw him. Just here."

"Turpy?"

Eloise nodded, still moving the light around, trying to see him.

Lorch found another torch and started scanning the ground looking for tracks. Hector, Kïïït, and the Nameless One ran over from where they'd been watching the show. "She thinks she saw Turpy," he said. "Fan out and let's see."

Half an hour later they regrouped, anxious. "Anyone? Anything?" asked Eloise.

"Princess, I did not see anything that looked like a track from him, but there are hundreds of people here, and the ground is badly trampled," said Lorch. "I definitely could not see the tracks of a dragged foot, but then, with his foot in a cast, his step and track would change."

"I'm sure I saw him," insisted Eloise.

"It's possible, certainly." Hector shook his head. "Even if he was here, it would have been easy for him to disappear into a crowd this large. And we don't know that he was."

Eloise's shoulders drooped. "Apologies, everyone. My eyes must have seen what they wanted to see, not what was there," she said. "False alarm, I guess,"

"It's still possible you saw him," said Kĩĩt. "It's not that implausible, and the dark of night hasn't helped our search."

"I appreciate the benefit of the doubt."

Lĩĩz and Mĩĩz ran up to them. "Mistress Eloise, are you OK?" asked Lĩĩz.

"You ran off so fast," said Mĩĩz. "I thought you'd been attacked by the itchies and had to go scratch your back on a tree. That's what I do when I get the itchies."

"No, no itchies. I just thought I saw someone I knew, and I wanted to have a few words with him."

"He must be a most exceptional conversationalist for you to run off stage like that," said Lĩĩz.

"I wouldn't say that. But he does know where a friend of mine is. I was hoping to persuade him to share that information."

"Oh. Well, come back to camp when you're ready. Máää is making up a pot of her realm-famous hot cocoa."

"Sounds perfect. We'll be along. And thanks for checking on me."

"Hot cocoa! Hot cocoa!" chanted Mĩĩz as the sisters ran back to their family.

Eloise looked at the others. "I'm sorry, everyone. He has me jumpy."

"It's OK, Princess," said Lorch. "It's better to be vigilant."

Swallowing her disappointment, Eloise followed the de Bongos back to camp.

It was immediately obvious why Prééëcîïíóöòúüùs de Bongo's hot chocolate might be realm-famous. It was rich and sweet, and she added some secret ingredient that made it thick, to the point of being less a drink and more like a pudding. It was the perfect antidote against the crisp night air.

Eloise listened in silence as Fortitude de Bongo led a review of their performance. They had done the same thing the night before, each member of the family having the chance to offer thoughts on what had gone well, what had not, and how they could improve. Eloise was grateful that no one pointed to her sudden exit as a problem. The coins had already been tossed when she ran off stage, so she'd not affected their livelihood.

Stomachs sated, she, Lorch, and the horses settled under the red cedar to get some sleep. They did not bother setting a watch since there were so many people around. Eloise still didn't know where they should go next, or how they might find Jerome. Maybe she'd been right, and Turpy was still around. The thought didn't help sleep claim her. Eloise's mind raced from thought to thought, eventually slowed to dawdling between worries, and finally settled into a deep, fitful sleep peppered with dreams of waving a torch around, trying to catch a glimpse of something she felt was there but could never see.

The attack was carefully planned, stealthily executed, and brazen. It started an hour after the moon settled below the horizon, leaving the night sky cloud-flecked and dark. If Eloise or the others had been awake, they might have heard the rustling of three dozen sets of furtive, clawed feet. Perhaps they would have smelled dank, dirt-scented fur. Instead, they slept and missed the warnings. The intruders were used to moving at night and in the dimmest of light, so were able to steal into the camp unnoticed.

A dozen furred bodies surrounded Eloise, noses twitching the air, checking for signs of danger. Another dozen encircled Lorch, swords drawn, silent and prepared. The rest guarded against the horses as best they could, ready and vigilant in the darkness, small, but determined.

The lead infiltrator made a paw signal to one of the smallest, an older one, who slipped a vial from a pouch and unstoppered it. A sweet-smelling odor wafted into the air, and she poured exactly three drops onto Eloise's lips. The sleeping princess woke enough to lick away the mixture, then fell back into slumber.

They waited, tense.

Eloise's arms straightened and stiffened by her sides. Her legs stretched out and her toes pointed. The one with the vial signaled back to the leader, who walked over and patted Eloise's hip until he felt the box containing the Star of Whatever. Satisfied, he gave another signal, and the dozen surrounding Eloise reached beneath her and picked her up like she was a board.

The motion and the unexpected rigidity of her limbs woke Eloise up. But before she could cry out, one of them stuffed a silencing cloth into her mouth—a rag that tasted like a wombat's handkerchief that had been snotted in for a year and a half without anyone washing it.

Which is exactly what it was.

Eloise tried to wriggle away, but the wombats held tight, bearing her toward the nearby stand of forest where. Eloise tried to spit out the foul-tasting scrap, but couldn't. She tried to yell, but only managed a grunt.

"Mistress? Are you alright?" It was Mîîiz, the youngest bongo, her voice quiet in the darkness. The wombats froze in place. "Are you OK? I can't see you. I was just having a private moment. Do you need a private moment as well?"

Eloise produced another muffled grunt.

"Máää, Dááà, everyone! Something's going on!" Mîîiz cried.

That woke Lorch, who sprang to his feet, then saw the furry bodies around him and the faint glint of drawn weapons. "Pri— Mistress! Mistress, where are you?"

The wombats carrying Eloise dropped her to the ground. She landed with an "Oof!" The wombats drew their swords, half pointing them at her and half pointing away, protective.

The three horses unfolded their forelegs in front of them, ready to lever themselves upright.

"Easy there," said the lead wombat to Lorch and the horses. "You be surrounded by sharpened steel. And that be our determination as well as our weapons."

Fortitude de Bongo lit a torch in the embers of their campfire and held it high, shedding light onto the stand-off.

For several long moments, no one moved. The wombats squinted into the light, and the only apparent motion was them adjusting the direction of their swords, and the dance of torchlight on blades.

Lorch tried again. "Mistress, are you OK?"

She choked out, "Uh-uh."

Fortitude De Bongo shifted the light so Eloise's stiffened body was visible.

A smaller, swordless wombat got close to Eloise's face. He narrowed his eyes and rubbed his chin. Then his eyes widened. "Master Shovelhovel!"

"Not now, RoyLee."

"Master Shovelhovel! Look who it be!"

"I be a bit busy here, RoyLee." The lead wombat squinted into the uneven light, ready to fend off an attack.

"No, Master Shovelhovel. Look. Look! It be the name lady."

"What name lady?"

"The naming lady! The savant!"

"*The* naming lady? Who helped us rename our gang?" Shovelhovel lowered the tip of his sword and squinted in Eloise's direction. He took a step closer and sniffed. "So it be. So it be. Her hair be short and white, and she be looking a bit older and thinner, but it be her for sure." The wombat reached over and took the rag from her mouth.

Eloise turned her head to the side and spat out the taste of wombat snot. Whatever was in her that kept her from moving had not affected her ability to breathe, swallow or speak. She wanted to scream, "Have you left your collective minds back in your burrow? What in the name of Çalaht's septic bunions are you doing here accosting me again?" But swords were still drawn, and from the look on Lorch's face, the odds of blood being spilled remained high. Eloise swallowed back her rage, and said with a calm she did not feel, "Hello, RoyLee. G'midnight, Master Shovelhovel. Nice to see you again. How are you all?"

"You know them?" asked Lorch, his hands still held in the air. "Who are they?"

Shovelhovel raised his sword, and cried, "We be the Pillagiarists—the gang formerly known as the Wombanditos and most definitely not the Womb-banditos, which would have been a stupid thing to name a gang —the fiercest gang with bad eyesight in all the realms! Heeyahhh!"

"Heeyahhh!" responded all the wombats.

"Shush, you! Trying to sleep over here!" yelled someone from a few camp squares away.

"Sorry, sorry there, neighbor," said Shovelhovel. He turned to his gang. "Sheath yer swords, mates. There'll be no kidnapping tonight."

❧   *21*   ❧

TEA WITH WOMBATS

While Lorch added sticks to the de Bongos' fire and put on a pot of water, the wombats carried Eloise's still-stiff body over to it and laid her near so she could warm up.

"Why is she like that?" demanded Hector.

"It be temporary," said Shovelhovel, waving him off. "Tincture of the wraith rose. But only the petals, not the rosehips, so it no be lethal or nothing. It just be part of facilitating the abduction."

Shovelhovel waved at the wombat who'd administered the first drops. She approached Eloise, pulled another bottle from her pouch and held it up. "Antidote. OK?"

"Yes, please."

"Slow or fast?"

"Is there a difference?"

"Fast hurts more. A lot more. Slow has to go in the eyes."

"Are we in a rush, Master Shovelhovel?" asked Eloise.

"Not anymore."

"Then slow will be fine." Eloise opened her eyes wide, and the wombat let two drops fall in each. Eloise blinked them in. There was an uncomfortable warmth to the drops, which spread out through her face.

Shovelhovel brushed dirt from his clothes. "Well, that being done, we'll be off then," said Shovelhovel. "It be late and all."

"Oh, I don't think so," said Eloise. "We need to chat. Lorch, could you please serve up some tea?"

"That be right kind of you, Mistress, but..."

"Master Shovelhovel, you have broken into my camp, drugged me, and attempted a kidnapping. From where I sit, and I can't yet, it looks like you have two options. You and yours can go off, and wait for me and mine to come after you, have a confrontation that will almost certainly be disagreeable, and then have you give me the information that I want. Or you and yours can accept my invitation to a cup of haggleberry tea, we can chat about things now, and skip all that other unpleasantness."

Shovelhovel hesitated.

"We have fruit rolls," added Eloise.

RoyLee tugged at Shovelhovel's tunic sleeve. "A fruit roll be sounding nice."

"Oh, I suppose," said Shovelhovel. He turned to the other wombats. "Settle in, folks. It be tea time."

Three dozen wombats took up most of the combined camping space. There weren't enough cups to go around, and the fruit rolls had to be sliced thinner than Eloise would have liked. Even so, it seemed pleasant enough, and the de Bongos and horses joined them. By the time everyone was settled, sipping, and nibbling, she'd regained enough mobility to sit up comfortably and hold a mug in both hands. She started with something she hoped was more or less neutral. "So, Master Shovelhovel, how's the new name working out?"

"It be a bit of a mess, as you just heard earlier."

"It did sound a little complicated."

"The name." Shovelhovel sighed, and all the wombats shifted, clearly uncomfortable. "The name thing be a bit of a mixed bag. You and your little business partner be right that we be needing a new name. Turns out, we be the only ones among all the gangs not to see the 'womb' in 'Wombanditos.' Them other gangs been laughing at us for years."

"I'm sorry to hear that. That must be difficult for you."

"But it be hard to change the name. We got no reputation with the new name, and we be having difficulty getting it to stick in the minds of others." He set his cup down on his saucer, and leaned forward, squinting in her direction. "It be why we be this far north. We be trying to get the new name, the Pillagiarists, to work on its own in a new place. But us being so fierce and all, people already be knowing who we are. So we be having to keep adding that bit about formerly being known as the Wombanditos."

"I guess it's good that your reputation is so strong."

"That be one way to be looking at it."

Eloise took a nibble of fruit roll and had another sip of tea. Jerome was usually the one to brew it, but Lorch seemed to have a flair for making it as well. Enough small talk, she thought. "So, what brought you here tonight?"

"You did, Mistress. Except we did not know it be you."

"Oh? So it was just a routine kidnapping?"

"A routine kidnapping? There be no such thing. Each undertaking must be planned down to the last detail if you be wanting it to go smoothly. But in this case, this was no to be a kidnapping, really. It be more of a thieving. Thieving, with a bit of kidnapping thrown in for good measure. Like a bonus."

"Thieving? What were you after?"

"We ourselves no be after anything, per se. It be more of a contract operation, being on behalf of..." Shovelhovel paused, like he was trying not to disclose something commercial-in-confidence. "On behalf of someone else."

Eloise waited.

Shovelhovel waited.

Eloise sipped tea.

Shovelhovel did the same, adding a bite of fruit roll.

"You realize that the identity of the person who asked you to do this and what they were after form the core of what I'm trying to learn, right?"

"I be understanding that."

Another sip each.

"Is there a problem?" asked Eloise.

Shovelhovel handed his cup and saucer to RoyLee, stood, and paced like he was trying to work it out. "It be a matter of reputation, like we be discussing. I can't be just giving out information because it's been asked for. It'd be bad for business. We be fierce and all, and that must be applying to everything."

"I see," said Eloise. She stretched her legs toward the fire, turning her feet at the ankles to see if the ability to move them had returned. It was improving, but she didn't think she could walk yet. "What if the information was conveyed under duress?"

"I beg your pardon, Mistress?" Shovelhovel stopped pacing. "What be you suggesting?"

"We could apply enhanced methods and force it out of you, such that you have no choice but to reveal the details, as much as you don't want to." Eloise pointed her toes at the fire.

Shovelhovel brightened. "I be liking this idea. It be fierce, just like us."

"And the best part is, we don't actually have to do it."

"No?"

"No. We can all agree to put it out there that that's what happened. You can make up whatever story you want to suit your mood and audience. You can change it as needed," said Eloise. "We can give you permission to tie as many bells and ribbons on the story of how bravely you resisted, and how, unfortunately, you had to yield your secret, despite valiantly withstanding a gruesome and painful attack on your person."

"I be finding that agreeable. I think we can be coming to a meeting of minds about this here approach," said the wombat. He rubbed the hair on his face, thinking. "Oh, that tale could be ripe! How the fiercest of the Pillagiarists—the gang formerly known as the Wombanditos and most definitely not the Womb-banditos, which would have been a stupid thing to name a gang—the fiercest gang with bad eyesight in all the realms, how their leader was captured and put to the greatest of suffering, but refused to divulge sensitive commercial-in-confidence information. No amount of plucking of eyelash hairs, or trimming of claws too close to the quick, nor excessive tickling nor exposure to unpleasant smells could make him budge."

"Oh, that be awful for you, Master Shovelhovel," said RoyLee, caught up in the telling. "How did you ever stand it?"

"With the greatest of difficulty and only through sheer toughness, grit, and fortitude of character, my boy."

"What made you give up the information in the end?" asked RoyLee.

"Loyalty to the wisdom. When they threatened to hurt our extended family, our wisdom of wombats, I had to give in and reveal what was being sought."

"No!" gaped RoyLee. "Those ruffians!"

Shovelhovel ruffled the hair on RoyLee's head and turned back to Eloise. "Deal."

A sigh of relief came from the bongos, horses, and Lorch, who'd all been following every word.

"Good," said Eloise. "And thank you." She flexed her knees to gauge their mobility. Better, and not too sore. "Do you need us to actually stage the nastiness, or can we leave that up to you?"

"No need to go to that trouble," said Shovelhovel. "I can be handling that side of things." He sat back down. "So, I only be meeting him the one time. He found me. Thin bloke. Bandaged foot like a Percheron had been dancing on it. Didn't give me his name. And truth be told, there was not much coin in the undertaking. It be his suggestion that we be kidnapping the person to make it more profitable. So kidnapping be the bonus."

"What did he want?"

"That wee box that be on your hip."

Eloise put a hand on it through her cloak. "What did he say it was?"

"A wee box on your hip. It no be my place to pry, and how much trouble could a wee box give? I no be pressing that matter."

"What were you supposed to do?"

"What we almost done. Sneak in. Secure you with the wraith rose drops. That be my idea because we have experience with it. I was to confirm the wee box was there. Spirit you away. Secure the box. Then three of us were to travel to deliver it while the rest be responsible for the ransoming."

"Travel?"

"He be leaving two days ago, maybe two-and-a-half. He said we should meet him at Acrostic Crossing."

The Nameless One snorted. It was his first contribution to the conversation,

"Acrostic Crossing. Where's that?"

"About two days for a horse at pace. The Nameless One and I have been there on campaign," said Lorch. "It is not a garden paradise."

"I have an aunty who used to live there," said Kïïït. "I visited once or twice as a foal. I remember it being dull as dirt. It was a podunk bump in the road with four inns and a monthly market."

"Four inns? Why so many?"

"It's on the main route to the Central Ranges. There seems to be enough passing traffic to keep them all in business."

Eloise turned back to Shovelhovel. "Did he give any indication at all why he chose Acrostic Crossing as a meeting place?"

The head wombat absently scratched behind his ear with a hind leg, then realized he was in public and straightened up. "No. Just said to be meeting him there. RoyLee, you be there when we met him. Be you recalling anything?"

"No, Master Shovelhovel. He just be naming the place and the when, but no the why."

"That be what I remember as well."

They all sat in thought, with only the occasional tea slurp or chewing of fruit roll interrupting the silence.

Prééècïïíóöòúüùs de Bongo took advantage of the lull to usher her children back to their beds after a polite round of g'nights from each of them.

More quiet thinking followed. Finally, Lorch spoke. "What do you think, Pr— Mistress?"

"I think what Master Shovelhovel described is consistent. Turpy tried to get the Star—the box before. So having him try again is unsurprising. We've seen him hire, or at least organize, others before. There were the rats at Gutrot House, if nothing else."

"If Acrostic Crossing is a way station for travelers, do you think he's going to the Central Ranges?" asked Hector.

"It's certainly possible," said Lorch. "But why?"

"Build a new life somewhere else?" suggested Kïïït.

"Seek asylum with the khan?" suggested Hector.

"Plot and perpetrate additional felonies against the crowns of the realms?" said Lorch.

Everyone looked at him.

Lorch blushed. "Apologies, Pri—er, Mistress. I might be experiencing some consternation around this whole thing."

"Understandable. Well, I think there's only one thing to do. We have to keep Master Shovelhovel's appointment with his client," said Eloise. "We'll leave for Acrostic Crossing at first light." She turned to the wombat. "Master Shovelhovel, can we offer you and your party a ride?"

22

HEAD SMACKERS

Between the wombat attack, the tea party in the middle of the night, and the time it took to recover from the wraith rose tincture, Eloise barely got any sleep before first light rolled around. She helped pack their things and ready the panniers, noting that everyone seemed a little slow to get going.

"Mistress Eloise?" asked a small voice. Mĩĩz had come over to where she was tying on her bedroll. "Will you and your friends share a last meal with us? Dáàä's making four-nut porridge."

Eloise glance at Lorch, who gave a small nod. "We would love to. Thank you, once again."

The de Bongo breakfast was a hot gruel of buckwheat groats cooked with almonds, cashews, pecans, and pistachios, sweetened with apple and pear. Like the de Bongo family itself, the food warmed and filled Eloise, and made her realize just how much she was going to miss them all. They had welcomed her and the others with an openness and completeness that she'd never experienced before.

When they finished eating, Eloise stood to help with the dishes, but Préëècĩĩíóöòùüùs de Bongo shook her antlers to wave her off. "We'll take care of that. You must be on your way."

"Thank you so much. You have all been so kind to us."

They all stood up, ready to say goodbyes, when Lîîîz nudged her father. "Dáää?"

"Go ahead."

Lîîîz held up a hoof. "Hold on. We have something for you." She and Mîîîz trotted over to the family's possessions and came back with two sacks. Mîîîz went to Lorch with hers, and Lîîîz handed hers to Eloise. "Something to remember us by," said Lîîîz.

Lorch peeked inside his bag and smiled. Eloise felt the weight and shape of hers and recognized it immediately. Each sack held a pair of bongo drums. "Are you sure?"

"They're the ones you played on stage, so we know you can sound good with them."

"Goodness. You're too kind. I don't know what to say."

"Thank you," said Lorch. "I look forward to playing them, and I will think of you each time I do."

"We hope so," said Lîîîz.

Eloise's mind raced, trying to think of something she could give in return. They were traveling light and had been since leaving Brague. The Çalahtist prayer beads that Odmilla had given her? Her travel copy of the *Scrolls of Çalaht*? The ring Jerome's mother, Seer Maybelle de Chipmunk, had given her? One of the traveler or witch stones that she'd recovered from what used to be in Melveeta the Elusive's stomach after she died and disintegrated? The three bags of groats that the queen of The South, Onomatopoeia, had given her?

None of them felt like an appropriate gift in this particular moment.

Lorch came to her rescue. "We have something for you, as well." He untied a flap from a pannier and brought out a muslin cloth tied with red string to form a bundle. He presented it to Mîîiz. "Can you share these with the others?"

"Of course," she said. "What are they?"

"Have a smell."

The little bongo carefully sniffed the cloth. Her eyebrows lifted, and she looked at Lorch. "What just happened to my nose?"

"How would you describe it?"

"Empty. Clear and empty. Very suddenly."

"That sounds right. These are sweets made with eucalyptus oil, corn mint oil, and peppermint oil. My mother gave them to me as a treat when I was a child, and I still have a fondness for them. In my family, we called them 'head smackers,' because they smacked out anything in your nasal passages. But the sweets monger here said they are called 'nosers' in the Half Kingdom."

"I think I like 'head smackers' better." Mîîiz took the parcel gently with her teeth. "Thank you, Master Lorch. You are most kind," she said around the edge of the parcel. She turned to her siblings. "Anyone want to try a head smacker?"

"Not just now, Mîîiz," said Fortitude "Once our friends have gone." He bobbed his antlers at each of them. "Boring travels to you all."

Eloise curtsied back. "Thank you."

Préë̈cîíióöòùüüs de Bongo came up to Eloise next, and in a soft voice, recited the proper farewell passage prescribed by Protocol. "May the road be smooth, the weather pleasant, may Çalaht light your path with her gap-toothed smile, and may you not be accosted by wild, marauding, bloodthirsty, ravenous bandicoots."

Surprised, Eloise leaned forward and offered her right cheek so the bongo could give her a Western Lands kiss—right cheek, left cheek, forehead. Eloise returned it, although she'd never done it with anyone who had antlers before. "Thank you," said Eloise. "Although, I have to confess it's not my favorite passage from the *Livre de Protocol*."

"Nor mine, Princess Eloise," agreed Préëëcĩïíóöòúüùs. "The anachronistic reference to bandicoots is offensive, even it is based in a certain degree of historical truth."

Eloise paused. "You figured out who I am?"

"As unlikely as it is for you to be here, yes, I did. Your name, for one, and the fact that Master Lorch almost called you 'princess' about a dozen times."

"I see." Eloise blushed. "Apologies for the deception, even if it wasn't very deceptive. And thank you again for the distinctly non-royal welcome you gave us. If you and your family find your way to Brague someday, please come to the castle and let me know. I would love to return the favor of hospitality. And I would love for you to play for my mother. She would enjoy your music."

"A performance for the queen. Now that would be something for the kids to remember, for sure. We would love to."

"Until then."

"Boring travels to you, Princess Eloise."

"Thank you, and boring travels to you all as well."

Hector lowered himself so Eloise could easily mount, and Lorch hopped up on the Nameless One. Kïïït shook a little to settle her panniers.

"Ready?" Lorch asked.

Eloise drew a deep, settling breath. "Ready."

They turned and headed out.

"Boring travels to you," called the de Bongo family, waving.

Eloise swiveled toward them and waved back.

She hoped she might see them again someday. Maybe she would be a better bongo player by then.

23

CLOSE ENOUGH TO FINE

As they rode out of Kääächööö, Eloise thought how good it felt to be on Hector's back again and moving, rather than sitting around trying to figure out what was next.

They stopped at the edge of the town to meet the three wombats who would travel with them: Master Shovelhovel, RoyLee, and the old female who had administered the wraith rose drops and antidote. Eloise felt wariness when she saw her and flexed her hands once again to check for any residual stiffness. There was none that she could tell. She slid off Hector's back so she would be closer to them when they spoke.

"G'morning to you," said Shovelhovel. "You be knowing me and RoyLee. And you met Seer Bunkerhunker before, but no be getting her name. She be our wisdom's seer, wise one, and healer. She also be my gran."

"Pleased to meet you, Seer Bunkerhunker. I'm Eloise."

"I know who you be," groused the old wombat.

Eloise formally introduced Lorch, Hector, the Nameless One, and Kïïit, and then Kïïit stepped forward. "Are you OK to ride on my back?"

"I no be sure, as I never be doing it before," said Shovelhovel. "Gran, you ever be having a horse as transport?"

"No. Nor do I be caring to do it now."

"Gran, I no be forcing you to come. No one be saying you have to do this."

"I be aware of that. But I be visioning what I be visioning, and my visions be telling me I'm going to be there whenever what be happening be happening." Her graying hair bristled, and she clutched a travel bag in front of her. "But I don't be having to like it."

Kïïit looked at Hector and the Nameless One. "This isn't going to work. Not with three of them. One might hold onto my mane, but the other two would have to claw into my back. We've not thought this through."

"I could have one in front of me," said Eloise. "And Lorch could have one in front of him."

"Possible," said Lorch. "But not ideal, if they're not used to holding on, or if we have to gallop suddenly."

The Nameless One tossed his head to motion at their baggage.

"Good idea," said Hector. "What about in a pannier? The two smaller ones could be on one side, and Master Shovelhovel could sit in the other."

"Would they fit?" asked Kïïit.

Hector considered the wombats. "They would if we repacked."

"Would that be more acceptable, Seer Bunkerhunker?" asked Eloise.

The old wombat's eyes unfocused for a moment as she checked in with whatever of the Unseen she was in touch with. Eloise had seen Jerome's mother, Seer Maybelle de Chipmunk, do this any number of times. It was eerie to see something so familiar echoed in another person this way.

Seer Bunkerhunker came back from wherever she was. "That be fine. Or as close enough to fine as we be getting."

Eloise and Lorch repacked their baggage to free up a pannier for the wombats, then Kïïït knelt down so they could climb in. RoyLee's eyes shone with excitement, Seer Bunkerhunker still looked wary, and Shovelhovel was almost as excited as Roy Lee, but tried to act blasé.

"Well, ain't that the grass strudel," said Kïïït as she stood. "That should work well. Let me know if you have problems or need anything. We're intending to keep up a brisk pace."

"I'll be doing that for sure," said Shovelhovel. "Gran, RoyLee, be you ready?"

They nodded, and the horses were off, heading out of Kääächööö and down the road toward Acrostic Crossing.

Lorch and the Nameless One led the way, with Eloise and Hector in the middle, then Kïïït and the wombats. The terrain was hilly, but not very steep, the morning air brisk, and with the three wombats snug in their pannier, they made good time.

RoyLee had a similar look to the one Kïïït had when she first left Stained Rock, but his interests were not grasses and bushes, but the broad shape of things. Eyes squinting, his nose twitching constantly, he tried to work out what was passing by him at a speed he'd never traveled before. "What be those greenish things to the left and right?" he asked.

"What greenish things?" asked Kïïït.

"They be green. Sort of shaped like a cone or an upside-down bowl. Or maybe a big ball. Some of them be red or orange or yellow."

"What, the trees?"

"Those be trees? Trees be more or less circular, not conical, bowl-shaped, or ball-like."

"They'd be circular if you were below them looking up," said Kïïït. "You're looking at them from more or less side on. That makes them look different."

"Oh. I be seeing now." RoyLee quietened and contemplated this revelation.

"Perspective," muttered Shovelhovel. "It all be a matter of perspective."

They traveled the whole day, slept rough that night, and continued the next morning. By lunchtime, they were getting close to their destination. Lorch and the Nameless One stopped at a copse of aspen trees. "Let's take a break, so we can arrive more refreshed and alert."

"I think we should wait until dark before we go into the town," said Eloise. "He'll be looking out for Master Shovelhovel and the others, but he won't necessarily be looking out for us."

"He might be," said Hector. "He was certainly watching us as we traveled the wrong way toward The South."

"That was before he damaged his foot. It's unclear how mobile he is and what remains of his ability to do surveillance," said Eloise. "Even so, I think we should assume he is at least wary, and at worst, as fully capable as he was before."

"What do you think he would do if he saw us?" asked Kïïït.

"If he sees us he may bolt," said Hector. "Or attack. Or hang back and watch. Or attempt sabotage. Or, or, or."

"In other words, we have no idea," said Eloise.

"Not really," said Lorch. "We know he is stealthy and keen. But I agree with you, Princess, that there is no benefit to us entering town in daylight."

"Princess?" said RoyLee. "Master Shovelhovel, what do he mean by 'Princess'? Why would he call the naming savant 'Princess?' Be they entwined in love?"

"A most excellent question, RoyLee." Shovelhovel squinted at Lorch, then Eloise. "Princess? Be you entwined in love, such that 'princess' be a title of affection?"

Eloise's face reddened. "No."

"Then be it possible that you be Princess Eloise Hydra Gumball III, Heir and Future Ruler of our sweet homeland, the Western Lands and All That Really Matters, here in what many might well be calling the middle of nowhere?"

"Yes."

"Then if I may be so bold, what in the name of Çalaht's webbed toes are you doing here? And why be you with us?"

"And will you be arresting us and sending us to the hoosegow?" asked RoyLee. "On account of our last encounter. Or on account of this one. Or both."

"No and no," said Eloise to RoyLee. "As for the rest of it, that's a somewhat long and complicated story."

"Humph." Seer Bunkerhunker got her unfocused look again, then came back. "That be explaining a thing or two."

"How so?" asked Eloise.

"What I be visioning be confusing. That, and the way these people be treating you. You being a princess makes the pieces fit together better."

"I see."

"I no be meaning to pry, Princess Eloise," said Shovelhovel. "But it might be safer for us all going into this if we be having a fuller picture of what's going on."

Eloise looked at Lorch, who lifted his shoulders.

"I suppose you're right, Master Shovelhovel," said Eloise. "Plus, we haven't really worked out the details of what we do when we get to town."

They found a sunny spot off the road where they could comfortably talk and wait for dusk. Lorch prepared a simple lunch of crackerbread spread with cashew and almond paste. The wombats, like the horses, spent half an hour browsing for a meal, then came back to where Eloise and Lorch sat.

Eloise let Lorch fill the wombats in. He sketched their journey in broad strokes, focusing mainly on the part that started with them leaving Stained Rock. He covered who they were, who Turpy was, explained about Jerome, and why they were after them.

"That be your friend with the naming business? He be in a bag. Oh, Master Shovelhovel, this Turpentine person be dangerous!" said RoyLee. "I no be wanting to meet up with him again."

"Now, RoyLee. I understand why you be saying that. But we be needing to see this through. There be coin in it if nothing else."

"I supposed there's the coin." RoyLee hunched down. "But I no be liking this."

Seer Bunkerhunker had been chewing a stalk of grass, listening. The old wombat leaned forward and pointed the stalk at Shovelhovel. "It no be about the coin now. Do you no get that? It be about much more than the coin."

"Gran, I—"

"Don't 'Gran' me. This be about right and wrong. It be about a dangerous person who should no be roaming the realms. If we need to be playing a part in whatever this is to stop him, then that's what we be doing. And we'll no be seeking coin as part of it."

Shovelhovel hunched down just as RoyLee had. "Yes, Gran."

"RoyLee?"

"Yes, Seer Bunkerhunker."

The old wombat turned to Lorch and Eloise. "You have a plan? I'd be hearing it if you do."

"Not yet," said Eloise.

"Then we best be putting one together. I be wanting to get back to our wisdom, and no be falling victim to this Turpentine fellow."

"I agree, Seer Bunkerhunker."

Lorch cleared his throat. "I had intended to hang back, identify him when we saw him, then capture him. I don't know how much planning is needed, or possible. We find him, then we grab him. There are more of us than him. With any luck we will have surprise on our side."

"Luck. I no be liking relying on luck," said Seer Bunkerhunker. "You best be thinking it through more. RoyLee!"

"Yes, Seer Bunkerhunker?"

"Could you please bring an old woman a bit of that crackerbread and nut paste?"

"Yes, Seer Bunkerhunker."

"Now, let's be putting all these heads together and come up with something a bit more clever than hoping for luck."

Eloise felt embarrassed. The wombat was right. They'd put far too little thought into what they would do when they encountered Turpy. "How exactly were you to meet up, Master Shovelhovel?" she asked.

"That no be completely worked out." Shovelhovel took a piece of crackerbread that RoyLee offered. "We're supposed to be leaving a message at an inn and then be waiting for a response."

"Which inn?" asked Lorch.

"That be an odd thing," said RoyLee. "He be saying that we be figuring it out."

"What?"

"That be what I said. I be saying that we be fierce but we no be having good eyesight. So why be making it hard? That be what I said to him," said Shovelhovel. "But he be saying 'security is important.' And so, if we be wanting our coin, we would go and figure it out."

"Too much mystery for my taste," said Bunkerhunker. "I no be trusting him."

"A well-placed mistrust," said Hector.

They spent the rest of the afternoon trying to come up with a reasonable plan.

There was not a lot of reasonable to be had. Just a lot of uncertainty.

❦ 24 ❦

ACROSTIC CROSSING

As they entered the town, the fading light was just giving up the ghost. It was immediately obvious that Acrostic Crossing was a baffling place by design. The town itself hid between a series of hills. The street names were meant to obscure rather than clarify, so one might have to go left at You've Gone Too Far, stop at Keep Going You Fool, or turn around at Must Go Straight.

They found the four inns that Kïïït remembered at the intersection of Dead End, which didn't come to a dead end, and Arch Circle, which was straight and distinctly arch free. Lorch pulled his black winter cloak around himself, drew up its deep hood, and left them standing in the shadows while he scoped out the inns for clues. Eloise watched as he moved from inn to inn, checking out the signs, looking in the windows, and having a quiet word with people either entering or leaving each establishment. At one point, he took out a scrap of hemp parchment and a piece of charcoal, and jotted something down.

"Most unusual," said Lorch when he returned. "Decidedly odd."

"How so?" asked Eloise.

"The inns do not seem to have names. Each sign is a somewhat awkward sentence."

"What kind of sentence?" asked Hector.

Lorch waggled the parchment a little. "They're made up of somewhat inn-related words." He pointed to the inn closest to them, then to his writing. "This is what's on the sign for that one."

Eloise read it out loud. "'Because every sleep tantalizes with premium luxury and audaciously classy elegance.' It sounds like a not very good advertising slogan."

"Other than bragging a little, does it tell us anything?" asked Hector.

"Not that I can tell," said Lorch. He pointed to a second inn and read the next sentence. "'Cooking lacks enthusiasm accommodation narrow if satisfactorily hygienic.' Not very enticing."

"I think they're puzzles," said Kiïit. "If not very good ones. Look at the first one. Lorch, were the words written out as a sentence?"

"No, they weren't. They were more of a list. Like this." He flipped over the parchment and rewrote the first one as a list.

Because

Every

Sleep

Tantalizes with

Premium

Luxury and

Audaciously

Classy

Elegance

"See?" said Kiïit.

"No, I don't," said Hector.

"Look at the first letter."

"Oh. I get it," he said. "It spells out 'Best place.' So what's the second one?"

Lorch again rewrote the words as they appeared on the sign.

Cooking

Lacks

Enthusiasm

Accommodation

Narrow

If

Satisfactorily

Hygienic

"Cleanish?" said Hector. "They've hidden the word 'cleanish?' Are these given by edict?"

"I think there is some sort of regulator who assigns them based on inspections," said Kīīīt.

"That's not exactly a ringing endorsement," said Hector.

Lorch read the next one. "Sobriety Not Our Concern Keep Enjoying and Relishing Every Drink."

"'Snockered?' Is that even a word?" asked Eloise.

"I think so, Princess." Lorch looked over at the inn. "From the outside, it looked the most derelict of the four. I could tell by a glance inside that liquid consolation definitely flows freely within its walls."

"I hope that's not the intended inn."

"I wouldn't put it past Felon Snotearrow McCcoonnch to choose such a place."

"No. I wouldn't either."

"What does the last one say?" asked Eloise.

Lorch held up the parchment to catch the last of the light. "Management Eschews Expectations Tasteful Helpings Evince Realistic Expectations."

"So 'Meet Here,'" said Eloise. "Master Shovelhovel, I think we found your inn."

"You be right, I think," Shovelhovel said. "RoyLee, you be remembering what to do?"

"Yes, Master Shovelhovel, I be remembering. I be going to figure out who be in charge and then deliver the message that we are here and ready to meet with that man about an object."

"And you be watching for the thin, limping man yourself, as you be having the best eyes of all of us."

"Yes, Master Shovelhovel. I'll be squinting right careful to see if I can spot him in there."

The young wombat scampered off to initiate contact.

RoyLee was gone fifteen minutes, with no sign of him coming out.

"Should we go in after him?" asked Shovelhovel. "Gran?"

Seer Bunkerhunker went unfocused briefly. "Nay. He no be in specific danger."

Another quarter hour passed. Then another.

Finally, the door creaked open and RoyLee emerged, smiling widely and listing from side to side. "Mashter... Mashter Shovelhovel, I be returning." The young wombat hiccuped.

"RoyLee? Be you alright?" Shovelhovel ran over to the wombat, but as soon as he got close, he juddered to a halt. "Çalaht smelling singed stinktree saplings! What happened in there?"

"I be having a very nishe time with Ïïïväään, the man in charge. He was very nishe to me. Very nishe." RoyLee wobbled as Shovelhovel guided him back to the shadows where the rest of them waited. "Hello, everybody. Nishe to see you again."

Eloise bent down. The wombat's breath could clean the grime off a dungeon floor with a single exhale. "What happened in there?"

"I went in and asked for whoever be in charge. That I had a mesh... A mesh... A shomething to shay to shomeone about shomething. Ïïïväään, he was at the bar. Did I mention that? Ïïïväään said I'd be having to wait a little bit, and would I be wanting shomething to ship... Ssssssip. Sip. Ship while I waited. On the house, he shaid. On the house. Ssssso I shaid thank you. And he gave me a mug of shomething that he called a Wombat'sh Friend."

"Oh, no," said Shovelhovel.

"Wombat's Friend?" Seer Bunkerhunker snorted, both amused and concerned. "I no be having one of those for a few decades. Not since your granddad be courting me. I no remember the imbibing, but well I be remembering the headache the next day. And the necessity for marriage shortly thereafter."

"Gran!"

"Truth be truth."

"It tasted like juniper punch," said RoyLee, looking dreamy. "It be spiced with cinnamon, Mashter Shovelhovel. Shinnamon."

"How many Wombat's Friends did you have?" asked Eloise.

RoyLee lifted up one paw, steadying himself on the other three as best he could. He held up two claws.

"Two," said Eloise.

RoyLee unfurled the rest of the claws on that paw.

"Five?"

The wombat waved his paw back and forth. "No. Shorry." Slowly and delicately, he lowered himself, hunched, and rolled onto his side just enough to free another paw. He extended another two claws.

"Seven? You had seven Wombat's Friends in an hour?"

"On the houshe," said RoyLee. "Ïïïväään... He was at the bar. Ïïïväään was very nishe to me. And very interested in me as a persh... Persh..."

"Person," finished Lorch.

"That's the one. Pershon." RoyLee rolled back onto his feet. "He was asking all about me. Me, and Mashter Shovelhovel, and Sheer Bunker-hunker. Lots of questionsh. Lotsh. Very comradely. Very friendly. Asked me about all my friendsh. And how we got here. Ssssso I told him about my new friends who helped us get here." He pointed to Eloise, Lorch, and the three horses. "I told him about you and you and you and you and you."

"Right," said Eloise. "Did you mention our names as well?"

"Of courshe I did. It would be dish... Dish... Dishrespectful if I didn't."

Lorch looked at Eloise. "It's possible we may have lost the element of surprise. I think we need an alternative plan, and quick." He scanned the dim stretches of Dead End and Arch Circle. "It might be best to split up somewhat. Some of us can remain, observing, while the others go into the inn and look for him."

"I agree, but I don't like it. Who knows what allies he has in there. Certainly, this Ïïïväään person."

"Ïïïväään wash very friendly," said RoyLee. "Told me to tell you to ashk for him." He wobbled again. "I'm not sure I be feeling sho good."

A noise came from behind the inn. It was the thumping of large, loping, padded feet. The sound drew closer.

"What the—" said Lorch.

It was a camel trotting right at them. On his back rode Turpy, snarling as he neared. It looked like he meant to run them down.

❧ 25 ❧

LOVELY NIGHT FOR IT

Camels had a reputation for foul language, rough opinions, orneriness, and excessive spitting. Eloise hadn't had much first-hand experience with them, but reputations were normally built on some sort of reality. Camels were generally not the sort of people you wanted to cross in a dark passage between buildings.

This one looked plenty scary. Having him come straight at her made Eloise's guts tighten. She didn't know whether to scream, fall back, or try to hold her ground.

A stray shaft of light from the inn caught Turpy's side. The sack! Even at a distance of several dozen lengths, Eloise could see something squirming and struggling inside. Fear of being trampled by a camel warred with frantic thoughts of how she to get the sack back.

As the camel came closer, something odd happened. He smiled. "G'evening to you all," he said. "Lovely night for it. I hope you enjoy your stay here in Acrostic Crossing. I don't particularly recommend that inn we just came out of. Ïïïväään the bartender isn't the friendliest of fellows." He drew closer. "Try the inn on the opposite corner, Cooking Lacks Enthusiasm Accommodation Narrow If Satisfactorily Hygienic. They do a lovely goldbeet and leek pie."

"Thank you?" said Eloise. It came out more as a question than a statement.

"El! El! Is that you?" The voice came from within Turpy's bag. "Are you out there? El! Help me! For Çalaht's sake, help me! El!"

"Jerome!" yelled Eloise. "Jerome!"

"Oh, is that his name?" said the camel. "Nice name."

"Shut up. Both of you. All of you!" snapped Turpy. "You! Camel! I told you to keep your mouth shut. Now shut up and run!"

"Sorry, sorry, sorry. You're right. You did say that. Sorry about that." The camel looked at Eloise's group as he drew level with them. "Not supposed to chat. This one doesn't like it."

"El!" screamed Jerome.

"Lorch! Hector! Everyone!" called Eloise. "Stop them! And get Jerome." They moved to narrow the space and try to impede the camel.

"Run, I say!" yelled Turpy. "Now!"

"Well, it was lovely meeting you all," said the camel. "Have a good evening and remember the goldbeet and leek pie." The camel sped up into a gangly, awkward gallop. It was a style of galloping that horses had sniggered at for centuries, but this camel was fast. Faster than any camel Eloise had ever seen. Faster, in fact than any horse.

The yammering camel and Turpy blew past them before they could capture him or snatch Jerome, then whizzed down Dead End and out of town. The only sound was the thunder of camel feet and snatches of his ongoing, one-sided conversation.

There was no point giving chase.

"Wow!" said Kiïit. "Look at that camel go!"

They all stared in the direction the camel had gone, watching as Turpy and Jerome disappeared into the dark.

"Is it possible for a camel to have longwalker weak magic?" asked Eloise.

"I've never heard of it before," said Hector. "But it's certainly possible."

"It'd appear it's more than possible."

"Ain't that the grass strudel," said Kïïït, eyes lit. "He was flying. How can he talk so much and run that fast at the same time?"

"Maybe he has a weak magic for incessant talking as well as for long-walking," said Hector.

The Nameless One struck a hoof to the ground, breaking the trance.

"You're right!" said Eloise. "We have to go after them." She turned to the wombats. "Can the two of you take care of RoyLee?"

"We be going with you," said Seer Bunkerhunker.

"Gran, I don't know," said Shovelhovel.

"I don't feel so nishe," said RoyLee.

"Seer Bunkerhunker, I—" started Eloise.

The old one waved her paw, cutting off Eloise's protest. "I be visioning what I be visioning. You'll no be the leaving us here."

"Right." Eloise turned to Kïïït. "Can you please lower yourself so I can help them back in the bags?" The mare dropped down. Master Shovel-hovel climbed into his side of the pannier on his own, but Eloise had to help both RoyLee and Seer Bunkerhunker into theirs.

"Best be putting RoyLee in front of me this time," said the old wombat. "If his reaction to the Wombat's Friend be anything like what I remember my own, I'll no be wanting him behind me, that's for sure. Him bouncing around on a horse no be making an unpleasant outcome any less likely."

"Would you rather RoyLee was on his own?" asked Eloise.

"There no be enough room for him or me with my grandson. And I'll need to be taking care of young RoyLee. Let's just be going, but best be making sure he be having enough room for heaving over the edge of the bag where it not be getting on me."

Within five minutes, the three horses were cantering down Dead End, following the trail of prints that the galloping camel had left behind.

❧ 26 ☙

NO ADVANTAGES

It's going to be a long night, thought Eloise as chill air bit through her travel cloak. She was grateful they'd rested a few hours before reaching Acrostic Crossing. Two hours into chasing Turpy through the night and they were still going strong. It would have been much worse if they'd been as exhausted as they had been after Mortimer Falls.

It took them an hour at a full gallop to realize that they weren't going to catch up with the camel. Not only was he fast, but he had the stamina to go for what seemed like forever. Galloping, or even cantering, on an unfamiliar road in the dark of the night was extremely perilous, so they slowed to a more sustainable and safer trot.

The easier pace gave Eloise the chance to have a moment with Lorch. "Where do you think he's going?"

"I'm not sure, Princess. I'm not even certain he's 'going' anywhere. Perhaps he was just leaving."

Eloise shook her head. "It's like you said before. He's deliberate. There's method here."

Kiiit spoke up from behind them. "This is the road to the Central ranges. I wonder what he wants there."

"I have no idea," said Eloise. "Lorch? Hector?"

No one had an answer.

"Have you been to the Central Ranges before? Is the nickname the 'Central Carbuncle' deserved?"

"I can't say, Princess," said Lorch. "Our campaigns didn't take us in that direction. Nor have I traveled there on my own. Nameless One?"

The horse shook his head.

"I didn't think so," said the guard.

"Kiiit?" asked Eloise.

"Nope-ity nope nope," she said. "Supposedly, I have an uncle there. Uncle Dougie. When I was a foal, he was my favorite uncle." Kiiit smiled, remembering. "He used to call me 'Kiiitty-cat', and I'd meow at him. He'd call me 'purr-fect,' and I'd pretend to chase balls of string. I now know that's an offensive stereotype, but I didn't know that back then. One day, he was gone. Just not there. Left without saying good-bye. I kept waiting for him to come back, but he never did. My mother —his sister—said that he headed into the tundra. That was years ago, so who knows if he's still there, or if he's even alive. We've not heard from him since."

"No?"

"The closest thing we ever had was a fourth-hand message from a trader who came through years and years ago. The message referred to Uncle Dougie by name, although it didn't quite get his last name right, and said that his family should be told, 'I am fine. I am us.'"

"Did that mean anything to anyone?"

"Maybe. I guess. I mean, the khan's people refer to themselves as 'the Us.' So if he fell in with them, he might say that. It could also be that his message had become garbled by the time it got delivered. My mother said he was a wild one, although I never remember seeing that side of him. She said that the ways of a settled herd were not for him. Everyone seemed to think it completely in character for him to leave and not look back. So I guess that's what he did."

They rode on, allowing a little distance between the horses. Lorch and the Nameless One led, their attention focused on the camel's trail. Hector didn't seem in the mood for conversation, so Eloise listened to the night sounds around her, which were dominated by the rustle of wind through pine needles. The hushed voices of Master Shovelhovel and Seer Bunkerhunker in discussion with Kiïit wafted through the clear night air. Only RoyLee slept, curled up in the pannier, having left what appeared to be six and four-fifths of seven Wombat's Friends splattered on the side of the road not far from Acrostic Crossing. Eloise was having trouble staying awake and was surprised at how alert the wombats were, until she realized that wombats, being nocturnal, would be used to these hours.

A while later, Eloise jerked awake from an uneasy riding doze. She'd been dreaming of talking to the spark of something in the Star of Whatever. It was a long, wordy conversation in which Eloise described the intricacies of Court and Protocol—totally out of character with her waking interactions with it. She'd been struck by its curiosity and command of nuance.

Eloise looked around to orient herself, and found Lorch and the Nameless One next to her, both lost in thought. Lorch's eyebrows were furrowed, and he sighed.

"Lorch?"

He straightened and looked at her. "Apologies, Princess. I didn't realize you were awake."

"Only just now." She suppressed a yawn. "What's the matter?"

"I have concerns, Princess."

"What sort?"

"What I seem to be worrying about a lot since we left Brague —resources."

"Ah."

"We're ill-provisioned for this journey. Winter will be hard upon us soon. I believe the winters in the Central Ranges deserve their reputation for harshness. Sleeping rough will not hold great attraction. In fact, it might actually set us back, if we have to spend a lot of energy trying to stay warm through the night. Yet, I fear inns and supplies will grow scarcer with each strong length we go. It is a sparse realm, a difficult realm of mountains and high ranges. Most of its peoples are nomads, so opportunities for resupply will probably be unreliable. None of us know the realm, and our maps do not provide as much detail as I'd like."

"Are you suggesting we turn back?"

"Of course not, Princess Eloise. We must retrieve Champion Abernatheen de Chipmunk. And I still believe we need to recapture the felon if we can, though he proves wily. I merely wonder if we have options other than blindly trailing along, hoping not to get too far behind. It does not sit well with me. None of this does. We don't hold any advantages, from what I can see."

Hector joined in. "I've been wondering about these matters as well. Plus, we have three more in our party. That adds to our concerns about mobility and food."

"True," said Eloise.

"And there's something else I've been wondering about," said Lorch. "Scope."

"Scope? What do you mean?"

Lorch took a moment to phrase his thoughts. "I guess I'm wondering what combination of factors would cause us to decide it was time to go home. Obviously, getting back the champion and capturing the fugitive would make it clear we could return. But what if either or both of those things doesn't happen? The realms are big. The Central Ranges are big. Trying to find a single person—let alone a person, a hostage, and a longwalking transport camel—could be impossible. Especially if that person does not want to be found."

Hector picked up the line of thought. "In other words, what constitutes an end state that we would find acceptable?"

"Time is a factor in this as well," said Lorch. "You are heir and future ruler. How long do you think we can be away from Brague without it becoming a multi-realm concern? The messages we sent ahead of us from Stained Rock are now hopelessly out of date. How long do we have until we must abandon this endeavor, appeal to the queen for assistance, or take some other approach?"

"I don't know." Eloise shifted uncomfortably on Hector's back. She'd thought a little about these concerns, but so much had happened so quickly that she hadn't given any of it full consideration. "All fair points. And to be honest, I really have no idea how to answer what you've raised. But I do know this. I'm not ready to give up just now. We know Jerome is alive—or he was several hours ago—and not that far out of reach. The time to declare success or failure, or to choose to return with neither of them, is not upon us yet. But I trust we will know what to do when we're faced with it."

"Yes, Princess," said Lorch. "I agree."

"I also agree," said Hector, and the Nameless One nodded.

"Lorch, as for your comment that we hold no advantages, I can't fully concur."

"No?"

"First, we aren't traveling with broken hands or a mangled foot in a cast. That can't make it easy for him, no matter what talents he brings to it. He would have to accommodate whatever pain he is in, and we know it must be substantial. Second, we have Seer Bunkerhunker. We don't yet know the extent of her abilities, how strong or accurate her contact with the Unseen is, but if it's anywhere near as strong as Seer

Maybelle de Chipmunk's, then she'll be able to help guide us and guard our safety."

"True," said Lorch. "Do you think the felon knows she travels with us? Do you thinks he suspects that she'll help us track him?"

"It'd be in character for him to know. He's methodical and thorough," said Eloise. "One wouldn't expect him to enter into an arrangement without knowing what he could about his potential associates."

"If he does know, it it might explain why he rushed off so fast. Maybe he thinks gaining distance outweighs any ability he fears she might have for tracking."

"Perhaps," said Eloise. "As for advantages, the last one we have us. We have more willing, clever minds to apply to whatever is going on than he does. Jerome's not going to make life easy for Turpy. The camel may be an unknown factor, but my first impression was that he was friendly, if not the brightest spark in the cooking fire." She made a gesture that took in their party. "Overall, I'd rather be on our side of the equation than his. And I continue to hope we can resolve this quickly."

"I hope so, Princess Eloise," said Lorch. "I truly hope so."

WELCOME TO THE CENTRAL RANGES

They moved on through the morning, following the distinct tracks left by the camel. The two-toed, hard-nailed, padded hoof prints stuck out like a beacon from the dirt road.

"He shows no signs of slowing down," said Lorch as they stopped mid-morning for a break. "He's barely broken stride since Acrostic Crossing."

"It must be amazing to be able to do that," said Kiïït. "I mean, we horses know something about running far and fast. But that's the grass strudel if anything is the grass strudel."

"I'd guess that camel is covering well over three times the distance we are," said Hector. "Maybe more."

"Which raises its own questions." Eloise took an orange from Lorch and peeled it from pole to pole in a single curl. "Why not take it easier when you know you are safely ahead? Why not try to lose us at one of the streams we crossed? What's the rush, and why no stealth?"

Eloise took out a handkerchief that she'd washed in a creek the previous day and laid the orange sections in a single row. She organized them from left to right in descending order of size and thickness, so she could eat them in ascending order from right to left. An orange at this time of year and in this place was an unexpected treat, brought for her and the others by Lorch from Kääächööö. At home, the ready availability of things like citrus fruit was an assumed presence. As she bit into the first section and tasted the sweet tartness, Eloise vowed she would never again take for granted things as simple as oranges.

They traveled the rest of the day, stopping finally at dusk to make camp. Exhausted, Eloise could barely keep her eyes open while their pinto bean, carrot, and turnip soup cooked.

"Kïïït and Seer Bunkerhunker seem to be becoming fast friends," Eloise said to Lorch as they watched the mare and the old wombat browsing for grass and leaves, and chatting.

"They appear to have similar tastes in food," said Lorch.

"I think it's more than that. I think Seer Bunkerhunker is sharing plant lore."

"Ah."

Seer Bunkerhunker plucked a tuft of grass and offered it to Kïïït, who sniffed it warily, said something, and then, at the wombat's encouragement, took a small nibble. Her eyes went wide and she laughed, which made Seer Bunkerhunker laugh as well.

"Any idea what that was?" asked Eloise.

"Laughing grass?"

Eloise smiled. "Why, Guard Lacksneck. Was that a witticism?"

"Apologies, Princess Eloise. I'll try not to do it again."

"No, no, no. Please witticism away," she chided. "They're pearls to be treasured."

Lorch's cheeks flushed pink. "Yes, Princess."

Later, sated with soup, they all sat near the fire and watched the night settle around them. Eloise found herself nodding off. "I think I need to get a few hours before it's my turn on watch."

"We be taking the watch all night," said Shovelhovel. "Wakefulness be coming easy to us, being nocturnal and all. Plus, we no be expending much energy moving about from place to place, being in the bag."

"That would be wonderful, Master Shovelhovel." Eloise yawned. "I think we all need the rest."

"You will wake me if there is any sign of concern, Master Shovelhovel?" asked Lorch.

Seer Bunkerhunker closed her eyes briefly, then waved a paw. "Rest deeply. I no be sensing any danger for your slumber tonight."

She was right. The night passed uneventfully.

Morning brought a freshness Eloise hadn't felt for days. "Let's get going. I feel today might bring something good our way."

It didn't. But it didn't bring disaster, either. Eloise was fine with a neutral result.

They followed the camel's trail, and found two or three places where Turpy had stopped and rested, and one where they had clearly spent enough time to light a fire.

Their journey took them higher and higher. The air began thinning, and winter snows threatened, but the weather held enough for the trek to be strenuous, but not unpleasant. She seemed to be managing her habits better, and hadn't needed the rosary or counting for a while. It was a relief not to have them gnawing at her quite so much.

As she moved in time with Hector's steady gait, Eloise thought about the box at her hip. Her dream of talking to the spark of something in the Star of Whatever had piqued her curiosity about the magical object. She was still wary of it—she had to be, having witnessed the awesome power it had channeled into the Purple Haze. Eloise was certain it had saved her life at Mortimer Falls. She was also certain that she'd communicated with it several times since first encountering it, in thoughts that expressed themselves in punctuation marks. Not very nuanced.

She felt like she *should* reach out to the thing and somehow get to know it better. But every time she was tempted to open up a conversation, she remembered Melveeta and how the thing had controlled her for more than two centuries.

On the other hand, she had no doubt that this thing tied onto her body was one of the most—perhaps *the* most—powerful objects in all the realms. What was she supposed to do with it? Wander around with it on her hip for the rest of her life, hoping that no one asked her about it? Hoping that what she should do with it would become obvious at some convenient time? She felt vulnerable with it, knowing there was at least one person who both wanted it and knew where it was. Who else might know? Who else might covet it?

She couldn't wait to get home and hand the thing to her mother. Or the Venerable Prelate Herself. Or the head of the Weak Magi Guild. There must be someone who knew about the thing and could see to it that no one ever Purple Hazed the realms again.

Did such a person even exist? She hoped so. Çalaht sitting on a seer-sucker serviette, she truly hoped so.

It probably made sense to establish some sort of rapport with the thing. It seemed wrong, or at least impolite, to only interact with it in times of extreme stress, like when she was plunging through the air. Was it capable of more than simplistic understanding and communication? If she opened herself up to it, would it engulf her? Ignore her? Chat to her, like in her dream? Reveal its secrets? Or would it just fling bits of almost nothing her way?

If she was honest with herself, Eloise felt two diametrically opposite feelings toward the spark in the Star of Whatever. It scared her to her core, and she wanted nothing to do with it. But it also sparked a profound curiosity in her, and she wanted to know everything she possibly could about it.

Eloise had no idea how to reconcile those two positions, so she let them hang in opposition to each other, like buckets on a peasant's shoulder pole.

Hours later at dusk, they repeated the previous night's activities: set a camp, organize food, light a fire and settle by it, leaving the wombats to keep watch. Eloise found herself nodding off again, this time lulled by a slow rhythm that Lorch beat out on his bongo drum. If she hadn't been so exhausted, Eloise would have joined him.

Once again, Seer Bunkerhunker checked in with her unseen forces and pronounced it safe to sleep deeply. For the second straight night, Eloise let herself drop into a profound, dream-filled slumber. And once again, it was full of chatty discussion with the spark of something. This time, Eloise chatted about what she knew of the various Western Lands queens and champions through the ages. Melveeta featured prominently, and the Star seemed to get wistful at the memory of Gwendolyn's champion. Over and over, her dream replayed the moment when she'd ripped the stone away from the old woman's frail hand, then jumped to the fast-paced decay that had turned her to nothing, leaving naught but bones to bury.

Sometime the following day, while Eloise contemplated her options with the Star of Whatever, the party crossed a bridge over a wide, slow river.

"Princess?" said Lorch.

"Yes?"

"That was the River Thurmond. Welcome to the Central Ranges."

Eloise looked around. "Where's the Adequate Wall of the Realms?"

"The River Thurmond is the boundary. The Adequate Wall of the Realms was only built where a boundary is on land."

"Right. Of course."

"So we be in the realm of the mysterious equine khan," said RoyLee. "I wonder if we will be seeing him."

"I'd no be counting on it, RoyLee," said Master Shovelhovel. "You'd be just as likely to run into our beloved Queen Eloise running around our realm. Both places be big."

"From his reputation, I don't know that we'd want to encounter him," said Lorch.

"Be he as fierce as we Pillagiarists—the gang formerly known as the Wombanditos and most definitely not the Womb-banditos, which would have been a stupid thing to name a gang—the fiercest gang with bad eyesight in all the realms?"

"That be what the rumors be saying. More so," said Master Shovelhovel.

"Then I be liking to meet him. Perhaps we can be learning additional fierceness from him. Perhaps he has ways that apply best to those with bad eyesight, like us."

"Perhaps. But we be needing to complete our task at hand more than we be needing to meet the khan. Plus, we be plenty fierce already, bad eyesight or no."

Eloise thought she'd be happy not to meet the khan. The prospect seemed both far-fetched and too much of a distraction. She decided to risk reaching out to the spark in the Star of Whatever. She had to start somewhere. "What do you think?"

But the magical stone was silent.

❧ 28 ❧

THE STEP OF THE STEPPE

Bjóöòrn Tóöòrúüùn didn't often regret taking on clients for transportation jobs. He loved his work, and he was good at it. He got to meet interesting people and see places he'd never otherwise visit. Plus, his speed and his stamina meant he could charge a premium.

As far as Bjóöòrn was concerned, being a longwalking camel transport for hire was an excellent gig.

Usually.

But this guy with the chipmunk in a sack was the worst.

He'd refused to tell Bjóöòrn his name. OK, fair enough. He wasn't the camel's first anonymous customer. But it meant that for days, he'd had to refer to the man as "Good sir," "My dear gentleman," and other vague appellations. "Would the good sir like a break?" "Is my dear gentleman in need of nourishment?" "Could the kind master possibly do something about the person screaming in his bag?"

But no. Good Sir was a surly, curt, monosyllabic so-and-so who had zero interest making amiable conversation. No matter how many times Bjóöòrn tried to lead him toward topics they might discuss, My Dear

Gentleman just told him to "shut up and keep moving"—as if Bjóöòrn wasn't capable of talking and running at the same time. Getting to know people was usually part of the fun. Being told to keep quiet made the trip so much more dreary.

And this trip was the dreariest of the dreary.

Now and then, Good Sir would volunteer a sentence. "Go faster, you indolent." Or "Stop jostling!" Once, Kind Master had offered a full soliloquy: "Watch it! You're making my teeth clack."

Bjóöòrn felt like replying, "Does my dear gentleman want speed or smoothness?" But he didn't. Bjóöòrn prided himself on putting the customer first and being polite, even to those who, like this one, didn't deserve it. His business was mostly word of mouth, so he kept his snappy retorts inside his skull.

Good Sir had zero clues how to ride. Not one. It was like he'd learned to ride from a drunken bucket of overcooked asparagus.

At least there was coin in it. Not huge coin, but commensurate coin. Enough to balm the rudeness and ignore most of the inconvenience. A camel had to make a living somehow, after all. Bjóöòrn took solace in the thought that there would be another job around the corner.

Not that there were a lot of corners here in the middle of nowhere. The grassy plains they'd been crossing for days seemed endless, monochromatic, and bland. Bjóöòrn had no idea how he'd pick up his next job, or how far he'd have to go to find it.

The camel's irritated musing was interrupted by a snarl from atop his back. "The house I'm looking for is in the next village. You'll be stopping there."

Fourteen words. A veritable speech. "Yes, sir," said Bjóöòrn. "It will be my pleasure."

Silence. No "thank you." No "much appreciated." But he'd gotten used to it.

The village—Not Much Point in Bothering—was nothing more than a clutch of tattered houses and an inn called Lowest Expectations that lived up to its name. The man directed Bjóöörn to a dilapidated A-frame cottage that listed precariously to the left and was surrounded by a wild, but cared-for, garden of veggies mixed in with flowers. The color and the variety of the plants surprised Bjóöörn, given the elevation and time of year.

The camel glided to a smooth halt at the front gate, then sat so Kind Gentleman could get off. The man eased his good leg over the saddle horn, faced the camel, and slid down. Half a length from the ground, his bandaged hand lost its grip and he slipped, landing hard on the foot with the cast. His leg buckled and Good Sir slumped to the dirt, decorating the air with a string of blasphemies.

Bjóöörn looked into the distance and pretended not to hear. There wasn't much he could do about it.

The man pulled himself up by hauling on the side of the camel. He tested his weight on his bad foot, winced, and took a tentative step. "Wait here," he snapped and limped toward the gate.

"Yes, sir. As you wish, sir. Does the good sir need me to fetch anything for him? I would be happy to do so."

Kind Gentleman slowly turned around and stared at the camel, saying nothing.

"Right, I'll just wait here. I can enjoy the scenery, and maybe chat with some of the local insects. There'll be grasshoppers in grasslands like this."

The man turned away and Bjóöörn watched him limp the fifteen lengths across the road to the gate, where he stopped and steadied himself. "Hoy hoy!" he called.

No response.

"Hoy hoy!"

Silence.

"Hoy h—"

"I heard you," grumbled a woman, standing up from a patch of celeriac. She held one of the root vegetables in her dirt-caked left hand. With her free hand, she wiped gray, fly-away hair back from her face, then adjusted her faded lavender croftwoman's tunic. The woman blinked focus into her rheumy blue eyes, which were set in a lined face that looked like it had seen a million sunsets.

"G'midday, goodwoman. I seek Dorianna Gangle."

"Do you now." The woman dropped the celeriac into a pail on top of a dozen more. She crossed her arms, looked at the man without moving toward him, and kept her silence.

"Do you perhaps know where I can find her?"

"Mayhap." The old woman bent down and picked a celeriac root from the pail. She wiped it on her apron to get rid of most of the dirt, then bit into it like it was an apple. She chewed and swallowed, her eyes locked on the man. "What makes you think she's anywhere close to these parts?"

"At one point, I had a degree of connection with the court of the Half Kingdom. I had a—let's call it a hobby—of collecting some of the more unusual bits of information I came across, especially if they were not well known—one never knows when something might be of value or provide an advantage. I became aware some time ago that the Step of the Steppe was known to ply her trade in podcasting in the Central Ranges hamlet of Not Much Point in Bothering." He lifted his casted foot. "I have need of her services."

"Do you now." It wasn't a question. She bit into the celeriac again, chewed, swallowed, and picked a stray fiber from between her teeth. "Who are you supposed to be, he who was once connected to the court of the king?"

"My name is Turpentine. As I said, I need the podcaster's help." Turpy paused. "I believe I need *your* help. Please, goodwoman."

Bjóöörn couldn't believe this was the same person who'd grunted, smirked, and commanded his way from the Half Kingdom to here. So he *did* know how to converse and be polite. He even used a name! Wonder of wonders.

The woman took another bite of celeriac. More chewing. "It looks to me like you have no need of me. You've already had a podcast episode."

"He was not the Step of the Steppe." Turpy waved a bandaged hand toward his broken foot. "This is not a fix, nor a healing. This was amateurish good intention wrapped in plaster."

The woman snorted and walked forward. "Who did the podcast? No, let me guess." She reached the gate, leaned across, and stared at the foot. "Lift."

Turpy steadied himself on the wooden fence and held up his foot. The woman slowly bobbed left and right, examining it like it was a basket of dodgy tomatoes that someone was trying to sell her as fresh. "From the color of the plaster, I'd guess Gertrude the Splinter of Hollyhoick. But her wrapping is not this neat. From the thickness and the shaping of it, it could be Bradley the Bandager of Whíïtfóöòrd, but he is too much a blowhard, and at the same time, too timid to take on difficult cases. And you would not be here if this was not a difficult case." She reached across the fence and poked the cast with her index finger, then wiped her thumb across it. She looked at the residue on her thumb, then rubbed it against her middle finger. "Oh for the love of Çalaht's bruised and battered bunions!" She shuddered and wiped the white dust on her garden apron, then spat on her apron and wiped it from there. "Täääradiddle. Nëëëville Täääradiddle of Kääächööö."

"Yes, goodwoman."

"That hack." The woman spat out a celeriac fragment. "Täääradiddle wouldn't know a podcast if it jumped out and yelled in his ear."

"Is that so, goodwoman?"

"I said so, didn't I? You're lucky your foot's still attached. Täääradiddle! Oh, put your foot down."

Turpy lowered his foot but still held onto the fence. "He spoke highly of you."

"It matters not if the sewer speaks well of the river."

"Pardon?"

"Coin? You best have coin, he who had the bad sense to be podcasted by a shonk."

Turpy patted a thin purse at his waist. "Some coin, yes."

"Then we can come to an arrangement, at least as far as your coin will go."

Turpy held up his bandaged hand. "Could you possibly do something about this as well?"

"How bad is it?"

Turpy waggled his broken foot. "At least as good as this."

"I'm a podcaster, not a handmaiden." Dorianna Gangle crooked an index finger into her mouth and dug some stray celeriac fibers from a back molar. "If you've coin enough, I'll do what I can." She turned and walked toward the A-frame house. "Follow," she yelled, without looking back.

To Bjóöòrn's amazement, Turpy smiled, then limped along behind her, the bag with the chipmunk swinging at his side.

29

THE SACK

Jerome did not think of himself as a hater. Sure, there were things he disliked. Jesters, for example, but that was a phobia, so "dislike" was probably the wrong word. Cream of cauliflower soup. Any form of dirge. Getting cockle burrs stuck in his fur. The word "candy." Badly brewed haggleberry tea.

Dislikes, but not hates.

Jerome *hated* the sack.

He despised it with a blazing heat he had never felt for anyone or anything. He loathed its confinement. He abhorred how its four thick canvas layers hid the outside world from him, leaving him completely unprepared for every jostle and thunk (and there were plenty of those). The bag not only hid the light, it also muffled the sounds around him, as well as the sounds he made. Communication was close to impossible —he'd screamed himself hoarse trying. The Çalaht-cursed thing was too hot during the day, too cold at night, too stuffy when closed, too tight all the time, and was an unappealing color.

Worst of all was the stench. The sack smelled like it'd had a previous life being used in the funeral rituals of herring. The reek of death, decay, and the sea were inescapable, and the smell rubbed its way into Jerome's clothes and fur. Twice, his tongue had accidentally made contact with the inside of the bag. The taste of septic wickedness had lingered for hours, and no amount of spitting nor wiping his tongue on his sleeve could dislodge the foul aftertaste.

He had to get out of this thing.

He had to get away from Turpy.

For good.

But how? Even if he could somehow get out of the sack, Turpy would just use his longwalker magic to catch him. And if Turpy found the sack compromised somehow, wouldn't he just get a different, probably worse one, and put Jerome in that?

Jerome couldn't tell how long he'd been in the bag. Some patched bits allowed fragments of light through, but he'd lost count of days. Had it been a week, maybe two, that he'd been away from Eloise and the others? He'd emerged from mind-numbness that first time to find Eloise upside down, running toward him, and then Turpy was airborne and somehow flying across a gorge, Jerome was screaming, and Eloise was falling down into a waterfall. Turpy had landed, and then Jerome was mind-numb again.

When he next regained awareness, he was in the sack.

Turpy let him out of the sack once or twice a day for his private requirements, but looped a crude noose around him so he couldn't escape. Jerome had barely had any food or spent more than three minutes at a time breathing fresh air.

No one Jerome heard through the sack or glimpsed in the rare moments he saw someone seemed to want to help him. Turpy somehow convinced all of them that Jerome's mind was enfeebled, that he suffered a debilitating, clinical-grade *Weltschmerz*, and that the jester kept him in the sack for his own safety. Screaming and pleading, which was all Jerome had available to him, only reinforced that story.

Then there was the boredom, which was excruciating.

It was the boredom that led toward unhelpful thoughts. He replayed those moments at the waterfall over and over, to the point where he was no longer sure if it had actually happened or if it had been some sort of fever dream. He hoped that's what it was—a fever dream, or a sack-induced hallucination, like the time he thought he'd heard Eloise's voice. He thought he'd heard her say "Thank you," and he'd immediately screamed "El! El! Is that you? Help me! For Çalaht's sake, help me!" He could have sworn he heard her say his name in reply. Twice.

But how could that be? Jerome had seen her go over a cliff. Or had he? Either hearing her say his name or her heading toward the bottom of a massive waterfall had been an illusion. The two couldn't both be true.

Yet he could have sworn he'd experienced both.

Jerome opted for the waterfall incident being the hallucination. Otherwise, how could Eloise be anything other than dead? That thought was too dreadful. He'd rather eat the accursed sack than have Eloise be standing with Çalaht.

Jerome gasped.

Eat the sack.

Eat. The. Sack.

Suddenly, Jerome realized exactly what he had to do.

At that moment, Turpy started screaming and spewing profanities. Someone—a woman, from the sound of her—was doing something to the jester that seemed very, very painful. Jerome sighed. This was the second time Turpy had hired someone do something like that to him.

Did Turpy like pain? Some people were like that. Maybe that's why he liked to inflict it on others. Maybe that's why he tortured Jerome by keeping him in the sack.

Crack! Aaahhh!

Çalaht splicing splotchy splines, it sounded like she was breaking his bones. Disgusting.

If this was anything like the last time, Jerome was in for a rather long and unpleasant wait.

Eat. The. Sack.

Jerome swallowed down rising bile, both at the sounds of mangling, yelling, and cursing from outside the sack, and at what he was about to do inside it. He spent a full two minutes psyching himself up, picked a likely spot, then began gnawing at the foul-tasting, hateful material surrounding him.

30

DISTURBANCE

For days, they threaded through mountains and valleys, their path heading inexorably upward. They still followed the camel's tracks, and Eloise could see that he'd slowed to a more sustainable pace—one that would be more comfortable for a damaged rider. The trail sometimes petered out, but they were able to pick it up again without too much trouble. Turpy and the camel, far enough ahead as to be unworried, made no effort to hide anything they did.

As she rode, Eloise decided that her dreams of the Star of Whatever were a nudge. They must be urging her to open up to it. She swallowed and gave it a shot.

It gave her nothing. The spark of something didn't seem interested in her at all. That's if it was even still there. She tried chatting like she did in her dreams, but got no response. She attempted simple phrases to no effect. She varied the topics to look for areas of interest. She sent the simple, single punctuation communication that had been successful in the past. She spoke to it at different times of day, both out loud and silently, using full sentences and fragments, trying every approach she could think of.

Nothing. The spark of something remained aloof and silent. The closest she got was a possible quiet, fleeting "—" from it, an impulse she'd never received before. Eloise figured she'd imagined it, but how could she actually tell?

Eloise knew the problem wasn't the box that contained it. They'd communicated through the box before. Was it a lack of emotion on her part? Absence of duress? Did it detect her wariness? Was it bored? Hiding? Sleeping?

How had Melveeta developed an affinity with the thing? From the way she told the story, it seemed like it just sort of happened. But it wasn't happening for Eloise.

Maybe the spark of something in the Star of Whatever was simply gone, and she may as well have been trying to communicate with a shoe. Possibly. Anything was possible at this point.

By the end of their fourth day in the Central Ranges, Eloise had given up trying to reach the thing. Her failed attempts were boring. Still, the dreams persisted, in which Eloise talked to the spark of something like the two of them were best friends. The topics they covered were not necessarily things of interest to Eloise, nor things she could even actually know, like rainfall statistics for Westie towns, the incidence of indigent mice in devotional houses, modern methods for making impromptu catapults, the relative advantages and disadvantages of bidents vs. tridents, all the known nicknames for Çalaht and Çalahtic oathing, the lineage of Eastern Lands monarchs, and the proper way to greet noble grasses.

Nonsense, in other words.

Toward late afternoon on the fifth day, they lost the camel's trail. The track came up to a wide, cold stream that cut through a bleak, high tundra. Search as they might, they could not find where the camel had come out on the other side, nor where he might have doubled back. They spent two hours with the horses splashing in and out of icy water in fading light, trying to see where they needed to go next, but there were no hints in either direction.

They gathered at the spot where the tracks ended. "I'm sorry, Princess Eloise," said Lorch. "There truly is no sign in either direction."

"Why here? Why now?" asked Eloise. "This looks to be in the middle of nowhere. Why would Turpy try to lose us here?"

"I suggest we prepare camp and reassess in the morning," said Lorch. "I'll prepare a fire so our equine friends can warm up."

After dinner, Seer Bunkerhunker did her usual pre-watch check-in with the unseen. She wrinkled her nose and stayed unfocused for longer than she had the previous nights. When she returned, she said what she'd said before: "Rest deeply. I no be sensing any danger for your slumber tonight."

"Gran?" asked Shovelhovel. "What's wrong?"

"It be the same as the past few nights, except it be a little different. Or maybe, it be different, but mostly the same."

"Ädëlë—I mean, Seer Bunkerhunker," said Kïïït, "do we need to set a different watch?"

"I no be sure. It be like I said, I no be sensing danger to your sleeping."

"I'll sit up with Master Shovelhovel," said RoyLee. "We can be handling any disturbance."

"I said, I no be sensing disturbance during sleep."

And there wasn't.

Not until dawn, when sleep was over.

They awoke to find themselves surrounded by horses in full battle paint. There were easily four score of them arranged in concentric rings around the camp, standing silent, ready for action. There was no hint of their arrival. They were simply there in the predawn stillness.

Instinctively, Eloise and the others jumped up and circled together, facing outward. Any chance to flee was blocked off. Lorch and Master Shovelhovel both reached for their swords, but Eloise held up a hand to stop them. She took a step forward. "G'morning to you all. What can we do for you?"

The horses stood there, silent, waiting.

"My name is Eloise. Who are you?"

"What, like the Westie queen?" The voice came from a stout stallion who stepped forward from the back. The other horses moved aside deferentially. To Eloise's eye, his breeding was so mixed as to be comical. His coat was a rich Palomino gold, but he had a Clydesdale's hoof feathers in white and the rugged build of a stock horse. His mane was long and unkempt, knotted into ropes of red that looked like he'd rolled in ochre. Perhaps he had—there was an ochre splotch in the middle of his forehead where a blaze might be. The horse shook his head at Eloise, disbelieving. "It appears your parents were ignorant, careless with your life, or both. From what I've heard, if the Western Lands queen found you bore her name, she would..." He trailed off, shaking his head. "There is enough unpleasantness in the realms without inviting more through stupidity."

He turned to a mare who was his exact opposite—slender to the point of lanky, with a dark bay coat, mane and tail, and minimal paint. She stood in the nearest circle. "Alana, is this them?"

The mare tilted her head. "Malakai, how many parties with two humans and three of the Not Us do you think we will find wandering across the tundra?"

The stallion bristled. "What of the wombats? Did your intelligence mention them?"

"They were mentioned as a possibility, but not a certainty."

Malakai lifted his head higher. "They don't look like spies to me."

"It is good that the Us have your keen spy detection abilities protecting the herd."

"Do not mock."

"Look, they fit the description of the savages that our intelligence received. It is up to His Alacrity to decide if they are spies or not. Not me, and certainly not you, despite your purity-given weak magic for spy detection."

"What are you talking about? I don't have a weak magic for spy detection."

"Exactly."

Ruffled, but not biting, Malakai turned back to Eloise's group, moving just a bit farther than he needed to so that his backside pointed at Alana. "You are to come with us. You can either do this willingly or unwillingly. I assure you that you would prefer the former, even if I personally might enjoy the latter more."

Eloise had never heard of these people and was not inclined to simply give anyone or anything up. She took another step forward, drew herself up, and put on her most imperious tone, learned from years of watching her mother. "Let's try this again, shall we? Good morning. My name is Eloise. Who are you and what do you want? And what nonsense is this that you think we are spies?"

"Right," said Malakai. "Alana?"

The mare stepped forward and approached Eloise and Lorch. She fixed one eye on the princess and spoke as if she was reading from a scroll. "You are traveling under the name Eloise Gumball, in direct contradiction to the Westie queen's prohibition against common offspring children using her name. Your human companion is allegedly Lorch Lacksneck, pretending to be one of the Queen's Guard, but he is clearly unsuited as such. The three of the Not Us were described, but only one, a Hector..." She tossed her head in Hector's direction. "Presumably that is you. Only that one and the mare, Kit or Kïïit or possibly Kîîit, were named. As I said before, wombats were given as a possibility, but only two were anticipated. Your route of infiltration into His Alacrity's realm was described in detail. We have been tracking you for two days. You have been moving with purpose toward the current camp of His Alacrity. The pieces fit. You are spies. Now, the Us do not have opposable thumbs, which means that things like capture and persuasion tend to jump quickly from words to action. Very blunt action. Malakai here might not be the greenest moss on the tundra, but he's ruthless when he needs to be. I suggest that you take up his offer to come willingly."

Alana backed away from Eloise, which gave her the opportunity to aim her backside at the stallion. "All yours," she said to him.

Eloise looked at her friends, who all nodded. "It would be our pleasure to accompany you to the camp of His Alacrity. Can we pack our things first?"

❧ 31 ❧

TARANTELLA

The hours of waiting while Good Sir was in Dorianna Gangle's A-Frame hovel were both exceptionally boring and disturbing for Bjóöòrn.

Boring, because the insects in the vicinity didn't seem to want to chat, and there were no other people of any species around. He tried his best with the insects, greeting grasshoppers, ants, and even a doodle bug with a friendly, "Hello there! My name is Bjóöòrn. What's yours?" But they all seemed too busy to talk. If they did speak to him, it was just to ask him politely to stand up so they didn't have to go around him.

The camel spent a lot of the time standing up and carefully sitting down again. Not a lot of entertainment in that.

The disturbing part was the screaming coming from the house— blood-chilling screams the A-frame did nothing to muffle. The old woman's home didn't dampen the horrific cracking sounds that preceded the shrieks, either, nor the profanities that followed them.

Crack! Aaahhh! (Profanity involving anatomy.) *Crack! Aaahhh!* (Profanity incorporating blasphemy.) *Crack! Crack! Aaaaaaahhhhhh!* (Multiple, stupendously offensive profanities strung together with anatomical blasphemy.)

"That must be why not many people come around these parts," Bjóöòrn said to a couple of nearby gnats. "Who'd want to be near those sounds for very long?" He was pretty sure they nodded in agreement, but they were gnats, so it was hard to tell.

Eventually, the screaming and profanity stopped, while the cracking continued. Bjóöòrn assumed the man—Turpentine? What kind of name was that?—had fallen mind-numb and was oblivious to whatever mangling was happening to him.

Dusk came, then night. Bjóöòrn nibbled grass, dozed, woke, chewed cud, and chatted to a couple of fireflies who pulsed phosphorescent yes/no answers until they had to move on. Some sort of glowing appeared every now and then that could have been candles or other fireflies, or something else, but Bjóöòrn lost interest in thinking about that.

Day dawned, and there was no sign of Kind Gentleman. The cracking had finished hours after the screaming had stopped, and now the house was silent.

Bjóöòrn allowed himself the luxury of wandering around Not Much Point in Bothering, and checked out Lowest Expectations, which turned out to be a nifty, hidden four-seater inn. "What do you have that a camel might enjoy, my good fellow?" he asked the innkeeper.

"Grass slurry?"

"Sounds superb." Bjóöòrn tried to chat, but the innkeeper ducked into his kitchen and the conversation petered out before it started.

Twenty minutes later, Bjóöòrn was served a dish of green mush that had a pleasant, piquant zing to it. "If I'm still waiting at lunch, I'll see you again, good sir." The camel paid a half coin—quite reasonable for the size of the bowl—and resumed his vigil outside Dorianna Gangle's home.

Late the next morning, Bjóöörn was trying to talk to an earthworm about soil boring techniques when Turpentine emerged from the house, hopping.

Hopping! No, it was a jig. He was jigging. Hopping and jigging and waggling his hands around like a flamenco dancer.

There was a distinct lack of bandages. None at all, from what Bjóöörn could see.

"Pardon me, but I'm going to have to wrap up our conversation," said Bjóöörn to the earthworm. "Good luck with your tunneling."

Kind Gentleman threw his arms wide and turned to the old woman, who'd stopped in the shadow of her doorway. "That was, without a doubt, the worst experience of my life!" He grabbed her by the shoulders and planted a kiss on each cheek. "Horrific! A misery!" He stepped back onto the porch, took her by the hand, and swooped her into a brisk tarantella, which she was completely unsuited to follow and immediately tried to get out of.

"The weak magic euphoria will wear off in half a day to a day," she groused, and pushed him gently away. "Best have this at hand when it does." She gave him a pouch from her apron. "Willow bark. The down from the euphoria comes heavy, and once the aches take hold, they spend a while before they settle out. The willow bark eases that."

Turpy seemed not to hear. "The torturers in the late king's dungeons could take some tips from you. Truly they could. But Goodwoman Gangle, you are a miracle. A Çalaht-kissed miracle!" He put his hand to his mouth and floated it away over and over like he was sending kisses to a stadium full of adoring fans. "Mwah! Mwah! Mwah! Mwah!" Then a last one at the Step of the Steppe. "Mwah!" Turpy untied the coin pouch from his waist. "Take it! Take it all!"

Gangle took the bag and slipped it into her apron. This was not an aspect of the euphoria she was inclined to dodge.

Bjóöòrn, who'd not yet received his coin, saw this and hoped there was another pouch somewhere else. The camel stood, anticipating Kind Gentleman's approach.

"I feel like I could run to the Sclerotic Wold and back! This. Is. Marvelous!"

"Well, don't. I won't have you undoing my podcast with shenanigans."

"Of course, Goodwoman Gangle, of course."

"Find somewhere to lie down for the rest of the day and the night. They'll have a bed at the Lowest Expectations. Use it."

"Of course, again, Goodwoman Gangle, of course."

"Now off you go. I have no more use for you, nor you for me. Shoo!"

Turpy spent a full fifteen seconds producing a bow so ridiculous and gilded with overwrought hand-waving that a Court suck-up would have been embarrassed by it. "Thank you, Goodwoman Gangle. Thank you. Thank you. Thank you. I shall be off to the Lowest Expectations."

"Goodbye then." The old woman closed her front door.

Turpy looked around, confused.

She opened the door, pointed, and said, "That way."

"Right. Right, right, right."

She didn't stick around for the second ornate bow.

Straightening, Turpy pranced off the porch, pirouetted, then tarantellaed over to the camel. "Hello!" He gave Bjóöòrn a bow that was as replete with gestures as the two he'd given Gangle. Then Turpy froze, and said, "Wait! Be right back." The jester danced back to the door and knocked a jaunty pattern of raps.

The door opened and an arm extended the chipmunk sack. Turpy took it, slung it over his shoulder, and made another ludicrous bow to the closed door, his free hand weaving through the air like a demented, bowing orchestra conductor. Then he minuetted back to Bjóöòrn. "Hello!" he exclaimed again.

"G'midday to you, good sir," said the camel.

"'Good sir,' you said? Did I not properly introduce myself? I am Turpentine Snotearrow McCcoonnch, late of the late King Doncaster's late court at Stained Rock and lately of nowhere in particular. Apologies for the belated introduction. You, master camel—sorry, missed your name—did a masterful job conveying me here with speed and grace and mastery. For that, I am grateful." Turpy followed this with a bow that included a spin, a click of the heels, and hand movements reminiscent of ocean waves. "You, good sir camel, have another task ahead of you."

"I do?"

"You do."

"Is there coin in it?"

"Of course!" Turpy patted his waist where his coin purse once was. He glanced down, confused, and looked around to see if he'd dropped it. He stared at the A-frame house, dramatically bumped his palm against his forehead, then turned back to Bjóöòrn and mugged a shrug worthy of rural amateur theater. "Of course there's coin in it, good sir. I, Turpentine Snotearrow McCcoonnch, late of the late King Doncaster's late court at Stained Rock and lately of nowhere in particular, would never ask you to undertake additional toil without suitable contribution. Never! Never, never, never! That would be un... Un... Unconscionable!" He looked up and down the dirt path that made up the main road of Not Much Point in Bothering like he was considering possibilities, or maybe formulating a plot. More to himself than the camel, he said, "You shall have your coin, both for your most excellent transport here, as well as for your next task."

Bjóöòrn reached his neck down so his face was level with Turpy's and tried to catch the jester's gaze. "Master Snotearrow McCcoonnch, I—"

Turpy looked at him. "Sorry, what was your name again?"

"Bjóöòrn. Bjóöòrn Tóöòrúüùn. I—"

"Pleased to meet you, Master Tóöòrúüùn." He swooped another rococo bow. "I am Turpentine Snotearrow McCcoonnch, late of the late—"

"No, no. No need. I got that bit. What is it that you want me to do?"

Turpy did a few jig steps and wagged his unbandaged hand, especially the thumb. "I no longer have need of your aid with transport."

"No?"

"No. As you can see, I am..." Turpy wiggled both hands and a foot toward the camel. "I am fixed. Good sir camel, I can convey myself henceforth. However, I need you to do something else. At the end of it, coin shall await you."

"OK." Bjóöòrn idly scratched his right front hoof on his left leg, wondering where this was headed.

Turpy swung out his arm, froze into a staged pose, and pointed down the dirt road. "I need you to head in that direction."

"Yes?"

"There is a plan, and I need you to convey some information."

❧ 32 ❧

NOSE SNORTING

It took two full days to reach the khan's camp. Eloise and the others rode in silence surrounded by the other horses. They crossed all manner of terrain, from conifer forests to tundra above the tree line, from high grassy plateaus to craggy mountainsides where steam rose out of cracks in the walls and ground—a reminder that volcanic activity was a constant threat. The khan's herd ran hard in disciplined formation. Even if Eloise had wanted to run for it, an opening never appeared.

Hector and the Nameless One were fit from being in the Royal Horse Guard and the Royal Guard Horses respectively, and Kïïït was used to hard work as a scullery mare. But the khan's horses had a ruggedness and impressive stamina that came from a life spent constantly on the move, and a practiced ease crossing the varying terrain. They spared little time for breaks, and rarely dropped below the speed of a canter, even when a narrow mountain pass forced them to travel single file.

By late afternoon, they made it to a rise that revealed the khan's camp below. A handful of sentry horses stood there, having watched their approach from several strong lengths away. Eloise saw a messenger colt shoot away toward the camp while the others blocked the path and waited for Malakai's group. He motioned for his herd to stop 100 lengths away, and trotted up to the guards. He approached the closest one, extended his neck forward, touched her nose, and blew a puff of air into the sentry's right nostril, while she did the same to him. They switched sides, touched noses again, and puffed into each other's left nostrils.

This struck Eloise as a surprisingly intimate ritual for warriors.

"It is good to see you, my brother," said the sentry.

"It is good to see you, my sister," Malakai replied.

"It is good you have returned to the Us," she replied.

"As we have taken the Us with us while we were gone, so it is good to be back with the Us."

One by one, Malakai exchanged this same nose puff and greeting with each sentry. The words were rote, but the feeling sincere.

Then Malakai went back to Alana, who stepped out through the horses surrounding Eloise's group. The stallion remained a formal distance away. "I give you my charge freely, Alana, daughter of Ganbaat and Altan."

"I take your charge freely, Malakai, son of Khulan and Gerel, and I will hold it sacred." They, too, approached each other, did the nostril puff, and then Alana moved to the sentries and greeted them with the same ritual.

Eloise was fascinated. If they had to go through this much rigamarole every time any of them met, how could they ever get anything done? Perhaps their lives were measured less by doing and more by being, or by some quality of these interactions, which is why they got so much focus. Who knew? One thing that Eloise did know was that her habits would not take kindly to having to blow up other people's noses all the time, or having them snorting up hers. She'd rather live in a hole.

Alana took Malakai's place at the head of the arriving party, and Malakai turned to Eloise and Lorch. "You will remain here," said

Malakai. "I will report news to His Alacrity. He will render a decision, or not, as he sees fit."

Eloise didn't like the sound of that, but stayed quiet. What "intelligence" could possibly have both described them and implicated them as spies? There was one likely answer: Turpy. This poisoning of the well was a very Turpy kind of move. She would not put it past him to be at the khan's camp, foot bandaged, whispering intrigues into His Alacrity's ear. Eloise realized she faced the same problem she met in The South. How could she prove who she was without anything that vaguely resembled proper paperwork and no diplomatic envoys paving the way? This trip to the Central Ranges wasn't even supposed to have happened.

Mess. Eloise didn't like mess.

As the other horses shored up the already impenetrable circles around them, Malakai galloped off to the camp below. At its edge, welcoming horses swarmed and jostled, bumped and reared, neighed and pawed the air. His distinctive gold coat remained visible for a few moments, and then he was lost in a boisterous mass that moved toward the center of the camp and out of sight, where presumably His Alacrity, Khan Nergüi Unbenannt Nimetuseta, conducted the nomadic equine equivalent of holding court.

Eloise and the others waited and watched.

She wouldn't call what the khan's people had a "camp." That wasn't the right word, even if it was the one they used themselves. Was it a camp if there were no tents, temporary shelters, fires, or other signs of encampment? She didn't think so.

What they had was a society. A sense of organization and order was everywhere, even with what must have been a thousand equines. Horses stood guard at strategic points around the area. Some were clearly practicing precision running like their captors had shown, others taught foals. A surprisingly large cluster all faced a single horse who led them in a series of extremely slow movements that had a dancelike quality. This was obviously similar to the warrior moves that

Lorch sometimes practiced, but with kicks, steps, pig-rooting (a term offensive to pigs), and rearing that were suited to their equine bodies.

But what stood out more than anything else was the overwhelming horse-ness of it all. Eloise was used to towns and villages with a mix of species. Here, at first glance, were horses and no one else, a huge society entirely of horse-kind. Eloise, used to a normal diversity, found the exclusivity of it shocking.

This, then, was the "Us" of the khan.

Eloise noticed that her captors were unnaturally quiet, barely shifting as the first hour of waiting dragged into a second. They were not rigid, but showed a disciplined stillness and alertness. Only their manes and tails blew when a gust of wind caught them.

Eloise and Lorch had slid off Hector and the Nameless One so they would not burden the horses while they waited. The two horses stood, each with a back leg cocked, resting, almost as still as the khan's horses.

Kïïït, however, could not stop fidgeting. Something bothered her. Kïïït barely kept still long enough for Eloise to help the three wombats out of their pannier. The mare stretched her neck, trying to see something, but there was nothing obvious to look at. She pushed to the front of the space that the khan's horses had left them and turned her head left, then right, peering toward the place where Alana waited with the sentries. Not satisfied, Kïïït tried to get past the inner circle of horses around them. "Excuse me," she said. "Sorry, but can I just slip through for a minute?"

"No," said a bay stallion.

"I'm not going anywhere. I just need to check something."

"No," he repeated. End of discussion.

"Kïïït, what is it?" asked Eloise.

"Nothing, Princess. I'm sure it's nothing." Kïïït walked to the other side of their space and resumed doing whatever she was doing. She'd look, mutter something to herself, then look again. Eloise wondered if she was deliberately trying to make a spectacle of herself, or if this was some sort of subterfuge. But the mare hadn't struck her as one prone to deception.

This restlessness went on for another quarter hour, then Kĩĩĩt went back to the bay. "Listen, sweetie, I just need to go forward a bit so I can see something. I won't try to run off. I won't try to get through all of you. I just need to move a bit closer to check something."

"No."

"You ain't fit for a turf war," she muttered, stepping backwards, careful not to tread on the wombats down below.

The bay chose to ignore her.

Kĩĩĩt was still, waiting patiently like the others.

For three minutes.

Then she was back to bobbing, weaving, and looking. The contrast to the stillness of those around her was sharp. Eloise wanted to teach her to knit or something, just so she had something else to do.

Finally, something bubbled over in the mare, and she reared up like she was trying to make herself seen. The circle of the khan's horses tensed, ready to respond. "Uncle Dougie!" Kĩĩĩt yelled. "Uncle Dougie, is that you?"

One of the sentries turned, looked at her, and trotted forward. A similar coppery sheen to his mane and coat betrayed a strong family line. There was no question, even to the most casual of lookers, that there was strong blood between them.

"Kĩĩĩtty-cat?" said the horse, a catch in his voice. "Kĩĩĩtty-cat?"

"Uncle Dougie!" squealed Kĩĩĩt. She burst through the horses around them, forcing her way to the sentry. They met halfway, and the mare flung herself at him with the unbounded enthusiasm of a foal. She slammed him with a "Whee!"

The horse took the playful body blow, circled his back legs twice, and then wrapped his neck over hers. Protective, comforting, welcoming. "Oh, my little Kiïïtty-cat," he cooed as she settled, leaning into him. "It's lovely to see you again."

"Uncle Dougie, I missed you. I missed you so much," she whimpered, snorting back tears. "Why did you leave me?"

"I didn't mean to leave you, little Kiïïtty-cat. But there's a story there. I look forward to telling it to you."

"If the reunion cuddles are done, word is coming," said Alana, motioning her head toward a messenger colt galloping up from camp. "Prepare to move on."

✵ 33 ✵

WELCOMING COMMITTEE

Alana led her party of horses past the watch point and down a trail toward the khan's camp. Kïïit's uncle had stayed behind, continuing his sentry duties, but he had given Kïïit one last nuzzle and said, "I'll find you down there. I want to hear everything, Kïïitty-cat. Everything."

"I'd like that. See you soon."

The walk down to the encampment was controlled and deliberate. It was as if the horses were making sure their approach was obvious, and no one in the main camp got spooked.

When they were 50 lengths away, the circle of horses closest to Eloise and the others slowed and stopped, blocking them from going any closer. Alana wheeled around to them. "You will stay here for now." It was a command, but also a request for cooperation.

"Yes," said Eloise. "We will."

"Good. Not many of the Not Us nor the savages get to see what you're about to witness. Consider it an unexpected—and unearned—privilege." Then she turned and walked toward the camp. The rest of the traveling herd went with her, save ten who remained to surround Eloise and her group.

Horses streamed toward each other from two directions. Alana's party of several dozen got as close as 20 lengths, then stopped and lined up. From the camp, hundreds of horses came forward, lining up opposite them in rows. The two sides assembled uneven teams, as if preparing for a game.

Or battle.

For three full minutes no one moved or spoke. Then a white horse with black spots—a Pinzgauer patterned like a Dalmatian—stepped forward so he was two body lengths ahead of the front line on the camp side. Again, he stood motionless, silent.

Without warning he reared up, and the entire line of the camp reared with him. They screamed blood-chilling neighs, flailing their forelegs like they would dash those across from them to death, then came down onto four feet and bared their teeth, hissing. The Pinzgauer shouted something in a language Eloise had never heard before, something deep, equine, and ancient. As one, the hundreds of camp horses slammed a right, front hoof into the ground. The Pinzgauer yelled something else, and the horses behind him answered with a left-right *stamp-stamp*.

The black and white stallion began a call-and-response chant in the unfamiliar language. The call sounded to Eloise like he exhorted those behind him to battle, and their response sounded like they all thought that was a great idea.

As one, they added a stylized stomping, kicking, head-weaving posture dance. It looked artificial, frightening, and lethal. Between the fierce chant and the dance's choreographed violence, it looked like they wanted to tear out the hearts of their foes with their teeth. Back and forth the chant went, from the call of the solo Pinzgauer to the response of the group behind him. The herd moved slowly forward in unison with stomped hooves, kicked legs, strained necks, bulging eyes, and protruding tongues.

It looked like the horse equivalent of declaring war.

Alana's line carefully drifted backward as the camp side inched forward, keeping the distance between them exactly the same. The Pinzgauer and his crowd threw themselves into chanting with an intensity that made the hairs on Eloise's neck stand up. With a final *stomp-stomp-stomp-stomp*, they froze, teeth bared, eyes wild.

Then they relaxed and silently moved back to where they'd started.

Eloise realized it was a welcome. Like the nose snorting, it was a ritual. The crazed-looking expressions and the vicious fighting motions were the camp's way of saying, "Howdy. Good to see you again."

Suddenly, Alana screamed like she'd been stabbed. All of her side joined in, neighing screeches ripping the air, then stopping with a single stamped hoof on the ground. She called out something in the same ancient equine tongue, but less menacing. Her soldiers repeated whatever she'd yelled.

Alana let the cry of words hang.

And then she began to sing.

Alana's voice filled the air, lilting and pure but strong and full of longing. The rest of her horses joined in, fearsome warriors blending into harmonies in a way that only a lifetime of singing together could produce. The words of the song were in the same ancient tongue, but this time, it was sweet and inviting. Even though Eloise could not understand what they were saying, she found her eyes welling up. The melody poured out yearning and love, the strangeness of lands visited and the comfort of hearths returned to, the sadness of those lost and the joy of bonds tied and hearts sated.

It was one of the most moving things Eloise had ever heard, made more so by the fact that she would never have expected to hear anything like it in the open fields of a grassy steppe, nor from some of the hardest, most disciplined people she'd ever come across. Eloise wiped away tears with the heel of her hand. She glanced at Lorch and saw he was doing the same. Kiïit and Seer Bunkerhunker openly wept, while Hector and the Nameless One stood at attention, blinking hard, and Master Shovelhovel and RoyLee sniffled.

With a long, final, soloed note that she held pure and sure, Alana finished the song.

There was silence on both sides.

Then the camp horses cheered and stamped, and the two sides rushed toward each other and began the ritual nose snorting. In the chaos of horse bodies, it looked like each was trying to greet all the others, although actually doing so would take forever. After a full quarter hour of this, horses began drifting off in pairs and clusters, friends reunited.

Alana rode back to where Eloise and the others waited.

"That was incredible," said Eloise. "Thank you for allowing us to see it."

"It is the way of the Us, nothing more and nothing less." She looked at the forward-most of the horses guarding them. "Anything?"

"Nothing."

"Good. Please follow me. I will take you to where you will stay until His Alacrity makes his decision."

Alana led them forward. They skirted the camp and rode toward a natural stone wall that was away from the main activity. As they drew closer, Eloise saw that the wall had a narrow opening in it, just wide enough that a horse might squeeze through. In front of the opening were six guards, four facing toward the gap, and two facing away. They straightened at Alana's approach. "Alana, daughter of Ganbaat and Altan," said the smallest of them.

No nose snort greetings this time. No returning of the formal form of address. Just a nod from the mare, acknowledging them. "Eight for you. Three of the Not Us. Five of the savages. You will keep them in?"

"Of course, Mistress Alana."

She turned to Eloise's group, standing in front of the cleft. "You should find it adequate. You may use your own possessions for comfort and whatever else you need. You might be tempted to attempt escape, but I suggest you don't. His Alacrity would not look on that with favor, and Malakai needs little excuse to ply his forms of dissuasion."

"How long will we be here?" asked Eloise. "How long until we can meet the khan?"

"To the former, I don't know. To the latter, I suggest the question is based on a flawed assumption."

"How do we communicate with you if we need something?"

"You don't."

"Right." Eloise looked at Lorch, Hector, and the Nameless One. "Anything else?"

They shook their heads.

"Then let's go."

"We will go first, if that's OK with you, Princess," said Lorch.

Eloise noted that he deliberately used her title. In other times, he'd been coy about that, but here, he was trying to assert her position.

At Eloise's gesture, he and the Nameless One moved into the break in the stone wall. Hector followed. As Eloise walked past Alana, the mare leaned forward to whisper something to her. "If you are not spies, it will be OK. If you are, it won't be. It is that simple with the Us."

"Then we should be OK," Eloise replied, face neutral. "Come, Kïïït. It has been a long few days."

Eloise went through the gap in the wall, and Kïïït followed with the wombats.

The narrow opening lasted no more than ten lengths before spilling them out into a field. It was beautiful—a surprisingly large circle of grassland 50 lengths across, with a copse of poplars and aspens. There was another plant dotted around, which Eloise had never seen. It grew ten lengths tall and looked like a huge, narrow pineapple poking out of the top of a yucca.

Eloise's gaze moved from the plants to the walls surrounding the field. Sheer cliffs 100 lengths high jutted up around it. The stark, uninviting walls hemmed in the area, making it clear that anyone inside wasn't going anywhere. It might not keep in birds, geckos, ants, or squirrels, but humans would be hard pressed to get away, and horses, who the open-air confinement was clearly meant for, would be stuck forever if they couldn't go back through the entrance. For certain species (elephants, giraffes, antelope, and yaks all sprang to mind), it was the perfect jail.

At least it wasn't a dungeon. Eloise could live with that.

❧ 34 ❧

THERE IS NO PLAN

Eloise and Lorch unloaded Hector, the Nameless One, and Kiïit, and helped the wombats out of the panniers.

"We might go graze for a while," said Hector. "The pickings have been thin."

"Good idea," said Eloise. "We'll get some food going as well."

"I be starving!" said RoyLee, and he shuffled off to a tussock and started nibbling.

"We might join RoyLee," said Master Shovelhovel, stretching his legs. "Gran?"

"I be coming," said Seer Bunkerhunker. "I think I see some cottongrass I'd like to try. I haven't had that in years."

As the horses and wombats wandered off, Eloise said to Lorch, "I'll gather sticks if there are any. We'll be wanting a fire."

"Yes, Princess," said Lorch. "I'll set up camp."

Eloise poked around their enclosure looking for things that might burn. Her mind kept returning to the equine ceremony she'd just seen, playing it back in her mind and feeling glad that Court welcomings were more civilized and involved less shouting, stomping, and facial contortions. Then again, they did sometimes involve the ear-bleeding sounds of the bombard, so maybe they weren't much better.

"Why, hello there! Nice to see you again!"

Eloise looked in the direction of the voice, vaguely recognizing it.

It took her a moment to locate him. He sat under a poplar chewing his cud.

It was a camel.

Turpy's camel.

"Hello," Eloise said to the camel. "I think we met very briefly, but not yet formally."

The camel heaved himself up onto four legs and pranced forward like he was the chairman of the open-air jail welcoming committee. "Good! You remember! Yes, it was brief. About a week ago. In Acrostic Crossing. My client was rather in a hurry. Hello, again. Again."

"So it appeared." Eloise approached the stranger.

"My name is Bjóöörn. Bjóöörn Tóöòrúüùn."

"I'm Eloise."

"Of course." The camel gave an overdramatic wink and a stage nod. "'Eloise.'"

Eloise didn't know what to make of that. "No, really. It is."

"Got it." Huge wink. Knowing nod.

"I beg your pardon, Master Tóöòrúüùn? Is something wrong?"

"No, no. Of course not." The camel looked left and right, like he was checking they weren't being overheard. "You're 'Eloise.' The bloke over there is 'Lorch,' The black-coated horse is 'Hector.' The mare is 'Kit' or 'Kïïit' or possibly 'Kîîit.' I don't have a *nom de guerre* for the other horse." He gave her another massive wink and leaned his head forward conspiratorially. "You're the s-p-i-e-s. Nice to finally meet you. I've been expecting you."

"We're not spies," said Eloise. This was getting annoying.

"I know, I know. He said you'd say that." Wink. Nod. Then the camel pursed his lips and said, "Your secret is safe with me."

"Were you the one who told the khan's people we were spies?"

"Yes." The camel leaned in closer, and whispered, "All is going to plan."

"What 'plan' are you talking about? There is no plan."

"He said you'd say that, too. Got it. No worries. There is no plan." Then he leaned in and whispered, "But all is going to plan." *Wink. Nod.*

"What are you talking about?"

The camel stood straight again and spoke too loudly, as if for someone else's benefit. "Nope. No plan. You're right. Well, best let you get settled in. Let you get 'set up,' as it were. Night will be upon us before we know it. Nothing to see here."

"No, nothing to see here at all," echoed Eloise, puzzled.

Lorch came over from their campsite. "Is everything OK, Princess?"

"Ah, 'Princess,'" said the camel. "Very good, Master 'Lorch.'" He emphasized the "ch" like it was a second syllable.

"This is Master Bjóöòrn Tóöòrúüùn," said Eloise. "He's the one who informed the khan and his people that we were spies. Apparently, all is going to plan."

"What plan?" asked Lorch.

"That remains a mystery."

The camel whispered again. "Nice to meet you, Master 'Lorch.' The plan is, indeed, in play and on track."

"Really, good sir," said Lorch. "What plan?"

The camel straightened again and used his loud someone's-probably-listening voice. "No plan. No plan at all."

Bjóöòrn Tóöòrúüùn struck Eloise as both daft and dangerous. Not a good combination. She tried a different tack. "We were about to have tea. Would you care to join us? We can talk about this plan of yours."

"Oooh, tea with the spies. How exciting!" cooed the camel. Then he realized his mistake. "Sorry, not spies. Not spies. But tea with the spies would be lovely. Thank you." Wink. Nod. "Also, the plan, that doesn't exist, is yours, not mine. A devious, clever not-plan it is."

"If you'll join us in a few minutes," said Eloise.

"Of course, of course."

"See you in a quarter hour or so?" she said. Eloise handed her meager collection of twigs and other burnables to Lorch. "I'll get a bit more. Perhaps you can light the fire?"

"Yes, Princess."

"Yes, 'Princess,'" repeated the camel. "Very good. Very good."

Half an hour later, Eloise, Lorch, and Bjóöòrn sat next to Lorch's small fire, a pot of haggleberry tea coming to a boil.

"Master Tóöòrúüùn," said Eloise. "Can you please do me the kindness of starting at the beginning?"

"The beginning? Sure." The camel cleared his throat. "I was born in The South near a small village called Pumpernickel Plains. My mother was a closet arranger by trade. My father was the son of a devotional house minder, and a stricter son-of-a..."

Eloise held up a hand. "Perhaps you needn't go quite so far back."

The camel tilted his head and nodded. "Start with my kindergarten schooling?"

"A bit more forward, still."

"Early, awkward attempts at dating? That one embarrassing encounter with a brachiopod who I accidentally referred to as a bivalve mollusk?"

"Ugh. I've done that. And they're so sensitive about it," said Eloise. "But maybe start when you met your client."

"That far forward?" He frowned, disappointed. "Are you sure? There's some interesting bits in there."

"If there's time, maybe we can circle back," said Eloise. "For now, let's start with that meeting."

"Right. Right, right," said the camel.

Eloise poured out the tea—a mug each for her and Lorch, and a small bucket for the camel, which he'd provided.

"I had dropped off my previous clients—two dozen rainbow toads who were attending a seance at a secret, undisclosed location exactly two strong lengths north-by-northwest of Acrostic Crossing. They hadn't booked me for a return journey, so I wandered back to Acrostic Crossing to grab a bite and a beverage. I often pick up work in the inns, so I make a point of stopping in. I call those 'inncounters.' Get it? 'Inncounters!' Bwahahahahaha!"

Eloise sipped her tea and waited for the camel to finish guffawing. She didn't feel obligated to acknowledge the lame joke. Bjóöörn was laughing enough for all of them. This was clearly a person who didn't mind the sound of his own voice.

"So, anyway, I was in the Management Eschews Expectations Tasteful Helpings Evince Realistic Expectations enjoying a trough of spruce beer and a plate of gingernut dessert gnocchi. I'd already been to the Cooking Lacks Enthusiasm Accommodation Narrow If Satisfactorily Hygienic—I can't remember if I mentioned that they do an excellent goldbeet and leek pie, although that evening I'd had their savory white bean tart, which was excellent, especially as they served it chilled with a mushroom tapenade. I'd also had tea at the Because Every Sleep Tantalizes With Premium Luxury and Audaciously Classy Elegance, which is about all I can afford there. That was after a jam scone at the

Sobriety Not Our Concern Keep Enjoying and Relishing Every Drink. I try to make it to all the inns, because you never know who will be where, and people need to know you're in town and available."

Eloise gritted her teeth, but kept up a smile. This was going to take forever.

"So you met your client?" prompted Lorch.

"That's right. Ïïïväään, the not-very-nice innkeeper, came over to me and said there was someone who wanted to see me in a side room—a possible client." The camel sipped from his bucket. "That is a very nice cuppa. Anyway, it was the client. Bandaged foot and hands. Not very friendly manner. Said he was in a real hurry and would pay in coin, but wouldn't disclose the destination or preferred route until we were underway. He also didn't mention the chipmunk in his bag when we made our agreement, which wasn't fair, because I charge by the person, even if it is on a sliding scale based on size and weight. But still, he should have known better. He grilled me at length about speed—how long it might take to get, say, from Stained Rock to Brague. And he very specifically asked if I was a longwalker, which struck me as rude, as one doesn't talk of these things in public, as I'm sure you know."

"At the risk of being rude as well, may I ask if you are?" asked Lorch. "I've never known a camel to have longwalker weak magic. It might affect..." Lorch looked around conspiratorially, then said, "the Plan."

"There is no plan!" said Eloise, exasperated.

Lorch gave her a knowing wink, then gave one to the camel as well. Eloise wondered if he was trying to win the camel's confidence or trick him somehow.

"Well, since you put it that way," said the camel. "Yes, I am a longwalker. Have been all my life, of course."

"Interesting. Very interesting," said Lorch. "So, the client hired you?"

"That he did. Ïïïväään, the not-very-nice innkeeper, popped in and said something about a wombat and Wombat's Friends. My client stood immediately, and we were out of the Management Eschews Expectations Tasteful Helpings Evince Realistic Expectations and on our way within minutes."

Eloise listened as Bjóöörn recounted in excruciating detail the journey from Acrostic Crossing to the village of Not Much Point in Bothering. When he got to the part with Turpy talking to the old woman, she remembered the name Dorianna Gangle from Nëëëville Täääradiddle at Kääächööö. He'd called her a "true foot hero" or something like that. But what had struck Eloise was the way he had said Gangle had a weak magic for podcasting. She'd never heard of that type of weak magic before, so it had stuck with her. Eloise was fascinated by the camel's description of the screaming that came from the house, and how Turpy had emerged dancing and free of bandages on both hands and feet. Could a podcaster heal hands? Apparently this one could.

Eloise shuddered. A fully restored Turpy in a dancing good mood struck her as a dangerous thing.

The horses and wombats wandered over and joined them, listening to the camel's tale.

"So then he shared the plan that you had put in place with his help," said Bjóöörn. "And may I say, it is a lovely, twisted, clever plan, and it's my honor to be part of it."

"Could you share your understanding of your role in our plan?" asked Lorch. He didn't bother with the wink this time.

"Of course. Master Turpentine told me I should head down a particular road, and turn left at Alba Querkey. If I followed that trail, I'd eventually find the camp of the Khan Nergüi, although how he knew where nomadic people might be at any time was a mystery to me. But he was right, and here I am. My client gave me explicit instructions—had me repeat them to make sure I got the wording right—about how to describe you, and how to make it known you were spies, whether I spoke to the khan directly or not. I haven't met him. Have you?"

"No," said Eloise. "Not yet."

"They tell me he's quite busy. Anyway. He said the khan would send a group of his people to find you, capture you, and bring you back to his camp. You would deny being spies, but then that's what spies do. But them bringing you here would serve your purpose, as you'll have successfully infiltrated the khan's encampment, and could proceed to spy to your heart's content. Like I said, very clever."

"That's daft," said Hector. "Absolutely bonkers."

"There be a logic to it," said Master Shovelhovel.

"So, anyway," said the camel. "One hundred forty-two, if you don't mind."

Eloise furrowed her brow. "I beg your pardon?"

"That's the number—142."

She shook her head. "Is that supposed to be a cipher of some sort?

"Coins, my new friends," said Bjóöòrn, smiling. "My fee."

"Your fee?" said Lorch.

"My fee. Very reasonable, given everything." The camel took a final slurp of his tea. "That was part of the plan. My client said the fee would be covered in full at this end of the endeavor by his co-conspirators, the spies."

"Right," said. Eloise. "And if I may ask, you found that a plausible scenario?"

The camel stopped talking, puzzled. His silence stretched while the wheels of his cogitation churned. It was the longest he'd been quiet since his first "hello." Finally, a look of incredulity marched across his face. "Çalaht conveying camelid cosmetics! I've been hornswoggled. I've been hoodwinked. I've been duped, bamboozled, and fleeced. I. Have. Been. Deceived!"

The camel stood up and said, "Excuse me." He walked 30 lengths away from the others, then he screamed. "Why does this keep happening to me? Why do I always let myself get fooled like that? I am such a dunce! I'm a Çalaht-certified, mind-numb..." On and on he went, berating himself as if he had no audience. Eloise felt embarrassed for him.

When he finished, he walked back to the group and sat back down. "Could I possibly have a bit more tea, please?"

"Certainly," said Lorch.

The camel sat with a blank expression while Lorch poured his tea. Bjóöòrn blew across it and took a careful sip. "So, there was no plan."

"No. No plan at all," said Eloise.

"And just to be clear, I'm pretty unlikely to receive any coin from you, right?"

"Sorry."

"It would've been a good plan, as far as plans go." The camel sipped tea from his bucket again. "A fine plan, indeed."

They all sat, hot mugs in hand, contemplating their situation and the jester's duplicity. Seer Bunkerhunker finally voiced the question they were all mulling. "Why be this Turpentine fellow wanting you a captive of the equine khan?"

"To cause us inconvenience and difficulty? To slow us down?" suggested Hector.

"Let's consider the simplest possible reason," said Eloise. "I think he just wanted to know where we would be so he could find us."

"Why?" asked RoyLee.

"The same reason he still has Jerome," said Eloise. "He wants something."

❧ 35 ❧

OBSERVATION

Turpy lay on his stomach looking through a spyglass. Below him was the largest horse society he'd ever seen. Doncaster had little to do with the Central Ranges or the equine khan, and interactions with that realm had been through a handful of emissaries who were not very informative or effective. Turpy didn't blame the late king. The other realms had so much more to offer the Half Kingdom than land that was either volcanic or meager and people led by someone who, from what Turpy had gathered, looked down on you if you only had two legs. Fanatics, the lot of them. No, that was the wrong word. Southies were fanatics. The khan's people were insular and snotty. All that guff about the "Us" and the "Not Us." Turpy had agreed with Doncaster's inclination not to engage.

He still didn't want to, but it was looking like he might have to.

From Turpy's vantage point, it had been easy to spot the humans in their enclosed area. Among so many horses, they stood out like bipedal lumps of awkwardness. They had that stupid transport camel with them. The quarter-wit had been fast, and gotten him where he'd needed to go, but five minutes into the journey Turpy had wanted to tie his yap shut. Thank goodness, the trip had constantly jarred his hands and bad foot. The pain was at least a distraction from the camel's verbal effluvium.

Turpy had expected that Eloise and the others might end up confined, but he had thought it would be in something more like a jail. That they were out in the open was a stroke of unexpected luck—something that had been in short supply since the Westie queen's evil spawn had shattered his thumb and failed to die in the Purple Haze, along with that shrew of her sister. And then his own brother—who barely knew how to tie a shoe, much less choose a side in a political struggle—had awoken at just the wrong moment and chosen the shrew over his flesh and blood. Gouache's betrayal stung more than Turpy cared to admit. After all he'd done for Gouache—bringing him to the castle, getting him a role with Doncaster, making sure he was cared for, fed, and housed—his brother's behavior was unforgivable.

"I've been a fool," Turpy muttered to no one. "An imbecile. What a waste of time." All those years maneuvering himself into Doncaster's orbit, then slowly, inexorably exerting more and more control. A whisper in the ear here. A hookah of prattleweed there. Nudge after nudge after nudge. Finally, Turpy had been poised to sit on the throne that he deserved as much as any person in the realms. More, if he was honest, since most of them had the mental prowess of banana slugs. To have it yanked away from him was intolerable. He'd never get another chance like that. If he'd been phrasing it for one of his jester routines, he might have said, "I have held the goblet full of life's wine, only to have it smashed from my hand."

That had a ring to it.

He'd liked sitting on the throne. He'd liked having access to the spoils of position. He'd even had the Thing in his grasp. He'd had such a short sip from the goblet full of life's wine. Now he was sucking a pebble plucked out of life's shoe, hoping to stave off thirst.

Less of a ring to it.

Turpy observed the walls of the enclosure that held the humans. One heavily guarded entrance. Steep walls. Half a dozen sentries ringing the top edge, posted out of view of those down below. Open area inside. Not many places to hide.

Turpy didn't have a plan yet, but it was percolating and would show itself soon enough. Originally, he'd thought he might be able to use the rat in the bag somehow. Get the Thing (he thought of it with a capital "T") as a ransom payment, maybe.

Percolate, percolate, percolate. It would come to him.

One thing was clear. The twins really should have killed him when they had the chance. It was stupid and weak of them not to.

Well, that was their problem, not his.

Turpy sat up, set down the spyglass, and dug out the pouch of willow bark Dorianna Gangle had given him. He pinched a generous wad and shoved it in his cheek. The residual ache in his foot and hands throbbed, and the willow bark eased it somewhat.

Even thinking about what she'd done to him still made him shudder. He'd known her healing involved weak magic, so he'd expected it to be gentle. Maybe a little uncomfortable.

Nope.

Her weak magic was one of the most complicated he'd ever come across. It had four distinct, related aspects: knowing where to break a bone, being able to break a bone precisely, knowing where and how to shove the broken pieces together, and then—somehow—encouraging them to reknit.

What she lacked was a weak magic for lessening pain.

If the process hadn't been so brutal, and if Gangle hadn't been so callous and methodical, it would have been fascinating. Instead, it hurt like Çalaht's elongated thumbs being yanked off, and he was grateful to have been mind-numb for as much of it as he had been.

Turpy closed his eyes and tried to recapture the marvelous feeling he'd had when he'd first come back to awareness. Drunk on the afterglow of the weak magic, Turpy had felt a lightness to his being that had been missing since their mother died years and years and years before. The euphoria had filled him and stayed with him for about a day, then dissipated.

He remembered clearly how, when he'd woken from mind-numbness, Gangle had sat on the other side of the room smoking a prattleweed pipe. The plant didn't seem to affect her the way it had the king. No synonyms. No babbling. No yearning for conversation. Turpy speculated that she was a highly tolerant, high-functioning, long-time addict. It made him wonder if Doncaster might have reached such tolerance over time.

He'd never know.

"Stand up," she'd said through a cough of smoke.

Turpy stood, expecting shooting pains in his foot. There were none.

Gangle left her pipe dangling in her mouth, held out her hands, then flexed them and rotated her wrists. She bit the pipe stem to hold it still as she spoke. "Do this."

Turpy had moved his hands slowly and carefully. First the fingers that had not been damaged, and then his thumb and wrist. They moved like they had when he was a teenager. "Amazing. Simply amazing," he said. He did the same with his foot. "Truly astounding." He walked around the narrow space, waggling his hands and testing his foot.

"If you ever need to escape a manacle like that again, I suggest you try a different approach," said Gangle. "I won't be doing another podcast like that for you. Ever. Understood?"

He hadn't told her how he'd acquired the injury. "Yes, Mistress Gangle. I understand."

"'Mistress Gangle,' is it now?" She snorted smoke through her nose. "Right. Off you go. I can't have you cluttering up my house forever." She'd scooched him out the door.

Now he relied on the willow bark to dull the residual ache. He wondered if he'd always have that, or if it would pass. If it was going to stick around, he'd need to find more of the bark. Maybe he'd need to go back to Kääächööö.

At least he could move freely again. He was going to need that mobility if he wanted to get the Thing back. Without it, he was just an out-of-work jester with no prospects. With it, he might sit on a throne again.

He picked up the spyglass, lay back down on his stomach, ignored the screaming coming from the bag (it was better than when the rat sang, which he'd started doing a few days before), and resumed his observation. At some point, he'd have to let the rat out again. Not now.

Percolate, percolate, percolate.

❧ 36 ❧

PANIC PLUS SOMETHING

It had taken Jerome longer than he'd expected to chew his way through the first, second, and third layers of the canvas sack. He was now working on the fourth and last. Jerome knew he had to be particularly careful now. It wouldn't be good to make a hole big enough to be discovered from the outside, but still too small to crawl out of.

If it had been a clean sack, or maybe made of a more palatable material, he'd have gotten through it in half the time. But battling the foul taste took more grit and determination than Jerome had brought to any task in years.

Fiber by fiber, he gnawed and spat, gnawed and spat, breaching the sack's integrity from within.

There was some risk that Turpy would discover what he was doing, so Jerome kept up a pretense of screaming. He hoped his deliberate screaming would sound similar enough to his previous genuine screaming that Turpy would leave him alone. The more he had screamed, the less inclined Turpy was to give him out-of-the-sack time. Jerome tried to use that to his advantage now, but screaming and gnawing were mutually exclusive tasks, the former slowing down the latter.

Gnaw. Spit. Scream. Psych himself up to continue. Repeat.

Every now and then, Jerome took a sparing bite of the withered apple that was his only companion in the sack. He thought about giving it a name—maybe Wiiilsööön—but he didn't like the idea of eating something with a name, so he left it at "apple."

Sometimes Jerome let himself sing badly instead of screaming, hoping that the sound would annoy Turpy. He'd been through the entire repertoire of Lyndia Thrind, circled back, and done it again and again, as badly as he could. He really gave it his all when he did "Send in the Jesters" and "Tears of a Jester," hoping it might needle Turpy. He liked to think it did, but had no evidence one way or the other.

Jerome tried to work out what was going on outside the sack. There'd been all the cracking and Turpy's screaming. What seemed like hours later, he heard Turpy have a conversation with the woman. Then smooth jostling, almost like dancing, which was strange, then a conversation with the camel (he'd seen it was a camel on one of his out-of-the-sack spells). Then a long period of movement, like they were traveling again. Most recently, the sack had been left in one place, and when he wasn't gnawing, screaming, or singing, he thought he might have heard Turpy talking quietly.

The sack had been still for what seemed like a long time. The spot Jerome was gnawing on was down against the ground, which was fortunate. That meant he could work on it without worrying that Turpy might see the movement and get suspicious. Also, Jerome had learned it was easier to chew downwards than upwards. Less tiring.

Then it happened. Jerome tugged particularly hard and, with a quiet ripping, the sack had a hole in it. He could see ground. Dirt and grass! By Çalaht's blessed bifurcated bronchus, he'd done it!

He worked faster now. This layer tasted different, and not quite as bad as the inside layers. Or maybe it was just different, being exposed to the outside world.

Turpy's muttering was clearer now. Jerome heard something about a "goblet full of wife wine." That didn't make any sense.

Jerome gnawed and gnawed, now getting specks of dirt in his mouth along with canvas fibers. Worried that spitting might make too much noise, he wiped his tongue on his tunic sleeve instead.

Within an hour, he'd made a hole large enough to get through.

He'd need to be careful. He'd have to ease himself out and stealthily observe the out-of-the-sack world, then make a calculated decision about his options, weighing them thoughtfully before making a careful choice...

Stuff careful.

Jerome squeezed out the hole and crawled on his stomach under the canvas to where he could see past the edge of the sack.

It was dusk. Turpy lay on the ground squinting through a spyglass. Below them was the largest herd of horses Jerome had ever seen. Stupidly large. Hundreds and hundreds.

Where was he? And why would there be so many horses in one place? Was it a convention or conclave of some sort? A festival? He didn't know of any local festivals that catered to equines, but that didn't mean there wasn't such a thing.

Think options, thought Jerome. *1) Stay here and deal with Turpy. 2) Stay here and try to hide. 3) Run toward the horses. 4) Run away from the horses. 5) Panic. 6) Combine option (5) with one of the other options (a very likely outcome).*

He chose option (6), combining (5) with (3). Jerome sprinted toward the horses. Anything had to be better than being in the sack or dealing with Turpy. He ran like his life depended on it.

Which, he was sure, it did.

As dusk claimed the day, Turpy peered through the spyglass at the land and the people below. The equines were doing horse things, both in the enclosed area and in the larger camp beyond. The few humans were doing human things, the camel appeared to be talking (of course), and the wombats were hidden in the grass; Turpy could just see them waddling about.

Behind him, the rat had stopped screaming, and the bag had been still a while. Thank Çalaht for small mercies. That probably meant he was asleep. It was something the rat had complained about; he'd gone on and on about the disruption to his sleep cycles. Then again, the rat complained about everything—the bag was too small, the apple was too old, he had requirements that were not being met, he needed to bathe. It had become background noise, and the torrent of complaints was one of the reasons Turpy couldn't be bothered letting him out very often.

Maybe the rat would still prove useful. If not, he could always toss the bag in a river and let the rat fend for himself. There were plenty of rivers in the realms. It would give the rat something to do besides complain, or emit that caterwauling he assumed the rat considered singing.

Turpy panned the spyglass across the scene below once more, trying to formulate the right plan to get the Thing back. Percolate, percolate, percolate. Negotiation was a possibility, but a thin one. Appealing to the equine khan to help him get his stolen property back was another (although it had only been in his possession a short while, so calling it stolen might be a bit rich).

As he swept the glass, something caught his eye. It was a movement of some sort, visible only for a split second as the spyglass moved past. It was blurry, which meant it was closer than the things he'd been looking at.

Strange.

Turpy moved the instrument back and forth until he located the blur again, then twisted the eye section to focus it.

Someone small was moving through the grass.

"No," said Turpy. "It can't be."

He pulled back from the spyglass to look at the spot where the motion was on the landscape. Then he glanced around. The sack was still there. That looked normal enough.

He looked back through the spyglass to see if the movement was still there. Perhaps he'd mistaken the tickle of wind on grass.

No. There was definitely someone running. Maybe "scampering" was a better word for it, but definitely moving at speed.

Toward the encampment.

"Not. Possible," snapped Turpy. The jester jumped up (He could jump! What a miracle!) and ran over to pick up the bag.

It was lighter than it had been. Turpy held it up and saw the hole. "Son of a Çalaht-cursed, suppurating sore," he snarled.

So much for percolating and careful planning.

Turpy took off.

Maybe he could catch the rat before he ruined everything.

❧ 37 ❧

SMASH AND GRAB

In the dim late-evening light, Eloise tried to light a fire against the coming night's cold. Normally, she let Lorch do this, but he was 20 lengths away discussing something with Hector and the Nameless One. Somewhere across the field, Kiïit, Bjóöörn, and the wombats nibbled grass, and the sounds of their laughter floated toward her. Eloise had decided it might be a good idea to get better at lighting a fire. You never knew when it might be handy. She'd watched Lorch do it often enough since they'd left Brague, and had tried it once or twice. She wasn't very good at it, and there was always so much to do to ready a camp for the night that it seemed inefficient for her to try when Lorch did it so quickly.

Not tonight. Tonight, the fire-starting would be on her.

Eloise took the flint and steel Lorch carried from one of the panniers, and gathered a small pile of things that she thought would easily catch alight—dead grass, fungus bits, plus a few dried seed heads from one of the pineapple-looking plants. She found a number of larger flattish stones—ancient things worn smooth by wind and years—and silently asked their permission. This was a bit like connecting with the spark of something in the Star of Whatever, but quieter. It was more like when she'd gotten the feeling that the traveler stones in Melveeta's stomach hadn't wanted to be left behind. Eloise stilled herself and focused on each stone separately. When she got the feeling that each was OK, she formed them into a protective fire circle.

Eloise placed her pile of kindling in the middle and struck the steel against the flint. The tiny spark flew wide. A second one bounced off the small pile rather than nestling into it. She struck again. Same thing. She tried holding the flint closer, so the spark had less discretion. Two dozen sparks later, one of them did the right thing, and the small, dry, fluffy pile released a tendril of smoke. "There we go," she said. She blew on it, gently encouraging. Several delicate puffs later, the moss and grass caught into a real flame. "Good," she said. She smiled at the small accomplishment, which she'd achieved just as night claimed the sky, and looked forward to settling by the dancing light and warming her hands.

A small, distant sound tickled the back of Eloise's attention as she lay the first twigs on the flame. The noise was high-pitched and seemed somehow familiar. Where had she heard that before? It wasn't mechanical, like the complaint of a carriage wheel in need of oil. It was more organic. More like a squeal than a squeak.

Eloise laughed quietly. The last time she'd heard a sound like that was at her champion's Naming Ceremony. Stoofy the jester had gotten too close to Jerome, and he'd gone into a full, blind panic. He'd hooned around the dais making a similar noise, and ended up under the queen's throne. It was a sound the likes of which had likely never been heard before in the Throne Hall, and probably never would again.

She couldn't believe it had only been a matter of weeks since then. It seemed like a lifetime ago.

Eloise looked up. Hector and the Nameless One stood with their heads high, fully alert, and ears twitching independently forward and back as they tried to locate the sound. Lorch, too, was trying to figure out what he heard in the dark.

Eloise stood, leaving the fire to catch fully on its own. "Jerome? Is that Jerome?" Hope fluttered wildly in her heart. It had to be him. Had to be. Who else would make that sound?

"I can't tell, Princess," Lorch called back. He narrowed his eyes and focused on listening.

The sound seemed to crest the edge of the surrounding cliffs, because it suddenly grew louder. It echoed around the enclosure's high walls.

"Jerome!" Eloise yelled. "Jerome?" She looked left and right, trying to pick out the source of the sound in the darkness. She stepped away from the fire so she could see better in the night.

A moment later, her eyes caught a hint of motion. Across the field, a small figure bounded down the face of the canyon wall, screaming like he was trying to outrun Çalaht's own judgment. It was him! He was alive!

"Jerome! Over here!" she yelled. "Toward the fire!" She wasn't sure Jerome could hear her over his screaming, so she moved to run toward him.

"Princess, wait!" called Lorch. "Look!" He pointed at the cliff.

It was another figure. It ran—there was no other word for it—down the cliff wall, a dark shape in the dark night. Its movements—*their* movements, for it was almost certainly a person—were impossible. Jerome had claws and the body of one ordained by nature to scale and descend trees. This person's motions made no sense. They did not face the wall like someone climbing down. They were side-on, moving like they were hopping from step to step down a tricky staircase, using little jumps that would make an ibex goat jealous.

Eloise stared at it, puzzled. The movement defied all logic.

No. Not all logic. It would not defy the logic of a longwalker's weak magic.

"Turpy!" yelled Eloise. "It's got to be Turpy!"

Lorch's instincts kicked in. He rushed to their gear, grabbed his sword, and hurried over to Eloise. The guard turned toward the noise, protective of her. At the same time, Hector and Nameless One rushed off the other way, toward Jerome's screaming.

"Over here!" yelled Eloise again. "Jerome, toward the fire!"

From what little she could see, Jerome was 30 lengths below Turpy on the cliff wall, and the jester was closing the gap as they descended. Jerome reached the bottom first, jumped across the top of five large stones, then zigzagged forward, screaming at the top of his lungs.

Seconds later, Turpy leapt down the final 20 lengths to the ground, landing in a crouch. Astounding. Bjóöòrn had described the change to Turpy's physicality, but it was another thing to actually see it. He was bouncing around like an acrobat. Even in the low light, he looked nothing like the near cripple who'd jumped across Mortimer Falls.

Turpy took a moment to look around and get his bearings, then he ran after Jerome. Where the chipmunk moved in an evasive pattern, Turpy shot ahead in direct pursuit.

"Stop him! Everyone, stop Turpy!" shouted Eloise.

Lorch ignored her command, running to stand in front of her, sword poised. Across the field, Kïïït yelled, "Got it!" She joined Hector and the Nameless One in a race to intercept the jester.

Master Shovelhovel's battle cry of "Heeyahhhh" rang out, and he was joined by RoyLee exclaiming, "We be the Pillagiarists—the gang formerly—

"Not now, RoyLee," yelled Shovelhovel. "Just run! Heeyahhhh!"

"Heeyahhhh!" cried RoyLee as they pelted across the field.

Moonlight poured over the cliff walls above, bathing the area in a sudden light. Eloise could now see Jerome shooting across the field, aiming more or less directly for her. She could also see that the horses would be able to cut off Turpy's pursuit.

Good.

Hooves clopped behind her as horses rushed through the prison's entryway. Eloise spun around and saw their equine guards rushing in to investigate. She whirled back to focus on her best friend.

Hector, the Nameless One, and Kiiit met and blocked Turpy's path. They jigged right and left, adjusting themselves, ready to take him on.

Turpy put on a burst of speed, feigned left, feigned right, and then dove through Kiiit's legs. He ducked, rolled, and came up on the other side of the three horses running just as fast as before. There were 20 lengths at most between the chipmunk and the jester, and Turpy was gaining fast. Hector, the Nameless One, and Kiiit turned and gave chase.

As Jerome approached, his screaming changed from an indistinct scream to "Elllllllllllll!"

Eloise moved to rush forward, but Lorch stopped her. "No! Just protect your champion. I'll stop the felon."

"Right." She crouched down, extended her right arm and patted her shoulder with her left hand. "Up here! Quick!"

The chipmunk raced toward her and when he was close enough, launched into a flying leap. He landed on her tunic sleeve, dug in his claws to gain purchase, and just like he had a thousand times when they were younger, clambered up to sit on her shoulder. He stopped, breath rasping, his tail fluffed rigid with fear.

There was no time to console or reassure, because Turpy was still running right at them. Behind the jester charged the Nameless One, Kiiit, RoyLee, and Master Shovelhovel.

Lorch crouched, sword ready, standing steadfast between his princess and Turpy. Eloise straightened and readied herself—although she had no idea what for. To negotiate, perhaps? Fight? Evade? Run?

A detached part of Eloise's mind realized this was a lot like what she experienced on the hockey sacking field. People running. Others trying to catch them. The threat of someone clunking into you. She played changer, so it was not uncommon for someone to barrel in her direction with the intent of ramming her. Except here, she was not holding a hockey sack, so there was nothing for Turpy to try to get away from her. No reason for him to run into her.

Unless he was going for Jerome.

Which he almost certainly was.

In a fraction of a second, the analogy pieced itself together as she braced herself to make a move. Was she playing changer? She had Jerome, so she assumed that was the case. What position did that make Turpy? Left flutter, an offensive position? Maybe he was more a right flutter—half offense and half defense. Maybe defensive girder. They tended to be the most aggressive.

Turpy ran at Lorch without slowing. When he came within three lengths, he flung his hand toward the guard's face. Sand pelted Lorch's eyes, nose, and cheeks. Turpy must have grabbed a handful when he slid past Hector, the Nameless One and Kiïit. Lorch, caught completely unprepared, flinched defensively. That was all Turpy needed. The jester jumped and landed squarely on Lorch's knee. There was the pop of tearing ligaments, a cry of pain, and Lorch crumpled to the ground.

Definitely defensive girder. And a nasty defensive girder at that.

Turpy ran squarely at Eloise and Jerome.

It was just the three of them. Eloise readied herself. It didn't look like there was going to be any negotiation. That left evasion and fleeing.

From nowhere, Seer Bunkerhunker hurtled forward and threw herself at Turpy's legs, entangling herself in them. Eloise recognized the move. The wombats had used it to capture her two years before, outside Mooondale after she and Jerome had visited Waft! An Autumnal Festival. The wombat's tripping was carefully calculated. Seer Bunkerhunker must have done it ten thousand times. She'd know exactly what to expect, and how her victim would land. If it was anything like what Eloise had experienced, Turpy would faceplant.

Except, he didn't. It must have been the first time Seer Bunkerhunker had tackled a longwalker. The effect was spectacular. Turpy hit her at full force, knocking her so hard she went rolling like an empty keg at the end of a long night of liquid consolation.

Instead of faceplanting, he became airborne.

The jester hadn't been expecting it either. He flew at Eloise with a surprised expression that matched her own. Then she saw his expression grow hard. He curled his body, tucked his head so it was out of the way, and led with a forward shoulder. Eloise barely had time to register what he meant to do, let alone react.

Turpy's shoulder and full body weight jammed into her solar plexus. Eloise's breath whooshed from her body, and she went hurtling backward. Jerome soared off her shoulder, his arms and legs flailing.

Eloise landed on the fireplace, her back directly on the spluttering flames. The circle of stones broke her fall, knocking whatever breath might have been left in her lungs. They bruised her ribs, shoulder blades, and neck, and it was sheer luck that none of them cracked.

Eloise gasped for air, and she could feel the heat of the fire as it tried to burn through her travel cloak and tunic. Before she could move, a dark mass shoved a knee into her guts, pressing her to the hot coals.

It was Turpy. With his left hand, he clutched Eloise's throat and pushed down with a straight arm, pinning her in place. He raised his right hand high.

In the thin moonlight, Eloise saw the glint of bare steel and the subtle curve of a knife.

38

GRAB AND SMASH

Eloise struggled for air, but none came. Turpy's grip on her neck was too tight. Blackness threatened to claim her as she tried to buck him off. She threw her arms up to protect herself, fully expecting her blood to come shooting out at any moment. Would he go for her face? Her heart? This was so brutal, so unexpected.

So typically Turpy.

Eloise expected the pierce or slash of his knife, but it seemed to be taking an awfully long time to arrive—certainly long enough for the fire to burn through her cloak and tunic and begin cooking the skin on her back.

Turpy twisted, digging his knee in further and exposing her side. His arm arced downward, and Eloise felt the blade's tug as it sliced into some cloth at her hip. Her cloak? Her breeks? This made no sense. Was he trying to... No, surely not.

Her clothes resisted the knife, then gave way. Turpy shifted the blade from his right hand to his left, grabbed at something, then was off her and running.

Eloise flung herself from the fire pit and rolled to make sure she was not consumed by flames. It hurt like Çalaht's own hair shirt biting into her flesh.

Two rolls in, she understood what Turpy had done. He hadn't been trying to cut her clothing or assault her. He'd cut through the hip sash and shoulder strap that held the Star of Whatever to her. He'd snatched the Star and was hurrying away with it through the chaos of horses and wombats chasing him, and horses from the khan's guard pouring through the narrow gap.

Eloise still hadn't caught her breath. "Stop him!" she coughed. "Stop Turpy!"

Jerome had been thrown several lengths away, and Turpy ran for him. Eloise thought he meant to grab Jerome again, but the jester didn't seem to see him. Jerome let loose another high-pitched squeal, but this one was different from the one just moments before. This time, it wasn't fear.

It was anger.

As Turpy ran past, the chipmunk leapt at him. Jerome caught Turpy's right tunic sleeve and held on as the jester tried to waggle him off. Instead of crawling up to his shoulder like he had with Eloise, Jerome went the other way—toward the cuff. He sank his teeth into the back of Turpy's hand.

Turpy grunted, moved the box with the Star of Whatever under his left arm, and whipped his right arm around, trying to dislodge the furious chipmunk. Jerome clamped down as hard as he could, biting through skin and muscle and making it down to bone. Blood seeped from his mouth.

Trying to get Jerome off slowed the longwalker down. If Turpy had been standing still, he might have tried to cut or stab Jerome. But he was still running, the Star of Whatever clamped to his side with his left arm, so there wasn't much he could do that didn't risk cutting off his own hand. Turpy windmilled his arm, then jerked it back and forth, trying to get Jerome loose. But Eloise's champion wouldn't budge.

Suddenly, there was a yell from another direction, this time to Turpy's left. "Where's my coin, you freeloader?" It was Bjóöòrn Tóöòrúüùn charging toward the jester. "Where's my payment?!"

The angry camel moved incredibly fast. It was camel longwalker speed against human longwalker speed, but the human was impeded, holding a box and with a raging chipmunk damaging his hand. Turpy tried to evade, but the camel intercepted him, ramming the jester as hard as he could. It was a perfect defensive girder move, and Eloise wondered briefly if camels played hockey sacking. The camel's tackle was accented by rage and multiplied by the force of his longwalker weak magic.

The impact knocked Turpy a dozen lengths through the air. The jester crashed hard to the ground, bouncing once, then twice. The camel's hit was hard enough to dislodge Jerome, sending him flying off the jester with a large chunk of Turpy's hand still in his mouth. The box with the Star of Whatever sailed off into the darkness. A moment later, it smashed into a rock, and Eloise heard the wood crack.

She dragged in a lungful of air, rolled to her knees, jumped up, and ran toward the fracas. The skin on her back stung as she pumped her arms. It would be a mess, she knew, but she'd have to deal with that later.

To one side, she heard Jerome spitting, clearing his mouth of jester flesh and blood. The thought made Eloise gag.

She saw Bjóöòrn run to where Turpy lay on his back, slightly dazed and panting. The camel pinned him to the ground with a hoof. "Give me my coin!" he bellowed. "Give me the coin you owe me! There was no plan. There were only lies. Lies! I trusted you. I helped you. I put up with your moods and your snarling and the way you maltreated the chipmunk because the customer is always right! Well, stupid me."

While Bjóöòrn harangued Turpy, the others caught up. Eloise joined the horses, and the wombats surrounded them.

"I... I..." wheezed Turpy. He slowly waved his bleeding hand in a "give me a second" motion, and then gestured at the camel's hoof, indicating that it was making it hard for him to breathe or speak.

Bjóöòrn shifted his foot off the jester and leaned down so his face was just a few weak lengths from Turpy's. "Where's my coin?!" Camel spittle flecked the jester's face.

Turpy shot the heel of his hand into the camel's snout. Bjóöòrn reeled back and the jester jumped up. Everyone moved to tighten the circle around him. The crowded space limited his options, but also limited what the others could do.

Turpy spun around once and spotted the weakest point—the wombats. He charged RoyLee and Master Shovelhovel, jumping one and side-stepping the other. With four long strides, he was clear again, and racing away, drawing on every bit of his weak magic.

Hector and the Nameless One led the pursuit, and the khan's guards charged after them. Eloise saw Bjóöòrn shake his head to clear the pain in his snout. The camel's anger had gotten the better of him; he'd let the jester get away, and he knew it. Now even more furious, he used his longwalker weak magic to pass the horses and run after Turpy. Eloise sprinted after them, and with a last spit, Jerome did the same.

Turpy's first instinct was to run for the entryway gap, but there were too many horses there. Instead, he rushed toward the nearest cliff wall, just a dozen lengths ahead of the raging camel, two dozen lengths ahead of 20 horses and, much further behind, a pair of very annoyed wombats.

"Scoundrel!" shouted RoyLee as he ran. "You be an unwashed, burrow-fouling menace!"

"Dastard!" added Master Shovelhovel. "Ne'er-do-well blackguard!"

"Lowlife wretch!"

"Caitiff!"

"Good-for-nothing miscreant!"

"Incorrigible creep!"

"Boys!" snapped Seer Bunkerhunker from somewhere behind. "Need I be washing your mouths out with soap?"

"Sorry, Gran," Master Shovelhovel called back.

"Sorry, Seer Bunkerhunker," said RoyLee.

The wombats kept running, but Eloise slowed and stopped. She'd never catch up and didn't want to further damage her burned skin. This one would have to be up to someone else.

Turpy was 50, then 30 lengths from the sheer wall of rock. But Bjóöòrn was fast, too, and looked like he'd be able to run the jester down. When he got close enough, he tried to bite Turpy, but his teeth clacked the air. Turpy ran even faster, but the camel matched him with his strange loping gallop. Bjóöòrn reached out with his head and managed to shove Turpy in the back. The jester stumbled for two or three steps, but recovered his stride and kept going, adding some evading zigzags, like Jerome had done just a minute or two earlier.

Eloise watched the camel crane his neck to the left then swing his head right, trying to hit Turpy with it. It grazed Turpy but didn't slow him. Bjóöòrn let the momentum of the near miss turn his neck to the right. "Where's my coin!" he screamed, slashing his head to the left like a mace.

It should have landed. It should have knocked the jester into the next realm.

But the camel's head swooshed past, finding nothing to hit. The unexpected lack of impact caught Bjóöòrn unaware, and the camel tripped and fell, sliding into the base of the cliff.

Turpy had done what he'd done at Mortimer Falls—jumped high and long. The leap took him out of Bjóöòrn's reach and toward the sheer wall of rock. Eloise watched Turpy fly upward in the moonlight and thought that surely he would bounce off and crash.

Turpy hit the cliff, and his "oof" was loud enough to echo. But he didn't bounce off. He slid down its face one length, and then another. He found something to grip with his bloody hand, but slipped again.

Then the jester stopped falling. His feet and hands dug in, and he clung to the vertical rock like a gecko 20 lengths from the ground. He was out of reach of all pursuers. Turpy held still, muscles strained, panting.

Eloise looked around for a stone to throw at him. She snatched a rock the size of an orange, took aim at his back, and flung it. The pain of her burn dragged slightly on her motion, and the throw went just wide, clacking into the cliff face four weak lengths to the left of the jester.

"You. Will. Not. Escape!" It was Jerome. The chipmunk latched onto the cliff wall and began climbing as fast as he could, claws digging. Eloise wasn't sure what her champion planned to do if he caught the jester, but she hesitated to throw more rocks in case she hit Jerome.

Turpy glanced down at the chipmunk, and then to the crowd below him. "Çalaht curse you all," he snarled. Then, as if he was jogging up a gentle incline on a lovely moonlit run, he scaled the cliff and hauled himself over the edge, leaving Jerome dozens of lengths below, scampering uselessly. Eloise watched as two of the sentries posted around the top rushed toward the escapee.

The jester stood, glanced at the approaching horses, and faced the crowd below. He bowed an ironic, ornate bow, like he might at the end of a performance. He lifted a single bloody finger in a final salute, then disappeared from view.

The sentries pursued, but Eloise knew they'd never catch him. Turpy was gone.

Gone, gone, gone. She wasn't sure if she was relieved, or more worried than ever.

❀ *39* ❀

HIS ALACRITY

Eloise hurried back to where she'd left Lorch. She found him trying to stand, but unable to put any weight on his right leg.

"Sit," said Eloise. "He's gone."

Lorch grimaced as he eased back to a more comfortable sitting position. "I think I hate the felon. There aren't many people I hate in the realms, but I'm making an exception for him."

"How bad is your leg?"

Lorch lifted his shoulders. "Bad enough."

"How bad is 'bad enough?'"

"I wouldn't want to ride. I wouldn't want to walk. I wouldn't want to stand."

"That's definitely bad enough. We're going to need to take care of that."

"Yes, Princess."

Eloise turned and showed him her back. "How bad does it look?" She heard the rustle of Lorch's clothing as he shifted forward for a closer look. He drew a sudden breath through clenched teeth. Eloise wasn't sure if it was from the pain in his leg or from what he saw. "Well?"

"Bad enough, Princess."

"How bad is 'bad enough?'"

"Your cloak and your tunic have burned through. There's redness over an area roughly the size of a dessert plate, as well as significant blistering. There's no charring or exposed muscle that I can see in this light."

"That's definitely bad enough."

"As you said for me, Princess, we're going to need to take care of that."

"It hurts like Çalaht's own fire poker," said Eloise.

"I suspect we'll need more than what we have in our provisions. Perhaps the khan's herd will have more extensive healing tools. Perhaps they even have a healer. They must, if there are so many of them."

Eloise nodded. "I'll ask when I can." She looked around. "I'll be back in a few minutes. Will you be OK?"

"Yes, Princess."

Eloise walked carefully to avoid disturbing her back. She wanted nothing more than to lie down somewhere and turn herself over to the ministrations of healing hands. It would be a while, though, before that could happen. She found the spot where Bjóöòrn had first run into Turpy. She closed her eyes and ran through what had happened in her mind—the camel's approach, his running into the jester, Turpy and Jerome flying. Eloise opened her eyes and walked in the direction they'd flown. She scanned the ground left and right, looking. It shouldn't be hard to find, assuming it was still there.

She sent a silent "?".

A pulse of green light came from 20 lengths away at the base of a winter-bare poplar. It shone through a crack in the box. Eloise hurried to where the Star of Whatever lay and carefully picked it up. The box had a crack a weak length wide in the wood along the top. She could see the Star through the crack, nestled in its padded cradle. She gently shook the box. It seemed secure. She tried opening it, but it was as reluctant as ever. The sash for her hip and the strap that went over her shoulder would both need sewing. She would get to that as soon as she could, although Lorch was better at sewing than she was. So was Jerome, for that matter. And most of Court. And probably most of the realm, whether they had opposable digits or claws or pods or cilia.

There was a rustle to her left, a pattern of movement she'd recognize anywhere. "Jerome? Jerome is that you?"

The chipmunk stepped forward, still panting from his run and climb. "El, I..."

He was interrupted by a racket coming from behind them. Malakai charged through the entryway, nostrils flaring. Alana was close behind, her sharp eyes darting left and right, taking in everything she could see. She stopped and called out, "Report!"

One of the guards trotted over and stood at attention. She rattled off what she and the other guards had seen. Malakai and Alana listened carefully, asking a few questions.

"I'll organize the search," said Malakai. "But if he's as fast as you say, we'll be hard-pressed to catch him." He pointed to two of the guards. "You and you. Come with me." The three horses cantered out through the entryway.

Alana walked over to Eloise. Jerome scuttled backward to get out of her way. "You're injured?" asked the mare.

Eloise turned and showed the horse her back.

"I see. And the other human? How damaged is he?"

"Bad. I fear he won't be able to walk for a while."

"Well, then it's good that one of the Not Us has deigned to carry him around."

Eloise wasn't sure what to think of that. Lorch and the Nameless One had such a close partnership that this skewed perspective on their relationship struck her as odd.

"I'll send for one who heals," said Alana. "She is with the Us, but is a savage like you."

Again, Eloise thought it best not to react. "Thank you."

Alana tilted her head and looked at Eloise with an expression that mixed bemusement and puzzlement. "There might be some need for explanations on your part."

"Oh?"

"Why the other savage attacked you."

"Yes," said a deep voice from behind them. "Explanations are most certainly in order."

Alana whirled around, swooped her head low, and kept it there. "Your Alacrity."

Eloise instinctively bowed as well, holding the box with the Star of Whatever close to her front and pressing the crack to her belly. The movement made her back sting even more.

A group of half a dozen horses approached from the direction of the entryway. Four of them closely surrounded a particularly large Brabant stallion with a chestnut coat and blonde mane, tail, and feathering. The Brabant stepped forward, walking directly toward Eloise. Even lit just by moonlight, Eloise saw that he was magnificently muscled in his neck and back. He came within six lengths and stopped. Eloise followed Alana's lead, saying, "Your Alacrity."

Unexpectedly, the stallion lowered himself to the ground, and with the changed angle, Eloise saw that there was something on his back.

Not something. Someone.

Another horse.

The horse on the stallion's back slipped off so he stood on the ground. It was all Eloise could do not to burst out laughing. The horse before her was the smallest one she'd ever seen—a miniature of a miniature. The top of his head, stretched high, would not have reached as high as Hector's knee. This was the equine khan? This was the mysterious and powerful leader of this disciplined mass of trained warriors?

Eloise was glad it was dark and her head was down. She suspected it was not the first time the khan's appearance had taken someone by surprise. Why was this not widely known? Perhaps this was why he always dealt with outside entities through emissaries and delegates.

Eloise kept her head down, but let her eyes stray upward. This was not dwarfism. His proportions were what one would expect, and Eloise had never heard of a dwarfish horse anyway. He was simply small. The khan's coat was an irregular patchwork of russet and white. His barrel body made him look like he might be in the family way, but obviously he was not. An ochre smear marked the spot on his forehead, equidistant from his eyes, where a third eye would be.

When he walked forward, it was suddenly clear why another horse carried him. It was not pride, nor the privilege of station. The khan moved painfully, heavily favoring his left foreleg and putting as little pressure on it as he could. The end of his leg curved sickeningly into a ball at the hoof, the bottom of it turned to the sky. As he moved, he limped along by walking on what should have been his ankle.

"Arise, Alana, daughter of Ganbaat and Altan. Arise," said the small horse.

"Thank you, Your Alacrity," replied the mare. There was honor and gratitude in her voice.

The khan limped forward and stood in front of Eloise. He spoke to Alana again. "This is one of our spies?"

"There is reason to doubt the intelligence we received, Your Alacrity," said Alana.

He looked at her. "Is there? Report." His voice was deeper than Eloise would have expected from one his size. His manner was commanding, but he held his authority lightly.

Alana relayed the situation as it had been reported to her, filtering out the unnecessary details. It was a swift, efficient, and more germane summary than the one she'd received.

When she'd finished, Eloise decided to step in. "My name is Eloise Hydra Gumball III. I am Future Ruler and Heir to the Western Lands and All That Really Matters."

The khan snorted. "Oh, I doubt that."

"I..."

"Hold your tongue, child." The khan limped two steps forward and looked at Eloise with one eye, then the other. "I've not yet met Queen Eloise of the Western Lands and All That Really Matters, but those who represent me say she stands strongly on the Protocol of the savages. If that is true, then I cannot imagine her allowing her daughter to roam the realms so unaccompanied, so vulnerable, and so randomly. She would not let said daughter arrive anywhere so substantial as into the presence of another monarch without fulsome and tedious preparatory negotiations, niceties, and ample diplomatic hoohah. It is much, much more likely that you, and those with you, are spies."

Eloise wondered what she was supposed to say to that. She'd just been assaulted. Her back felt like she could roast potatoes on it, and her cloak and tunic kept sticking to the damaged skin and pulling away, which wasn't helping her mood. Plus, she was certain that where her back wasn't burned, she'd be bruised from landing on the fireplace stones. Eloise was in no mood to convince anyone of anything, much less the Çalaht-can-take-him tiny head of this Çalaht-forsaken carbuncle of a realm.

Probably not a good time to let her feelings out.

Eloise breathed slowly to calm herself. Still bowed, she shifted the Star of Whatever to her left hip so she could gesture with her right hand.

As she moved the box, a pulse of green light shone through the broken lid. She quickly covered it with her arm.

The khan said, "I—" and then he caught a glimpse of the emerald glow shining through the crack. His head jerked up like he'd been kicked in the jaw, his eyes rolled back in his head, and his tongue lolled. It was like he was visiting the La La Realms.

A moment later, his whole body shivered like he was shaking off rain. He lowered his head and craned his neck around. "Herd Rememberer!"

A horse who'd hung back stepped up. "Yes, Your Alacrity?" He was even more deferential to the khan than Alana. A quiver in his voice betrayed fear.

"I call on the herd rememberer to act as my witness and as memory for the herd," said the khan to the horses nearby. Then he turned to the herd rememberer. "What did I say when I last came back from my connection to the Purity?"

"You said, 'We must prepare to receive the Light Bearer.'"

"Then you said?"

The herd rememberer lowered his head sheepishly (a phrase offensive to ovine beings). He coughed, swallowed, and paused as long as he thought he could. "I said, 'The Light Bearer? I thought you gave no truck to myths.' And then I apologized, as I apologize again now. My apologies, Your Alacrity, for commenting on what you said and doubting your words. My role is to remember, not comment. I have learned that."

The khan's eyes still looked a little far away. "I am again humbled to have touched the Purity with such directness," he said. Then he turned to his horses. "The Light Bearer has arrived."

"The savage girl spy is the Light Bearer? Impossible!" exclaimed the herd rememberer. "She is not one of the Us."

The khan looked at him, face unnaturally still.

The herd rememberer gasped, realizing his mistake. "Oh, no. My apologies, Your Alacrity. I've done it again. Please—"

"Silence," the khan whispered.

The horse squeaked off the rest of what he was burbling.

The khan shook his head slowly at him, looking like it took every bit of his self-control to not say more. He turned away from the herd rememberer and shuffled a step closer to Eloise. The small horse held his head up as high and straight as he could, although his head was still not as high as her waist. He cleared his throat and said, "I am Khan Nergüi Unbenannt Nimetuseta. I have been expecting you. The Us have been expecting you. Not you *per se*, but that which you carry, and so, by extension, you. You will please come with me." He pointed his nose toward the cracked box. "Bring the Light you bear." He turned his head toward Alana. "Have the dream wife see to the other injured human, then bring her to the clearing for this one."

"Yes, Your Alacrity."

"We are done here," he called to everyone around him. "Let's see if we can get through the rest of the night with less incidence of damage and knavery." With a final, "Come, please," to Eloise, the khan turned and walked away. His manner was so dignified and commanding that it overcame his awkward gait and diminutive size.

He was, Eloise thought, regal.

She stepped to her pannier, and took out her just-in-case dress, thinking it could be torn into bandages. Eloise turned and found Jerome a few lengths away. "I'm sorry. I'll be back as soon as I can."

"It's OK, El. Go."

Without another word, she followed the khan out of the open-air jail.

❧ 40 ❧

THE DREAM WIFE

Walking through the encampment was eye-opening. As Eloise had glimpsed when waiting above, there was a lot of society going on—horses on watch, horses sleeping in carefully aligned ranks, horse families nestled together against the chill, speaking in low voices, even laughing, and guards standing at strategic points around the camp, alert for intruders.

In the thin illumination of moonlight, she was again struck by the lack of structures and other demarcations of built civilization. Even people who spent their lives traveling from place to place tended to have bags, pots, pans, tools, and weapons. Beavers, bees, and birds all built things in one way or another. So did ants, spiders, wasps, and bagworms.

But apart from a few personal adornments, there were no objects at all.

To Eloise, it was such a foreign way to be in the world. How very different to town life. How very, very different to court life. But it also seemed very free. Unencumbered by the trappings of settled life, these horses could spring up and be on their way before she drew two breaths. Presumably, their main needs were finding plants to browse, water to drink, and perhaps a place for shelter in bad weather, although given how many of them there were, that last one was doubtful.

It made Eloise think about the objects she was attached to, and what she might shed if she had to move about the world with even less than she carried now.

They came to a low rise and the khan's manner changed from going somewhere to having arrived. This was his clearing? It was hardly a clearing at all. The land was tundra, so what had been cleared? Moss? Lichens? It was just an open space with a screen of loosely clumped boulders to one side that might give a modicum of privacy. Perhaps "clearing" was more of a formal name than a descriptor, but it would have been like putting a chair in a courtyard and calling it the Throne Room.

"Please sit," said the khan. "I will be with you in a short while." Without waiting for her response, he limped off and ducked behind the boulders.

Eloise looked around. No seats. No fire. Not much to lean on. She didn't want to go too close to where he was, so she found a small boulder in the other direction, wadded up her just-in-case dress as a makeshift cushion, and sat down side-on to the stone, since she couldn't lean back on it.

She didn't get the sense that he was testing her in the way the Southie queen, Onomatopoeia, had, leaving her waiting as a show of power. But he was gone long enough for drowsiness to set in, a desire for sleep that was so strong, it battled with the pain of her burns, and won. Eloise dozed off with her right shoulder against the boulder and her head lolling forward and back.

She awoke with a start when a hand gently touched her upper arm. The sudden movement disturbed the injuries of her back, and she sucked in a sudden inhale.

The hand belonged to a woman. Eloise looked into her eyes, which in the dark of night had a piercing blackness to them. She wore an ochre splotch at the wisdom eye in her forehead, which immediately reminded Eloise of the ochre mark on the khan's blaze. The woman's hair was a mass of waist-length ropes—matted strands that might once have been braided but had long given up any pretense of neatness—tied mostly behind her. She wore breeks below a knee-length shift that looked like it would barely provide the slightest nod in the direction of warmth.

"Apologies, young lady." Her deep voice sounded serious, which went with the deep look in her eyes. She came across as one who spared few words and had almost used up her quota for the day. "I didn't mean to startle you."

"I... It's OK," said Eloise, standing. "I can't believe I fell asleep like that."

The woman gave her an "it happens" shrug, but said nothing else.

"I'm Eloise. I—"

The woman's eyes went wide. "You're joking."

"I—"

"Your tongue has a Westie lilt. Were your parents daft? The Westie queen would have your liver sealed in a gallipot and stored on a shelf labeled 'Stupid Things' in less time than it would take for you to say, 'Not such a good idea.'"

"So people keep telling me."

The woman crossed her arms and angled her head, silently considering Eloise. Then she pointed her index finger at the ground and drew a circle in the air, indicating that Eloise should turn around.

The princess complied.

"Hmmm," said the woman. Without asking, she raised Eloise's travel cloak, and repositioned her so her back caught more of the moonlight. "Humph," she said.

Eloise heard the khan's labored hobble coming up from behind her. His awkward gait had a sound as distinctive as its look.

"Dream Wife. You're here," he said. "Finally."

The woman gently lowered Eloise's cloak. She quickly turned and bowed to him, her ropy hair falling forward, hiding her expression. "Yes, Your Alacrity."

Eloise followed her lead.

The khan looked at the dream wife, irritated. "Where are your means of treatment? No ointments or unctions?"

The woman didn't look up. "Like me, she is a human female of the savages," said the dream wife. "She will want privacy for what I need to do. I shall take her to my tent and treat her there. Once I'm done, I'll return her to His Alacrity, and she'll be in a better state for the interview His Alacrity wishes to conduct."

"Privacy?"

"Privacy," the woman said.

"Privacy." The khan said the word like he was tasting a new species of sour grape. "She will not speak to me as you treat her here?"

"Does His Alacrity wish her to feel humiliation?"

"No."

"Is His Alacrity trying to torture her?"

"No."

"Does His Alacrity have an interest in human anatomy?"

The horse snorted. "Hardly."

"Perhaps His Alacrity is more curious about the application of the healing arts than His Alacrity has let on previously?"

"There is no change there."

"Then His Alacrity should take my counsel on this."

The khan gave an exasperated snort. "So be it."

"She will also likely be in need of food," she said. "I shall feed her."

The horse rolled his eyes sarcastically. "Anything else?"

"Probably not. But it will not be before the sun rises."

Another derisive snort. "Send a messenger colt when you are ready to return her here." He looked at Eloise. "You will be treated, fed, and brought back. Is this acceptable?"

"Yes, thank you."

"Until then." The khan turned away and hobbled back to his screen of boulders.

When he was 20 lengths away, the dream wife rose from her bow. She threw her hair ropes back over her shoulders and silently watched the khan's retreat. When he had finally limped out of sight, she turned to Eloise. "You are able to follow?"

"Yes, thank you," said Eloise. "May I ask your name?"

"My name?" said the woman, vaguely puzzled. "I have been the dream wife many more years than I was anything else. That is how the Us refer to me. You may do the same."

Then with a nod in the direction they would go, she led Eloise from the clearing.

41

POULTICE

The dream wife's tent was tucked away at the edge of the encampment, which is why Eloise had failed to see it before. The moonlight caught it in full shine, and Eloise saw it was painted with a speckling that would camouflage it against the tundra landscape. The structure was six lengths wide and made of an octagon of canvas supported by eight poles and as many guide ropes, which were staked into the earth and anchored by stones. The dream wife lifted a flap and waved to Eloise, inviting her to enter in front of her.

The inside was lit by a small fire pit that had been banked down for sleep. The tent still held its warmth, and Eloise relaxed into its comfort as she stood still, blinking, and gave her eyes time to adjust.

The tent's furnishings were spare: a grass mat as a bed, a couple of folded blankets, a sack with six scrolls poking out, and a closed wooden chest that took up a quarter of the interior space. On it was a pair of pots and a kettle that looked like it had seen a hundred years' worth of fires.

Eloise stood near the pit and looked around at the tent's inside walls. They were decorated in a riot of swirls, glyphs, and symbols that hinted to Eloise of half-remembered lessons from her Oracles and Insights classes. Her first impression was that the images were random, but then patterns emerged. The largest spiral was painted to look like it emanated from the smoke hole in the center of the roof. Other spirals dotted the center of each panel. There were lines of star shapes where the number of points increased from six to seven to eight, then upward, to one with 21 points. There were symbols that looked like they should form words from a language lost to time. These were woven in and out of crude representations of animals—a slithering snake, a sly jaguar, a flitting hummingbird, and a soaring condor. The tent's marking combined to give off a feeling of some unknown weak magic.

The dream wife pointed to the sleeping mat. "Please sit. I'm going to need light." She then took several sticks from a pile of wood stacked neatly against one wall, laid them in the fire pit, and puffed the coals back to flame.

Eloise sat cross-legged on the mat. "Did you attend to Lorch? Is he OK?"

"The one dressed as a guard? His knee is severely sprained, and I bandaged it against swelling and to give it support. He's lucky it didn't dislocate or break."

"Can he walk? Or ride?"

"If pressed, he could probably do the latter if he was able to mount, but it would be uncomfortable. He won't be much inclined toward the former for a few days."

"I see," said Eloise. "Thank you for helping him."

The woman nodded an acknowledgement. "Let me see what I can do for you."

Eloise held out her just-in-case dress. "I thought this might be useful."

"There is not much call for dancing among the Us."

Eloise looked at her. "Pardon?"

"That is a dress for dancing. The closest the Us get to dancing is the welcome ceremony you witnessed."

"I see." Eloise held her eye, then saw the dream wife slowly wink. "Oh. You jest."

"Indeed. As serious as the Us are, humor is valued," she said. "I assume you're volunteering your dancing dress for bandages?"

"Yes."

"That shouldn't be necessary, but we can hold it in reserve." She folded it, spent a moment touching the material, ran her finger along a seam, and set it down next to the wooden chest. "Now, can you remove your cloak?"

Eloise unclasped her cloak and held it in front of her. Seamstress Lint-trap would not be pleased with the state it was in. Or maybe she would. While the material had burned through, and as painful as her back was, the cloak had prevented a much worse injury.

The dream wife took the cloak from Eloise and folded it neatly with the burned spot on top. As she had done with the dress, she spent a moment feeling the material and looking at the stitching. "Hmmm," she said, and put it on top of the dress.

"You'll need to set your box aside. Can I put it with your other things? I won't disturb it."

"That's OK. I'll do it, thanks." Eloise stood, took the two steps to the trunk, and tucked the box under the dress and her cloak. She handled it in a way that kept the crack covered, and only a hint of green light escaped.

"Obviously, I'll need your tunic off so I can work with your back. Fortunately, it doesn't appear to be stuck to your skin. Can you raise your arms above your head?"

Eloise got them part of the way up, but the burns hurt too much. "I don't think so."

"Can you do this?" The dream wife leaned forward and held her arms like she was going to dive into a lake. "Otherwise, I can cut it off."

"I'd rather you didn't." Eloise gritted her teeth and made the diving motion.

The dream wife eased off the burned tunic. Eloise straightened and crossed her arms in front of herself, feeling chilled and exposed. The old woman folded the garment burned-side up, again rubbed the material between her fingers, then placed it on the cloak. "Please lie on your stomach."

Eloise complied. She turned her face to the tent wall and listened as the dream wife opened the lid of her wooden chest. She rummaged around in it, and Eloise heard the light clink of small glass jars mixed with the rustle of cloth. She turned her head and watched the dream wife duck out of the tent and return minutes later with a pail of water, which she set next to Eloise. She then brought out a candle, lit it, dripped wax onto a low stool, pushed the thick end of the candle into the wax, and waited a few moments while the drippings hardened and held the candle upright. It smelled of soy and lavender.

The dream wife dipped a cloth into the bucket. "There might be some discomfort," she said. "But I need to make sure it's clean. The water is cold. That will help with the swelling."

Being dabbed with the cloth was like being hit with a snowball. It stung and was unpleasantly wet and cold. Eloise focused on keeping her flinching to a minimum.

After a particularly bad flinch, the dream wife said, "There is no need to maintain a silence. You have my permission to swear."

"You would have me swear? As in oath, like a sailor?"

"Yes. You have my permission to use language that an ocean bass would think salty."

"Whatever for?"

The dream wife snorted in a way that reminded Eloise of the khan, dipped the cloth, and dabbed the freezing water onto Eloise's back again. "Pain management. I find that those who stay silent when I work on them can tolerate much less than those who utter, or even scream, oaths. Usually, the fouler the better."

"Is this a second witticism?"

"Not at all."

At Court, swearing was definitely on the No No list, especially for princesses who had Protocol and the reputation of their family name to consider. Eloise rarely heard her mother say anything stronger than, "Çalaht kiss my soul," which was the sort of thing only pious little old ladies said. It wasn't like Eloise had never heard swearing, and creative oathing was something one could admire in a way. But to flat-out swear in front of a stranger was just awkward.

"I'll pass, thank you," said Eloise.

There was the sound of a jar being unstoppered. "I need to debride the area. This might sting a little," said the dream wife. She sluiced an acrid fluid directly onto Eloise's burns.

A sound like bubbling evil came from her back, and it felt like a million fire ants were having a hootenanny on her skin.

"Ffffffffffffffffffffffffffffffffffffffffffffffffffar out!" screamed Eloise. "Çalaht dodging deranged, demonic, decoupaged darts! That hurts! A lot!"

"Thought it might," chuckled the dream wife. "One can tell you don't swear much."

"When one is raised as I was, one doesn't."

"Hmmm."

A few more dabs with cold water and the stinging was gone. "Next, the aloe vera," said the dream wife. "Then honey. And then a poultice of chickweed, comfrey, plantain, and slippery elm."

"The aloe vera I know," said Eloise. "But why that combination for the poultice?"

"The plantain juice soothes and protects from infection. The comfrey is similar, in that they both ease the anger from the wound, speed healing, and whisper to the skin that it needs to grow anew. The slippery elm and the chickweed are also to soothe the inflammation."

"And honey?"

"It is very healing for wounds, if you are lucky enough to have some."

"I've not heard of honey used in this way. By what accord with the bees did they grant you the privilege of using their honey?"

"Accord? Privilege? Listen to the way you speak." The old woman shook her head slowly. "The knowledge of the healing qualities of honey is centuries old. But the bees guard themselves fiercely against exploitation."

"As they should."

"Exactly. As they should." The dream wife wiped on the aloe vera and then the honey as she spoke. "I did not come to an accord, although it is a privilege to have reached a place where they honored me with some of their honey and gave me permission to use it for healing. I got to know a hive, and in particular, the hive's queen. She had a curiosity about the ways of the equines—I was already living with the Us—and I was curious about the ways of bees. We spent many afternoons passing the time together, sharing what we knew. When the Us moved on, she gave me the gift of some of the hive's honey."

"That's lovely," said Eloise.

"It was. The bee queen had an amazing mind. You would know that the world is revealed to us through our senses. But you would also know that a snake experiences the world very differently to, say, a hummingbird. The queen was able to convey to me how the world appeared to her through her compound eyes, her antennae, and how she could hear air movements in a way that is similar to how we detect sounds."

"Fascinating."

"Yes, it was nothing short of mesmeric. If you have the chance to converse with bees, I encourage you to do so." The dream wife finished with the layer of honey, then said, "I'll apply the poultice now. You will need to let me tie it on by wrapping a bandage around you. Is that acceptable?"

Eloise nodded. The poultice was surprisingly heavy, a thin cloth laden with the mix of herbs and then placed against her back. The dream wife put a second layer above this, a sort of breathable cloth that reminded Eloise of fancy wet weather gear. This would act as a protective layer above the bandage. The dream wife fixed the top and bottom of the bandage to her using strips of cloth passed under Eloise at the bottom of the ribs and just at the armpits. She then had Eloise sit up, which again made her feel exposed and vulnerable. It had been years since anyone other than her handmaid Odmilla had seen her in such a state (ignoring the soldier's cold incident after Mortimer Falls, which she most certainly would). The old woman wound a long, narrow cloth around Eloise from the bottom of the bandage to the top, overlapping each circle of the wrap.

The dream wife tied off the bandage at the top near Eloise's shoulder. "That should keep it snug and prevent leaks. Is it too tight?"

"No, thank you."

"Keep the bandage in place for three days," said the old woman. "I'll change it then. You and your companions will need to remain that long, at least."

"You do not change it more often than that?"

"Some do. I don't. I worry about disturbing the healing process unnecessarily."

"I see," said Eloise. "I will speak with the others about the timing of what you said."

"Of course." The dream wife reached inside her wooden chest and pulled out a clean linen shift. "This should fit you well enough. I'll see to the repair of your clothing. Now, food."

42

THE RING

The old woman dug into a rucksack and pulled out a linen bag. "Porridge? Oats are one of the foods I have in common with the Us. I don't eat a lot of grass, but we share a fondness for oats, when we can get them. They'll eat them whole, of course. I prepare them in the way of humans—I hull them so they're oat groats, steam them, and then roll them flat. Better texture. Less picking of husks from the teeth."

"That would be lovely, thank you. I believe that's how Chef makes them at home." Eloise's back still ached, but with the poultice and the aloe vera, she was much more comfortable.

She watched the old woman put water from a different pail into a battered metal pot, shake in a generous helping of the flattened oats, and set the pot on the fire to cook. She handed Eloise a wooden spoon. "You can stir?"

"Yes."

"You will answer questions now?"

Eloise hesitated. What choice did she have? The woman had been kind and patient with her burns, and she had helped Lorch. If she meant harm, then she wouldn't have bothered with either. It might give Eloise a chance to practice answers she would later need to give to the khan. "Of course."

"Tell me about your ring."

"My ring?" Of all the questions she might have asked, that was the last one Eloise expected. She splayed out the fingers of her right hand and pointed to the ring she wore on her middle finger. It was a silver band engraved with the ornate knot work of the Central Ranges. "This ring?"

"Yes."

"Well, OK," said Eloise, wondering how this could possibly make a difference to anything. "It was a gift." Eloise poked the spoon into the pot and stirred gently.

The dream wife watched her, waiting.

"Right, it was a gift from Seer Maybelle de Chipmunk, my mother's court seer. Seer Maybelle is the mother of one of my fellow travelers. Did you meet a chipmunk when you treated Lorch?"

"Yes. Nervous type. Chattered a lot."

"That is her son, Jerome," said Eloise. "You'll have to pardon his manner at the moment. He's had a bad few weeks." And she hadn't yet had time to talk to him and find out just how horrible they'd been. She feared the worst, but at least he was alive, and seemingly sound in body.

"So you travel with your seer."

"Jerome?" Eloise smiled. "No, no, no. Jerome Abernatheen de Chipmunk is my champion."

The dream wife knitted her brow. "Your champion? Why would you make one such as he your champion?"

Eloise was taken aback by the directness of her question. "What do you mean, 'Such as he?' What 'such' is that? His species? His size?"

"Those things don't matter," scoffed the dream wife. "I refer to his lineage. The gifts of prognostication, the ability to tap into the Unseen, the wit to interpret the hints and nudges from the tools of divination—these things travel from blood to blood to blood. When they are as strong as they are in your Seer Maybelle, it seems impossible for them to miss her direct issue."

"Do you know her?"

The old woman stared at her, silent, her face expressionless. Eloise held her gaze. After a full half minute, the dream wife nodded slowly. "The ring you wear was a gift to her from me."

Eloise's mouth dropped open. She looked at the ring, then back at the woman. "Oh. Really?"

"Really, indeed." They sat in silence. Then the dream wife said, "Stir the oats, child. The taste is not improved by burning."

Eloise brimmed with questions. How had Seer Maybelle and the dream wife met? How long ago? How well had they known each other? What mysteries had they shared? Was the ring a token of friendship, an obligation, a meaningless formality? What gifts of the Unseen did they share in common? Which were different? If the ring represented some sort of deep tie, then why in the world would Seer Maybelle give it to Eloise?

"To be clear," said the dream wife, "she presented you with this ring. She did not give it to her son."

"Correct."

"And he does not tap into the Unseen? Not at all?"

Eloise thought a moment. There was that string of fake prognostications at Ye Olde Public Inn in the village of Colander. That had been weird and strangely accurate. But it was an outlier, and hardly conclusive. Eloise lifted her palms. "What can I say? I've known him a long time. He really doesn't have his mother's talent. There might be the odd fluke of insight, but for as long as I've known him, Seer Maybelle's gifts have not manifested in her son."

"I see. Did she try to train him? Expose him to the Unseen forces as a guide? Help him get to know them?"

"I think she tried, maybe? But he hasn't spoken to me about it. You'd really have to ask him."

"I might do that. My attention before was on the guard's knee. I'll find a few moments to speak with him." The dream wife grasped the edge of the pot with a cloth and took it from the fire. She used the wooden spoon to serve up a bowlful each.

"Thank you." Eloise took hers carefully. She lifted a spoonful and blew across it. "May I ask—"

"No. No questions now. Eat. You need to speak to His Alacrity. We have kept him waiting long enough, and probably to the edge of his patience. Eat, so we can go."

❧ 43 ❧

INCONCLUSIVE, BUT NOTED

A sliver of sun was just peeking above the eastern horizon when the dream wife sent a messenger colt to alert the khan that she and Eloise were on their way. The tight bandages, the discomfort in her back, the unfamiliar feel of the borrowed shift, the lack of travel cloak, the Star of Whatever balanced on her right hip, and the rough blanket draped over her shoulders—all these made Eloise feel awkward as they walked to the khan's clearing.

She shouldn't feel nervous, but she did. Eloise had spoken to plenty of nobles. She'd interacted with the Southie monarch just fine (well, eventually, anyway). For that matter, she'd been raised by a queen. How hard could it be to talk to the head of the Central Ranges?

And yet there she was, feeling nervous, unsure what the equine khan would say or do. This must be what it's like to stand before her mother in the Receiving Room, she thought, if colder and with less furniture.

They found the khan sitting down on a circular mound that was only slightly larger across than the khan himself. The mound was cleared of stones and was raised like a dais and situated so it afforded an uninterrupted view of the rising sun in the morning and the setting sun in the evening. The small, club-footed horse faced the herald of the new day, his eyes closed, his breathing deep and rhythmic.

The dream wife stopped at a respectful distance and stood, motionless, while the khan finished his contemplations. Eloise still thought of this as "iron ring staring," from the training leading up to her Thorning Ceremony. She closed her own eyes, turned to face the sun, and let the calm of the moment fill her.

Several minutes later, the khan took a final, long, deep breath in through his nostrils and blew out a lungful of air in a single sudden rush. He then held the exhale for a long moment, opened his eyes, and resumed normal breathing.

He turned to the two of them. "You may approach."

The dream wife stepped forward and bowed. "Your Alacrity," she said. A moment later, Eloise did the same.

The khan looked Eloise up and down. He glanced at the box containing the Star of Whatever, then seemed to deliberately avoid looking at it from then on. "You have been tended?" he asked.

"Yes, Your Alacrity," said Eloise.

"Fed?"

"Yes, Your Alacrity."

"Then let us begin. Tell me..."

The dream wife quietly cleared her throat. The khan stopped and looked at her. "Yes?"

"Your Alacrity, if I may say something before you continue?"

He looked at her, reading her expression, then sighed. "If you must."

"Your Alacrity, I believe she is who she claims to be."

The khan snorted his now-familiar dismissive snort. "Is that of consequence?"

"I think it is, yes."

"Explain."

"I think who she is might affect the tone and manner of His Alacrity's interaction with her. It might influence the extent to which His Alacrity tries to meet the apparent intention of His Alacrity's vision and the visions of those who preceded you. It could even influence His Alacrity's level of politeness and friendliness."

The horse lifted his head and tilted an eye at her. "Are you suggesting I have issues with politeness?"

The dream wife held his eye—not something Eloise had seen in their previous interactions. "Of course not, Your Alacrity. It would be ridiculous to suggest anything of the sort." But her monotonic voice was drained of all inflection.

The khan snorted again.

The dream wife kept silent.

Snort.

Silence.

Long, exasperated snort.

Extended, long-suffering silence.

"Fine," said the khan, finally breaking eye contact. "Your concern with regard to politeness has been noted." He looked again at Eloise, but continued speaking to the dream wife. "Upon what do you base this conclusion of yours?"

"No single thing. Instead, several observations added together." The dream wife gestured at Eloise as if she was a shopkeeper's mannequin. "Her manner of speech is from the Western Lands and All That Really Matters and is reflective of a Court education."

"Accepted. Continue."

"The quality of her garments is exceptional and costly."

"Accepted."

"Her capacity to swear is almost non-existent. Regarding this, she said, 'When one is raised as I was, one doesn't.'"

"Inconclusive, but noted."

"Her companions refer to her as 'Princess Eloise.' It is reflexive."

"Again, inconclusive, but noted."

The dream wife took Eloise's right wrist between her thumb and index finger, lifted her arm, and pointed to the ring. "She wears this."

"Oh. Interesting."

"You recognize it."

The khan nodded, thoughtfully. "Yes, I do."

"Then you would accept the most logical reason it would come into her possession would be if she was associated with the Court of the Westie queen."

"Logic would lean in that direction, although it could have been thievery."

"She allegedly travels with the son of the seer to whom I gave it."

"Do we know he is truly her son? You know rodents. They can look very similar."

"I shall not dignify that, Your Alacrity. I cannot say it if it is him or not, as I haven't spoken with him in any depth. But the way the pieces of this particular puzzle fit together indicates that this is, indeed—as unlikely a conclusion as it seems—Princess Eloise Hydra Gumball III."

"I see." He sniffed the air like he was trying to smell out the truth. "And the matter of spying? How they were targeting our encampment?"

Eloise decided it was time to speak up for herself. "A fiction, Your Alacrity. It was perpetrated by the one who attacked me last night, Turpentine Snotearrow McCcoonnch, the former jester to the late king of the Half Kingdom, my uncle, Doncaster Worsted Halva de

Chëëëkflïïïnt, and was conveyed in ignorance by the transport-for-hire camel, Bjóöòrn Tóöòrúüùn."

"Humph," grunted the khan. He turned back to face the morning sun and closed his eyes as if he wanted to return to his earlier contemplations.

Then the khan appeared to reach a decision. He hauled himself up onto his three good legs and looked straight at her. On top of his mound, they were roughly eye to eye. "We shall consider you to be who you say you are until evidence proves otherwise. As such, I welcome you, Eloise Hydra Gumball III, to my realm, the home of the Us, the Central Ranges. You shall have the rights and responsibilities of a representative of Queen Eloise Hydra Gumball II of the Western Lands and All That Really Matters."

"Thank you, Khan Nergüi."

"You have eaten. Can I invite you to take a morning tea with me?"

"Thank you. That would be lovely."

"Dream Wife, you will serve?"

"Of course, Your Alacrity."

The khan limped down from his mound and stood next to Eloise. "I must graze first. You will accompany me, and we can talk. Then tea."

44

OAT CAKES

Eloise strolled along as the khan browsed the sparse tundra plants. Given how cold and inhospitable the landscape was, it had an amazing variety of species.

"Do you eat cottongrass?" he asked. "Or maybe you'd like some arctic willow?"

"No, thank you," said Eloise. "I've not had those before. Are they suitable for human consumption?"

The khan chomped a mouthful from a red-leafed bush and said, "I have no idea. You'd have to ask the dream wife. The needs of humans are not a major concern among the Us."

"I see."

Small talk was not, apparently, his strong suit.

The khan moved from plant to plant, carefully guarding his use of his bad foreleg. Eloise remained a respectful distance away and watched as he nibbled a little here and a little there before moving on to the next one. It wasn't clear if this unfocused method of eating was because he liked variety, or if he was trying not to affect any single plant too much. Perhaps both.

Eloise took another crack at conversation. She knew little about him, his realm, or his people, so wasn't sure which direction to head. "So, does His Alacrity think it will snow soon?"

The khan stopped mid-chew and looked at her. "Do I think it will snow soon? You're asking me about the weather? Of all possible topics, that's the one you choose?"

"His Alacrity asked me about food. The weather seemed like a safe and neutral topic until we get to whatever it is that we'll really be discussing."

"Hmmph." The small horse bit off a chunk of arctic willow, chewed, and swallowed it. "Soon. Within days, perhaps even today, the great mare of winter will embrace us with her pure white coat. We have seen the first hints of it in the air already." He leaned down and tore off a mouthful of tussock. "There. We've covered the weather. Shall we talk about what one is planning for the weekend? Perhaps the latest gossip about Lyndia Thrind?"

Eloise did not reply.

The khan continued his breakfast as the surrounding encampment worked itself into the buzz of the day. Already, the first warrior prac- tice sessions were underway, and colts and foals rushed to gather for their lessons. Everything struck Eloise as purposeful and serious.

"So, tell me," said the khan. "How did you come to possess that which you carry?"

Eloise lifted her hand to show the ring. "This?"

"No."

Eloise held forward the box with the Star of Whatever. "This?"

Some of the Star of Whatever's green glow slipped past her fingers. The khan flinched and looked away. "Yes. That."

"Of course, Your Alacrity."

But there was no "of course" about it at all. How much of the story should she reveal? Where should she start? Could she even trust him? If the Star of Whatever was everything she thought it was, what would stop him from coveting it or trying to take it from her? With a thousand horses at his command, the Star would be his in a heartbeat. He'd referred to her as the Light Bearer, but was that even a good thing? It could be a curse or a death sentence just as easily as it could be a badge of honor or a blessing of some sort.

It was all a worry.

Counterbalancing all of that were those same thousand horses. They were loyal, respectful, and eager to follow the commands of their diminutive, half-crippled leader. He ruled with toughness, but not cruelty. There had to be *something* they all saw in him. Otherwise, why let him rule? It's not like he could physically dominate even the smallest of them.

It was their honoring of him that made Eloise take the plunge and choose to trust him.

So she started with, "My sister and I were fogged at the command of Turpentine Snotearrow McCcoonnch," and took it from there. Within two minutes, the khan had stopped eating and was giving Eloise his full attention. She covered the journey into the Purple Haze. following the inner tug she felt, finding Melveeta, ending the spell, Melveeta's death, and bringing the Star of Whatever back with her. She didn't explore just how magical she thought the Star was, but suspected the khan had a sense of it from the way he flinched when he looked at the light coming through the crack. As they neared the dream wife's tent, Eloise finished with, "I hope my mother, or maybe one of the Court mages, will have some sort of insight about what to do with it."

The khan stared at Eloise. "That's a remarkable tale," he said. "Extraordinary. If it's even half true, it's one for the bards."

"I don't know about that. It's all so recent," said Eloise. "I'm still not sure what to think about it all, and it's far from over."

They found the dream wife standing at her doorway, waiting calmly. Next to her, a horse stood with much less calm. It was the herd rememberer, looking as twitchy and uncomfortable as he had during the night.

The khan saw the horse and huffed. "You sent for him?"

The dream wife nodded. "It seemed likely there might be things that needed remembering."

The khan snorted, but said nothing.

The dream wife had placed two blankets on the ground, and bowed as the khan sat on the larger one. She motioned for Eloise to take the other, but remained standing herself. "Would His Alacrity like his usual tea, or something different this morning?"

"Haggleberry."

"Haggleberry?" The old woman said the word like her sovereign had just requested snake spit tea. "As His Alacrity wishes." She looked at Eloise. "Princess Eloise?"

It was the first time any of them had used her name and title. Progress.

"Haggleberry sounds wonderful," she said. "May I help in any way?"

"That won't be necessary, thank you. Would His Alacrity like oat cakes? They were just baked and are still warm."

The ruler of the Central Ranges did something Eloise had not seen before—he smiled. "What do you think?"

"One does not wish to presume anything about His Alacrity's preferences or proclivities." The dream wife was also smiling, and the exchange had the feel of practiced banter. "What if His Alacrity's fundamental position on oat cakes has changed? One would not want to offend His Alacrity by proffering unwanted oat cakes."

"Is it not one's duty to the Us, to one's khan, indeed, most importantly, to one's self, to be alert to changes in circumstances?"

"Of course, Your Alacrity."

"Would a shift in one's khan's fundamental position on oat cakes not be considered a change in circumstances?"

"As much as an opinion on a foodstuff can be considered a 'circumstance,' yes."

"Dream Wife, have you detected such a change? Have you communed with the Purity, perhaps, and encountered the tendrils of a prophecy dealing with an alteration regarding oat cakes?"

"No, Your Alacrity. No oat cake-based prophecies have been encountered in my connections to the Purity, nor with regard to any other aspect of the Unseen. No divinatory reading of tea leaves, motes of dust, candle wax dripping onto hemp parchment, candle wax dripping onto water, casting of dice, casting of dominoes, casting of beans, observation of stars, observation of clouds, observation of the footprints of ants, scrying, crying, gazing at the spots of a palomino, drawing of coins from a sack, drawing of circles, listening to the howling of dogs, the clipping of fingernails, the clipping of toenails, the tossing of rose petals, the metaphoric tossing of biscuits, the drawing of lots, nor lots of drawing, the use of rods, the pattern of sticks, nor waving of wands—none of these things have portended a change to His Alacrity's attitude toward oat cakes."

"Did you try reading the breezes? Gazing at shadows? The wafting of smoke? The burning of writing onto bark? The splattering of mud? The patterns of spider webs? The falling of ash from incense? The direction of comet tails? The smoldering of laurel wreaths? Reading the rainbow patterns from oil dripped on a lake?"

"Is His Alacrity implying that I have not been thorough?"

"Of course not."

"As I said, I have not detected anything that might lead one to indicate that His Alacrity's position on oat cakes may have changed, is currently changing, or is likely to change any time soon."

"Very good. Then you should comfortably and with confidence conclude that oat cakes would be welcomed this morning," the khan said, smiling. "Especially when still warm."

"Then I shall fetch them." The old woman ducked into her tent, pulling the flap down behind her. Then she poked her head back out. "That was a 'yes?'"

"That was a yes."

"Right. No change since I came in here?"

"Not yet, no."

"Good." The tent flap came back down.

❧ 45 ❧

THE LIGHT BORNE

Eloise watched the back-and-forth between the khan and the dream wife, bemused. She wondered if the dream wife was the only one who was allowed to interact with the khan that way, or if he became that familiar with others, too. Certainly the herd rememberer, standing there like a bent carriage wheel, did not look like he ever bantered with his khan. The exchange also struck her as something Jerome would have come up with. It was the sort of conversation the two of them would have had—at least they would have before he'd spent all that time in a sack. Eloise felt a lump growing in her throat, and swallowed it down. She hoped Jerome was OK. She couldn't wait to talk to him.

Eloise snugged the blanket she wore more tightly around her, careful not to pull too tight against the fresh bandages. There was an awkward pause while she and the khan listened to the dream wife rustle around in her tent preparing tea. Eloise tried again with conversation. "His Alacrity said last night that I came to him in a vision. Is that correct?"

"Not you, *per se*. The Light itself," he said. "But more importantly, I saw that it was being borne toward us."

"Why?"

"Why have a vision? It is part of my duty as khan. I connect to the Purity, as have all khans before me."

"No, I mean, why is this Light of His Highness's vision important, or that His Highness's vision indicated that the Light was being borne?"

"Two very different questions," said the horse. "Why the Light is important is not clear. It has come to me in visions ever since I began connecting to the Purity as khan. But I am just the latest. It has come in the connections to the Purity for khans stretching back as far as the Us can remember."

"What do you know about this Light?"

"Only that which the Purity chooses to share with me, which is not a lot. That which it shares, and that which remains from memories of previous khans." He lifted a chin and pointed to their witness, who took half a step back, having been noticed. "Herd Rememberer would know more," the khan said. The herd rememberer stayed motionless, his expression blank. "Although, 'know' is the wrong word. He can recite, but recitation is not the same as knowledge. He can recite the connections to the Purity experienced by khans past as far as his limited learning allows."

"Limited learning?" asked Eloise.

"He was apprenticed to the herd rememberer. But the herd rememberer fell ill and passed to Çalaht's green fields well before her time, having only transferred a portion of her memories to him. Ever is it thus when one of the herd rememberers passes to graze at Çalaht's side before they complete the apprentice's training."

Eloise furrowed her brow. "Is His Alacrity saying that the herd's memories and histories rely on one person and an apprentice? That seems like a single point of failure problem, and one that would have been noticed and remedied long ago."

The khan tilted his head—the equine equivalent of a shrug. "The Us do not write and do not stay in one place. So our histories are oral. The Us are philosophical about the losses this approach introduces. One does not just become a herd rememberer. It requires particular skills. People with those talents do not arise among the Us very often."

"And since one herd rememberer can never convey all of his or her memories, then part of your history disappears with the death of each herd rememberer."

The khan gave another head tilt. "When parts of the herd's memories are lost, we think of it as a chance to shed the burdens of the past. At some level, we celebrate that." He sat quietly for a few moments, like he was trying to figure out what words to use. "As you said, it's impossible to remember everything. Even if a herd rememberer completes all of his or her training, there will be gaps. There are always gaps. Surely there are gaps in your own histories. It must be the same among the savages and the Not Us as it is for the Us. Even with your writing and your scrolls, not all can be captured. If something is important enough, we remember. It might be turned into one of our chants or a song and spread more widely. The Us has its bards, which is a weak form of herd remembering, as well as our herd rememberer. But if something is not so important, then it may fall into the gaps of time and memory, and be lost."

The dream wife carried out a tray laden with an oversized teapot, two tea cups with saucers, and a plate of oat cakes. She set the tray on the ground between Eloise and the khan, went back in, and brought out a small, ceramic, hollowed-out half-cylinder the length of Eloise's forearm and decorated with purple red peonies. She set this before the khan, hollowed side up, and Eloise realized it was shaped like a trough, similar to what she'd seen equines drinking from in taverns like the Splintered Dray, but delicate, refined, and tea-sized, rather than liquid consolation-sized. She set a cup and saucer on the ground in front of Eloise, hefted up the pot, filled the khan's trough, then filled Eloise's cup, releasing the tangy smell of haggleberry tea. Eloise breathed in the aroma. It was spiced, but not in a way Eloise recognized. Ginger? Peppercorn? A hint of cinnamon? It smelled wonderful, and she wondered if Jerome, with his staunch opinions on haggleberry tea, would approve.

The dream wife put a small plate next to the khan's trough, served him three cakes placed in an overlapping triangle, then offered the plate to Eloise, who took two and set them on her saucer exactly opposite each other, on either side of the cup. The dream wife filled the second teacup, put half an oat cake on her saucer, then stepped back to stand next to the herd rememberer.

The herd rememberer was not included in the tea ritual. Eloise assumed he was there to remember and nothing else. Still, it seemed a little rude. Then again, it's not like the servants at court were invited to share tea with her mother.

The khan blew across the ceramic trough to cool the steaming liquid. Eloise lifted her cup and did the same.

"So, the khans of the Us have had visions of the Light for centuries," he said. "These visions have been consistent, but maddeningly vague. The herd rememberers have recalled 'the Light,' 'the Emerald Light,' 'the Deep Green Light,' and other variations glowing away in their encounters with the Purity. We knew there was significance and hidden meaning, but we never knew what it was. This ongoing message meant that it was *always* the first thing taught from one herd rememberer to the next, and the first thing recorded from any khan's connection to the Purity."

"I see," said Eloise. She sipped her tea and enjoyed the unexpected blend of flavors. Eloise beamed at the dream wife. "Magnificent. Truly splendid. Thank you." She savored a second sip and lowered her cup. "So, if I understand, that answers the first question—why it's important to you: all those vague visions. And the second question? The Light being borne?"

"Because the Light was always just *there*. But I was the first one in all those generations who saw that it was on the move, that the Light was coming to us," said the khan. "And here, we're on unfamiliar territory, because there was always another aspect to the vision. The Us were to 'render unto the Light that which it needs.' It was recorded with many words over many years, but it was always more or less that. My own vision gave me clarity that we were to 'give the Light its desires.' But, again, what that means in practice is unclear."

"It's a stone. What wants could it possibly have?"

The khan gave another head tilt and sipped the tea from his trough in one long, watery slurp. A moment later, he let loose an epic belch.

At this, the dream wife smiled. "I'm glad it was to His Alacrity's taste. More?"

"Please."

"You haven't touched your oat cakes. Is there a problem with them? Or have you changed your mind?"

"When I have a chance to eat one, I'll let you know."

While the khan and the dream wife continued their oat cake dance, Eloise pondered what it might mean to "give the Light what it needs." She thought about the spark of something in it. What desire might an entity with the apparent mental capacity of a single punctuation mark have?

"So, what does the Light want?" Eloise asked.

The dream wife and the khan looked at each other. The horse spoke. "You are the Light Bearer. You'll need to tell us."

"I have no idea."

"None?"

"None."

"Well, that's not convenient," said the khan.

The dream wife poured another round, and they sat quietly sipping and thinking, all watched by the herd rememberer, who had calmed down and was now just observing them.

"I have a question," said the khan.

"Yes?" Eloise broke off another half oat cake, but didn't nibble it yet.

"What can you tell us about the Star of Whatever? You described to me the circumstances under which it came to you, but you haven't said much about the Star itself. What do you know or what have you discovered? There has to be a reason khan after khan has had visions. And there has to be a reason you have brought it here. The need, the desire of the Light must be buried in there somewhere."

"Hmmm," said Eloise. "Let me think."

This was exactly the conversation she didn't want to have. She hadn't told anyone about her experience of the spark of something in the Star of Whatever. Not even her sister, Johanna, while they slogged through the wasteland of the Purple Haze. She didn't think she wanted the first people she told to be this hobble-legged king, the old woman, and the nervous horse with the memory training.

"I'm not sure what to say," Eloise said. "It's a stone. It glows. It's magical. Apparently, very magical."

The khan went unfocused for a moment. "No, that's not it. There's something else."

The dream wife did the same. "I agree."

They sipped tea, nibbled oat cakes, and waited. The herd rememberer looked like he would doze off.

Then an idea dawned. Maybe it wasn't supposed to be her choice. Maybe it should be up to the spark of something to decide what it wanted—whether it would like to be revealed or not. So, even though it was as silent as the stone it was, Eloise formulated her query and sent the spark of something a probing "?".

The green light in the Star of Whatever pulsed faintly in response. Eloise saw it, and noticed that the khan did as well—the horse looked like he'd been hit in the jaw.

Eloise perceived a "...". That was one the spark of something hadn't used before, but she understood it to mean "hold on." Eloise held up an index finger, silently asking the others for a few moments. Then she closed her eye and waited.

And waited.

The wait was so long that she began to question the "...". Had she made it up? But then, what about the pulse of green light?

Then it came. A ".".

It felt like assent.

Eloise opened her eyes again, set the box on her lap, and rubbed the cracked lid lightly. "I have permission. Let me tell you about the spark of something that is in the Star of Whatever." She told the others of how Melveeta had guided her to perceive the small sense of consciousness residing in the stone, and how when she was connected to the enchantment woven by Gwendolyn the Irritable's champion, Eloise was able to communicate with it, and how she cajoled the spark of something to end the spell. She also shared how she thought the Star of Whatever had somehow saved her life when she went over Mortimer Falls. Eloise mentioned the odd dreams she'd been having, and ended with her attempts to enter into a relationship with the spark of something, explaining that it had remained incommunicative, and that the "..." and the "." she'd just had from it were the first hints that it even still existed since she'd plunged into the waterfall.

The khan and the dream wife let her speak uninterrupted. Both of them occasionally dropped into their unfocused look, as if they were trying to verify her story with the Unseen.

When Eloise finished, the khan drew a slow breath and nodded slowly. With a last check in with his connection to the Unseen, he said, "Yes. That was it. That was the thing you needed to tell us. And it's clear to me how we can help."

He looked at the dream wife and she nodded.

"How?" asked Eloise.

"The Us can help you facilitate your connection to the spark of something in the Star of Whatever."

"You can?"

"I believe we can," agreed the dream wife.

"Is that a good idea? It basically ate Melveeta the Elusive. She developed an affinity with it at Queen Gwendolyn's command, deployed a spell using it, and the Star of Whatever took over what remained of the broken pieces of her life and kept her alive and in pain for 200 years. I don't know that it can be trusted. And I don't know if anyone can be trusted with it."

"It's your choice, Princess Eloise," said the khan. The horse stood and drew himself into his most regal posture. "From what you've said, and from what I've gleaned from the gap-filled memories of the Us, the spell you described from Melveeta the Elusive on behalf of Gwendolyn the Irritable was rooted in jealousy, greed, anger, revenge, and hatred. There's no surprise the result was what it was.

"But hear this, young princess. I am Khan Nergüi Unbenannt Nimetuseta. It's my duty to the Us to connect to the Purity. And there's a reason we call it the Purity: what we touch is that which is purest in all the realms and in the Unseen worlds beyond. But it's more than that. It is purity that we must bring to our encounters with it. That purity in our being protects and guides us. It's a tool and an attitude." The khan indicated the dream wife with his chin. "We can guide you to experience the Purity. If you do so in connection to the Star of Whatever, it will almost certainly bring clarity to that which connects you to the stone and this spark of something of which you speak. Is it guaranteed? Of course not. Is there danger? There is always danger. But if I had a fear, my fear would be that if you didn't achieve that kind of clear communication, the real danger to you would lie in uncontrolled, untrained, and unguided interactions with it. If it would 'eat' you, it would be more likely to do so through your ignorance."

The dream wife raised her hand, and the khan nodded for her to speak. The old woman unfolded her legs and stood as straight and proud as her monarch. "Princess Eloise, this is what we know—what *I* know, what His Alacrity knows, and what the Us know. This is how we can provide the Light that which it desires. And how we can have the best chance to protect you from Melveeta the Elusive's unpleasant fate. Please grant us permission to do this."

"I see," said Eloise. They certainly seemed sincere in their desire to help, and confident in their ability to do so. There was no question she was nervous about the Star of Whatever. No, nervous was the wrong word. She was petrified of it. The thought of ending up enthralled to a force beyond her control for centuries, like Melveeta, or accidentally perpetrating a similar evil made Eloise want to fling the Star of Whatever into the Gööödeling Sea and run in the other direction.

But she wouldn't do that. It wasn't the right thing to do. Melveeta had given the Star to her. Had given it "unto" her. Like it or not, it was Eloise's responsibility. She thought through what the two of them had said, and something about their words clicked into place like long-lost pieces of a jigsaw puzzle. If there was a way to be able to control or communicate with the spark of something, and if she could do so reliably and safely, if there was the chance that she could avoid being consumed by it, then that was a chance she had to take.

Eloise stood up, shifted the Star of Whatever to her left hip, and curtsied as best she could wearing breeks and an outsized tunic. "Thank you, Khan Nergüi Unbenannt Nimetuseta. I would be grateful for your aid." She bowed slightly to the dream wife. "And for yours."

"Very good," said the khan. He turned to the herd rememberer. "Noted?"

"Noted, Your Alacrity," said the other horse. "It will be remembered for the Us."

"So, what do I need to do?" asked Eloise. "I hope it doesn't involve singing."

"No singing," the khan said. "But do you have any experience with prattleweed?"

UNPLEASANTNESSES

Eloise awoke lying on her side in an unfamiliar bed. Her surroundings were completely dark, and she suffered the same momentary waking disorientation she'd felt every day over the past weeks.

She ran through the mental routine she'd developed to help orient herself. Am I alive? (Yes, as far as she could tell.) Am I in danger? (Not obviously.) Is the Star of Whatever here? (She felt for it—yes, it was.) What realm am I in? (Not sure yet.) Are there marauding bandicoots nearby? (Again, not obviously.)

Eloise rolled onto her back, gasped at the pain, said something her mother would not have condoned, and rolled back to her side as everything rushed back in a flash—the fight with Turpy, Jerome, Lorch, the burns, the dream wife, the khan—all of it.

Including agreeing to that ceremony. Çalaht slandering slovenly, slimy, sluggards, what was she thinking? If her experience in the Southie devotional house was anything to go by, this was going to be an unmitigated disaster.

Eloise thought back to the end of the morning's discussion. The dream wife had cleared away the tea dishes after offering the khan a final few oat cakes, which he'd gobbled down. Then he'd said, "We'll need a few hours to prepare for the ceremony," and hobbled off to do whatever was on his agenda.

The dream wife had watched him go, then said, "It's been a long night for you. I suggest you get some sleep. It'll be another long night tonight."

The mention of sleep made Eloise stifle a yawn. "I'll go back to my friends and rest there."

"No," said the dream wife. "Stay here. In my tent. You should prepare for the ceremony in solitude. I'll send a messenger colt to your companions... Wait, no, I shall go myself. I can convey any messages for you and do so faithfully."

The thought of schlepping back to the others had made her feel even more tired, but she wanted to see Jerome. Needed to see him. "My champion is..."

"Will your champion not understand your need for rest and recuperation?"

She was right. He would. Reluctantly, Eloise agreed to stay.

Which is how she found herself in the dream wife's pitch-black tent wiping sleep from her eyes and wondering where she might go to have a private moment.

The tent flap opened briefly, revealing a late afternoon sky before the light disappeared as the dream wife slipped in and the flap closed behind her. "Ah, you're awake. Good," she said. "We'll be starting the ceremony once the moon rises two hooves' worth above the horizon, which will be a few hours, but we have some distance to cover first. I'd offer you something to eat, but it's best to approach the ceremony with an empty stomach, given what will likely happen. Do you need anything?"

"How are my friends?"

"The others? The human rests. The swelling in his leg appears to be lessening a little. The Not Us and the wombats send regards. The chatty one of the Not Us chats and chats with one of the guards she calls 'Uncle Dougie,' although his name here would not translate to anything close to that. The chipmunk—" She cracked the flap again. "The chipmunk is here."

Jerome eased into the tent. "Hello, Princess Eloise Hydra Gumball III."

Eloise sat up. "Hello, Champion Jerome Abernatheen de Chipmunk."

"Good to see you."

"Good to see you as well."

If the dream wife had not been there, Eloise would have scooped him up and given him a massive hug. But that didn't seem appropriate, so a moment of silence lingered. Instead of the hug, she asked, "How are you doing, Jeroboam?" She hoped her use of a nickname managed to convey, *Oh, Çalaht, I thought you were dead, and it must have been terrible, and I was worried sick.*

"It's not been a good few weeks. I'm hoping that's behind me now. How's your back, Eloigning?" She took that use of her nickname to mean, *Yes, it was miserable, and I hate that jester with all my might, but we can't really talk about that right now, can we?*

"Hurts, but it's better now that it's bandaged and treated." Which she hoped conveyed, *I've missed you.*

"That's good." Which she took as, *Me, too.*

She gave him a good-to-have-you-back wink.

He winked back.

There was another awkward pause. Despite the nicknames and the wink, this was definitely not the conversation Eloise wanted to have, or would have had if they'd been alone, or even with the others. She'd barely glimpsed him since his return, and they hadn't spoken about his time under Turpy's control. That seemed like forever ago, somehow, but it had only ended the night before.

Jerome cleared his throat. "So, are you really going to do this thing, Eluviation? Even with the vision herbs, the sweating, the vomiting, and the numerous other likely unpleasantnesses, just for a visit to the La La Realms?"

"Vision herbs? Sweating? Vomiting?" Eloise looked at the shadowy shape of the dream wife. "I haven't heard about any of that. What 'numerous other likely unpleasantnesses' are we referring to?"

"You've been asleep, or I would have explained," said the dream wife. "Besides, those are not the things to focus on. What you need to focus on is opening yourself up to Purity. The rest is externalities. This is all about internalities."

"Right," said Eloise. Her habits poked their heads up above her mental parapet and waved hello. She'd not been niggled by them recently because of being so busy, and then the pain and distraction of being burned. But she knew that her habits would have something to say about a night of sweating, vomiting, and "other likely unpleasantness-es." They'd go kicking and screaming.

Not good. Very not good. Eloise felt her heartbeat pulsing at her throat and starting to speed up. "I'll be fine," she said.

Jerome swallowed. "So will I."

Eloise looked at him through the darkness. "What do you mean, Jereed?"

Jerome nodded toward the dream wife. "I've been invited to partici-pate in the ceremony as well."

"Really?"

"Really."

"I have a knack with these things," said the old woman. "My sense is that your friend would be served by connecting to the Purity."

Eloise wasn't sure what risks this entailed, but Jerome had been through a lot, and she wasn't sure he was up for whatever it was. "To what ends?" she asked.

"To his own ends," said the dream wife.

"That's not an answer."

"No, it isn't," the old woman agreed. "But it will have to do."

"El, it's OK. I'm good," said Jerome. "Really."

"Are you sure?"

"Are you?"

"No. No, I'm not," said Eloise. "Not at all. Not the tiniest least bit sure. But I have the feeling that I need to, so I'm going to."

"Then we are the same amount of sure." Jerome walked over to Eloise and took her hand in his paws. "I also get the sense that whatever-it-is is something I need to do." He gave her hand a little squeeze. "Come on, El. We got this."

Eloise felt Jerome's delicate paws press her fingers. His presence calmed her. That did not happen very often. Usually, she was the one calming him (over and over and over). But Jerome wasn't running around the tent in a panic. If he could control himself, then she could control herself too.

She gave him a small squeeze back. "Right. OK." She nodded acceptance. It wasn't exactly convincing, but it would do.

The dream wife moved to her wooden chest, took out a small pouch, and let the lid close with a small thwump. "His Alacrity awaits us. Shall we go?"

"Hold on," said Eloise, standing. "You told me to prepare. I haven't prepared."

"That was a flexible instruction," said the dream wife, going back to the tent flap. "You slept. That will do. You needed the rest."

"Are you sure? You don't need me to do anything else?"

"Well, ideally, you'd have a few months to ready yourself for something like this. But we don't have that, so we'll just adjust."

"Right," said Eloise. "A few months."

"You'll be fine. The unpleasantnesses are unpleasant, but by no means fatal," said the old woman. "Please, we need to go, as I don't know how fast you can walk."

"Jer? What do you think?"

"Princess Eloise, I think we can handle any unpleasantnesses."

Eloise took a deep, steadying breath. "OK. You're right. I'm sure we can."

The dream wife picked up a folded blanket. "You may bring my blanket from the bed. The walk there will be cold. And of course, bring your box and that which resides within." She lifted the tent flap. "Shall we?"

Eloise stood, wrapped the blanket around her shoulders, picked up the Star of Whatever, and stepped out into the cooling evening air.

❧ 47 ❧

DRUNKEN PIEMAN SLICING

The three of them walked through the encampment in a direction Eloise had not been before. Horses of all ages and colors watched them pass. One or two of the foals gawped, but the rest kept their expressions stoic, even if their eyes betrayed curiosity. She wondered how often humans or chipmunks went among them.

From the look of it, not very often.

They appeared to be heading toward a cluster of hills that preceded a range of mountains that rose beyond. Eloise adjusted the blanket so the edge covered her head like a hood, and hugged it closer, careful not to pull on her bandages. The dusky clouds hung dark and low, looking like they were trying to decide between rain and snow.

The walk helped warm her up, but the word "unpleasantnesses" kept rattling around in her head, riling up her habits. The word was maddeningly vague. Were the unpleasantnesses physical? Emotional? Psychic? Generic? Specific? Her imagination, fueled by the nudges of her habits, began running scenarios: parts of her being cut or pierced, ritual burning or branding, forced facial tattooing, singing in front of others, or things coming out of places she'd rather they didn't in ways she couldn't control. All of those things could be classified as "unpleas-antnesses," and were things she would rather not have to endure. Espe-cially the singing. And the things coming out of her. But really, all of them, along with the hundreds of other possible unpleasantnesses she could conjure.

Eloise's breathing raced, her pulse sped, her guts clenched, and her mouth did a fair imitation of a desert. She knew herself well enough to know that tears and despair were likely not far behind as her mind raced to fill in the uncertainties with unmitigated disasters.

"Time to count," she said to herself. Eloise reached for the Çalahtist prayer beads Odmilla had given her, but of course, they weren't there. They were back in the dream wife's tent in her burned travel cloak. She thought about the burned spot and what might have been damaged. Not the beads, thank Çalaht. They were in a pocket nearer to the front. Eloise suddenly felt almost naked without her travel cloak. Burned or not, she would have felt better with it on.

Even without beads, it was definitely time to count. Eloise whispered the numbers under her breath. "Two, three, five, seven, eleven, thir-teen, seventeen, nineteen, twenty-three..."

She counted her steps, assigning each a sequential prime number, which she had to concentrate on remembering as they got larger. She also knew that when she got to 521, 523, and then 541, that would be the equivalent of 98, 99, and 100, and she could circle around and start over from two again. This gave her sets of 100 steps.

She could accumulate these using a pattern she once heard about called the Drunken Pieman's Slicing. That sequence came from the maximum number of servings, whether wedges or odd little chunks, that a drunken pieman could get slicing across a round pie if he didn't care how neat or messy the results were. Eloise imagined the pieman as a tall, skinny man with dark thinning hair and a mustache to make a walrus jealous, wearing a version of Chef's striped kitchen garb and wielding an overly large knife. She pictured him glassy-eyed from liquid consolation, stumbling into his shop and grabbing a steaming pie from the cooling rack—sometimes apple, sometimes boysenberry, sometimes brunchberry, sometimes pumpkin, sometimes pecan—and slicing away with drunken abandon.

One cut gave two servings. Two gave four. After that is when it started getting interesting, which Eloise knew because she'd contemplated this sequence over many breakfasts, making experimental cuts into griddle cakes. Three cuts could give seven pieces because it could have a little triangle bit in the middle. Four cuts gave eleven bits. Five yielded 16. Six could be made into 22 serves. And so on.

Johanna had thought Eloise's pancake-cutting obsession a little weird, especially when Eloise insisted on trimming the griddle cakes so they were as round as she could get them. Looking back, Eloise had to admit that might have been taking things a bit far. Still, she'd found it fascinating.

Between walking through prime numbers and then grouping them using the results of the drunken pieman's butchery, she managed to distract her habits enough that she no longer felt the need to run screaming for the horizon. It was a lot of mental work to avoid antici-pated, even wildly speculated, unpleasantnesses. But at least it worked.

Eventually, Eloise felt calm enough to notice her surroundings once again. The dream wife led them across the tundra, following a path that was sometimes there and sometimes not. Jerome walked ahead of Eloise, his manner contemplative, his steps methodical. There was no scamper at all in his movements. While Eloise had been off in the land of pies and primes, she'd fallen behind some 20 lengths. She picked up her pace to catch up.

From the look of the sky, it seemed they'd been hiking at least two hours—long enough for the moon, slightly waxed from the night before, to have heaved itself fully into the sky, where it lit the unfa-miliar trail. Eloise wasn't quite sure what constituted two hooves' worth, but it was two fingers high already. As night fell, the tempera-ture dropped, and the distant clouds, now closer, seemed to be deciding on snow.

They crested one hill, skirted another three, and then headed straight for the closest and smallest of the mountains. Before she knew it, the trail steepened and their walking tended toward climbing. If it got all the way to clamber, Eloise would have to figure out a way to tie the Star to herself so she'd have both hands free. But it wasn't that bad yet

Halfway up, Jerome broke their quiet. "Does this mountain have a name?"

"The savages and the Not Us call it Wretched Mountain. You will see why soon enough," replied the dream wife. "The Us know it better. They call it Mount Enigma. They know it for what it is."

Jerome tasted the name. "Mount Enigma. Moun-tuh En-ig-ma."

"That's a much better name than 'Wretched Mountain,'" said Eloise. "It isn't the mountain's fault if people have a problem with it."

The dream wife nodded. "The name alone is proof that sometimes it takes more than eyes to see what's in front of you."

"My mother says that," said Jerome. "All the time."

"Then she is wise," said the old woman. "Now, let's continue in silence. It's not much farther, but the last part requires focus and care. Here..." The dream wife waved Eloise toward her. She took the blanket from Eloise's shoulders, and had Eloise put the box with the Star of Whatever to her side. The old woman then made a swift set of folds and wraps that turned the blanket into a kind of cloak or snug poncho that encased Eloise's torso and head, but had the bottom tied tight so the Star of Whatever was held firmly in place.

"Interesting," said Eloise, testing the movement the arrangement allowed. "And comfortable. Perhaps you'll show me how to do that."

The dream wife nodded a smile, and they were off again.

The trail sloped upward, and Eloise felt the extra stress on her calves. The dream wife glided forward as if she did this all the time. Perhaps she did, or perhaps living with the equines, who were so much stronger and had so much more stamina than she did, had forced her to this level of fitness. But Eloise was less used to the strain on this particular set of muscles. That, and the press of the bandages bothering her, made her more fatigued than she felt she ought to be.

They topped a rise, and Eloise and Jerome both gasped. Before them was a blasted-out landscape of boulders and rubble, almost completely surrounded by a rock face that reminded Eloise of their open-air prison. Here, however, what should have been tundra was devoid of all apparent life. Not a plant nor a tree nor grass was visible anywhere. It was like Çalaht had gone into a rage and slammed her staff into the ground, leaving destruction.

"You should see it in daylight," whispered the dream wife. "The lichen and mosses share a blood-red tinge. It looks like the aftermath of a particularly gory battle. It's magnificent. And horrific." She pointed to a path. "We'll traverse along the edge. It's narrow, so mind your step. Trust me, you don't want to trigger a rock slip."

The three of them picked their way around boulders and across rocky debris toward the edge and picked up a near-invisible path that worked its way up and around. Eloise focused on stepping where the dream wife placed her feet, and was grateful to have both hands free to steady herself. The invisible path the old woman followed often canted dangerously toward the stony desolation below, and every pebble that loosened and tumbled away made Eloise worry that a rock slip would follow. Even Jerome, as light and agile as he was, slipped more than once on the treacherous trail.

Here, there was no need for counting.

They skirted the edge of Çalaht's wrath until they came a third of the way around to a cleft in the wall. It was just four lengths wide at the mouth, and revealed a steep incline leading inward. The dream wife turned and went into the cleft without looking back.

Up they went.

In one way, the going was easier since it lacked the loose rocks. In another, it was harder, since the incline was uncomfortably steeper than a walk, but not quite a climb—more like an awkward, onerous staircase, but lacking actual steps. Plus, it was much darker here, since the moonlight didn't peer down into the narrow slice between the cleft walls.

It occurred to Eloise that if the khan was waiting for them as the dream wife had said, then he must have already come this way. How could that possibly be? Did he limp to the top? If so, then he was incredibly tough, given that his leg seemed to cause him pain with every step. Or was he carried? If so, how did he stay on when going up this kind of slope? Did he clamp on with his teeth? Was he tied on somehow? The dream wife would be able to knot a rope. Or was there a different, easier path to get where they were going that didn't involve scaling this mountain that was indeed wretched?

Perhaps this torturous route was meant as some sort of test, perhaps a way to soften up the resolve of those who would undergo the ceremony she and Jerome were facing.

Eloise made her way higher and higher, ignoring the sweat that soaked through both her bandages and her shirt and dripped down her face. She dabbed her forehead with a dirt-covered sleeve and worried that, even with the blanket, she'd be chilled when they finally stopped.

That is, if they ever stopped.

Finally, Eloise glanced up and saw what looked like the top edge of the side walls. Above them, at the far end of the trail, an archway spanned the rock-lined corridor. Just in front of it, back-lit by a perfectly placed slice of moon, Khan Nergüi Unbenannt Nimetuseta stood waiting, his profile a silhouetted, calm majesty gazing at the starry sky.

Eloise, the dream wife, and Jerome climbed up toward him, stopping several paces away. The khan blinked like he was coming back from somewhere, turned his head, and motioned them forward. The dream wife stepped past her sovereign, walked so she stood under the arch of rough-chiseled stone, and turned to face the other three. The khan limped a quarter circle so that he, too, was looking uphill at her.

The dream wife closed her eyes, breathed deeply, waited a few moments, then opened them again and began speaking. "You have arrived, coming of your own free will. Is this true?" Her voice had the singsong of ritual.

"Yes, this is true," said the khan. At his nod, Eloise and Jerome said the same thing.

"You would seek to touch the Purity?" asked the old woman.

"Yes," they all said.

"Then let us start and let us all be worthy of that which the Purity will grant us." She turned and walked the rest of the way through the arch. "You may follow."

Saying nothing, the khan limped after her.

Eloise cleared her throat to catch Jerome's attention. She raised an eyebrow at him—one last are-we-sure-this-is-a-good-idea? look.

Jerome shrugged a silent you-don't-have-to-do-this-if-you-don't-want-especially-after-the-way-you-embarrassed-yourself-in-The-South-with-the-Southie-queen-at-the-devotional-house look.

Eloise shrugged back a you're-right-I-didn't-exactly-cover-myself-with-glory-but-there's-something-here-that-feels-unfinished look.

Jerome nodded a yeah-that's-what-I'm-feeling-too-also-how-did-he-get-up-here-with-a-leg-like-that reply.

Eloise nodded back an I-was-wondering-about-that-too-and-I-really-hope-this-is-not-a-stupid-idea look.

Jerome furrowed his brow with an are-we-going-to-stand-here-exchanging-looks? look.

Eloise didn't reply to that. Instead, she took a deep breath and stepped through the stone archway.

❧ 48 ❧

MAY YOU BE CLEANSED

Stepping through the archway was like walking into the underworld. The area, just 20 lengths across, was shaped like a round, roofless, stone yurt. The smell of sulfur assaulted Eloise, and all around her steam drifted up through cracks in the ground. In the very center of the space, something glowed orange-red. The dream wife and the khan walked them toward it, and Eloise saw it was a pool of molten earth—exposed, threatening, bubbles popping in slow motion. The heat of it warmed her instantly, and its light brushed everything with an eerie, amaranth glow. It was like they'd brought her to the exact spot that gave the Central Ranges its nickname of the Central Carbuncle.

Four carmine-red blankets lay in a semi-circle near the lava pool. One of them had a smaller square of material in the middle, an intricately woven ceremonial cloth with wide bands of a deep red the color of the tundra plants, narrow bands of mantis green, and thin lines of pink and yellow. In the middle of the cloth sat two decorated clay pots. One was the size of a blood orange and sealed with wax, while the other was open-lidded and as big as an overly enthusiastic potato. There was a twig with small, red, furry leaves, and next to that, a long-handled spoon, like something used to stir a very small pot from a long way away, or perhaps to look down a flamingo's throat.

A rustle came from a dim corner. Standing next to what looked like an odd pile of neatly-stacked cleaning supplies was the herd rememberer. He stepped forward and sat on the rightmost blanket, curling his legs under him. Gone was most of the nervousness Eloise had seen in him previously. His eyes looked more focused and sharp. It seemed that in this place of sulfur and steam, he felt more comfortable in his role as herd rememberer. The horse sat with just a little fidgeting, ready to notice everything and remember it for the Us.

The dream wife eased down onto the blanket with the ceremonial spread. She sat on her knees, her back straight. The khan lowered himself onto one of the simple blankets to her left and faced the fiery pit.

"Sit," said the dream wife, waving Eloise and Jerome to the blanket on the left of the khan.

Eloise sat on her knees in an imitation of the dream wife. She placed the Star of Whatever so that it was touching her hip and away from the others. Following the khan's lead, she let her gaze rest on the glowing hole. Jerome, his face serious and his expression closed, settled on the other side of the blanket, closer to the equine monarch.

The khan looked at Eloise and Jerome. "The way of the Us is the path of fire," he said. "To touch the Purity is to sear away all that is false and burn off any pretension. To touch the Purity is to expose one's self to the heat of truth, and to see what that blaze scorches away and what truth it leaves behind."

There was a swirl of something above the khan's head.

Snow.

Specks of it fluttered down, but the heat coming from the pit and the steam from the cracks warded it off, dissipating it before it could settle. Eloise worried what this might mean for their walk back. It would be colder and even more treacherous than the journey there.

But first, there was this ceremony to get through.

The dream wife lifted her arms to the side, palms upward, and began chanting in the ancient horse tongue. The khan closed his eyes and joined in. When the horse herd had used their language for their greeting the day before, it had sounded severe, guttural, and aggressive. Now, as their chant blossomed into a song, that harshness fell away. Eloise still had no idea what the words meant, but from their tone and manner, it sounded like they were calling down the sacred and imploring the Unseen to come to them. Eloise closed her eyes and quietly, self-consciously, added her humming to their sung invocation. Jerome did the same.

When the song finished, the old woman picked up the long-handled spoon. "I ask for the gift of fire so we may honor the air." She leaned low and reached the spoon toward the hole, scooped up a small blob of the molten earth, and dropped it in the open pot. Whatever was in there burst into flame. The dream wife let it burn for a second, then with a sharp puff, blew it out, producing billows of smoke. She held the pot in both hands, lifting it first toward the pit and then toward the sky. "I call on the spirits of sage, of thyme, of eucalyptus, and of wormwood. May your blessings be upon us. With your smoke, we honor the air around us, and cleanse ourselves so that we may be ready to meet with the Purity."

The old woman took the smoldering pot and stood in front of the khan. She lowered it so it was in front of his face, and he stretched his neck forward to mingle with the smoke. The dream wife then circled him widdershins four times, waving wafts of smoke over him. When she'd finished, she stopped at his front, bowed, and said, "May thee be cleansed and free of attachments and desires as thee approach the Purity. May thy connection bring all that is good to the Us."

"So be it," said the khan.

"So be it," echoed the dream wife.

She stood before Eloise. The old woman did not bow, but held the pot forward. Eloise leaned into the smoke and focused on the smell—

earthy, acrid, peaty, and sweet, all at once. The dream wife circled her, bathing Eloise in the smoke. After the fourth circuit, she stopped in front of Eloise and said, "May thee be cleansed and free of attachments and desires as thee approach the Purity. May thy connection be clear, and thy insights profound."

"So be it," said Eloise.

"So be it," said the dream wife.

She then repeated the smoking with Jerome, saying, when she was done, "May thee be cleansed and free of attachments and desires as thee approach the Purity. May thy connection open up that which lies dormant within thee for the good of all involved."

"So be it," said Jerome.

"So be it," replied the dream wife.

The old woman then walked over to the fiery opening in the earth, getting much closer than Eloise thought was safe. She poured out a palmful of the smoldering contents into her hand, held it up to the sky, then sprinkled it into the pit. The plant fragments sparked and danced, igniting and disappearing in a shower of tiny flares. She put a palm on either side of the pot and bowed toward the place of the rising sun and then in each of the other cardinal directions, as well as earthward and skyward. With a last bow toward the heat of the earth, the dream wife put the smoldering pot back down on the ceremonial cloth.

Eloise noted that the dream wife had not included the herd rememberer in the smoking ritual. His role was strictly as an observer, not a participant, and he did not seem perturbed by this.

Next, the dream wife picked up the twig and plucked five of its crimson leaves. She made a small fan of them and then, as she had with the pot, she bowed with them to the four directions, the earth and the sky. The first leaf she gave to the lava pit. The second she put in her mouth. The third she gave to the khan, who also took it into his mouth. She moved to Eloise and Jerome, opened her mouth, lifted her tongue, and showed the leaf there. "This is minder leaf. It prepares you to be mindful," she lisped. "Don't swallow. Anything. Spit when I say."

Eloise took her leaf and placed it under her tongue, hoping it wasn't toxic. Or unwashed. She wasn't sure which would be worse.

For the chipmunk, the dream wife tore a small corner from the leaf and only gave him that, saying, "We need to be careful because of your size."

Jerome nodded, took the fragment, and popped it in his mouth. The dream wife went back to her blanket.

The four of them sat there facing the glow, letting the leaf do whatever it was supposed to do.

It slowly filled Eloise's mouth with a dull bitterness, not unlike the taste of a bad almond. Unpleasant, but tolerable. Then a tingling spread from below her tongue, up her cheeks to the roof of her mouth. Also unpleasant, but nothing to complain about. If these were the "unpleasantnesses," she'd be OK.

Eloise's mouth trickled, then flooded with saliva, pooling and gathering. It teased, then threatened to either go down her throat or dribble out of her closed mouth. The tingling grew into a fizzing, then a full-on buzzing of her entire mouth. It vaguely reminded her of the sensations she'd felt during the Thorning Ceremony—there was that same sense of discomfort that had to be endured.

When Eloise thought she couldn't take it anymore, the dream wife finally stood, walked toward the lava, and spat—once, twice, thrice. The leaf and spit sizzled and spluttered into the heat of the open earth.

Next, the khan did the same, approaching the hole with his awkward gait, and then expectorating leaf and saliva. "May the Purity find me worthy," he muttered, his words less distinct than they had been before. He must have a similar mouth buzz going on.

Relieved to be rid of the thing, Eloise stood and made her way toward the hole. Its heat pushed back at her, and when she spat, it consumed the globule in a hissing instant. "May the Purity find me worthy," she slurred in a whisper.

Jerome was next, but he just sat there, eyes closed, his face pulled into a tight grin like he was trying not to laugh. The dream wife waited a full minute for him, and then another. Her expression went from patience to curiosity. Eventually, she looked at Eloise and nodded for her to do something.

Eloise leaned over. "Jerome?"

No response.

"Jer? Are you OK?" She poked his shoulder gently.

The chipmunk jerked upward and his eyes shot open. "El! This. Is. Amazing!" Jerome slurred through a mouthful of drool. "Did you feel that? All the tingling? What mouth feel! And the taste! The subtle flavors of the leaf! Did you catch the oak-filled base notes slipping in and around the tinge of bitterness? And the top note of persimmon? Sublime. Just sublime."

Jerome suddenly looked around, remembered where he was, and clapped a paw over his mouth. "Sorry. Sorry, sorry, sorry." He mastered his features into a neutral expression.

Everyone waited for him.

"It's your turn," Eloise said to him quietly.

"My turn to what?" asked Jerome.

"You really missed it?"

"What did I miss?" Jerome glanced around. "Surely I didn't miss anything."

"You're supposed to spit into the pit."

"Spit. In the pit. Really?"

"Yep."

"And you did that?"

"Yes."

"Isn't that unsanitary?"

"Just do it."

"Right. Right, right, right." Jerome stood with attempted dignity, strode toward the pool of molten earth, drew his head back, and hoicked out the biggest chipmunk loogie in the history of all the realms. Where the saliva from the others had dissipated in the air above the heat, Jerome's leafy expectoration splatted wet and phlegmy against the surface, then skidded along in a little ball like a stone skipped on a lake. It sizzled until it had evaporated into nothingness.

The others looked at him.

"What?" said Jerome. "Did I do something wrong?"

"No," whispered Eloise. "It was impressive. You just need to do it two more times."

"Spit twice more."

"Yes."

Jerome turned to the pit and with great seriousness, spat twice more into the hole. These spits weren't as impressive as his first try, but they still had a drama to them. He turned back to Eloise.

"That OK?"

"Sure. That's fine. Now you say, 'May the Purity find me worthy.'"

The chipmunk drew to his full height, threw his arms wide, and declaimed as if to an auditorium, "May the Purity find me worthy."

It jangled against the solemnity of the moment. Again, the others looked at him.

"Now what?" he said.

"You're not reading the room," said Eloise.

"Oh."

"Would you like to sit back down?" said the dream wife.

"Sure. Of course." Jerome resumed his spot on the blanket.

"And maybe stay with us this time?" she added.

"Right. Right, right, right. Sorry."

❦ 49 ❦

MELVEETA'S ADMONITIONS

The old woman picked up the second pot and opened its wax seal. The aroma blossoming out was both familiar and mysterious. Clove dominated, but it was mixed with something vaguely mentholated, and there was an astringency to it as well. The dream wife stood and bowed with the pot, as she had with the smoking bowl and the leaves. "May these vision herbs guide thee to the Purity," she said. "May this sacred mix bring truth and insight."

She knelt in front of the khan, pinched a wad of the plant matter and held it up for him. He opened his mouth, took the herbs, and neither chewed nor swallowed.

"May thee find thy way to the Purity," said the dream wife. "May the Purity find thee a worthy representative of the Us."

The khan nodded, then lay down on his blanket. Within moments, his breathing slowed, his tongue lolled, and he seemed to have gone to the La La Realms.

The dream wife sat in front of Eloise. "Are you ready?"

"I think so." Eloise pointed at the pot. "May I ask what's in there?"

"The contents of the vision herbs is not something that is normally shared, certainly not outside the Us."

"Right," said Eloise. "It's just that it's possible I'm a bit sensitive to things."

The dream wife cocked her head, considering. "I would not recommend trying to replicate this just from a list of ingredients, Princess," said the old woman. "The proportions matter. Greatly."

"I won't be trying to replicate anything, I don't think. In fact, I give you my word that I won't."

"So be it." She tilted the pot so Eloise could see inside. "There are shavings of seeker's root. Some crushed, dried leaf from the mage's mire tree. There's an element of prattleweed, but not the seed, as we mentioned. Petals from a howler flower. Petals from the blossom of the agnostic's mistake. Petals from a heretic's blindness rose—the yellow ones, not pink or white. There's shredded bark of the wanderer's revelation bush. Plus, I add some mandarin zest for flavor."

"That sounds like it would blow the back of your head off," whispered Jerome.

"It could," the dream wife said. "Touching the Purity is not a game, and not without danger. There are those who seek to touch the Purity and do not come back, or who come back changed in a way that marks them for the rest of their lives. Make no mistake, this act has consequences, especially if done incorrectly." She looked back at Eloise. "You may back away now, should you feel it too unsafe or risky, or if you feel you are unworthy or unable to proceed. A spiritual journey like this, even under guidance like mine, is a choice. *Your* choice. The Us never force it upon anyone. Do you understand?"

Eloise nodded.

"Do you wish to stop?"

Eloise wanted to yell, "Of course I want to stop. This kind of thing is not me at all. This is a bad, bad, bad idea. Pass! Hard pass!" But she didn't.

That would have been fear speaking. Fear and her habits, who didn't like straying into such territory.

Beneath it, Eloise truly wasn't convinced that this was a good idea. She certainly didn't want to make a fool of herself the way she had in The South.

But it was more than that. She had seen what the Star of Whatever had done to Gwendolyn's champion. Melveeta's last words had been unequivocal: "Do not let it eat you the way it ate me. Speak to no one of it, and find a way to make sure it is never, ever, ever used again."

Eloise had broken the Don't Speak About It rule more than once. She could live with that. And she was positive she didn't want to be eaten by the thing and end up a desiccated husk like Gwendolyn the Irritable's champion. And if this ceremony was going to open her up to the Star of Whatever, wouldn't that make her more vulnerable to its caprices?

Without question.

And that made her nervous. Very, very nervous.

But...

There was always a "but."

But if she was to follow Melveeta's third admonition—to keep it from doing harm again—Eloise felt at the core of her soul that she had to somehow get to know it, to become familiar with how it worked. She needed to understand it, or to at least divine what made it tick, tock, ting, and tong.

Without that, she'd only have Melveeta's retelling to go on.

And that wasn't enough. Not at all, if for no other reason than Melveeta had proven unreliable at best.

When it came to the Star of Whatever, Eloise needed a truer kind of knowing if she was to guard against its misuse.

Eloise looked down at the box holding the stone and the green glow emanating through the crack. She realized there was something else going on that she had to admit: she *wanted* to know how the Star of Whatever worked. She wanted to understand the magic behind it, magic that had faded from the realms since Back When. Melveeta had brought her into her Purple Haze spell, which had given Eloise a direct sense of what magic could do, and what it felt like.

And she wanted to experience that more.

This desire to engage with strong magic scared her more than anything else—more than any unpleasantnesses that her habits feared, more than touching the Purity itself or whatever else this ceremony would entail. She feared being lured into it, corrupted by it, or lulled by it. She feared somehow unleashing something she had no idea how to control, channel, or turn off. She feared what temptations might be revealed. And she feared not being up to the task.

It wasn't like there was anyone she could turn to for knowledge or help. None of the mages these days would have more than a theoretical understanding of strong magic. They'd be ignorant of what the Star of Whatever might or might not be able to do, and would, at best, possibly find some dust-encrusted scrolls that might relate.

No, they'd be worse—they'd be "learned." "Curious." "Fascinated." They'd want to conduct studies, poke and prod the thing, and undertake tests. It would be all mind and no heart, and certainly wouldn't come from a place of experience.

The mages would be no help at all.

She'd be on her own.

Well, so be it. She knew better than anyone alive what the Star of Whatever was capable of—or maybe it was the spark of something within it that was the issue. One or the other. Or both.

And that, right there, was the problem. It (or they) had to be neutralized, but to do that, she needed to know more about it (or them). If this ceremony could help achieve that, then she knew what she had to do.

Eloise straightened and saw that the dream wife was looking at her curiously, still waiting for some sort of response. "Yes," said Eloise. "I'd like to continue."

"So be it." The dream wife looked Eloise up and down as if assessing her size. She measured a careful wad of the herb mix that was somewhat larger than what she'd given the khan. "This stays in your cheek as long as you can stand it. Then swallow when you must. Clear?"

"Clear." Eloise opened her mouth and took the vision herbs. They tasted much as they smelled—clove, menthol, a touch of anise, the mandarin the dream wife had mentioned, and something that reminded her of an ill-tempered lemon. Eloise used her tongue to tuck the wad between her left cheek and gums. It reminded her of Commodore Stúüùbing, the alpaca who had taken them from Port Port to Haze Town on the *Barco del Amor*. He always had a chaw of something in his mouth, and was forever spritzing little streams of goop overboard.

"May thee find thy way to the Purity," said the dream wife. "May the Purity find thee a worthy receptacle for truth."

Eloise nodded a thank you.

"Please lie down on your side," said the dream wife. "Place your box as close to you as you can. Keep contact with it if you can."

Eloise stretched out on her left, facing Jerome. She slid the box with the Star of Whatever beneath her head like a pillow, which seemed as good a spot as any. The polished wood felt smooth against her cheek.

The dream wife adjusted her position so that she was in front of Jerome. "You heard all of that?" she asked.

Jerome nodded.

Now the old woman looked Jerome up and down. "As before, we need to be careful. I've not acted as the dream wife for one of your size and species before. I'll err on the side of caution, as we can always add a little more if needed."

Again, Jerome nodded.

The dream wife pinched out the tiniest speck of the herb mix. Jerome opened his mouth and she dropped the meager portion onto his tongue, which Jerome then retracted. He closed his eyes like a sommelier considering an unfamiliar vintage.

The old woman bowed with the pot toward him. "May the Purity find—"

Jerome flopped over backwards, splatting on the blanket, arms and feet pointed to the sky. Eloise sat halfway up as the dream wife leaned forward to see if he was OK. He was breathing and had a stupid grin pasted across his face. The dream wife gently prodded him with her pinky. He responded just enough to mumble something about "tannins" and "*terroir*." Then he dropped mind-numb into the La La Realms and was gone.

The old woman shook her head slowly and said to Eloise, "He should be alright. Lay back down." She lifted the bowl toward Jerome's inert body and said, somewhat perfunctorily, "May thee find thy way to the Purity. May the Purity find thee a worthy receptacle for truth." And then added, "Good luck with that."

Eloise lay back down. She wasn't feeling anything at all. The buzz of the crimson leaf had faded, and the vision herbs just seemed to produce drool. Perhaps you had to be somewhat susceptible to them for them to work, and maybe she wasn't.

If nothing was going to happen, this would be a long, boring night.

Or maybe she'd just fall asleep. She yawned, trying to keep her mouth closed.

50

ACCORD

Eloise heard something that sounded like code.

Tap-tap-tap.

Pause.

Rap-rap, rap-rap, rap-rap.

Perhaps a signal between conspirators?

She opened her eyes.

Eloise sat among stacked sacks of potatoes in a room off the kitchen at Castle de Brague. It seemed to be part pantry, part scullery, part root cellar, and part staging area for rubbish—which made neither functional nor hygienic sense. Nor did it look like any room she'd ever seen.

Dream logic, Eloise thought. *And stupid dream logic, at that.*

Tap-tap-tap.

Pause.

Rap-rap, rap-rap, rap-rap.

The sound came from behind her. She stood, careful not to topple any of the potato sacks or piles of dishes.

Tap-tap-tap.

Pause.

Rap-rap, rap-rap, rap-rap.

Not behind her. Beneath her.

A trapdoor, half obscured by bags of potatoes.

Eloise hauled half a dozen sacks out of the way, grasped a rusted iron ring and pulled. The door budged, but was heavy, like it wasn't meant for frequent use. She planted her feet, grabbed the ring with both hands, and hauled upward. The door lifted grudgingly. Careful not to let it flop down, she opened it as far as it would go in the cramped space, resting it on three full sacks, one of which was labeled "Yams R Us." A second read "ProTuberAnces," and the third was hand-lettered with "Dictaters." The accompanying motto was "You will eat these spuds and you will like it."

The trapdoor revealed a well-lit staircase guarded by oversized brown mice as large as corgis. They wore chain mail, gauntlets, and snarls, and pointed their drawn swords at her.

"Pardon me," said Eloise, stepping carefully into the stairwell. "I think I need to go this way."

"Thee shall no pass!" screeched the brownest of them.

"Thee shall no pass!" echoed the others.

"Why ever not?"

The screechy mouse opened his mouth to say something, but didn't seem sure what. "Because!" he shouted.

"Because!" shouted the rest.

"Please?"

The corgi-mice wavered, glancing nervously at each other.

"She said 'please,'" whispered a light-brown one at the back, shaking like he'd seen the shadow of a demon. His sword-nicked ear and whiskers, which bent at right angles, trembled. "Politeness! What do we do?"

"It's a trick!" yelled Screechy. "Just you wait! Any moment now she'll be trying…" He paused, barely able to bring himself to say the next word. "Kindness!"

The other corgi-mice gasped and quivered their swords in her direction.

"That's, that's unthinkable!" cried Ear Nick.

"You seem like such nice people," said Eloise. "I'd be most grateful if I could go past."

More gasps. Two of them dropped their swords and ran away into the darkness in tears.

"I like your uniforms," said Eloise.

"Hold steady," commanded Screechy. "She doesn't really mean it. Keep your nerve."

The remaining mice bunched closer for safety, still blocking the way.

"Ten-hut!" boomed a voice from lower down. The too-big mice snapped to attention, swords still pointing at Eloise. A long-eared hare hopped up the stairs from below. He wore epaulettes, a pinz nez, a fez, and nothing else, and leaned forward to squint through his glasses at Eloise. "So, you finally heard," he said.

"Heard?" said Eloise.

He did the *tap-tap, rap-rap-rap* pattern on his noggin. It thocked on his skull like a hollow log. "Heard that."

"Yes, I heard it."

"Like I said, 'finally.'" The hare puffed his chest and waved back the mice. "Quickly, now. Go on down," he said to Eloise. "He will be ready to speak when you arrive."

"Thank you." Eloise stepped past the mice. "Nice to meet you all."

They gasped one last time and let her pass.

Down the staircase she went, descending into a profound darkness. The steps felt rough-hewn beneath her feet, and she guided and steadied herself by touching the wall with her right hand, its surface changing from dirt to stone, sometimes dry, sometimes damp, often unexpectedly slimy. At first, the smell was earthy and loamy, but that gave way to dust, mold, and dankness.

Every now and again, the *tap-tap, rap-rap-rap* would echo up from below. It kept her going. This felt unlike any dream she'd ever had—too real, too present, too linear.

After going down a lifetime of steps, Eloise saw a glow of light small enough for her to wonder if her eyes were playing tricks on her. But it grew brighter as she drew closer, until the stairs flattened out into a green-lit chamber slightly larger than the pantry/scullery/root cellar where she'd started.

Eloise knew who she'd find at the end of it—the spark of something in the Star of Whatever. She walked carefully toward the brightest point of light until she saw the being.

There he was.

Eloise always did her best not to judge other species by their looks. For one, having an overly human-centric frame of reference was inappropriate. She would have to deal with a variety of people (both human and non-human) if and when she became queen, and her mother always said that looking at things through eyes that were too human was a handicap. For another, from her discussions with other species and from what she'd learned in her Peoples and Populations lessons, beauty was very much in the eye of the beholder. She might not care for the look of a proboscis monkey's nose, but to them, the bigger the hooter the better. She might think a red-lipped batfish's lips, a shoe-bill's beak, or a blobfish's blobs were weirdly red, too shoe-like, or overly blobby. But if she'd learned anything it was that attractiveness came in many, many, many, many forms, and the heart craved what the heart craved. A huge honking nose, creepily red lips, a massive, shoe-like beak, or a body that was basically an ill-formed gelatinous blob would ring *someone's* bell.

She understood all that.

But she couldn't help herself. By Çalaht's missing back molars, this was the ugliest creature she'd ever met.

The look of him, even in this dim, strangely green light, stopped her where she was. He was vaguely shaped like a mole, but hairless, about ten weak lengths long, and squinty-eyed, like his kind never saw light. His legs were thin and short, and his bare tail looked like an afterthought—not stumpy, but more like a pinky to one's thumb. Most prominent were his front teeth. Four massive incisors, two above and two below, protruded like a beaver's nightmare, as if he had to chew his way to get anywhere.

He thumped his strange pinky tail on a crystalline floor, and the chamber filled with the *tap-tap, rap-rap-rap* sound.

He'd been the source of it. He was the one she was supposed to see.

"What?" he said to her. "I can feel you looking at me. What's the matter?"

"Nothing. Nothing's the matter."

"Haven't you seen a naked mole-rat before? You were expecting a kitten down here? Or maybe one of those baby pygmy hippos everyone always 'oohs' and 'ahs' at? Perhaps a wee red panda or a cute little meerkat pup?"

"No, not at all," she said. "Of course not."

"Then stop staring."

"Right. Sorry," Eloise said. "Didn't mean to offend."

If this was supposed to be the Purity, his manner did not strike her as particularly pure.

"My name is Eloise."

"We've met."

"We have?"

The naked mole-rat looked at her, or at least in her direction.

"Right, we have," said Eloise, knowing he meant their several punctuation-short communications. They were certainly nothing like this. But presumably, that was the point. "Do you have a name?"

The naked mole-rat clacked his huge front teeth together in thought. "What do you call me?"

"I think of you as the spark of something in the Star of Whatever." It felt weird saying the words out loud.

"Call me Sparky, then."

"Sparky?"

"Is there a problem with 'Sparky?'"

"Not at all."

"You weren't traumatized as a child by someone named Sparky?"

"No. I don't think I've ever met a 'Sparky' before."

"Then Sparky it is."

"Right," said Eloise.

"And what should I call you?"

"How about my name? Eloise?"

"No, if I'm going to have a nickname, you should have one as well. How about 'Weezy?'"

"What? No!"

"Lizzie."

"No."

"Lola."

"Huh-uh."

"Ellie."

"No. Not that, or 'El.' A friend calls me those. I'd rather not mix the two."

"Lisa?"

"No."

"Elpfundri."

"Where did that come from?"

"Dunno. Aloyse?"

"Pass."

"Running out of ideas here. It's down to 'Weezy' and 'Loulou.' Your call."

"Neither, thank you."

"Loulou, then. That's it, I'm calling you Loulou."

"I'd rather you didn't."

"Loulou it is. Done."

They stood there, looking at each other.

She had no idea what to do next, so she just stood there. The mole-rat didn't seem inclined to help her. He scratched at his armpits using his strangely long teeth. Doing this caused him to involuntarily thump his tail in the *tap-tap, rap-rap-rap* pattern.

It was disconcerting to know where it came from.

Eloise sat down on the chamber floor so she was closer to his eye level. "I'd like to come to an accord."

"Why?"

"I'd like us to get along."

"Again, why?"

The real answer was that she thought the Star of Whatever was the most dangerous thing in in all the realms, but it seemed impolite to put it that way. "You have a lot of potential inside you. I think that it would be good if that potential was not used as it was in the past two centuries."

"Yeah, that one was a doozy."

"A 'doozy?' That's what you call killing thousands and ruining half a realm? A 'doozy?'"

"Not to mention absorbing almost all the magic in all the realms. I think that qualifies as a 'doozy.'"

"So you're aware of that? You know what you've done?"

"Not as such," said the naked mole-rat, who had stopped scratching and now gave Eloise his full attention. "While you're here, in this place and in this manner, I have enough of a connection with you to be able to see into your thoughts and memories. I got it from you."

"I see."

"I must say, this works much better than you trying to connect through your dreams. Does the fifth Earl of Upper Psyllium really dance such a bad gavotte?"

"I wouldn't know. He died half a century ago."

"Your dreams are yammering word salad."

"Sorry."

"The other one was the same."

"Other one?"

"The one you called Melveeta. She kept dreaming of wart cream. Who dreams of wart cream? Or medicaments in general?"

"Thrilling."

"Exceptionally." The naked mole-rat sat down in front of her, mimicking her posture. "Before we enter into any kind of 'accord' there's a change you need to make."

"Change?" asked Eloise. "What kind of change?"

"You have to stop thinking of me as stupid."

"I don't think you're stupid."

"Don't lie. You do. You think of me that way because my ability to communicate with your world, the 'outside' world, is limited to what you perceive as single pulses. You think I'm being chatty if I manage to send you something as complex as '!?!'. Yours is a bias toward verbal expression. Not everyone is good at that, and that doesn't mean they're stupid."

It was true. She'd thought of the spark of something in the Star of Whatever as some sort of idiot savant at best. If Sparky was an accurate representation of the Star's true essence, she'd been wrong.

"So be it," Eloise said. "If this is who you are, and not some bizarre vision-herbs-inspired mind trickery, then I'll freely acknowledge, and let go of, my bias."

"That will do," said Sparky. "What terms do you propose?"

"Terms." Eloise hadn't thought that far ahead. "We're going to negotiate terms?"

"Isn't that what accords are about? Terms and behaviors? Agreements and outcomes?"

"Let's start with behaviors," said Eloise. "I propose a few things. First, and foremost, I demand that you do no harm. Not to me, not to my friends or family, not to anyone."

"Sorry," said the mole-rat. "That one's off the table."

"Why?"

"It is like demanding that a knife never cut. A knife can cut for good, cut for bad, or cut neutrally. But which of those a particular cut is depends on your perspective. Are you cutting a carrot? The carrot might not like it. Are you waging war? If you cut your enemy, is that for good or ill? Even your Melveeta, who cast that doozy of a spell in anger and pain, a spell I amplified according to her unspoken wishes—even her spell was created in service to her monarch. Your Melveeta thought she was helping her queen."

"Interesting," said Eloise. "And yet healers are able to take on a vow of 'First, do no harm.'"

"True," said the mole-rat. "But they don't say that to their scalpels. They say it to their fellow healers."

"So you're more the scalpel than the person."

"Close enough. Care for some tuber?" The mole-rat produced a large chunk of some indeterminate tuber and offered it to her.

"Thanks so much, but I might pass," said Eloise.

"Your loss." Sparky gnawed at the tuber.

Eloise saw that he could move his front teeth independently, spreading them and closing them at will, which she found particularly creepy. Whatever she'd expected from touching the Purity, it would never in a thousand years have been watching a naked mole-rat's odd teeth attacking an oversized tuber.

"OK, terms," said Eloise. "And let's be frank, shall we? Melveeta warned me not to let you 'eat me.' I do not wish to be tethered to a spell, wanted or unwanted, for any amount of time, much less a couple of centuries."

"Agreed," said Sparky. "But let me tell you something about your Melveeta. She *wanted* to be part of that spell. She was casting it with every fiber of her being. She wanted it to be as powerful and as enduring as she could make it, and she gave herself fully to it. I simply did what she bade me to do. If you don't do that, I won't do that."

"Fair enough. Next, I ask that you provide me guidance, should I be in a circumstance that requires it, especially when it comes to any magic that involves you."

"I can live with that, with the caveat of, 'To the best of my ability given the circumstances involved.' It's not like I'm watching the outside world and thinking about it all the time. You keep me in a box. My ability to communicate is limited. My options for acting in any particular moment are likewise limited. Even this…" he indicated his mole-rat body, "… is a construct. A fiction created to facilitate this wee interaction of ours. So, I agree to a best efforts stance on this point."

Eloise scratched the back of her hand, thinking. "OK. How about communication? Can we communicate more than we have until now? Can you be more verbal in a way that works better for me, now that you know me somewhat?"

"Possibly. This bridge between us will linger. We might be able to foster it. I'll certainly try if it helps me avoid dreams of that stupid earl gavotting."

"I think that covers it, then," said Eloise.

"I have terms," said Sparky.

"Oh?" Eloise couldn't imagine what he could want. "Go ahead. I'm listening."

"You don't just get rid of me. You don't just bury me in a hole or chuck me in a ravine, never to be seen again. You accept that there is, as you've said, a spark of something inside the Star of Whatever. You are the Light Bearer. You shall bear the Light."

That sounded a lot like being stuck with him. Possibly forever.

"Best efforts," said Eloise. "And subject to change, but with consultation, if at all possible."

"No. Not good enough. Too waffly."

Eloise didn't like this limitation of her options, but wasn't sure what she could do about it. Probably nothing. "Fine," she said. "I agree."

"Good." The mole-rat chewed a bit more tuber. "Next, you take me out of that blasted box a little more often."

"You want me to agree to cast spells? I can't do that."

"No, that's not what I'm talking about. That blasted little box is boring. I had all that work I got to do for all those years. Now? Nothing. It doesn't have to be constant. Just so I'm not cooped up all the time."

"Fine. Agreed, if I can work out how the thing opens and closes reliably."

"Good enough." The naked mole-rat took a couple of steps closer. "Here's the big one."

"Yes?"

"Our agreement is between us. You and me. It is non-transferable and non-inheritable. If I encounter one who is not you, especially without prior discussion and consent, all terms of this accord are suspended in the first instance, and terminated if it is clear there's been a breach."

"You're saying you have to stay with me for this agreement to apply?"

"Yes. Until some other future accord is reached. I won't be handed around like a bauble."

Eloise sighed. That meant no giving him to her mother or one of the more learned mages. Well, realistically, she'd already come to that conclusion. "Agreed."

The naked mole-rat extended his strange little hairless front paw. Eloise took it between her index finger and thumb.

"Loulou, we have an accord," said Sparky.

"Yes, Sparky, we have an accord," agreed Eloise.

51

SOAP

J erome blinked to awareness and found his feet dangling in the air. He was being carried by the scruff of his neck toward a barrel full of water. "Wh— what's going on?"

Yer deaf. Deaf and blind. Deaf and blind and mute." The voice— female and gruff— came from whoever was carrying him. She pronounced the words "deef" and "blinnd" and "moot." A country-woman's accent. Not one from Court.

Jerome tried to crane around to see who it was. He glimpsed enough of her to see that she was another chipmunk. Old, wizened, gray-furred, and yet somehow strong as a bricklayer and big enough to carry him like a pup.

"Eyes forward, yer," she said, tightening her grip on his neck and shaking him a bit. "I've enough disappointment in yer without yer adding 'scrabbling around unpleasantly' to the list."

They reached the barrel and, without warning, the old chipmunk shoved Jerome' face-first into it and swished him back and forth like a dishcloth. The water felt like melted glacier.

She was trying to drown him!

The old chipmunk hauled him out of the water and held him dripping above it. She swiveled her wrist so Jerome faced her, and studied him. "Nae. Not there yet," she said.

"Not where?" said Jerome.

"Not clear." She dunked him back into the icy water, swirled him around some more, and heaved him back out.

Jerome gasped, shook himself to fling off the frigid water, and spluttered, "For the love of Çalaht don't—"

Splash.

Swish.

Out.

Pause, ignoring his scrabbling.

Splash.

Swish.

And out.

The matronly chipmunk held Jerome above the barrel, her eyes boring into him. "Yer nae see nor hear, nor do yer speak with the tongue of our line. The soap ought to fix that. It'll clean yer blockages. Hold yer breath again, sonny."

Another short plunge, a bit more waggling in the water, then the chipmunk plonked Jerome onto a drainboard next to the barrel, grabbed a bar of soap, and began scrubbing hard in his right ear. The soap had the smell of tea tree and mustard seed, and lathered like a cyclone hitting a bubble bath. Jerome squirmed and ducked, trying to get away, but the old chipmunk kept a firm grip on his scruff and kept scrubbing.

"Stop it!" he yelled. "You're not my mother!"

"Nae," she said, swapping the bar of soap to his other ear. "I nae be yer ma. But yer blinnd and deef and moot all the same. Mayhap if them that came after me had done a better job, yer might see and hear and speak the way those in our line do. Hold yer breath."

Another dunk. At least she'd warned him that time. There was some underwater ear scrubbing, and then she hauled him back up.

"Eyes closed," she said.

Jerome barely had time to squint them shut before he felt a soapy washcloth going after his face. She seemed to be trying to clean his eyelids, but his nose, lips, and cheeks came in for a scouring as well.

After what felt like an hour and a half, but was probably only 20 seconds, she said, "And rinse..." like she was mumbling the steps of a recipe she'd made a thousand times. She plunged him back into the near frozen water, spun him back and forth a few times, then pulled him back out.

Jerome spluttered water and gasped, "What do you mean I'm blind, deaf, and mute? I see and hear and speak just fine—"

This time, she stifled his protest by soaping the inside of his mouth with the cloth. Jerome gagged and was grateful to be shoved in the water again so he could get the taste of tea tree and mustard out of his mouth.

When the old chipmunk hauled Jerome up again, he yelled, "Madame! That will do! Unhand me!"

"Unhand yer?"

"Yes, unhand me!"

"As yer wish."

The old chipmunk let go of him, and Jerome dropped back into the barrel for one last dunking.

He dog-paddled (a term that canines find offensive) his way to the barrel's edge and dragged himself over it. The old chipmunk stood there, arms folded, and Jerome kept a wary eye on her as he squeegeed the worst of the water from his fur and licked the back of his paw a few times, trying to get the lingering taste of soap residue off his tongue. Then he straightened, clasped his paws behind his back, and looked her in the eye with as much dignity as he could manage while dripping wet. "Madame, I ask you again. What do you mean I'm blind, deaf, and mute? And why are you washing me so, so... With such vigor?"

"Do yer see, hear, or feel the Unseen?"

"Not really."

"Do yer see, hear, feel, or intuit the signs of divination?"

"No."

"Do yer speak words of prognostication?"

"Not usually, no. There was this one time in a place called Ye Olde Public Inn in the village of Colander when I—"

"Nae, yer don't. Tis clear enough. Like I said, yer deef, blinnd, and moot."

Jerome allowed himself a shrug. "What can I say? It's not my way."

The old chipmunk's fur bristled, and she gestured with the bar of soap. "Not yer way? Not yer way! To be speaking such, yer must be wanting another taste of this." She moved to snatch him again, but Jerome managed to avoid her this time. He scampered to the far side of the barrel, trying to keep it between them.

"I'll ask you not to do that again, Madame."

"Yer be needing this worse than I thought. I be trying to clean out whatever be clagging yer ability to be of the lineage—of seeing that which can be seen with the inner eye to see it, of hearing that which can be heard when one listens to the winds and whispers and silences, and of speaking that which needs be spoken to them that needs be hearing it."

"Madame—"

"No need to 'madame' me. 'Mamó' will do."

"Mamó?"

"I prefer that to 'Nanna,' 'Gran,' 'Granny,' 'Gammie' (which sounds like I have a gammy leg), 'Mimsy' (which makes me think of borogoves), 'Nonni,' 'Nai nai,' or even 'hey, yer, old lady.'"

"Nanna? You're serious—we're related?"

"Yer Ma be my great-great-great-great-great-great-great grandlassie or some such. I no be fully clear on how great the number of 'greats' needs to be, but yer get the idea. The line from me to thee be straight and true."

"I, uh... Really? You're really my great-great-something-or-other grandma?

She nodded.

"Then allow me to say, 'Pleased to meet you?'" He didn't mean for it to come out as a question, but this was confusing. How could she possibly be here and alive?

Oh. Wait.

That was it.

She wasn't alive. This was a Purity thing. *She* certainly wasn't "real," even if she seemed very real. The taste of her soap had certainly seemed real enough.

"I can hear yer thinking from over here, sonny. It nae be that hard."

"Perhaps not for you." Jerome stuck a claw in his ear to clear out some suds. He looked around for a towel, saw none, and wiped the suds on his leg. "How is it possible that—"

"That nae be the question at hand. I mean, yer mother be a clear channel. Yer gran was a clear channel. Yer great-gran was nae slouch when it came to the Unseen, even if she had an unfortunate tendency to glossolalia. I cannae understand why yer be different from all of them that came before you."

"I just don't have my mother's gifts. That's been obvious since I was a pup."

"Obvious to whom?"

"To my mother, if no one else. To me. To my Oracles and Insights instructors. To this one elderly badger my mother hired to—"

"Yer a bit inclined to gabbing on a bit. Our kind must be willing to talk, so that be there. Mayhap there be other qualities that the Sight can hang onto. Maybe there are manifestations of the Sight that yer nae aware of. Do yer like silent sitting?"

"Not so much."

"Experience a feeling like you been somewhere or done something before, even though that cannae be the case?"

"No."

"See things when you touch objects that belong to others?"

"No."

"Powerful dreams?"

"No."

"Can yer sense when trouble's a'coming?"

"No. Usually trouble arrives first, and then I notice it."

"Heal others with yer open paws?"

"Definitely not."

"Do yer know when a herald is going to arrive with a message from someone and who it's from before the herald shows up?"

"Nope."

"Prophetic dreams?"

"Sorry."

"Be yer uncanny lucky?"

"Sadly, no."

"See floating blobs of light?"

"No."

"See shadows or smudges in the air?"

"No."

"See colors around folks when yer look at them?"

"No."

"Do wee bairns stare at you?"

"Not more than normal."

"Can yer tell if one who is in the family way will be having a boy or a lass?"

"No. But I could see how that might be helpful."

"Do yer hear music in the distance, but cannae locate it?"

"No."

"Feel unexpected hot or cold places in someone's home?"

"No."

"Do yer ever dream yer someone else?"

"No."

The old chipmunk put her fists on her hips, getting exasperated. "There must be something! There has to be."

Jerome gave his shoulders a resigned lift. "I don't think there is."

"I cannae believe that. Do yer like tea?"

Jerome brightened. "Why, yes! Yes I do! I. Adore. Tea. Especially haggleberry tea. There's nothing better than a good cup of haggleberry tea. I savor it. Love it. Tea is my thing!"

"Then maybe there's something there we can work with. Can I offer yer a cuppa?"

"Mamó... It was 'Mamó,' right?"

"Yes."

He bowed politely to her, his fur still dripping. "Mamó, I would be most grateful for the opportunity to share a cup of haggleberry tea with you."

"Well, then, there yer go. Perhaps I can learn yer something about seeing the Unseen in its dregs."

"I'd... I'd like that," said Jerome.

And he found that he meant it.

❧ 52 ❧

EMANATIONS

E loise blinked open her eyes.

She was once again near the open lava pit, lying on her side with the box containing the Star of Whatever beneath her head. Her muscles ached, her back burned like she'd been flayed, and her guts felt like they'd been spilled out, danced on by a battalion of rhinoceros ballerinas, then put back in upside down.

"Ah, there you are," said the dream wife. She leaned over Eloise, covering her with a blanket, and dabbed her forehead with a cool cloth. "You'll start shivering soon. The various unpleasantnesses will follow. Be ready, but it's best if you just go with it."

"Right," croaked Eloise. Her voice sounded like her vocal cords had been taken down to a river, pounded on rocks by a washer wench, twisted to get the water out, then put back in her throat. "I should go with the post-shaking unpleasantnesses."

"Not so much 'post' shaking. More during. It sort of all happens at once." The old woman pointed at the items stacked to one side. "Don't worry. I have towels and buckets at the ready. And a change of clothing if needed."

Eloise's habits prickled at that. Buckets? Towels? Spare clothing? That didn't sound good. If she hadn't been so exhausted, her habits would have sent her backing away from whatever was coming as fast as she could.

But given how she felt, there'd be no backing away anywhere.

Come on, she said to herself. *Get a grip. How bad could it be?*

Very bad, her habits replied. *Very, very bad.* And with the aid of her habits, Eloise started imagining all the things the unpleasantnesses could involve, based solely on needing buckets and spare clothing, even ignoring the towels.

She tried to ignore the worry welling up in her, and the baby-octopus-suckers-on-her-skin feeling that she was starting to experience. Was that caused by the after-effects of the vision herbs, or was it just her habits giving her something to go spare about? Eloise couldn't tell. She ran her tongue around the inside of her mouth. It felt as dry as a scorched scone, and about as flavorsome. Here and there in her cheeks and gums, she felt flecks of what she hoped were the remnants of the vision herbs and not anything worse. But she'd seen the khan with his tongue lolling on the ground, and some of what was in her mouth might well taste of dirt.

Had her tongue been lolling on the ground too? Ugh. She began imagining all the ways eating dirt could be bad for her: causing her breath to smell like soil, triggering digestive distress by eating substances not meant to be swallowed, or even ingesting the source of untold agues.

She definitely needed a distraction.

Eloise looked at Jerome. He was in the same supine position as before, but was making slow gestures that looked like he was miming tea drinking, complete with an elevated, pointy pinky claw. He looked both very dignified and ridiculous. Was he trying to impress someone in the La La Realms?

She looked beyond Jerome to where the khan lay. He, too, was under a blanket, and his body shook with constant, violent spasms. Sweat poured from him, dripping to the ground below. There was enough of it to form a small rivulet, which snaked its way toward the lava pit.

Without warning, there was an explosive, lingering, almost artistic blast of air from the back end of the khan's blanket. Incredibly, it sounded exactly like the opening notes of an old Court fanfare often played at state funerals called "Looketh! Yonder Agave Monger Hath a Hooter the Size of a Barnacle or Perhaps a Melon!" This unexpected semi-musical offering was followed moments later by an extended belch that rumbled up from the equine monarch like a driverless cart thundering down a mountain road, and then splattered out of him like a spilled load of half-rotted lettuces squelching an octet of hurdy-gurdy grinders.

Impressive. Truly astounding.

The tremors struck Eloise suddenly and forcefully. One moment, she was marveling at unlikely gaseous horse noises. The next, she was shaking like she had Çalaht's own delirium tremens. Eyes closed, Eloise felt her teeth clack, her torso and limbs shake, her stomach gripe, and her entire body dampen and then drip. Eloise couldn't maintain any control. No assertion of will could stop what was going on.

It went on and on and on. Hours' worth. A lifetime's worth. And there was nothing she could do about it.

At one point she opened an eye and saw Jerome that was also under a blanket, quivering like an introverted jellyfish forced to give a speech in front of a stadium full of oration critics. His unpleasantnesses took a higher pitched form, a piccolo performance to the khan's booming. Eloise didn't care to imagine which instrument her own unpleasantnesses resembled, but was pretty sure it was some freakish combination of tuba, cymbal crash, and the reedy, brain-exploding whine of a bombard.

"Unpleasantnesses." What an inept euphemism. This was just plain nasty, perhaps the foulest experience of her life. She wasn't sure any amount of connection to the spark of something in the Star of Whatever was worth this kind of ignominy.

Thinking of the Star of Whatever brought back memories of the naked mole-rat. How strange that encounter had been. Was it real, or was it just some sort of vision herb-induced mind blip? She suspected the latter, but at least part of her hoped there had been some reality to it.

There was only one way to find out. Mentally, she reached out to the spark of something. *Sparky? You there?*

The green light in the stone pulsed briefly. In her mind came the words, "Hey, Loulou. Nice to hear from you. And so soon! Not that my sense of time is any good."

"So it was real?"

"Apparently real enough. But now's not the time. You have other stuff going on, it would appear."

"Right."

"See you, Loulou."

"See you, Sparky."

Then it was gone.

That the spark of something in the Star of Whatever was still there helped. It hadn't all been for naught.

Eloise let herself go into the experience as best she could.

$$\maltese \quad 53 \quad \maltese$$

RETURNED

By dawn, it was done. Buckets, towels, and, to Eloise's embarrassment, a change of clothing had all been necessitated. But at least it was over.

The khan and the dream wife asked her and Jerome about their experiences. Eloise gave a not-very-detailed summary, focusing on the naked-mole rat who had appeared to her, but omitting the depth of her encounter with Sparky.

Jerome spoke of having tea with an ancestor, but she could tell that he wasn't being forthcoming either.

Still, what little the two of them said seemed to satisfy. "Whatever happened to you when you approached the Purity, some sort of cosmic requirement has been met," said the khan to Eloise. "In my connection to the Purity this time, there was no mention of the Light itself, nor of it being borne. That's a first for me. And perhaps a first for two centuries' worth of khans. I can't say for sure, since we will have to see what happens in the future, but it would appear that the obligation of my lineage has been met."

The horse then gave a thorough account of his own vision for the benefit of the herd rememberer. It had to do with herd alliances and equine politics, and it left Eloise yearning for a nap.

The khan stood and said, "It's time for you to return with the dream wife. It takes me longer, and I prefer to make my way on my own."

"Do you follow the same path as the one we came up on?" asked Eloise.

"There may be many ways to approach the Purity," said the khan. "But there is only one way to reach this particular place."

"That's incredible. And you do it unassisted."

"Always," he said. "I believe it's part of the process. The day I can't make this particular journey for the Us is the day I shall no longer be the khan."

Eloise was again amazed at how tough the small, commanding horse was. She wasn't sure what she should say, so she simply said, "Be safe."

"Always." He nodded to Eloise and then to Jerome. "Now go, so I can get started."

The dream wife tied the blanket around Eloise again so the box with the Star of Whatever sat comfortably at her hip. Then they said goodbye and left the khan to limp back slowly on his own.

The next few hours passed in a blur of exertion, exhaustion, and treacherous footing. The dream wife led Eloise and Jerome back through a fresh covering of snow. The trudge down the steep incline past the archway threatened to become an unwelcome icy slide. Worse was the unstable footing in the area Eloise thought of as Çalaht's Devastation. Thanks to the snow, it was easier to know exactly where the dream wife stepped, but it was harder for the old woman to be sure of where she should place her feet. Her every movement disturbed the even purity of the snow, revealing glimpses of the blood-red lichen and moss she had mentioned on their way up. Several times she teetered on an unsteady spot, and twice the old woman slipped badly enough to send her sprawling. If it bothered her, she didn't show it. She stood, brushed herself off, and carried on with stoic determination.

Eloise kept Jerome ahead of her so she knew where he was. His manner going the other way had been somber and serious, but now there was a different quality to his silence. He seemed chastened, or chastised, perhaps. Whatever had happened on his journey did not appear to have left him feeling jolly.

Well, the same could be said for her. There was no need for counting on the return trip. Instead, Eloise replayed her encounter with Sparky in her head, committing every word firmly to memory. She wanted to be able to return to it and mull over the implications.

They came down off Mount Enigma, skirted the three hills at its foot, and crested the one closest to the herd. They reached the khan's encampment close to midday, and the dream wife took them back to the open-air jail. It had not yet been two full days since Eloise had walked out of there behind the khan, but it felt like a lifetime. She noticed that the narrow passageway into the clearing was more lightly guarded—just two horse sentries, one facing forward, one facing back, and neither paying much attention. She was desperate for sleep, a chance to let her body heal for a few hours, and some time to sort through everything that had happened, once her brain was not fog-bound with fatigue.

The moment she and Jerome made it through the gap in the wall, she heard a voice yell, "Princess! Princess, it's you! Are you OK?" Lorch hobbled over and stuttered to a halt in front of her. "And Champion Abernatheen de Chipmunk, you're here too. Good. I've been... I've been concerned for you both. We all have been."

"Guard Lacksneck, I—"

Before she could say anything else, Hector and the Nameless One rushed over. Moments later, so did Master Shovelhovel, RoyLee, Seer Bunkerhunker, Kïïït, Bjóöòrn Tóöòrúüùn, and a horse Eloise finally recognized as Kïïït's Uncle Dougie. They crowded around, peppering her with questions.

"Are you hurt or injured?" asked Lorch.

The Nameless One gave her a simpler are-you-OK? look.

"How's your back?" asked Hector.

"Did something happen to your clothes?" asked RoyLee. "You're not dressed as you were."

"Did ye be doing their ceremony like they told us?" asked Seer Bunkerhunker.

"Do you need something to eat, perhaps?" asked Master Shovelhovel.

"Did anyone say anything about me?" asked Kiïit.

Eloise laughed, overwhelmed. "It's lovely to see you all," she said. "I'll happily answer any and all questions, but we've had a long night, and a long day before that, and truly, more than anything, I need sleep. I'm sure Jerome feels the same. Right, Jerome?"

She looked around to get his agreement, but the chipmunk had curled up beneath one of the nearby yucca tundra trees and was already snoring.

"Right," said Eloise. "I guess I feel the same."

"Of course," said Hector. He turned to the others. "Shall we give her some space?"

Eloise looked for a tent or shelter. "Is there a place I could..."

"Over this way, Princess," said Lorch. "Please come with me."

He led her to a secluded spot near the cliff face and away from the entryway, where he'd put up a tent and laid out her sleeping roll. "The ground is littered with rocks and stones, Princess. I've moved as many as I could, but it's not all that comfortable. I've taken the liberty of padding your sleeping roll with an extra two of my own blankets."

"Oh, Lorch, this looks amazing. Thank you."

"My pleasure, Princess. I'll leave you to it. I'll stay nearby, in case you need anything."

"An hour or two of sleep should do me. If you could please wake me up at mid-afternoon? There's much to discuss."

"Yes, Princess."

He left her, and Eloise crawled under the blankets fully clothed. She had just enough wakefulness to think, *It's nice to be back with everyone.* Then she, like Jerome, was spicing the air with snores.

❧ 54 ❧

CONSIDERATIONS

When Eloise woke, she immediately realized that more than a couple of hours had passed. Her body had the heaviness of a long sleep, and a dusky light filtered over the edge of the surrounding cliffs and into her tent. She lay still for a few minutes to gain full wakefulness, and realized that the light was gathering, not fading.

Not dusk. Dawn. She'd slept half a day and through the night. At least.

It wasn't what she'd intended, but it was probably what she'd needed.

She couldn't hear anyone stirring yet, so she allowed herself an unexpected luxury: time to lay there and just think. So much had happened since Jerome had appeared scooting down their prison's cliff face, and that ignored the couple of weeks since they'd left Stained Rock.

It felt like a lifetime.

Someone else's lifetime. That's how distant it all felt.

There was so much she had to consider. Turpy's escape, for one. That's where this whole thing had started, and it remained the biggest problem.

This was something she'd have to talk over with the others.

She was still very far from home and hadn't made contact for much too long. Would the khan be willing to spare a messenger to let her parents know she was safe and wouldn't be too much longer? He might do that for her.

But was that true? Would she be home soon? There was still the matter of Turpy. On the other had, there were other considerations, not the least of which was the injury to her back. It would need more tending soon. Eldridge the Apothecary, who still creaked his way around the halls of Castle de Brague, would have the salves, unctions, and poultices she'd need to heal as best she could. The dream wife had given her first aid, and it had helped, certainly. But she'd seen Eldridge work miracles on soldiers who'd come home from campaigns with the most horrid burns. If she'd learned anything from the apothecary, it was that speedy and early treatment were crucial. That, alone, made getting home sooner rather than later a good idea.

It was something to add to the discussion she'd have with the others.

Eloise wondered if she needed to do anything else here among the khan's herd. She didn't think so, and it felt like a task completed. But she didn't know the ways of the horses, and it seemed like Protocol was not followed here at all. She didn't want to leave in a way that caused offense, but had no idea how to avoid creating a diplomatic situation. Perhaps the dream wife could help with that one. Or she could just be straight with the khan and ask him directly. He might be open to that.

Then there was the Star of Whatever.

Sparky.

The naked mole-rat, with his strange movable teeth and hairless body, must have been some sort of metaphor. A convenient representation of the spark of something. Obviously, there couldn't actually be a mole-rat in the Star of Whatever, and Melveeta hadn't said anything about one. Who knew why the vision herbs, the Purity, or some strangeness in her own mind had thrown up that particular characterization. Maybe it made him more relatable. If so, it was only barely.

More than anything, the encounter with Sparky needed cautious and thorough consideration. Had she touched the Purity in the way the khan and the dream wife had meant her to? They hadn't said otherwise when she related her experience. Maybe whether she'd done it "right" or not didn't matter. Was her vision-herby meeting with Sparky akin to what Melveeta said she'd had with the magical stone—an affinity? Did this constitute a relationship of some sort? Would it mean that Eloise could command or control him? That was a scary thought. She had no interest in exploring the stone's magical potential, Sparky or no Sparky.

Well, maybe a little. Maybe there was a smidgeon of interest.

And that in itself was dangerous.

She patted her hip to feel if the box was still there. It was, still tucked into the wrap the dream wife had tied around her. Eloise silently reached out to the spark of something. *Sparky? Are you there?*

There was no response, but the quality of the silence was different. It wasn't the blank unresponsiveness from before. It was more like it was simply asleep, or otherwise occupied.

Eloise permitted herself a sigh. Thinking about her encounter with the naked mole-rat, she recounted the commitments she'd made to the spark of something. That all felt very real. No fakery or brain burp hallucination there. Those commitments felt as binding to Eloise as any contract drawn by magistrates, witnessed by the First Advisor, and signed and sealed using her mother's signet ring.

She was going to have to honor their agreement.

Even if the Star could only do the barest of what Melveeta had described—like the disruption of magic in close proximity—Eloise needed to know if that would happen around her when she had the Star. If nothing else, there might be some safety considerations. What if someone relied on their weak magic for something critical, and suddenly found it unexpectedly gone?

Eloise needed to test it somehow.

But how?

There was one person among them who she knew, with certainty, had a known, readily available weak magic.

She hauled herself out of bed to face the brisk dawn of a new day, and ducked out of the tent to find her potential test subject.

❧ 55 ❧

LEFT FLUTTER RUN RUN HYPOTHESIS

The camel looked confused.

"I beg your pardon?" said Bjóöòrn Tóöòrúüùn. "You want me to do what?"

Eloise had found the camel on the far side of the clearing, browsing grass on his own.

"I need you to run at me," said Eloise. "As hard and as fast as you can."

The camel looked at her. "Are you sure?"

"I'm absolutely sure. Try your best to tag me."

Bjóöòrn gasped, scandalized. "I can't do that. It would be wrong. It would be unseemly for me to even attempt to tag you, your being a princess and all. Çalaht forbid I should succeed, or accidentally flatten you."

Eloise looked at him for a moment. "Do you play hockey sacking?"

Bjóöòrn smiled. "Does a Çalahtist devotional house minder count the coins in his collection dish? Does Lyndia Thrind warble the odd song from time to time? Do horned lizards squirt blood from their eyes?"

"Horned lizards can squirt blood from their eyes?"

"You bet!"

"So, that's a 'yes' to the hockey sacking, then?"

"That's a 'yes.' Where I'm from, all camels play hockey sacking, coach hockey sacking, watch hockey sacking, wager on hockey sacking, create art about hockey sacking, discuss hockey sacking with their dear old gran, or do one or more of the above at the same time. We're practically born with hockey sacks in our mouths."

"Well, good. I play changer at hockey sacking. I can handle it if you try to crash into me." Eloise looked at him. "What position do you play?"

"Left flutter."

"Really? I would have thought you more the changer type, like me. Or maybe a middle splendid."

"When I was growing up, I played a lot of changer. So did my brother Bééènnÿ. But when we made it onto the village team, they already had a really good changer—a dromedary. Her name was Ägnetha Ämplehümps. She could flip a hockey sack up, bounce it from hump to hump while she loped down the field, and then flick it for a goal like it was a magic trick. So Bééènnÿ and I moved to other positions."

"Ägnetha Ämplehümps. I think I've heard of her. Didn't she play for the Fërndälë Abstract Concepts?"

The camel laughed. "No, no, no. That was her sister, Ännï-Frïd. Ägnetha Ämplehümps played for the Nëw Vällëy Non-Threatening Inanimate Objects. People make that mistake all the time.

"Anyway, you understand hockey sacking," said Eloise. "So just pretend that's what we're doing, but a touch version, not full contact, and try to tackle me."

Bjóöòrn tilted his head at her, still wary. "Can you at least tell me why?"

"I'm testing a hypothesis."

"What hypothesis?"

"I don't think I can tell you. If I do, it might affect how you carry out your part of the experiment."

"Right. Then I shall remain hypothetically ignorant."

"I wouldn't put it that way, but yes," she said. "Just go over there, pretend I've got the hockey sack, and come at me."

"As you wish, Princess."

Bjóöòrn walked 30 lengths away from Eloise and turned to face her. "Ready?"

"Ready."

He loped toward her and lunged. Eloise easily sidestepped him.

"Look, thanks for that, but you're not really trying," said Eloise. "This isn't going to work if you don't give it your all. I need you going full speed."

"Right. Full speed. Got it." He walked back to his starting position. "Ready?"

"Ready."

"Coming."

The camel ran at her, but as he got to the halfway mark, Eloise yelled. "Hold on." Bjóöòrn eased to a stop as Eloise walked over to him. "That's not what I'm looking for."

"What do you mean?"

"I mean, I've seen you run. I saw you with Turpy on your back. I know what you're capable of."

"Oh," said the camel, understanding. "You want me to *run* run at you. Like I do for clients."

"*Run* run. Yes."

"I see what you mean. The confusion is your talking about hockey sacking. I'm..." He looked embarrassed. "One's not allowed to *run* run during a game. It would be unfair to the others. And unsportsmanlike. I have to save that for off the hockey sacking paddock."

"I see. That would make sense."

Lorch and Jerome appeared. "Can we join you, Princess?" asked Lorch.

She'd hoped to conduct her experiment in private, but Lorch and Jerome knew about the Star of Whatever, so it wouldn't hurt for them to be there. "Certainly."

"What are you doing?" he asked.

"She's conducting a secret experiment," said Bjóöòrn. He lifted his head up, proud. "I'm an ignorant hypothesis."

"I see," said Lorch.

"OK, let's do this." Eloise and the camel walked back to their spots.

"Ready, Princess?" asked Bjóöòrn.

"Ready. *Run* run away."

This time the camel ran at her at full tilt. His longwalker weak magic turned his legs into a blur of motion, and he streaked across the open space, screaming, "Cowabunga!"

This struck Eloise as a strange thing to yell. It sounded like it might be offensive to bovines. Perhaps it was a camel thing. Or a camel hockey sacking thing.

Eloise placed a hand on the box containing the Star of Whatever. It lay nestled at her hip inside the blanket she still wore. She braced herself, watching the camel come ever closer. He was, indeed, *run* running at her. She waited for the magic-dissipating effects of the Star of Whatever to kick in, disrupt his longwalker weak magic, and slow him. *Any moment now*, thought Eloise. *Any moment now.*

Any moment never came. Bjóöòrn lunged at her at full speed like she was a changer holding a hockey sack. He tagged her, but his speed and momentum accidentally sent her flying. Eloise managed to roll, so she didn't land on her back, and she just stopped herself from clunking into one of the pineapple yuccas.

"Princess!" yelled Lorch.

"El!" yelled Jerome.

They ran over to her, finding her winded but slowly standing up. "I'm OK. I'm OK," she wheezed. Eloise gave Bjóöòrn a thumbs up. "That was good. Let's try again."

"Try again, El?" whispered Jerome. "You just stood there and let him hit you."

"I didn't think he would. Or could." She waved at the camel, indicating that he should return to his starting position. "Go ahead, Bjóöòrn. I'll be with you in a minute. Let me catch my breath."

"El, what's going on?" said Jerome, his voice still low.

"He'd be a good left flutter," said Eloise. "That's his position." She drew a long breath and blew it out slowly. "OK. I think I'm ready."

Lorch held up a hand. "Princess, may I ask the nature of the experiment you're conducting?"

"I'm not sure I'm ready to say."

"Princess, if I may be so bold. I think it highly unlikely that I'll stand here and let a camel run at you without some sort of explanation first."

"I'm with Lorch on this one, Eloise," said Jerome quietly.

"I suppose." Eloise turned her back to the camel, who was once again 30 lengths away, and fished out the box with the Star of Whatever. "I'm trying to test this."

"Test it how, Princess?"

She told them some of Melveeta's story about her earliest experiences with the Star of Whatever, and how she first discovered that it disrupted the weak magic of those who were near it. "I'm trying to figure out if it still does that, or if that was just something Melveeta managed to tap into two centuries ago."

"I get it," said Jerome. "If this thing is doing what you think it ought to be doing, then it will somehow hinder his running, because he has longwalker weak magic that can be interfered with."

"That's what I was thinking."

"It doesn't seem to have worked," said Jerome.

"No. That particular experiment did not support the hypothesis."

"Princess, do you need him to run into you?" said Lorch.

"I was trying to give him a reason to go as fast as possible. And I was trying not to let him know what I was testing."

Lorch frowned. "I see. Perhaps he can run past you. Come close, but not with the goal of tackling you."

Eloise thought about it. "I guess that should work."

"Shall I let him know about the change of tactics?" asked Lorch.

"Good idea," said Eloise. "Tell him to get as close as he can while still going past."

"I'll do it," said Jerome. He pointed to Lorch's injured leg. "I'll get there faster."

"Right," said Lorch. "Of course."

Jerome hurried over to Bjóöòrn and explained the change in strategy.

"Got it!" called the camel.

Eloise gave him a thumbs up, hid the box back in the blanket, and braced. "Ready!"

Bjóöòrn *ran* ran toward her. The Star of Whatever again had no effect, and he whooshed past at full speed, coming within weak lengths. The air around him sucked her into its wake, and—oof!—Eloise went flying again.

She stood and dusted herself off. "Maybe just a little farther away next time. OK, Bjóöòrn?"

"OK." He jogged back to his starting position, and Jerome returned to stand and watch with Lorch.

Eloise tucked the Star's box into the blanket and braced.

The camel *ran* ran.

Eloise went airborne as Bjóöòrn blew past. This time, she managed to land in a pineapple yucca.

"Good, good," she gasped as she slowly stood up. "Let's give it another go."

"Princess, no," protested Lorch.

"Hold it, Lorch," whispered Jerome. "Let me try."

While the camel walked back to his spot, the chipmunk went over to Eloise and helped her brush a smear of moss from her breeks. "You know that to the outside observer this looks spectacularly bone-headed, right?"

"I can imagine."

"Part of the reason it is boneheaded is that you're failing to conduct your experiment with sufficient deftness."

"I beg your pardon?" Eloise rubbed her short hair to remove residual dust and yucca fragments. "What do you mean?"

"Your methodology is flawed."

"How so?"

"Experiments provide insight into cause-and-effect by showing what outcome results from manipulating a given factor."

"Yes, and?"

"You're not manipulating any factors, except maybe the distance between you and the camel when he passes you. But to the outside observer, you're just getting repeatedly blown over, while randomly hoping to discover something."

"Fair point."

"If you're going to insist on continuing with this line of inquiry, the least you can do is manipulate an experimental factor and see if you get a different result."

"Right," said Eloise. "I'm open to suggestions."

"Hmmm..." Jerome walked around her, considering. "Maybe if you take the box out of your blanket. Hold it in plain sight, instead of hiding it. It's just us—me and Lorch. We already know about it. And you don't have to tell Bjóöòrn what it is. To him, it'll just be a box."

"Right," said Eloise. "I can live with that."

Eloise went back to her starting position. She eased the box back out, held it tightly to her front, and said, "Ready when you are."

Run run. Wheee!

Eloise picked herself up. "I'll try holding it out in front of me."

Run run. Whoosh!

"I'll try holding it above my head."

Run run. Whoa!

Eloise took the hand Lorch offered, and hauled herself back off the ground. It was getting harder each time, and she didn't know how much more experimental curiosity she could tolerate. Plus, she suspected her back might be bleeding.

"Is the problem the box?" whispered Jerome.

"It could be. You can imagine that it was designed to have some sort of dampening effect on the Star of Whatever. But I don't know how to open it. In fact, it hasn't been opened since he went in there."

"He?" asked Jerome.

"I think of the Star as a 'he.'"

"Does that strike you as odd?"

Eloise looked at her champion. "Maybe?"

"The box does have a crack," said Lorch. "Could that somehow be useful?"

"Good thinking," said Eloise. "I could try to aim it, perhaps. It's worth a shot, anyway."

Eloise resumed her starting position. "Ready when you are," she called to the camel.

"Are you sure about this, Princess Eloise?" Bjóöòrn replied. "I'm starting to feel bad about how many times this has not gone your way."

"You're only doing what I've asked of you."

"I know, but I'm worried."

Me, too, thought Eloise.

"It's fine," she called. "Come on. I'm ready."

The camel launched himself in her direction, his speed once again incredible. Eloise held up the Star of Whatever and pointed the cracked side of the box at Bjóöòrn. *Come on, Sparky,* she thought. *Help me out here, buddy. Please, please, please, please, please.*

The spark of something in the Star of Whatever didn't verbalize a response, or even send one of its single punctuation marks. But if *felt* like Sparky had replied, *Sure, why not?* With Bjóöòrn seconds from flying past her once again, Eloise felt something. It was the tiniest of pulses—a fraction of a tingle of a blip.

The effect on the camel was instantaneous and profound. His speed dropped from magnificent to normal. The unexpected deceleration threw off his running and messed with his gait. He stumbled and tripped, sliding the last five lengths.

Eloise easily sidestepped him as he skidded to a stop.

"What happened?" asked Bjóöòrn.

"I think I managed to successfully manipulate an experimental variable," said Eloise.

"Well, it hurt."

They tried it another half dozen times. Eloise was able to connect with Sparky just enough to consistently slow the camel once he was within ten lengths.

The Star of Whatever works, thought Eloise as she went back toward their camp with the others. *Now that really is scary*.

❧ 56 ❧

PLAN A AND PLAN B

After Eloise's experiment with the Star of Whatever, they all gathered for breakfast—two humans, a chipmunk, three horses, three wombats, and a camel. RoyLee and Master Shovelhovel had prepared a porridge of polenta spiced with cinnamon and vanilla.

"Ain't that the grass strudel," said Kïïït when she tasted hers. "I had no idea you could do that with cornmeal."

"It's the spices that make the difference," said RoyLee. "At home, this is a special treat, since normally we just eat grass, roots, leaves, and fungi, if we can find them."

"I be partial to the odd fungus, that be for sure," said Seer Bunkerhunker.

As Eloise ate her first, and then second, bowl, she told the others what she had gone through since she'd left them, keeping it light on details. When she relayed her experience with the vision herbs, she said even less—just that it was a guided journey under the dream wife's direction, and that she'd had some insights that meant something to her, but not anyone else. It seemed to satisfy everyone's curiosity.

Conversation waned, and Lorch handed around mugs of haggleberry tea. Jerome sipped his and gave Lorch an appreciative nod—high praise from the chipmunk.

Eloise took hers and let its heat warm her hands. She was definitely feeling bruised from the morning's scientific undertakings, and was nervous about what the results had revealed.

Seer Bunkerhunker slid her empty bowl away from her and leaned over to Master Shovelhovel. "Will you be asking her, or be it up to me?" she whispered.

"Gran, I was trying to find the right moment."

"This seems to be a fine moment, if you ask me," said the elderly wombat.

"Ask me what?" said Eloise. "Assuming the 'her' you're referring to is me and not Kïïit."

"No, I be meaning you," said Seer Bunkerhunker. "What's next?"

"Next?"

"She means, do you have a plan?" said Shovelhovel. "Much has happened since RoyLee, Gran, and I joined you. And it seems like the circumstances now be changed."

"That's true." Eloise blew across the edge of her mug and took a sip. Jerome was right—Lorch's tea was excellent. "That's very true."

"And we've come such a long distance," added RoyLee. "I bet I've traveled farther than just about any wombat I've ever met, save Seer Bunkerhunker."

"And I've been grateful for all of your help," said Eloise. "Your help and your companionship."

"Thank you," said Shovelhovel. "But Gran be right. We be needing to think about what's next for us, given how long we've been away from our wisdom."

"I've been thinking about it too," said Eloise. "I'd say the choices are simple. Plan A: we go after Turpy. Plan B: we go home. Anyone have any other options they can think of?"

"Not at the moment," said Hector. "But it would be worth noting that 'going home' wouldn't have all of us ending up at Castle de Brague."

"Noted," said Eloise. "Would anyone care to speak for or against either plan?"

Lorch raised his hand. "What speaks in favor of Plan A is that the felon should face justice. One could easily argue that we have a duty to ourselves, to our society, and to our Crown to ensure that he does so. Especially since he was our responsibility, and he escaped."

"Anyone want to add to that?"

Hector raised a hoof. "I'm not averse to pursuing Turpy. If that's what needs to be done, that's what needs to be done." He stood for emphasis. "As you said, Princess, we either go after him or we leave him be. Truth be told, going after him feels hard and uncertain. Winter will not make our tracking easy nor our travels comfortable. Not going after him feels like quitting, and leaving someone dangerous on the loose. But if we decide to pursue him, where would we look?"

"That's a good point," said Lorch. "He could be anywhere."

"As a longwalker," said Eloise, "he could have gone anywhere and back again already. You've seen how he moves, especially now that his injuries are healed."

"Not going after him doesn't have to mean failure," said Hector. "In fact, it could be turned to advantage."

"How so?" said Eloise.

"Guard Lacksneck, the Nameless One, and I all have some degree of training and ability in tracking. But there are those for whom that is a life's work. We could follow Plan B, go home, and encourage the queen to despatch professional trackers to pursue him."

"If our beloved queen puts a price on his head, then bounty hunters will jump on the chase," said Lorch.

"Will the trail not be too cold?" asked Eloise.

"Perhaps. But how much warmer is it now?" said Hector. "We're already dealing with a cold trail. With winter on us, it will be cold in more than one sense of the word."

"True," said Lorch.

Jerome raised a paw. "Duty comes into it, but there is more than one duty at play." The chipmunk's voice was low, reflecting the somber mood he still carried. Everyone had to lean forward to hear him. "We do have a duty to justice. But Princess Eloise has a duty to her parents and her realm. I can only imagine that the queen's tolerance for the princess's traveling across the realms is limited. Princess, at some point, your duties at Court assert precedence. That is especially true if we take into account Hector's point that others could be sent after Turpy. I want him found and brought to account as much as any of you. More." Jerome swallowed, and his voice wavered. "You have a need for healing. So does Lorch. And you have duties at home that call you. I don't know how much longer you can put off answering that call."

"Fair points, Jerome," Eloise said. He was right about the healing. And he was right about her duties at home. Protocol and Court waited for her like a patient, if condescending servant. Or perhaps like an impatient tyrant. She allowed herself a small sigh, then looked at Kı̈ı̈t, the wombats, and the camel. "Do any of you wish to add anything?"

"It be your choice," said Master Shovelhovel. "It not be up to us." Kı̈ı̈t and Bjóöòrn nodded agreement.

"Right," said Eloise. "Right, right."

They sat in silence, contemplating all that had been said. Lorch poured another round of tea, and the only sounds were sipping and slurping.

"So, Princess Eloise," said Lorch. "Which plan is it?

Eloise set down her mug and stood. "I think the odds of us finding Turpy are pretty low. Probably impossibly low. As you said, we have no good idea where to even start looking, save where we last saw him, which was there." Eloise pointed to the top of the cliff where Turpy had left them with a single finger salute. "I say, let's go home. Let my mother send some trackers after him. Jerome's right. There's only so much running around the realms that's appropriate, and we almost certainly crossed that line a long, long time ago."

"I agree with you, Princess," said Lorch. "The right path is to go home."

"Hear, hear," said Hector. "To going home."

⚜ *57* ⚜

STILL NOT A MUSHROOM

Kïïït volunteered to let their equine hosts know that Eloise and the others intended to leave at first light. "I'll check with Uncle Dougie first," she said. "He'll tell me if there are ceremonies or rules or expectations or whatever that you need to be aware of."

"Thank you, Kïïït," said Eloise. "I appreciate it very much."

Eloise tried to help tidy up after breakfast, but Master Shovelhovel and RoyLee refused to let her. "You be having quite a few days, from what you be telling us," said Shovelhovel. "We'll be taking care of this. You go be resting so you be ready for traveling."

She went to tidy her sleeping roll and get her gear ready to go, but that didn't take very long. Nor did the discussion she had with Lorch, Hector, and the Nameless One about which route home they should take, as their maps did not cover the Central Ranges in enough detail to be useful. Lorch offered to speak with one of the Us to get guidance.

Which left Eloise with something she'd not experienced in far too long —an idle moment. She decided not to let it remain idle. She went to her pannier and found a needle and thread to see to some repairs. The

349

result wouldn't be as sturdy as anything Lorch would fix, nor as precise as Jerome's needlework. She guessed that even Hector and the Nameless One could probably sew better than her. Still, it would be passable, and some items were best done by one's self. Despite her determined efforts to the contrary as a child, she still remembered the stitches Seamstress Linttrap had taught her more than a decade before: the backstitch, the whipstitch, the running stitch, and her favorite, the running-backstitch, which was stronger than a running stitch, but not as laborious as using just backstitches.

Eloise found a warm, sunny spot with a nice view of the tundra and a boulder to lean against, and set to work.

She'd been sewing for almost an hour and was putting the final touches on the pieces she was mending when she heard the sound. Sniffling. Faint sniffling from a little way off. Did someone have an allergy? No, there was no sneezing. Just the sniffling. Delicate, little sniffles mixed with the occasional sigh.

It took her a few minutes, since it had been years since she'd heard him do this, but she knew who it was. Eloise tied off the last stitch in a perfectly acceptable if slightly too large knot and used her teeth to break off the extra thread. She poked the needle through a piece of cloth to make sure she didn't lose it, set down her work, and went to look for the sniffer.

Eloise found Jerome 20 lengths away, sitting by himself behind a large rock. He, too, had picked a sunny spot with a nice view of the tundra, but there was nothing sunny about his demeanor. He was wrapped in a blanket against the tundra chill, and was, as she suspected, crying.

"Hey, Jer. What's up?"

He didn't look at her. "Nothing."

"Can I join you?"

"You're the princess. You can do what you want."

This wasn't good. He didn't throw being a princess at her very often. Eloise sat down next to him and stared at the stark beauty before them.

She said nothing for a good ten minutes while he continued his sniffling.

Finally, she said, "You want to talk about it?"

"There's nothing I would like to do less."

"Fair enough."

Another ten minutes passed.

"How about now?" she asked.

"Nope." Jerome sniffled again and drew his blanket closer. "You go ahead, though. What are you thinking about?"

"I was trying to estimate how many stones there are in the tundra." Eloise held up her thumb in front of her and angled it sideways like an artist considering her subject. "I narrowed the area of my counting to a section of the landscape about the size of my thumb. I counted the stones I could see and multiplied by a factor to account for the ones I can't. There's a lot of guesswork in it, because I'm assuming an even distribution of stones, even though that's a ridiculous assumption. I then applied that number to the rest of what is visible." Eloise rotated her hand, stepping her thumb along in even increments, like the hand of a clock moving across its dial. "I then extended my calculations to account for parts of the tundra hidden from our view. That doesn't account for the varying scattering of stones, nor the fact that different conditions allow different numbers of stones to be seen, depending on things like clouds and the angle of the sun."

"Yeah? So, how many stones are there?"

"A bunch."

Jerome snorted a laugh. "That'd be about right."

"Yes, it seems about right to me. Perhaps as many as a whole bunch." She gently nudged him with her elbow. "Go ahead. What were you thinking about when I got here?"

"Everything. Nothing."

"There's a lot of scope in that. Anything in particular about everything and/or nothing?"

Jerome hesitated. "The champion thing. I've been thinking about the whole champion thing."

"Oh? That's interesting," said Eloise. "So have I."

"Really? What have you been thinking?"

"No, you go first. I went first with the stone counting thing. It's your turn."

"Right."

Jerome hunched his blanket closer around him. His whiskers trembled, and he wiped the back of one paw across his eyes. He shifted so he faced her.

"Princess Eloise Hydra Gumball III, I have been a disaster as your champion from the start." He counted off on his claws. "I botched the Naming Ceremony. I have been tossed into a bowl of punch—by one of *us*, mind you. I was locked in a dungeon cell in The South, then again in the Half Kingdom. I was kidnapped by a loon who kept me in a sack for days at a time. Said loon dragged me into the heart of the most desolate place in all the realms. I had to chew a hole through the world's most disgusting sack to escape. He then managed to attack you and cause you one of the worst injuries you've ever had—an injury that will leave you permanently scarred."

"It's been a hard time for you. I understand."

"Ya think?" Jerome stood for emphasis. "I failed to keep you from being fogged. I didn't even know you'd been fogged, and I wasn't part of the search party that went after you. I got you arrested in The South because I was speaking, which in turn caused you to have a difficult time with Queen Onomatopoeia. There's plenty more, but that gives you a sense of it."

"So maybe things will smooth out from now on." Eloise ran a hand along the top of the brittle winter tundra grass. "I've still got a lot of princessing ahead of me. You have a lot of championing ahead of you. It'll average out over time."

"No. It won't."

"Why not?"

"Because I *don't* have a lot of championing ahead of me. That's where you're wrong."

"How so?"

"Because you need a different champion. I said it when you first asked me. I said it before the Naming Ceremony. And Çalaht knows I've proven it over and over in the weeks we've been on this journey." Jerome clasped his claws in front of him. "Princess, for the love of everything Çalaht-blessed, don't. Just don't. Don't keep me as your champion. Everyone—you, me, the realms—everyone will be the better for it."

She sat there, arms crossed, letting the moment stretch. "Are you done?"

Jerome swallowed and looked like he was carefully considering her question. "Yes, Princess, I've said what I have to say."

"Good. I have something for you."

"What?"

"Wait here." Eloise got up and went to where she'd been sewing. She reassembled the pieces of what she'd been working on and returned to Jerome, holding them behind her back.

"Good, you're still here," said Eloise.

"You tell me to wait, I wait."

She brought what she carried from behind her back. It was a small, sheathed blade. "Champion Jerome Abernatheen de Chipmunk, I return to you..."

"Don't. El..."

"That's 'Princess Eloise,' please. Champion Jerome Abernatheen de Chipmunk, I return to you your champion's sword." She held out the sword in its scabbard and pointed to a spot on it. "Look. I fixed the buckle and sewed the strap. *I* sewed the strap. It will stay on you again."

Jerome didn't move or say anything. His eyes flashed from surprise to embarrassment to hurt to confusion to anger and back again.

"Please, take it and put it on." Eloise lifted it a little closer to him. "Come on, Jerome."

"Princess Eloise, this is a mistake. I can't. I just can't."

"Jerome. Don't do this to me. I still want you as champion. I need you to be my champion."

"Why? Because my mother said something? Because she had a vision? We both know that's not reason enough."

"Your mother's vision has nothing to do with it."

"No?"

"No. Not anymore. Maybe then, but not now."

"Then why? I'm useless. I'm worse than useless. I'm an active drag on everything. I mean, look at what's happened. You're *here*, for Çalaht's sake, because you came after me. You should be home, enjoying the comforts of court and castle and Chef's finest haggleberry tea. And you would be, were it not for me shooting my mouth off over and over."

"I won't deny it. That's all true enough. Everything you've said is true." Eloise knelt down so she could look him in the eyes. "You know what else is true? You're loyal and devoted. You helped us get money with strangely accurate fake prognostications. You bamboozled and defended me against the happy clappers. You used Gordon the Noisome's ear hair to great effect when guards were swarming at Castle Blotch. You have given counsel and support. And you're my friend. And as my friend, I'm asking you to continue being my champion."

Jerome looked down at his feet, slowly shaking his head. Tears streamed.

"C'mon, Jeramiad. Take the sword and put it on."

Silence.

"Jerome, I need you to be my champignon. At least for now. At least until we get home."

The chipmunk's head snapped up. "What? What did you say?"

"I said I need you to be my champion, at least for now. At least until we get home."

"You did not. You said 'champignon.'"

"Did not."

"Did too! You said you want me to be your mushroom! I knew it!"

"Did not."

"In your mind, you think 'champignon' and not 'champion.' And that time it came out."

"I'm sure I said 'champion.' Why would I want you to be my mushroom?"

"It's what you said!"

"Is not." Eloise gave him a sly look. "And if it is, what are you going to do about it?"

"I can't believe you've resorted to a joke we've been telling since we were five."

He stood looking at her, hands on hips, blinking tears. Then he said, "Fine. Give me that," and snatched the sword from her outstretched hand. The chipmunk slid it over his shoulder and gave her a short, perfunctory bow. "Princess Eloise Hydra Gumball III, it is my honor to continue to be your champion, at least for now." His words were rushed and had no sense of ceremonial grandeur. "Do not call me your mushroom again." He turned and stomped off.

From behind, Eloise saw him wipe the back of his hand across one eye and then the other, then shake his hand to fling off the tears.

It wasn't 100 percent clear if his indignation was genuine or mock.

❦ 58 ❦

REPAIRED

T he messenger colt arrived mid-afternoon. "Dream Wife would see you again," he said. "At your earliest convenience."

Eloise had expected to hear from her, being fairly certain the old woman would want to change her bandages, if nothing else. And here it was. Eloise was embarrassed that she'd not been as kind to her wounds as she needed to be, but there was nothing she could do about it now. "Thank you for letting me know. I'll come now."

"I'll tell her you're on your way." And he was gone in a clatter of hooves.

Eloise told Lorch where she was going and walked the now familiar path to the dream wife's tent. She found her standing outside, waiting, and accepted the invitation to enter.

Inside was dark and warm, as it had been two days before, only this time it was more of a comfort than a strangeness.

Without wasting time on pleasantries, the dream wife said, "If you'll strip off, I can change your dressings. Then we can have a last cup of tea before you leave. That is, if you're amenable."

"That would be lovely." Eloise began disrobing, starting with the dream wife's blanket. "Thank you for letting me use this," she said, folding it neatly and moving to put it next to the dream wife's trunk.

"Please keep it. A small gift. If you like, I'll show you how I tied it after tea. It's cold, and you have a long way to travel."

"That's very generous of you."

Eloise took off the rest of her borrowed clothing and lay facedown.

"Humph," said the dream wife when she saw the bandages. "Careful not to move. This might tickle." She took a thin, sharp blade, slid it under the edge of the bandage with the sharp edge facing upward, and sliced the length of the binding to expose Eloise's back. When she saw the state of the wound, the old woman sucked sharply through her teeth. "Have you been on campaign since I last saw you?"

"Is it that bad?"

"It's worse. It looks like you've been wrestling a flock of ill-tempered cassowaries."

"Oh."

"I trust whatever it was, it was worth it?"

"Probably, yes," said Eloise. "I thought my back might be bad."

"If you weren't leaving, I'd confine you to bed for a fortnight to prevent further infection and scarring. As it is, even healed, your back will look like you've been meted out 50 lashes. You're lucky you're not feverish."

The dream wife cleaned and dressed the wounds. Eloise swore even more than previously, her best being, "Sainted Çalaht sarcastically salvaging sabotaged sapsucker saltboxes! That really hurts! A whole lot!"

"Really, that's not great swearing," said the dream wife.

"Sorry."

"You will need this seen to regularly by your healers at home. Don't skimp on the opportunity to have it taken care of properly. They will have more tools at their disposal, and might be able to mitigate the scarring. I don't treat burns often among the Us, as the equines avoid having much to do with fire."

"I'll do that," said Eloise. "I promise to get it seen to."

"Properly seen to."

"Yes, properly seen to."

With the thick, globby poultice in place and covered by a top dressing, the dream wife again had Eloise sit up as she wound a long, narrow cloth around her torso from the bottom of the bandage to the top. Like the first time, it was snug enough to prevent leakage. "That should last you until you get home, with any luck. You can leave it on for a week, easily, and longer if needed. If it has to be changed on the way, make sure you stop at a reasonably sized town, and only let a skilled herbalist look at it. Don't just allow any random 'healer' to put any old thing on it."

As the dream wife tied off the top of the binding, Eloise asked, "Do you think the khan might be willing to send a messenger to my mother's court to let her know we are OK, and that we are returning?"

"The odds are good he's done so already, but I'll check and make sure."

"I'd be grateful. They'll be worried."

Eloise reached for the borrowed linen shift to put it back on, but the dream wife held up a hand. "Not that." She opened the lid of her trunk and pulled out two folded items.

Eloise knew exactly what they were. "My tunic! And my travel cloak!"

"I've cleaned and fixed them. I hope you don't mind how I've done it." The old woman first held up the tunic with its back facing Eloise. There was no sign of the burned spot. In its place was a motley patchwork of fabrics sewn together like a quilt. From the front, it would look totally normal. From behind, it would surprise whoever might be looking.

"It's amazing," said Eloise. "How did you find the time?"

"I found the time," said the dream wife. "And now..." She handed Eloise the tunic, waited for her to put it on, and then picked up the travel cape. The old woman unfurled it to show what she'd done.

Like the shirt, it had been mended to hide any hint of burn damage. Instead of a patchwork fix like the tunic, it had a single piece sewn into the middle of it—a square of material with wide bands of a deep red, narrow bands of dark green, and thin lines of pink and yellow. "Do you recognize it?" asked the old woman.

"It's your ceremonial cloth. You used it two nights ago. I admired it then, and I'm astounded now that you've done this with it."

The dream wife nodded. "I didn't make the choice lightly. I wove this myself, and even dyed the threads it was made from. Put it on." She held it up so Eloise could slip on the cloak. "With this, even more than with the tunic, a part of me goes with you. May it protect you, may it warm you, may it keep you safe. May it guide you, may it bring you peace, and may it remind you of the spirit of the Us."

"Dream Wife, I will treasure it."

"Good." The dream wife reached out a weathered hand and patted Eloise on the cheek. "Good."

Unease filled Eloise. She needed to gift something in return. The dream wife wouldn't expect or demand it, but Eloise needed there to be reciprocity. She needed to make at least a token gesture.

Eloise reached for Seer Maybelle's ring, ready to slip it off, but the dream wife caught her eye and gave the barest shake of her head. She knew what Eloise wanted to do. And the message was clear: not that.

What then? All she had with her were her clothes and the travel cloak.

A travel cloak lined with pockets ingeniously sewn by Seamstress Lint-trap. Eloise ran through a mental inventory of what should be in those pockets: the prayer beads Odmilla had given her, her travel copies of *The Scrolls of Çalaht* and the *Livre de Protocol*, the ornamental bags of groats Queen Onomatopoeia had given her, her small multi-purpose knife.

The knife! Sure, she needed it for meals and a thousand other cutting tasks that popped up in her travels. Like her hair. She'd used that knife to hack off her hair when Melveeta's blood had soaked it and her habits screamed and screamed at her to do something about it. There was a lot of Eloise in that knife.

Which made it the perfect gift.

"If I may," said Eloise. She reached her right hand into a pocket in the travel cloak and drew out the knife. She turned it so the handle was toward the dream wife and offered it to her. "Please accept this token of my affection. Perhaps you can use it to harvest herbs or help with your sewing. And perhaps if you do, you might think of me and my gratitude for all your kindness, and for guiding me to engage with the Purity of the Us."

The dream wife took the knife and balanced it across her palms. She bowed with it to Eloise. "My thanks. It will always remind me of the young princess spy who brightened my life for a few days."

❧ 59 ❧

THE GRASS STRUDEL TO BEAT
ALL GRASS STRUDELS

Eloise returned to find Kïïït in discussion with Lorch, Jerome, Hector, and the Nameless One. She was explaining the Us's approximation of protocol, and how it related to food. The mare was at her most verbally enthusiastic, and as Eloise joined the group, she noted that Kïïït wore a daub of ochre on her forehead.

"Uncle Dougie said the Us don't do rituals around food the way other people do," explained the mare.

"So, banquets and feasts, that sort of thing," said Hector. "They don't do them? Not at all?"

"That's what Uncle Dougie said. And I guess it makes sense."

"How so?" said Lorch.

"A banquet is a kind of celebration, but it's a celebration in a form that's outside how they think. And if you ask me, it's a good thing. I'm a scullery mare, or I was, anyway, so I know what a kitchen is like when there's a feast afoot. It's a misery. A pure misery. It ain't fit for a turf war. You have Cook shouting orders left and right, and all the fires that need stoking and pots that need stirring and then scrubbing, and the yelling when someone can't find their favorite ladle, and the stress around making sure there's enough cumin in the sauce and that the cos lettuce is crispy and not mealy, and how dare you even look at that bowl of berries they're for the king and his guests and were you dropped on your head as a foal?" Kiïit gasped a quick breath. "And then there's the whole thing with serving, which I mostly didn't have to do because I don't have thumbs or fingers, but once they made me dress up in one of the server's outfits and they put the bowls right on my back so I could bring them in in a way that seemed fancy but it was just stupid because who wants to eat curried cream of cauliflower soup when it's been balanced on someone's back and has dribbled over the sides of the bowl because it's nigh on impossible to walk from a kitchen to a banquet hall with eight bowls of hot soup on your back and not spill a little? Am I right? Am I right? I'm right!" Kiïit stopped and saw the others staring at her. "Sorry," she sniffed. "The curried cream of cauliflower thing was traumatic."

"It's OK, Kiïit," said Eloise. "Keep going. You were talking about how the horses don't do banquets?"

"Yeah, right. Sorry. Anyway, Uncle Dougie said the Us just eat what's around, and spend, like, zero time on food preparation. They're nomadic, so meals aren't something they think about the way other people do. They eat this, they eat that, and they move on. Uncle Dougie said they do have a few rituals that have to do with eating, but it mostly happens spontaneously, like when they come on an unexpected patch of something edible or it's a particular time of year. So there's a Welcoming of the Gray Thistles ritual, and an Honoring of the Fescue ceremony. But they won't spend time gathering ryegrass and orchardgrass and bahiagrass and lucerne and make a big salad for everyone to sit down and eat."

The Nameless One snorted once and nodded.

"I agree," said Hector. "It sounds very functional."

"'Functional' is a good word for it," said Kiïit. "But the point is, you shouldn't take offense that they're not throwing a banquet or reception in your honor or anything like that. It's not their way. The way of the

Us is that they will do any honoring and say what needs to be said when you arrive and when you leave."

"Right," said Eloise. She stood with her arms wrapped around her front, feeling the constraint of her new bandages.

"Princess, I need to ask you something. I was going to ask you about it before, but could never get a moment with you, and besides, I've only really just decided what I want. Being with the Us and seeing my Uncle Dougie again have been the best, just the best. It's the grass strudel to beat all grass strudels, and I've seen a lot of grass-strudely things since we left Castle Blotch. Princess, I'm so comfortable here with the Us, comfortable like I've never felt before in my whole life. So I was wondering if you might be OK with me not going back with you, especially since there's no Sock for me to be hauling, or even a cart to haul him in. If that's OK and you don't mind and it isn't an inconvenience or anything."

Then the torrent of words stopped, and Kïïït stood there with the most hopeful, worried, wide-eyed expression Eloise had ever seen on a horse.

"Oh, Kïïït." She put an affectionate hand on the mare's neck. "It's fine. You don't need my permission, but you certainly have my blessing. I'm glad you've found a place you want to call home."

Kïïït beamed a massive smile. "Princess, you truly are the grass strudel. His Alacrity—that's Khan Nergüi—he said when he gave me my forehead mark that I could help the Us better understand the Not Us and the savages, since I've been a Not Us all my life and I've lived and worked with the savages—sorry to use those terms but those were his words, although they are not mine but you get the idea, and I guess if I'm going to live with the Us I might need to get used to saying them which strikes me as odd but I'll get used to it I'm sure but anyway, thank you so much I'm really grateful for all you've done for me and I'm going to miss you all so much and I'm going to miss everything but I really want to be here for now anyway..."

Eloise gestured for her to slow down. "That's really good, Kïïit. I'm sure you'll be happy here. We'll miss you, too. Maybe some day you can use your knowledge of the different ways of life to be an envoy or ambassador for the Us. That way you could have your hooves in both worlds."

"Do you really think so?" Kïïit took a step backward, raised her head as high as it would go, and in a mock herald's voice said, "Presenting Am-bass-a-dor Kïïit of the Cen-tral Ran-ges." She laughed and gave a dismissive head shake. "Wouldn't that be something? Hah!" She gave Eloise a quick horsey curtsy. "If it's OK, I'll say goodbye to the others, and let Uncle Dougie know I'm definitely staying."

"That's fine, Kïïit," said Eloise. "And good luck."

The mare curtsied again and trotted away, tail up, saying "Am-bass-a-dor Kïïit of the Cen-tral Ran-ges" over and over, laughing each time.

"I'm going to miss her grass strudels and her turf wars," said Hector.

The Nameless One nodded and gave Hector a light bump with his hip.

"Me too," said Hector. "I liked having her around, too."

Thirty minutes later Master Shovelhovel, Seer Bunkerhunker, and RoyLee found Eloise.

"Princess Eloise, may we be having a moment of your time?" asked Shovelhovel.

"Yes, of course," said Eloise. "Does this have to do with your journey home? I assume you're going back to the Half Kingdom where your wisdom is."

"That's what we be wanting to discuss. Gran and I, we be wanting to return to our wisdom. We've come to an arrangement with Bjóöörn Tóöòrúüùn to carry us there. It would take too long on foot, and I'm not sure Gran's up to that much walking."

"I'd be fine," snorted Seer Bunkerhunker.

"Yes, Gran. Of course you would."

"But the Divine One gave us a finite number of steps in our time in this realm. Why waste steps like that when there's a perfectly good camel amenable to be helping out?"

"It's OK, Gran. You no have to be being defensive about needing a ride."

"I no be being defensive. And I no be needing a ride. And we're not here to talk about me."

"Truth, Gran, truth. Princess Eloise, it's young RoyLee here we be meaning to talk to you about."

"Yes? Is there an issue?"

The three wombats fidgeted, but said nothing.

"RoyLee?" said Eloise. "Is there something you wish to say?"

"Yes," said RoyLee. "And no."

More fidgeting.

"Sorry, which is it?" asked Eloise.

"Yes, I be wanting to say something, but no, it not be mine to say," said RoyLee. "It be Seer Bunkerhunker's visioning, so I be thinking she should be saying it."

"Seer Bunkerhunker, is there a problem?"

"It no be a problem, I don't think. It's like RoyLee be saying, I be visioning. Didn't mean to, but there it be."

"And?"

"I be visioning that RoyLee no be coming home with us."

"Oh? Really?"

"I be seeing him at your Westie court."

"To be clear, it's not my court. It's my mother's. But you see him coming home with us?"

"Not exactly yes, but not exactly no. It be more like I be seeing him in among all the Westie court people. Lots and lots and lots, none of whom I be recognizing, but all of them being gathered for some sort of something. An event? A celebration? Twas not clear. But RoyLee be there, and he be wearing frills and such. And he be comfortable being there, like he's been there at least a little while."

"Right," said Eloise. "I see. Is there more to it?"

"No," said Seer Bunkerhunker. "That be it. It no be like the Unseen sent me a herald. It be glimpses."

"So..." Master Shovelhovel coughed, covering his nerves. "So we be wondering if you might be willing to let RoyLee go with you instead of with us," said Shovelhovel. "We're no trying to fob him off or anything."

"Of course not," said Eloise. "RoyLee has shown himself capable, resourceful, and reliable. There's no fobbing involved in this matter at all."

"That's very kind of you," said Shovelhovel.

"What do you think of this, RoyLee?" asked Eloise.

"I no be wanting to wear frills," he said. "That'd be awful. But the rest —the bit about being at court and being comfortable there—that I like the sound of."

"The thing is..." Master Shovelhovel's voice trailed off, and Eloise suspected he was coming as close to blushing as a wombat could. "The thing is, we no be having the coin to pay for his returning with you. We may be the Pillagiarists—the gang formerly known as the Womban-ditos and most definitely not the Womb-banditos, which would have been a stupid thing to name a gang—the fiercest gang with bad eyesight in all the realms. Heeyahhh."

"Heeyahhh," echoed RoyLee automatically.

"But this caper with the kidnapping, and more broadly, the stealing, cheating, and thieving in general, well, it no be very profitable for us.

Even before we made a deal with that person whose name I don't want to say and tried to kidnap you (before we knew it was you, of course)—even before then we were thinking of trying our hand at activities that required a degree less fierceness and rubbing up on the wrong side of the queen's laws."

"Oh," said Eloise. "Like what?"

"Novelty stoneware mugs," said RoyLee.

"Mugs? Like drinking mugs?"

"That be right," said Master Shovelhovel.

RoyLee jumped in. "We done some test ones, like mugs shaped to look like a wee little carriage, or a mug to look like you be drinking out of a tree stump, or a plain, beautiful mug with beautiful writing on it that be saying something surprisingly rude. Oh, we be having so much fun thinking these up."

"But why mugs?" asked Eloise.

"That way, we could still say that we be mugging people, especially if we charged them really high prices. We could still claim to be the fiercest gang with bad eyesight in all the realms, on account of all the muggings."

Eloise smiled. "I see."

"But we no be having the coin to pay for RoyLee's journey with you, even if you be willing to have him. It be taking more than we have to engage the camel, who's given us extremely reasonable rates. We be having to pay the balance of his fare when we be getting home."

"Right. I don't think it's a matter of your paying for RoyLee. I think other matters take precedence."

"Like what?" asked Shovelhovel.

Eloise straightened, assumed her most regal posture, and took a step to tower over the young wombat. "RoyLee, do you make this choice of your own free will?"

"Yes, Princess."

"Do you promise to serve our queen and the Western Lands and All That Really Matters faithfully and with an open heart and mind?"

"Why, yes, Princess. Of course."

"Do you promise to put aside the ways of lawlessness and abide by the rules and decrees of our queen and our land?"

RoyLee grimaced. "You no want me to be breaking laws?" He rubbed his chin with the top of a claw. "But, we Pillagiarists—the gang formerly known as the Wombanditos and most definitely not the Womb-banditos, which would have been a stupid thing to name a gang —the fiercest gang with bad eyesight in all the realms. Heeyahhh—"

"Heeyah," said Shovelhovel rotely.

"We always be living outside the laws. No one be telling us what to do or when. Laws be for chumps. That be what Master Shovelhovel always be saying."

"Well, I don't know that I *always* be saying such," said Shovelhovel.

"RoyLee be right," said Seer Bunkerhunker. "You be saying it most every day. 'Laws be for chumps. And we no be chumps, right, mates?' And then everyone be yelling 'Chumps, chumps!'"

"Gran, no!"

"Truth be truth."

"Be that as it may," interrupted Eloise. "RoyLee, that's correct. If you come with me, you'll need to obey the laws of the realm."

"I see."

They all stood there quietly, giving RoyLee time to assimilate this foreign and novel idea.

"Princess, you'll no be thinking I'm a chump if I follow the laws?"

"No, RoyLee. I'm the one asking you to do it. There's no chumpiness involved."

"Right." RoyLee stood up on his back legs and carefully bowed to Eloise. "As strange as your request be, I'll be doing my best to honor it."

"Then I would be delighted to have you come back with us. We will find an appropriate place for you at Court. I'm sure my mother would be happy to do that."

"That be very kind of you, Princess," said Master Shovelhovel. "May I make a small suggestion?"

"Yes?"

"Perhaps you no be telling the queen about the kidnapping and thieving and all. We may be the Pillagiarists—the gang formerly known as the Wombanditos and most definitely not the Womb-banditos, which would have been a stupid thing to name a gang—the fiercest gang with bad eyesight in all the realms. Heeyahhh."

"Heeyahhh," said RoyLee.

"But we no be needing the queen looking for us."

"Your secret is safe with me." Eloise smiled. "Çalahtspeed to you for tomorrow, Master Shovelhovel and Seer Bunkerhunker. I'll make sure RoyLee is cared for."

As the three wombats walked away, Eloise could still hear them.

"I be telling you she'd be saying yes," said Seer Bunkerhunker.

"Yes, Gran."

"I be a seer. I be visioning. I told you she'd say yes."

"Yes, Gran."

"You should be listening to me more. You no be needing to be shy about talking to yon princess."

"Yes, Gran."

"She be a very nice young lady. And approachable. Before we go, you should probably be apologizing to her again for trying to kidnap and ransom her."

"Yes, Gran."

"Twice you tried. So two apologies."

"Yes, Gran."

Eloise smiled and went looking for the others.

60

A HECK OF A WAY TO SAY GOODBYE

In the pre-dawn darkness, Lorch finished knotting his pannier onto the Nameless One, then lifted RoyLee and settled him into it. "Is that comfortable?"

"Thank you, Guard Lacksneck."

"'Lorch' is still fine."

"OK. Thank you, Lorch."

Eloise was dressed and ready for the journey. She wore the repaired tunic and travel cloak as well as the wrapped blanket to shield off the wintry chill. The box with the Star of Whatever was nestled once again in the blanket's folds at her hip.

She stood next to Bjóöörn, who was sitting as low to the ground as he could. Seer Bunkerhunker refused Eloise's offer to help her into her side of the camel's pannier. "No, no, no," said the wombat. "You'll no be there after we be parting ways. I must be being able to get in and out of this on my own."

"It's easy, Gran," said Shovelhovel from the other side of the camel. "You just sort of flop in."

"I'll no be flopping. That I can be promising you."

After more to-do, the old wombat did, indeed, flop into the bag, and settled in for the ride.

Malakai and Alana stepped through the cleft in the cliff unannounced and trotted over.

"G'dawn to you," said Eloise.

"G'dawn. Let it be known that we will guide you to the edge of His Alacrity's realm," said Malakai.

"Oh?" said Eloise.

"Yes, it is so. His Alacrity has decreed."

"Malakai, you don't need to be so dramatic," said Alana. "Princess, His Alacrity has asked us to take you to the border. We know the fastest route that will take you back to the Western Lands and All That Really Matters."

"Thank you," said Eloise. "We'd appreciate your help."

"Plus, it gives us a chance to make sure you don't go bumbling around our realm again," she said. "Once was plenty."

The Nameless One snorted, but Eloise chose diplomacy. "We'll be ready in a few more minutes. What about them?" asked Eloise, pointing to Bjóöòrn and the wombats.

"The savage knows the realm," said Malakai. "He will not get lost."

"Right."

"We shall await you on the outside," said the stallion. Then he cantered back through the cleft.

Alana shook her head as he went. "Malakai's prone to the dramatic, and he doesn't even know it," she said. "Plus, he has a flawed sense of direction, always favoring the direction of the sun. It'll be me guiding you. Just don't let him know that you know that."

"Understood," said Eloise.

"See you in a minute," said the mare, then made her way out.

Eloise looked at Lorch and the Nameless One. "Everything in order?"

"Yes, Princess."

"Where's Kïïït?"

"She slipped away about an hour ago."

"She's gone already?" said Eloise. "That's sad. I wanted to say goodbye."

Hector joined them, with Jerome already on his back. "It will be good to be moving again."

"It will be good to head home," said the chipmunk. "I think I can hear my bed calling me from here."

"Let's head out then." Eloise hoisted herself onto Hector's back and followed Lorch and the Nameless One into the opening.

❦

WHAT MET THEM WHEN THEY EMERGED TOOK ELOISE'S BREATH away. Every single horse of the Us stood across from them in careful ranks and perfect stillness. Front and center was the khan himself, painted up as if for war. The dream wife stood to his left and slightly behind. To the far right Eloise glimpsed Kïïït, not quite as still and straight as the others, but statue-like compared to her normal peripatetic, chatty self.

Eloise and Hector moved to the front, and Lorch and the Nameless One fell in slightly behind and to her left. Bjóöòrn and the wombats took the same position on the right.

At a nod from the khan, the dream wife strode toward Eloise. She stepped between Hector and the Nameless One, stood at Eloise's thigh, and turned to face the lines of horses.

Khan Nergüi reared up, his bad leg dangling, and screamed. His voice seared the air with a cry both fierce and heart-rending. Behind him, a thousand horses did the same, their cries overwhelming.

Then, as one, they came down and stamped the ground, a *thwomp* echoing forever in the sudden silence.

It sent chills down Eloise's spine.

Stomp.

Stomp-stomp.

The khan began another call-and-response chant in the ancient equine language, leading his people in a kicking, head-weaving, stamping posture dance that slowly crept forward. It was different to the one Eloise had witnessed before. Their delivery was just as fierce, just as energetic and loud, but instead of the sense of greeting, this one evoked farewell.

The dream wife quietly translated the chant:

As you leave

My hooves strike sparks on this red-tinged land.

A warning. A promise. A threat.

I may live. I may die. The difference is slim.

But surely my foes will tremble and flee

As I step step step step toward them

Lightning eyes. Thunderous hearts.

While I await your return

I will dance the songs of the living and the dead

For one more day.

They finished with a last *stomp-stomp-stomp,* their necks straining left and right and their eyes wild and bulging.

Then the horses relaxed and went back to where they'd started, reforming their lines and resuming their stillness.

They waited.

Eloise waited.

Eloise realized they were waiting for her. She whispered to the dream wife, "What do they want?"

"Your response, of course."

"What?" Eloise felt her mouth going dry. She'd addressed crowds at court before, but never one this large or this daunting. "I don't know the language. What am I supposed to do?"

"Your response, young princess spy, is up to you."

"Right. Right, right, right."

Should she make a speech? Recite a poem? Launch into an interpretive dance?

Not likely.

Her stomach flipped when she realized what the horses were expecting. Alana had done it when she'd responded to the arrival chant.

Alana had screamed. And then—oh sweet Çalaht, no!—she'd sung a song.

Jerome swiveled around and gave her an Are-you-OK? look.

She replied with a No-not-in-the-least-you-were-not-there-before-they-screamed-and-sang-neither-of-which-I-particularly-want-to-do-in-front-of-a-large-village's-worth-of-horses-thank-you-very-much look.

He nodded an I-see-what-you-mean look. He glanced around at the horses, then back at her with a Can-I-be-frank-for-a-moment? look.

Eloise shrugged an If-you-must-but-say-something-useful look.

Jerome squinted a Do-it-anyway look at her.

Eloise's eyes went wide, and she gave him an Are-you-out-of-your-Çalaht-benighted-mind-no-way look.

Jerome fixed her with a Princess-Eloise-Hydra-Gumball-III-get-over-yourself-and-put-on-your-big-girl-princess-foundation-garments-and-do-what-needs-to-be-done look.

Eloise felt her face flush. She shook her head—fractionally, but firmly.

Jerome nodded—slowly, but decisively.

She shook her head again and stared at him.

The chipmunk just stared her down.

She shot him a Fine-but-don't-expect-anything-but-a-sack-of-wet-ashes-and-snail-barf-in-your-Yule-stocking-this-year look.

Eloise leaped off Hector, threw her arms wide, and before she could give it any more thought, let loose a solid, gut-fueled yell to match the khan's. To her surprise, her companions joined in, screeching along with her. Hector, the Nameless One, and Bjóöòrn reared up and pawed the air. When she stopped, they did, too, landing with a solid thunk. The sound echoed, not like a thousand horses, but clear and long.

A few of the horses across from her nodded approval, and the corners of the khan's mouth might have twitched with the briefest of smiles.

That's the screaming like a loon part finished, Eloise thought. *Now the hard bit. The singing.* She swallowed. *Don't think, don't think, don't think, don't think, don't think, don't think...*

Eloise opened her mouth and let fly with the most meaningful, impassioned, stirring song that she knew:

"There's a lady who knows all that glitters is groats..."

Her rendition of the first line of "Three Bags of Groats for My Sweetheart" was deliberate, lingering, belted out, and fueled by a bravado that Eloise did not actually feel. Her nerves gave her voice a vibrato that added to the poignancy.

On the second line, Jerome joined in, adding a top end to the melody. By the third, Lorch had snatched his bongos from where they were tied onto the Nameless One's back, and he and Hector added in their voices. Lorch tapped a simple bongo beat, and the Nameless One *clop-clippity-clopped* a blending, syncopated rhythm. By the fourth line, the wombats and camel had lent their voices as well.

Together, the impromptu choir infused the song with harmonies Eloise would never have dreamed them capable of. It must have been born of the many, many, many thousands of times in the past months that one of them had sung, hummed, warbled, or just thought about That Song (or sometimes That Infernal Song), as the song's creator, Jaminity Delgado Blister, sometimes called it. Their voices filled the equine encampment with an unexpected beauty and grace.

When they got to the end where the singer convinces his sweetheart to trade the three bags of groats for true love's first kiss, they crescendoed, belting out the last words with such gusto that it was either the realm's best homage to Jaminity or the realm's worst parody of Lyndia Thrind, the song's most famous singer.

Either was OK with Eloise.

They finished.

Silence.

Then a thousand horse whistles, hoots, and stomps roared approval.

"Well," said the dream wife. "That seems to have worked."

"I guess so," said Eloise.

The khan said a few more unintelligible equine words and the assembly broke. The khan limped painfully forward toward Eloise and her friends, followed by Malakai and Alana. Instead of the horses heading in every direction to get on with their day, they fell in line behind their monarch.

"He would have a word with you, Princess," said the dream wife. Then, to the others, she said, "If you would please form a line, side-by-side, to her right."

"What's this?" asked Eloise.

"Tradition," said the dream wife. "And an honor. I've never seen him do this for any who are not of the Us, except for me."

"Are you not of the Us?"

The dream wife raised one shoulder. "Usually, I think so. But because of my species, it's not always clear."

The khan hobbled over until he stood in front of Eloise, and a line of horses snaked behind him. "Princess Eloise, I wish you Çalahtspeed for your journey home."

"Thank you."

"Please extend my regards to Queen Eloise Hydra Gumball II and give her my best wishes for a continued peaceful coexistence between our realms."

"I'll do that."

"Would you do something else for me?" asked the khan.

"Of course."

The small stallion looked uncomfortable. "I need you to deliver a specific message."

"Yes?" said Eloise.

"Please tell Queen Eloise, 'That thing about the thing with the thing and the other thing that got kind of thingy—it's no longer a thing. Let's move on.'"

"Should I actually understand that?"

"Please just deliver the message. She'll know what I mean."

"It will be my pleasure."

"Do you need to practice it to make sure you got it right?"

"Got it. 'That thing about the thing with the thing and the other thing that got kind of thingy—it's no longer a thing. Let's move on.'"

"Thank you. Now we will say farewell in the way of the Us. Please lean down." When she was closer to his face, he said, "It was good to have had you with us, my sister," said the khan.

Eloise guessed at the correct reply. "It is good to have been with you, my brother."

"It will be good when you have returned to the Us," said the khan.

"It will be good to return to the Us some day," said Eloise.

Then the khan extended his neck forward, touched Eloise's nose, and blew a puff of air into her right nostril. It surprised her completely, and she only just managed not to jerk backward. Her habits screamed, *Horse snot! Horse snot! Horse snot up your nose!* Eloise kept her face steady as they switched sides, touched noses again, and puffed into each other's left nostrils. Then they stepped back from each other, and the khan gave her a nod, then moved to stand in front of Lorch.

At least that was over.

But it wasn't. Malakai moved to stand in front of her. "It was good to have had you with us, my sister."

A thousand horses! She was going to have to do this with a thousand horses! "It is good to have been with you, my brother."

"It will be good when you have returned to the Us," said Malakai.

"It will be good to return to the Us some day," said Eloise.

No, no, no, no! Nose touch. Horse snot right. Nose touch. Horse snot left. Nod. *No, no, no, no!*

Next, it was Alana's turn: ritual words, nose touch, horse snot right, nose touch, horse snot left, nod, done. Next was a stallion Eloise wasn't sure she recognized, followed by the mare who was a sentry, then the most serious foal she'd ever met, then one of the messenger colts. It struck Eloise as a strangely intimate thing to do with someone you didn't know at all, and each one of them made the gesture with sincerity and seriousness.

It was a heck of a way to say goodbye, and Eloise wondered what kinds of agues might be shared between horses and humans through the medium of airborne mucus.

It took half a day to say goodbye to everyone. Kïïït was there somewhere in the middle, whispering, "Thank you, Princess," between nose puffs.

"Good luck to you, Kïïït," said Eloise, and then, breaking the nose puff protocol, she threw her arms around Kïïït and gave her a hug. The mare smiled, gave Princess Eloise a gentle nuzzle, then moved on.

When they'd finished, Eloise had exchanged breaths with every stallion, mare, filly, colt, and foal. She found it both one of the most disgusting and most incredibly bonding experiences of her life.

Last was the dream wife, who performed the same ritual, but added a hug at the end. "Do they still say 'Boring travels to you' in the Western Lands and All that Really Matters?"

"Yes, they do."

"Then, boring travels to you, Princess Eloise Hydra Gumball III. And as they say among the Us, 'When you leave, you shall remain. Where you go, there we shall be.'"

"That's lovely," said Eloise. "Until next time."

"And who knows? Perhaps there actually will be a next time."

"I hope so."

"If the Purity wills it, it will be so."

61

ESCORTED

They rode out of the horse encampment in bright winter sunlight. Malakai, Alana, and a squad of half a dozen warrior horses initially led them back the way they had come.

Eloise felt a lightness she'd not experienced in weeks. Home. They were finally going home. Whatever mess was left behind (Turpy, for example) would be someone else's problem. She could live with that.

Less than an hour after their departure, they stopped at a fork in the road.

"This is us," said Bjóöòrn.

"So soon?" Eloise felt suddenly sad.

"I'm afraid so."

They helped the wombats out of the panniers, then gave them their space so RoyLee could have a private goodbye with his elders. Eloise overheard snatches of the conversation: "...be being polite..." "...no be starting a sub-chapter of the gang...." "...be paying careful attention..." "...tell my ma..." "...told you that you be being a smart one. Don't disappoint..." "...miss you..." "...love you, too..."

When they loaded them back up, all three were sniffing back tears. The camel took the left fork. RoyLee watched them go until they rounded a bend and were gone.

"They'll be alright," said Eloise, giving his shoulder a small squeeze. "And so will you. I'll make sure of it."

"Thank you, Princess," sniffed the wombat.

Malakai and Alana set a fast pace, alternating periods of cantering and trotting. They avoided galloping, as it was too taxing for a long journey, but never slowed to a walk. The landscape blew past, silent, cold, and stark, and once again, Eloise was struck by the discipline and stamina of the khan's warriors.

Mid-afternoon, they left the well-signposted trail they were on, headed through a patch of scrub and traveled cross-country, following a route that had not seen feet nor hooves in years. They crested hills and splashed through streams skinned by winter ice. They skirted forests and tried to avoid gaining or losing too much elevation that they'd have to reclaim. It was exhausting, and Eloise felt thrilled to be out of confinement, unburdened of her cares (for now, at least), and moving fast and free again.

At dusk, they reached a fast-flowing river in a gully far below, traversed by a half-heartedly maintained rope-and-board bridge. It was clearly a relic from a time that had shown it more care, or at least had more travelers necessitating its upkeep. Now it was missing planks, and its ropes looked so old that Çalaht herself could have been the one to tie them in place.

Malakai and Alana stopped in front of it, with the six warriors halting and coming to attention to one side. "When you cross this bridge, you enter the Western Lands and All That Really Matters," said Malakai. "Within 20 lengths straight ahead of the bridge, there's an obvious, if disused, trail. Follow it, and eventually you'll reach something that could actually be called a road. Go right. Keep going. Find the first town you can. Your maps should be good from there."

"Is it possible to go down and cross the river instead of using the bridge?" asked Lorch.

"Of course. It will take about three days," said the stallion. "The Us use the bridge. It requires care, but it's doable."

"Do you know how recently it's been used by the Us?" asked Eloise.

"No more than five years hence. This is not a regular route for us."

"I see," said Eloise. "Well, thank you for guiding us here. I'm sure you've saved many days on our trip."

"We will go now," the stallion said. "My suggestion is you make your way over as soon as possible. Dusk approaches, and you don't want to cross when there's no light. Or you can make camp and cross in the morning."

"You're leaving now?" asked Eloise.

"We have discharged our obligation," said Malakai. "There's no need to linger."

Alana coughed a stage cough. "Malakai."

"Yes."

The mare stared at the stallion, waiting.

"What?" he asked.

She kept staring.

"No," he said.

"Yes," she answered.

The six other horse warriors in the squad suddenly stiffened and did their best to look as invisible as six horses standing at attention could be.

"What?" asked Eloise.

Malakai turned to her and drew himself to his full height. "I have asked Alana, daughter of Ganbaat and Altan, to help me be aware of when I say things that others might find insensitive so I don't come off as a 'tight-withered old nimrod,' as she puts it. Apparently, this is one of those times."

"Not 'apparently,'" said Alana. "Is."

"Alright!" he snapped. "I got the message." He turned back to Eloise. "Apologies if I spoke in an insensitive way. I do not wish to be a tight-withered old nimrod. And I believe in self-improvement."

"That's fine," said Eloise. "I hadn't noticed anything."

Malakai turned to Alana. "She hadn't noticed anything."

"She noticed. She's just being polite."

Malakai turned back to Eloise. "You were being polite?"

Eloise gave a small, reluctant nod.

"This is difficult," muttered Malakai. "Anyway, we must go."

"Of course." Eloise bowed to Malakai, Alana, and the other horses. "Thank you all for bringing us here. That was most generous."

"It was generous of His Alacrity," said Malakai. "All thanks can be directed to him whose command it was."

"There. That right there," said Alana. "That's what I'm talking about."

"What? No. Again?" The stallion seemed genuinely flabbergasted. "How?"

"We can talk about it later." Alana bowed to Eloise and the others. "Goodbye, Princess Eloise, Guard Lacksneck, Champion Abernatheen de Chipmunk, and young master RoyLee. Fare thee well, Hector de Pferd, son of Ferdinand de Pferd and Ethel de Pferd. And you, too, One Who Has No Name."

They returned her bow.

Alana took a step forward, leaned over, and whispered in Eloise's ear. "I'm glad you turned out not to be spies. That would have been very messy. It's worked out for the better, don't you think?"

"Yes, all told," Eloise whispered back. "It has."

"Wind be in your mane," said the mare.

"Boring travels to you."

Alana winked at her, stepped back, and turned to the warriors. "Form up!" she barked. The squad of six stiffened even more to attention and slightly adjusted their positioning. "Lead on, brother Malakai."

Malakai wheeled and set off at a trot, the squad making a tight formation behind him. They rounded a bend and were gone.

62

LOON BRIDGE

"Right," said Eloise to the others. "Home, then. What do you think? Camp or cross?"

Eloise, Lorch, and Jerome, with RoyLee tagging along, checked out the bridge, while Hector and the Nameless One, tired from the hard ride, rested and cropped some tussocks.

Jerome took half a dozen steps onto the bridge and bounced on it to see if it was sturdy under his small weight. It barely wobbled. "I'd have no problem with it unless it completely fell apart when I was in the middle," said Jerome. He unpacked a dried apricot the size of his head, took a nibble, then gestured with it, pointing at the horses. "It's them we need to be concerned about, of course."

"Let me try," said Lorch. He stepped onto the bridge with Jerome and jostled it. "It seems like it should hold."

"It would be good to make it into our realm tonight, even if it's just across the border. It would feel more like home," said Eloise.

"I see no reason not to continue, Princess." said Lorch.

They gave Hector and the Nameless One a few more minutes, then lined up to go across. Jerome went first and made it to the other side with the bridge barely swaying. Lorch followed without incident, and the Nameless One crossed like he was walking on the Queen's Boulevard in Brague.

It was Hector who had a problem. Three-quarters of the way across, there was the crack of breaking wood, and his back right leg plunged through a plank. Hector lost his balance and buckled, landing heavily, and the old ropes creaked and shook.

"Steady there," called Lorch. "Don't flail. You don't want it swinging more than it already is. Are you OK?"

"I think so," said Hector. "I scraped my leg pretty badly, but it doesn't feel like it ripped open." He craned around to look at Eloise. "Princess, do you see any blood?"

"Not from here, no."

"Good," said Lorch. "Can you lift yourself back up to a standing position?"

Hector pressed his front legs into the bridge floor and tried to push himself upward. No luck. He tried again, but couldn't get the purchase he needed to draw up the sprawled back right leg. "I'm afraid I'm going to need help."

The Nameless One looked at Hector and snorted something at him.

"No, I don't think that's necessary," replied Hector. His voice was strained, and it sounded to Eloise like he was embarrassed.

The Nameless One snorted again, more insistently.

"What's he saying?" called Lorch.

"I'd rather not say. It'll be OK. I'll get out of this in a minute."

A snort, a stamp, and a head waggle from the Nameless One.

"Hector, please," called Eloise. "What's he saying?"

"Nothing, Princess."

"Hector."

Jerome recognized The Tone. It worked, even from three-quarters of a rickety bridge away.

"The Nameless One is suggesting a halter be placed on my head. The Nameless One would drag me forward with it."

"A halter. Really?"

"Yes, Princess."

"Isn't that... Sorry, but horses find that demeaning, don't they?"

"Yes, Princess. It is a return to barbarism. That's why I'd rather not use one."

"But would it work?"

Hector paused, swallowing. "Possibly. It could provide useful leverage if pulled correctly."

"So a halter is a reasonable suggestion, given the circumstances?"

Another pause. "Sadly, yes, Princess."

Eloise said nothing else. Hector tried several more times to extricate himself from the bridge.

"Equine Designate de Pferd," said Jerome gently. "Night falls."

Hector humphed. "Fine. You're right. Guard Lacksneck, I'll need you to fashion a halter from some rope. It needs to be sturdy since you'll be pulling on it."

Lorch knotted a rope to form a set of loops to go around Hector's nose and over the top of his head behind his ears. He took a second rope, tied it to the bottom of the first, and let Jerome walk it out to Hector.

"Sorry, mate," said Jerome as he slid it over Hector's head. "Really sorry. It won't be long."

"It's... it's what needs to be done. But..."

"Yes?"

"I'd rather it wasn't a matter for joking."

"I've had a lot of my propensity for joking excised by this trip. Whatever's left can easily avoid this matter."

"Thank you."

"No problem."

At the far end of the bridge, Lorch tied the other end of the rope in a loop and slipped it over the Nameless One's neck. "Ready?"

"Champion Abernatheen de Chipmunk, I suggest you aren't on the bridge when we do this," said Hector.

"That's OK. I can hold, and just be here if you need me."

"I don't want to have to worry about whether or not I might step on you."

"Right." Jerome gave one of his excessive, hand-wavy bows and said, "Equine Designate de Pferd, I shall leave you to it." He ran up and off the bridge.

"Ready!" called Hector.

The Nameless One stepped forward to take up the slack in the rope, making it taut, but not pulling. He craned his neck around so he could see Hector and snorted.

Hector gave a small nod, which put a wave in the rope. "It's OK. Let's just get it over with."

"Do you need me to push from behind?" yelled Eloise.

"I'd rather you weren't on the bridge," said Hector.

"We'll see how you go."

"Pull!" called Hector.

As the light dimmed from dusk toward dark, the Nameless One leaned into the rope, pulling on Hector's head. Hector heaved with his front legs and pushed up with the one back one. The forward tug gave him the additional force he needed to get back to a standing position. The fourth leg came up, but he couldn't pull it through. "Keep holding me," called Hector. "My hoof's caught." Cautiously, he tugged on his right leg, but it wouldn't come free. "I can't tell how, but my leg's stuck."

"I'm going to come have a look," called Eloise.

"No, I'll do it," said Lorch. "Please, Princess, don't risk it."

"You're on the wrong side. You'd have to climb over him to get to his leg. And Jerome and RoyLee are too small to tug effectively, if that's needed. I'll do it."

"Right, Princess. Be careful."

Eloise stepped carefully onto the bridge, grasping the ropes that served as handrails. The planks were covered with deep green lichen that looked gray in the dimming light, and the rush of water far below became louder as she moved forward over it. Eloise eased her way down the slope, making sure she always had three firm points of contact. "Left hand, right foot, right hand, left foot," she said to herself. It was the same mantra she used when rock climbing or bouldering.

She passed the halfway point, and the bridge's slope changed from downward to upward. "Almost there," she said to Hector.

"Take your time," said Hector, his voice strained by the pull of the halter. "I'd rather you were careful."

By the time she reached him, it was fully dark. "How're you doing?"

"It's unpleasant, but tolerable. Rather like having one's teeth rasped when they get too long."

"Mine don't do that," said Eloise. "I'm going to run a hand down along your leg."

"Mine do. If you don't get them rasped, one's teeth get sharp. My dam was always on us foals about having regular raspings."

Keeping a firm grip on the handrail rope, Eloise squatted and used her other hand to feel from the outside of his right thigh past the joint of his hock and down toward his fetlock. "There's the problem," she said. "Somehow, the bridge planks have moved. Your leg is caught between hoof and fetlock at the pastern between two boards.

"Right," said Hector. "It feels a bit like that, although I think the circulation is cut off, as it's tingling."

"Try moving your leg slowly upward so I can feel what's going on."

Hector lifted his leg. Eloise felt the constraining planks pinch inward. "OK, I can tell what's happening. Just a minute."

Eloise gripped the plank and pulled. The other one came up. She pushed on the lower plank, and they both went down. "I need to wedge them apart somehow so your foot can slip out. Plus, my weight's on the wrong one. You're going to have to let me climb under you so I can change my position and pry them apart."

"Are you sure that's a good idea?"

"No. Not at all. Ready?"

"Ready."

Eloise wrapped an arm around his leg to keep herself steady and shifted so she faced the way she'd come. She put her knees on the lower plank and slid both hands under the upper one. "On three. And just know my face is right here when your hoof comes free."

"I'll be careful."

"One, two, three." Eloise pulled up on the plank behind his pastern and shoved with her knees down on the closer one. The ropes holding the planks held tight, but there was just enough flex that she created a gap. "Now!"

Hector slowly pulled on his leg, but his hoof still jammed.

Eloise strained harder. "Just yank it!"

"Yes, Princess."

Hector gave a sudden jerk and his hoof flew free. He overbalanced and scrambled as the Nameless One pulled him forward. The freed hoof caught Eloise in the temple as it went past, knocking her onto her back. "Ease up! Ease up on the rope!" yelled the horse.

The Nameless One stepped forward to give slack, and Hector came to a stop. "Princess, are you alright?"

Eloise lay on her back rubbing the side of her head. There'd be a bruise before she knew it, but she was grateful he'd clunked her backward and not sideways. She wasn't plummeting into the ravine or dangling from the ropes. So, bonus. "Just... Just finish getting across. I'll be there in a second."

She grabbed the ropes for safety and felt the motion of the bridge as Hector finished his traversal. Eloise looked at the stars emerging as each footfall gave the bridge a little jolt. *That could have been worse*, she thought.

When Hector was all the way off, she gave her head a last press with her palm and eased back up. "Coming," she called and stepped forward.

A bird landed on the frayed rope handrail in front of her. It was the scruffiest, most unkempt yellow-billed loon Eloise had ever seen. His left eye was missing, his upper beak was split, with a chunk of it skewing off in the wrong direction, and his feathers looked like he'd recently flown backward through a cyclone. He staggered (and smelled) as if liquid consolation from the local public inn made up the bulk of his diet.

He turned his one eye toward her and stared.

"Yes?" said Eloise.

"I..." His voice sounded like he had a three-century long hookah habit. He cleared his throat like he was trying to dislodge his liver and spat. "I know who you are."

"Do you?"

"Yes, I do."

"So what? Lots of people know who I am."

"But *I* know who you *are*. And I *know* who *you* are. *And* I know *who* you are."

"Very clever," said Eloise. "Ish."

"Princess," called Lorch. "Are you okay?"

"Fine. Be there in a sec." Eloise turned her head so she was staring at the loon with the same look he used on her. "Obviously, you have me at a disadvantage. Who you are?"

The loon gargled more phlegm and spat again. "He told me not to tell you."

"He who?"

"Him. Then again, he also told me not to let you know I was helping him watch. But me? I work different. I like to let 'em know I'm there. It gives 'em something to think about. Like you're gonna do now. I'm gonna be living in your head without paying a tithe. For me, that's the fun bit. Some of the fun bit, anyway."

"Princess? Is someone there?" called Lorch through the dark.

"No one important," Eloise yelled back.

The bird ignored the jibe. "Having said all that, I'd be grateful if you'd not tell him about our little chat," smarmed the loon. "You've seen what he can be like." The loon spat again and feigned boredom. "Just know we're there. Watching. I may have just the one eye, but I see plenty. Plenty, plenty, plenty."

Then, without another word, he flew off, a ghost with disheveled wings and a grating manner. As he rose, he barked his crazed loon laugh over and over.

"Who was that?" asked Lorch when Eloise made it to the other side.

"Some loon." Once RoyLee had joined them, she gave a quick recap of her conversation with the one-eyed bird.

"That sounds serious, Princess," said Lorch. "We'll need to be vigilant with our night watch."

"And during the day," added Hector. "Who knows when someone will try something."

"Let's find a spot for the night." Lorch led them off the path and away from the bridge to make camp.

❋ 63 ❋

XROSSING

The night passed without incident, but everyone was jumpy. The loon's cackle echoed in Eloise's mind, keeping her from dropping off to sleep. As he'd predicted, he was living tithe-free in her head. That made her angry, which also kept sleep at arm's length. A frost as thick as wedding cake icing didn't help. They hadn't prepared for sleeping rough in winter. Thank Çalaht for the dream wife's extra blanket.

She listened to the others sleeping. Jerome was having a tea nightmare. He kept mumbling, "Too hot! Water's too hot! You'll bruise the leaves!" RoyLee also spoke in his sleep, exclaiming, "We're the Pillagi..." over and over, but never managing to say the word "Pillagiarists" all the way through. Lorch sat on watch, sighing over and over, a sure sign he was ruminating contingencies. Only Hector and the Nameless One slept deeply, a perk of their exhaustion after the day's ride and Hector's near miss on the bridge.

Eloise must have finally dozed, since she found herself waking to Hector on watch and a rising sun gleaming over the glistening ground.

"G'morning," croaked Eloise. "Blessings of the day."

"Blessings of the day to you, Princess," said Hector. "I trust you slept."

"I eventually reached a reasonably close approximation. It will have to do."

"We've a long day ahead, and I'm sure we're all keen to get started. I'll get the Nameless One and we'll graze while you break fast."

Lorch insisted on a cooked breakfast, and Eloise was grateful for the warmth of porridge sprinkled with dried apricot shreds and cashew crumbs. They finished, tidied, packed, and loaded the horses—all before the sun had given the night's thick frost much of a hard time.

Lorch and the Nameless One went first, and they retraced their steps back to the bridge, turning right onto the path that led away from it. Half a day's ride later, they came to a row of wooden stakes in a swath of cleared land stretching left and right as far as they could see.

"What are those?" asked Jerome. "And why?"

The stakes had been placed with incredible precision—each was exactly five lengths apart and they protruded uniformly from the ground for one and a half lengths. From the look of them, they'd been there a while—the sturdy ironwood was weathered and caked with lichen.

"Look," pointed RoyLee.

Where the row of stakes crossed their path, an official-looking box sat on a pole at just above waist height. The box would once have been grand, but now stood sentry with faded paint, a bent hinge, and a resigned sag. The lid had a rusted metal sign with embossed lettering pitted with age. It read: "Wall of the Realms, Western Lands and All That Really Matters—Central Ranges, Zone 4,302, Section 83. Obey all instructions inside."

"This is the Adequate Wall of the Realms?" said Jerome incredulously. "I thought it was finished everywhere. Years and years ago."

"It's supposed to be," said Eloise. "'Border to border to border to border to border and back.' One 'border' for each of the four and a half realms."

"This isn't a wall. This is the idea of the possibility of a wall, officious-looking box notwithstanding."

"This must date from the earliest days," said Hector. "Before every-thing had the word 'adequate' added to it."

Lorch opened the lid. "There's a logbook. And a list of instructions. Beautiful quillmanship. All those swirls and loops make it fancy and hard to read."

"Let's hear them," said Eloise. "The sign says we have to obey them, and goodness knows we wouldn't want to disappoint a rusted old sign."

"Or the long-dead petty official who authorized it," said Jerome.

"Exactly."

Lorch cleared his throat like an overwrought thespian preparing to recite an ill-metered sonnet. "Herewith are the Instructions for Trav-elers Xrossing into the Western Lands and All That Really Matters at this Sometimes-Occupied, Royally Designated Border Xrossing Checkpoint. Instruction the First: Determine if there is one or more border guards and/or customs agents on duty. If so, congratulations! The attending border guard and/or customs agent will either arrest you, impound your goods, gather levies and imposts, or, in some cases, send you on your way."

"That sounds a bit grim," said Hector.

"Instruction the Second," continued Lorch. "In the event that this royally designated border xrossing checkpoint happens to be unat-tended, proceed as follows: Sub-Instruction the A: Face in the general direction of Brague. If you are unsure which direction that is, please consult the arrow at the base of the pole supporting this royally approved box."

"There be the arrow," said RoyLee. He oriented himself in the direction it pointed and stood at attention.

"Sub-Instruction the B: Determine if you have anything to declare, either situations or items. Note that all wrongdoings, contraband, infractions, prohibited substances, and compromising personal circumstances are considered declarable."

"That's rather comprehensive," said Eloise. "That really could be almost anything."

"Sub-Instruction the C: Facing Brague and speaking in a loud and clear voice, declare your declarables as follows. State your name, your occupation, the month, the year and, if you know it, the day, as well as your normal place of residence, followed by each and every one of those things that you self-assessed as being declarable. Assume that someone can hear you, which might or might not be the case. Sub-Instruction the D: Enter the relevant details in the Queen's Royally Authorized and Recognized Xrossing Logbook affixed below these instructions."

Lorch flipped open the cover of the Queen's Royally Authorized Xrossing Logbook. "Wow, this has been here a while. This first entry is decades old. Apparently a herbwoman residing in Splït Ïnfïnïtïvë considered her stock of pukeweed, her possession of strong opinions on the use of onion-poultices, and her frequent use of the word 'ain't' to be declarable circumstances. Hmmm." He flipped a few pages. "A retired herald from Skullcruft has declared his extreme attraction to the sound of his wife whispering her shopping list." Flip, flip, flip. "A tinker from Unmitigated Catastrophic Disappointment has declared a box of near-valueless oddments." Flip, flip. "A gravedigger with a business called No Bits Left Behind has declared..."

"Hold it," said Eloise. "Unmitigated Catastrophic Disappointment? A tinker? What's the name?"

"Harold Salubrious Clapper," read Lorch.

Eloise shook her head. "Sorry, doesn't ring a bell."

RoyLee was still facing Brague, standing uncomfortably at attention. "So, do we make declarations or not?"

"What's the last entry in the book?" asked Jerome.

Lorch turned to the back, then flipped forward, looking for the last page with writing. "Uh... Six decades ago. A baker from Loosely Interpretive Nuances declared a sack of red runner beans sourced from a backyard gardener whom he suspects of having dumped them in paint. He was traveling with a croupier transporting 'admittedly loaded dice.'"

"I think we're pretty safe to give it a miss," said Eloise. "But I might let my mother know the state of border security at this particular 'xrossing.' Not that she's overly fussed with such things. Now, if I may..." She took a step across the line represented by the ironwood stakes, took a deep breath, and sighed. "There's no place like home," she said. It made her feel like clicking her heels in joy, but instead, she turned to the others and said, "I welcome you back to the Western Lands and All That Really Matters. Now, let's see how fast we can get home, shall we?"

$\mathbb{X}$ 64 $\mathbb{X}$

LIKE A SNEEZE

As they traveled Bragueward, winter seemed determined that they would enjoy the sights of every locality they passed. Eloise had seen plenty of snow over the years, but had never spent so much time actually in it. As they moved through hamlets with names like Bottomless Hinchley, Snaketopiary, and That Cluster of Hovels Near Ned's Old Shed, Eloise got very good at distinguishing different types of snow as it fluttered, slashed, and splatted down.

To pass the time, she made up names for various kinds. "Marble marbles" were little hard balls of snow that got under foot or hoof and were slick to walk on. "Vanilla pudding" was snow with a skin on top and white sludge below. "Devotional house minder's misery" was snow blown so hard and so high that it covered the doors of dwellings. (Eloise imagined legions of devotional house minders digging their way out so devout practitioners could come in and worship Çalaht.) "Hoof flop" was the palm-sized bit of compressed snow tossed up by a horse's hoof while at a trot. "Half Kingdom horror" was snow mixed with dirt, giving it a muddy color. (She didn't know if they actually had it in the Half Kingdom, but liked the alliteration.) "Warrior darts" was wind-blown snow crystals capable of slicing any exposed skin. "Wedding cake" was snow piled in even layers (although she only saw one example of this). And her favorite (or least favorite, depending on if she was in it or looking at it through a window) was "arrowproof super chunk chunk corn crud on toast," a miserable combination of snow so hard one could carve it (the arrowproof part) covered by heavy wet chunky snow (super chunk chunk) under a layer of wet granular snow which melted during the day and refroze at night (corn crud), mixed with powder snow on a heavily trafficked part of a road defiled by previous passersby and frozen into a crusted mess (crud on toast).

Naming types of snow gave Eloise a way to distract herself from the things that were bothering her. First (and always, it seemed) was the Star of Whatever. She checked in with Sparky now and then, but he was quiet, just metaphorically nodding a sort of "Hello, Loulou" and going back to sleep. She didn't consider this a breach of their accord, but it might have been nice to pass the time getting to know him better.

Nope.

Then there were her bandages, which seemed to have adopted the motto, "Life is better if you itch like you have hives, an undershirt made of badger dandruff, a ragweed allergy, and a colony of lice living on your skin." The worst of it was that between the winter weather and all the layers she had to wear, it was impossible for her to reach and scratch any of the itchy spots. If they stopped for a break and she could find a surface that wasn't laden with snow, Eloise would back up to it and rub against it, providing a few moments of blessed relief. But mainly, the itching was maddening, especially when combined with her ongoing inability to attend to her habits, which constantly niggled at her.

And yet again, Jerome had "Three Bags of Groats for My Sweetheart" stuck in his head, and would randomly sing, hum, or yodel almost-correct snatches of verse or melody. This gave Eloise a chance to enjoy another few thousand repetitions of That Song in her head.

Even more insidious than the itch, her chivvying habits, and the endless looping of That Song was the one-eyed loon. Him, and Turpy, and who knew how many other people. She kept looking for them—

behind the bare branches of the trees they passed, or the hedges at an inn where they stopped for a meal. Eloise imagined eyes following her, boring into her, watching, watching, watching, even if she couldn't see anyone actually doing it.

It was maddening.

She mentioned it to Lorch, who nodded in agreement. "I know what you mean, Princess," he said. "I call it 'watcher's haunting.' One is watching for something in particular, and the idea of it shapes everything into glimpses of it."

"Have you seen the loon?" asked Eloise. "I'm seeing him everywhere."

"No, Princess. I assume he's there—him, the felon, or perhaps someone else the felon might have hired—but I've not seen any of them."

The days melted together, a melange of different types of wintry unpleasantness, false sightings of spying eyes, itching, ignoring itching, scratching and making things worse, more itching, counting to distract from itching and her habits, and mediocre meals taken at inns with names like How Now Brown Chow (horrid), Yam Shack (Lorch and RoyLee liked it), and The Underachiever's Kitchenette. The sameness of the journey dulled her senses, and the hypnotic clopping of hooves sent her to the La La Realms more than once.

The attack came at night.

They were trying to cover a few extra strong lengths in the dark to reach an inn called Grub in the Scrub, which Lorch's map promised was there. The name seemed more appealing than the one in the previous village called The Beguiled Spile, serving only items decanted with a spile. Jerome had spent the last three strong lengths thinking of foods that might require a spile. "I've come up with maple syrup (or any other edible tree sap, although I don't know of any others), and beer, ale, palm wine, and other forms of liquid consolation," he said. "So, what do they serve if spile food is their niche, their *raison d'être*? You can't get salad from a spile. You can't get nuts or veggies from a spile. You can't get fruit from a spile, although if you shoved a spile into a ripe plum, you might get a trickle of plum juice, but I don't think that's what they mean. You can't get—"

"Jer, if you want, we can go back and see." Eloise did her best to keep her voice neutral.

"No, thank you. Not even if Çalaht her Divine self was in there working the spiles. I can't imagine anything worse."

"I can."

"What?"

"Speculating about it *ad nauseam*."

Jerome humphed. "Well, pardon me, Princess Eloise, for having a curious and inquisitive nature."

Eloise went back to thinking about what one should call the snow they were currently wading through—smooshed yam? Lumpy spud puree? Cauliflower curse?

Something hit her from the right, knocking her off Hector in a single wallop. The angle of it spun her a quarter turn and Eloise landed face-down in the snow, which muffled her cries and filled her mouth with cauliflower curse. A fraction of a second later, something or someone was tearing at her back, ripping at the dream wife's tied blanket.

It was a panther—dark, silent, and strong, with a dangerous and accurate leap, and built like an arsenal of weapons.

He's going to kill me. Eloise's mind raced. *This can't be it*.

"Princess!" yelled Lorch.

"El!" shouted Jerome.

There was a faint hiss of steel as both drew their swords, but it was drowned out by the muffled thud of hooves as Hector and the Nameless One wheeled to face whatever was going on.

The panther flattened Eloise with one paw square on her neck, holding her head immobile. Eloise squirmed and bucked, expecting an assassin's bite or the slash of lethal claws.

Instead, what she felt was rummaging. His great paw moved up and down her side, looking for something.

The Star of Whatever!

"The Star!" she spluttered, spitting out snow. "The Star! He's after the Star!"

The horses rushed forward but hesitated, the risk of hurting Eloise too high. Hector spun, ready to double-barrel the panther with both back hooves, but didn't have a clear opening.

"Princess, cover your head!" shouted Lorch as the Nameless One maneuvered to make a foreleg strike.

RoyLee threw himself into the fight. The wombat scrambled from his pannier, squinted to see whatever he might, and launched himself in the general direction of the commotion, screeching a wild, "Heeeeeeeeeeyaaaaaaaaaahhh!" He landed on the back of the panther's head, dug in his claws until they drew blood, and bit down on whatever was closest—the cat's ear. The panther growled and shook his head trying to dislodge the wombat, but RoyLee held on.

Jerome saw RoyLee's folly and matched it. He ran to Hector's flank and flung himself at Eloise's attacker, his champion's sword slicing the air in front of him. The chipmunk landed and sank the blade into the cat's neck. It drew blood, but failed to damage anything vital.

The panther roared and shook himself, but the wombat and the chipmunk held on. Jerome pulled the sword from the scruff and jabbed downward again. This time, it tore into the cat's shoulder muscle and lodged into bone.

"Now!" yelled Lorch. The Nameless One saw the opening and reared. But before he could strike, something flew at his eye and he flinched away. It was the loon. The one-eyed bird swooped and dove at the horse over and over, harrying him, neutralizing his attacks and forcing Lorch to clutch a handful of mane to stay on the Nameless One's back.

In the blur of dark, struggling shapes, a third was suddenly there—Turpentine Snotearrow McCcoonnch. Turpy ran into the fray at long-walker speed. He threw an elbow that slammed the side of Hector's head with a loud thud. He smashed a kick into the Nameless One's knee—almost the exact same move he'd pulled on Lorch in his last attack. Turpy then rushed to where the panther struggled to keep Eloise pinned while the wombat and chipmunk did as much damage as possible.

"I'll get it," snarled Turpy. "Just get them out of here and keep those idiot horses away."

"Right," grunted the panther. With a last shove, he ground Eloise into the snow, then leapt toward Hector and the Nameless One, taking Jerome and RoyLee with him.

The moment the panther was off, Eloise heaved out of the snow, swinging wildly and struggling for air. A random blow glanced off Turpy's temple. He shook it off and countered with a fist directly into Eloise's solar plexus. The pain staggered her and she fought to stay upright as she gasped wintry air. Turpy grabbed at the dream wife's blanket, pulled a dagger, and sliced at Eloise's side where the Star of Whatever hung. The princess flailed and kicked, but Turpy's punch had left her limp and ineffective.

Splat! The box with the Star of Whatever fell from the blanket and hit the snow, its trailing length of sash still attached to it.

Turpy shoved Eloise back a step and fumbled his dagger as he stooped to pick up the box. Instinctively, Eloise yelled, "Lorch!", and as the jester's fingers brushed the lid, she stepped forward and kicked it like a hockey sack. It arced toward the guard. With a changer's deftness, Lorch caught it by the sash and held it dangling.

It was a beautiful kick. If she'd been on the hockey sacking field, she would have gotten a point. Possibly two, if someone other than Jerome was keeping score.

"Go!" Eloise yelled to Lorch. "Keep it safe!"

Lorch and the Nameless One spun and galloped away.

"Get it," yelled Turpy to the panther. "Whatever it takes."

The panther dislodged RoyLee and Jerome by slapping them against a tree, then sprinted after the horse and guard. He was bleeding, and winced as he moved. Eloise doubted he'd catch them.

The Star of Whatever would be safe.

"You..." barked Turpy. He grabbed her by the collar and brought her face close to his. "You filthy, ridiculous excuse for a..."

Eloise took a fraction of a second while Turpy raved, and thought, *I really don't believe in violence. It solves nothing. There's way too much of it around, and it's ineffective and inelegant.*

Then she reared back, lifted her right leg, and grabbed the jester's tunic. She stomped hard on his foot while pulling him toward her and snapped her forehead forward. A bit like a sneeze, but more.

She'd been aiming her head for the fleshy part of Turpy's nose, but missed. Instead, her hairline collided with the top edge of his left eye socket and the bridge of his nose.

That would have to do.

So would the heel of her boot crushing his instep.

The sounds of cracking bone and collapsing cartilage were accompanied by Turpy's screams. He juddered back, limping, and covered his face with his left hand.

Eloise felt the impact down to her teeth. A blossom of agony flowered across her skull and down the back of her neck. She was amazed at how painful it was. *It's supposed to hurt him, not me*, she thought.

Then again, from his screaming, she guessed it might have.

The jester lunged a backhand swing at her, which she moved to avoid. Both of them slipped and the blade of Turpy's hand caught her throat.

She hit the ground on her back, once again landing on her burned skin. Eloise swallowed several times to see if the blow had damaged her windpipe. There'd be a bruise, but she could breathe and swallow.

She rolled onto her side and saw Turpy holding a hand to his injured face. The jester grimaced and limped in the direction that Lorch, the Nameless One, and the panther had gone.

Eloise lay in the snow rubbing at her neck, listening to the loon cackle as he flew off after Turpy.

❧ 65 ❧

GRUB IN THE SCRUB

Grub in the Scrub turned out to be an unexpectedly elegant inn with an all-night kitchen in the middle of a hamlet whose only other distinguishing features were a shop called Candle Me With Care, another selling bread and damaged fruit called Batard and Bruised, and an architect specializing in devotional house design called In Çalaht We Truss.

"You really don't think we should go after Lorch and the Nameless One?" asked Eloise as they stepped into the inn's courtyard. She held a handkerchief filled with a bundle of snow against her forehead, hoping to mitigate the swelling and bruising.

"No, Princess, I don't," said Hector. "They know where we're headed. It makes sense for them to consider it our rendezvous point and come back here."

"I guess."

"The three of you go inside, get comfortable, and have something to eat. I'll order a warm bran mash and keep an eye out for Lorch and the Nameless One."

"I no be hungry," said RoyLee. "I'll be watching with Equine Designate Hector."

"No, RoyLee," said Eloise. "You were very brave back there..."

Jerome quietly cleared his throat.

"You and Jerome, both. Please come inside and let me get something for you to eat."

"I'll no be shirking duty, Princess Eloise. I no be being no shirker, and I'll no be starting with the shirking now."

"It's not shirking to take care of yourself. Tell you what. You come in and have dinner, and when Hector needs a break, you can have the next watch."

"That be acceptable, Princess," said RoyLee, bowing to her.

"Good. Why don't you head in and find us a table for three?"

"Yes, Princess." The wombat waddled into the inn.

"He's taking this very seriously," said Jerome. "I like that. Did you see him go after that panther mercenary? Didn't even hesitate."

"No, I didn't see. I was occupied at the time. But I'm grateful to him, and to you, Jerome. And you, Hector."

"They should never have gotten that close, Princess," said Hector. "We'll need to adjust what we do from now on."

"Let's let Lorch and the Nameless One return. Then we can adjust as needed."

"Right. Agreed."

Grub in the Scrub was packed with diners from wall to wall. Eloise found RoyLee with the *maitre d'*—a glass frog who nodded at Eloise and Jerome as they entered. "Good evening, madame, sir, and welcome to Grrrrrub in the Scrrrrrub, your home for dining excellence," said the frog in the plummiest voice Eloise had heard since Elgin Lëëëäääfäään-nïïïhïïïlääätööör at the Legs Not Arms. The frog sat up on his hind legs and gestured with his forelegs, a posture that would have made a Protocol instructor proud, but which had the downside of displaying his transparent abdomen. Eloise tried not to stare at his internal organs as the frog gestured toward RoyLee. "Young sir here tells me you'd like a table for three, and that you do not have a reservation."

"That's correct," said Eloise. "Any openings this evening?"

"Usually, I'd have to say not a chance. But you're in luck. One of our regulars has had to give up his usual table."

"Oh?"

"Yes. He passed away yesterday, and we have a strict policy to only serve living patrons."

"Has that been a problem in the past?" asked Jerome.

"A few years ago, a family of cicadas kept bringing in the exoskeleton of their deceased grandfather, who had a standing reservation with us," said the glass frog. His heartbeat sped up visibly at the memory. "They insisted their grandfather was still with them, and therefore we had to honor his reservation."

Jerome grimaced. "Hence the 'No dead bodies' rule."

"Indeed, good sir. Now, as I said, our former patron's sad ill fortune is your good luck this evening. Follow me, please."

The frog led them to a table close to the fireplace, and said, "Your serving wench this evening will be Zëphÿr, and she'll be here in a few minutes. If I may be so bold, I recommend the chef's blueberry blintzes with a side of potato latkes and a bagel."

"Thank you," said Eloise. "We'll keep that in mind."

"Enjoy your meal," he said, bowing, giving them one last glimpse of his innards squishing around.

"I'm not sure seeing a frog's insides is conducive to digestion," said Jerome. "Do we have coin enough for this place?"

"We should. Lorch was the one who suggested it."

Zëphÿr turned out to be a giraffe weevil, whose red wings and extended, jointed neck were as unexpected as the *maitre d's* visible guts. "Can I bring you any liquid consolation to start the meal?"

"No, thank you. I think we'll just order," said Eloise. "The *maitre d'* suggested blueberry blintzes, latkes, and a bagel. Is that still available?"

"Yes, mistress."

"I'll have that."

"Me, too," said Jerome.

"I be having no idea what said 'blintzes' be," said RoyLee.

"They're like blini," said Jerome.

RoyLee gave him a blank stare.

"Palatschinke?"

Blank stare.

"Crepes?"

RoyLee furrowed his brow. "Creeps?"

"Crepes," said Jerome.

Blank stare.

Eloise mimed rolling something with her fingers. "Blintzes are sort of like a kind of rolled griddle cake with a filling."

"Oh." RoyLee's brow furrowed more. "Why they no be called 'rolled griddle cake with a filling' then?"

"Because they're blintzes," said Jerome. "That's diff—"

"Good point, RoyLee," interrupted Eloise. "Try it, and if you don't like it, you can get something else."

"Blintzes, then," said RoyLee to the serving wench. His expression made it look like he was going to marshal his way through a culinary ordeal.

"Very good," said Zëphÿr. "Given how busy we are, it'll be about an hour. Are you sure you don't want some liquid consolation?"

"No, thank you," said Eloise.

Zëphÿr left them to wait.

Jerome pointed to Eloise's forehead. "Let's see it now."

She removed the snowball hanky. "How bad is it?"

"A most splendiferous bruise, Ellorissimo. Truly magnificent."

"Glad you approve." Eloise put the hanky back. "At least head wounds heal quickly."

"I think you'll be enjoying that one for a while."

"Fantastic."

Dinner was a slow-arriving pleasure. The three of them ate, delighted by the food, but tense as they waited for news of Lorch. They allowed themselves dessert—Eloise had the rugelach, Jerome the sweet noodle kugel, and RoyLee the almond chocolate chip mandelbrot—and then a round of haggleberry tea, and then another.

By the third pot of tea, the inn was emptying out, but by the fourth, the glass frog was showing Lorch to their table. He carried a sack and looked tired.

"Lorch!" Eloise jumped up. "Thank Çalaht you're here. And safe."

"Yes, Princess." He paused, seeing her bruises. "You're injured. What happened?"

"Our beloved princess," said Jerome, "conducted a personal inquiry into high-impact, forehead-based self-defense through directly applied means on the fugitive from the queen's justice."

Lorch furrowed his brow at the chipmunk, then looked back at Eloise. "You sank a kebby on the felon?"

"If by 'sank a kebby' you mean I slammed my forehead into his face, then yes."

"Please tell me everything," said Lorch. "But first..." He handed Eloise the sack. "The, uh, object of interest is in here."

"Oh, thank you." Eloise took it, relieved to have the Star of Whatever back. A missing-something-twitchiness she hadn't been conscious of eased as soon she took the bag, put her hand inside, and felt the box. Was this a sign that the spark of something had started latching onto her somehow? Maybe, but still, it felt good to have Sparky returned. "Thank you for keeping it safe. How did you evade the panther? Did Turpy catch up?"

Lorch dragged over a chair, ordered blintzes, sat, and described a manic race through unfamiliar ground in the dark. He ended with, "Ultimately, the panther was injured so the Nameless One simply outmaneuvered and outpaced him. Once we lost him, we were able to circle back. I expected I'd find you here and was very glad when I did."

"Turpy?" asked Eloise. "And the loon?"

"There was no sign of the felon. The bird was there for a while, and then he wasn't."

"They're out there somewhere," muttered Jerome.

"Yes. We'll have to be vigilant," said Lorch. "Day and night. And ready for another attack."

Then it was Eloise's turn. She described the end of her encounter with Turpy, from when she'd kicked the box.

RoyLee jumped into the story. "It all be happening so fast. The panther, he be knocking Jerome and me off," said RoyLee. "I be scrambling up and trying to work out what be going on when I see Princess Eloise. The Turpy fellow be holding her and yelling at her and then wham! She be clunking him. Wham! I be shocked. Wham! I'll bet that woke him up. And then he was all go-go. Off he be going like a jitterbug."

Lorch slowly shook his head. "Back home, we call it a 'Lower Glenth housewarming,'" he said. "Apparently, either administering or receiving one, or both, was a way for certain yokels to initiate a new home."

"That's stupid," snorted Jerome.

"You'll get no argument from me there. But it was a tradition. One I was happy not to perpetuate."

"A 'goat's hello,'" said RoyLee. "I've heard it called that."

"A 'Half Kingdom handshake,'" added Jerome. "Or a 'musk ox mambo.'"

"I once heard the Venerable Prelate Herself talk about the methods employed by the Pietistic Sisterhood," said Eloise. "She said that when they were having one of their more rigorous theological 'discussions' with another sect, and didn't have ax handles at hand, they'd do that instead and call it 'the Divine One's anointing.'"

"Good one," chuckled RoyLee. "That's what I'll be calling it from now on."

Lorch finished his blintzes, declined dessert, and said, "I'll organize a room for you, Princess. No need to suffer sleeping rough after tonight."

Eloise fought back a yawn. "I'd be grateful. And we have the coin?"

"Brague is just five days' more ride from here. A week at most. We have coin enough for a night."

POWER TO THE PEOPLE

They rode out after a breakfast of the best pumpkin spice babka Eloise had ever had, which was saying something, because Chef did a mean babka. Thinking of Chef and her babka twinged Eloise in a way she hadn't expected. Sure, she wanted to go home, but thoughts of babka made her actually feel homesick for the first time in weeks. Eloise allowed herself the luxury of yearning for her own bed, for her comforter, her bath, her hairbrushes, her favorite scrolls, the chance to get back to some semblance of normal, and to have her habits finally stop pestering her. She could put away Odmilla's beads for good and do a lot less counting.

It would be good to be home.

It would also be strange. So much had changed, and she was pretty certain she had changed, too.

That was assuming they got there. Eloise chose to let herself believe that might actually happen now.

The day's ride proved uneventful, as did the next, and the one after that. Strong length by strong length they headed toward Brague, and Eloise saw the paths become trails become something that might pass for a road. This slow, steady improvement was matched by hamlets becoming less sparse and villages more common. All that made it easier going.

The weather, however, was a different matter. It seemed to have a chip on its shoulder, as though fall, summer, and spring had called it names, so winter felt it needed to prove something. Eloise imagined winter saying, "You think you're so awesome with your flowers and buds? Your ripening fruits and seeding grasses? Your harvests and color changes? Well, check out these huge, wet flakes driven by gale force winds, and these icicles hanging like daggers on every roof, eave, and conifer."

A childish weather tantrum. Winter was being a complete brat.

Eloise hunched into her blanket and pulled her travel cloak closer. Unconsciously, she patted the box at her hip. Having the Star of Whatever inside a tied blanket hadn't been secure enough. After dinner at Grub in the Scrub, she'd gotten out a needle and thread, found the pieces of sash Turpy had sliced up back at the equine encampment, and had sewn them back together. It had been on her hip ever since.

Jerome sat watching her do it, his whiskers and claws twitching with every snagged, uneven, and gathered stitch. "You sure you don't want me to help with that?"

"Nope. I need to do this one on my own."

The job might have brought Seamstress Linttrap to tears (and not in a good way), but she wanted her energy in it, and no one else's. It also gave her something to do aside from worrying. So far, the coarse repair was holding just fine, and the Star of Whatever was back where she felt it should be for now—attached to her side.

As exhausting as the winter travel was, it was more exhausting to be constantly on the lookout. The snow meant visibility was low, and it felt like there was constant opportunity for another sneak attack. They were careful to travel only in daylight, and spent the nights in inns, both for the shelter and the protection of crowds. The days of travel took their toll on everyone. Eloise suspected that being so close to home helped keep everyone civil. That, and the fact that it was too Çalaht-cursed cold to do anything other than just keep going.

Three days out from Brague (in normal, reasonable weather), they reached the Queen's Roadway, an actual carriage-friendly road that would take them to Scoff, back to For the Love of Çalaht You Two Cut It Out, through either Itchy or Itchier (if they were still called that), to the First Night Inn (formerly the First Knight Inn), and finally home.

"That's something I'm grateful to see. I didn't think I'd ever say that about a road, but there you go," said Eloise.

"It's a welcome sight indeed, Princess," said Lorch.

"I can almost smell Chef's mushroom bisque from here."

"Mushroom beast?" asked RoyLee. "Who'd be eating a mushroom beast? And how beastly could a mushroom actually be? Most fungi I be meeting are pretty tame fellows. Hardly beastly at all."

"Not 'beast,'" said Eloise. "'Bisque.' It's a soup."

"Why not call it mushroom soup, then? That would avoid the whole unfriendly fungi issue."

"Yes, RoyLee. I'll let my mother know your concerns."

RoyLee's eyebrows narrowed. "There's no need to be bothering our queen with such matters. Unless you be thinking they be of sufficient import."

"I was kidding."

"Oh. Right. Sorry, Princess Eloise. Wombats don't always be picking up on sarcasm or irony so good. Our bad eyesight means we don't be reading faces well and be relying more on tone. A flat delivery be getting us every time."

Jerome had a dreamy look on his face. "Do you think we could convince Chef to do one of her acorn squash and kale lasagnes? As a sort of welcome home treat? She does that cashew ricotta with it. I think I could dive into one and not emerge for a week, especially if it was kept in a warming oven."

"Oh, good idea," agreed Eloise. "Both the lasagne and the spending a week in a warming oven."

They reached Scoff at dusk and went straight to Perfect Consumption, where Elbowbagette was on duty. She bowed as Eloise, Lorch, Jerome, and RoyLee entered the main room. "Hi, my name is Elbowbagette. I'll be your serving wench and night clerk this evening. Can I interest you in a room?"

"Yes, please," said Eloise. "What do you have?"

"We have a queen bed studio room with a view of the courtyard. The bed frame was handmade by a local craftsman using naturally fallen timbers where permission was asked of all insects and other people living in the wood. To be clear, all people were given the option of either remaining in the wood and becoming part of the bed or taking a mutually agreed upon allowance, determined through neutrally administered arbitration, and locating to another fallen timber that was not earmarked for this project."

"That sounds—" started Eloise.

"The ropes are braided and woven from pure, locally grown hemp, inspected and certified to be *cannabis sativa*, and are rated to hold three-quarters of a strong weight. The mattress cover was woven by the Non-Indentured Goodwomen's Cooperative, using a means of production they own as a group, and who share all proceeds from their work equally, regardless of any individual member's particular ability to contribute to the cooperative's output."

"I—"

"The mattress stuffing is straw reclaimed by orphans from a local thresher, and consists of a balanced mix of barley and oat stalks, but specifically omits wheat, as the production of wheat as practiced in this region is conducted in a way the workers voted to call 'an example of exploitation' and 'likely to cause aggregate disharmony.' The bedside table is—"

"That sounds fine," interrupted Eloise. "We'll take the one room. Also, there are two horses who will want a stable so they can shelter from the snow."

"The stable element of our complex has adopted an open-door, communal structure and your horse companions are welcome to take part in the accommodation and meal arrangements for no specific amount of coin, but should they wish to volunteer an hour or two of their time, it would be welcomed. This open-door, communal structure was set up as a way to show solidarity and support for the often-oppressed underclass of equine workers who urgently need to rise up against those who hold a metaphoric, and in some cases actual, boot on their collective necks."

"Do you have any potato soup?" Jerome batted wide, innocent eyes.

"That will do, Jer," said Eloise. "Thank you, Elbowbagette, for letting our horse comrades use the stables. I'll let them know."

"Don't thank me. They should thank the brave, forward-thinking members of the equine collective."

"OK..."

"As for your referring to them as your 'comrades,' I doubt it. You don't strike me as being part of the revolutionary struggle." Elbowbagette looked her up and down. "Also, there's no need to go let them know anything. I'm sure one of the collective's tireless executive members, a role rotated among five of them on a week-by-week basis, has already welcomed them and offered hospitality. The executive is keen to investigate situations involving possible and actual exploitation." She gave Eloise a piercing look.

"Oh. The horses? They're not being exploited, I assure you."

"Spoken like a true exploiter."

"No, really. No one's exploiting anyone."

The serving wench-cum-night clerk pointed at Eloise's clothing. "One cannot be dressed such as you and be free of the taint of exploitation. But that's OK. We'll take your coin all the same." Elbowbagette raised a fist to shoulder height. "Power to the people."

RoyLee raised a fist. "Right on!"

The others looked at him.

"What?" he said, slowly lowering it.

"I'll show you to your room." Elbowbagette shook her head as she led them up a set of stairs.

❦ 67 ❧

TWICE, THRICE

They were up and breaking fast in Perfect Consumption's dining room just after dawn.

"I had the best night's sleep I've had in ages." Eloise stifled a yawn as she spooned rice syrup onto her breakfast. "That Non-Indentured Goodwomen's Cooperative makes a heck of a mattress."

"Would any of you like more locally sourced, wildcrafted, steel-cut oats soaked overnight in filtered, artesian water with a stick of ethically sourced cinnamon?" asked Lorch as he ladled another bowlful.

Jerome held up his bowl. "Yes, please. And you forgot the bit about a percentage of the proceeds going to support an underprivileged family of nomadic yaks wandering homeless in the remotes of the Eastern Lands."

"There's that, yes." Lorch ladled another serving for the chipmunk.

"How can the yaks be being homeless?" asked RoyLee. "If they be being nomadic, like the serving wench be saying, then they be having no home by choice. That no be making them 'homeless.'"

Jerome looked at him. "I think you and I are going to get along just fine, young sir."

Half an hour later, with stomachs full and a "balanced, nutritious, and locavore-approved" lunch tucked into their panniers, they left Perfect Consumption. It was a glorious, blue-skied, windless day. The temperature was several degrees warmer than it had been—warm enough for Eloise to untie and stow the dream wife's blanket, but not so warm as to melt the white-flaked world around them and turn it to mush. The fine breakfast, the solid night's sleep, the improved weather, the enticing lunch ahead, and the relative nearness of home had Eloise feeling ebullient for the first time in a long while.

They picked up Queen's Roadway near the inn, and just outside Scoff, crossed the intersection with the Whacking Great Hole Greater Park Area Boulevard, a trail as piteous as its name was glorious. A massive sign with a large, red arrow read, "Visit the Whacking Great Hole, the Hugest Hole in the Realm!" and in small letters below, "Please Don't Die While You Are Here."

They passed the "boulevard" and kept going along the Queen's Roadway.

Thirty lengths later, Eloise paused. "Hold on, everyone."

Hector stopped and craned his neck to look at her. "Yes, Princess?"

"This may seem silly, but I have a hankering to visit the Whacking Great Hole."

"Again?" asked Jerome. "Really? I mean, it's the hugest hole in the realm, so I get that bit. But home beckons, doesn't it?"

"It's the 'once, twice, thrice' thing."

"Oh, I see."

"What be 'once, twice, thrice?'" asked RoyLee.

"Have you never been to the Whacking Great Hole, the hugest hole in the realm?" asked Hector.

"No. I no even be hearing about it before. What be it?"

"A big hole in the ground," said Jerome.

"And?" RoyLee waited.

"And nothing." Eloise shrugged. "It's a big hole in the ground. And you can buy overpriced refreshments. But people come from all over to see it."

"So the 'once, twice, thrice?' thing be what then?"

"There's supposed to be an old saying," said Lorch. "'Everyone should visit the Whacking Great Hole at least once for good memories, twice for good fortune, but thrice is a curse.'"

"That no be a very catchy old saying."

Jerome threw his arms in the air. "Exactly what I said. Remember? But without the odd grammar."

RoyLee leaned forward, still curious. "How many times be you visiting the Whacking Great Hole, the hugest hole in the realm?"

"Just the once," said Eloise.

"And? How be it?"

"The hole itself is..." Eloise lifted her palms upward. "Well, it's a great big hole, like we said. And if you like that kind of thing, then it is about as great as it gets."

"And did you have good memories?"

"Good enough, I guess. We were looking for my sister, but didn't find her. Uncle Doncaster..." Eloise was surprised that her voice caught at his name. She cleared her throat. "King Doncaster, and I guess Turpy, had taken her there. They'd seen it before and wanted to share it with her, and I guess get their good fortune. But she was gone when we got there. So that was disappointing. Other than that, it was OK." Eloise paused. "RoyLee, do you have any interest in seeing it?"

"Of course!" exclaimed RoyLee. "I be a wombat. Wombats no be hole aficionados or enthusiasts. We wombats be hole experts, hole immersives, hole connoisseurs! I be very, very keen to be seeing the Whacking Great Hole, the hugest hole in the realm. I be having a professional interest."

"Right, then." Eloise turned to the others. "What do you think? Shall we get ourselves some good fortune?"

"If you wish, Princess Eloise." Lorch didn't sound very enthusiastic.

❧ 68 ❧

STILL WHACKING GREAT

An hour later, they stood in front of the tiny wood booth with the sign that said, "Whacking Great Hole Greater Park Area Tourist Complex." The shack still had ample copies of "Your Guide to Seeing the Whacking Great Hole Without Dying" lining the wall at crazy prices, and it was tended by a bored-looking skink wearing a ranger's cap and a khaki tunic, along with a khaki blanket to help her stay warm.

Eloise suspected it was the same skink who had been there before—she had a button pinned to her tunic that read, "Hi, My Name is _____. Welcome to the Whacking Great Hole, the Hugest Hole in the Realm. Please Don't Die While You Are Here." Eloise's suspicion was confirmed when the skink opened her mouth, covered a yawn with her paw, and used a bored voice to say, "Hi, My name is _____. Welcome to the Whacking Great Hole, the hugest hole in the realms. Please don't die while you are here. How may I help you?"

"Hello, _____," said Eloise. "Nice to see you again."

The skink looked at her, face neutral.

"We met you a few months back?"

The skink gave no sign of recognition. "Welcome back to the Whacking Great Hole, the hugest hole in the realms. Please don't die while you are here."

"That's OK. You would meet a lot of people in your job. It's wrong of me to expect you to remember us."

Jerome piped in. "We had our friend Alejandro Diego Ferdinando Felipe Esteban Iglesias Desoto de Lugo with us?"

The skink gasped, and blushed. "Al baby. Is he here? Is he with you?" She craned her neck, looking around. "I... I don't see him with you. Where is he?"

"He's elsewhere, traveling and singing with a friend."

"Oh." The skink deflated like a pufferfish at a belching contest and resumed her resting state of ennui.

"We thought we'd visit the Whacking Great Hole again," said Eloise. "To get our good fortune."

"That will be two coins each. Twelve for the six of you." The skink looked at them all. "Are you a family?"

"Uh, sort of?" said Jerome. "Not really, but kind of, maybe. Why?"

"If you're family, then it's only ten coins."

"That's OK," said Eloise. "We're happy to support the excellent work you do here."

RoyLee tugged on the leg of Lorch's breeks, and asked, "We be having to pay to be seeing the hole?"

"No, young sir, you do not," said _____ in her said-this-a-million-times voice. "Seeing the hole is free. You're paying for the maintenance of this booth, for us telling people not to die here, for maintaining the refreshments stand (I recommend the lemonade, it's very refreshing. Although it's closed today, as it's off-season), for someone to pick up the crud that people leave behind, for—"

"Thanks, but we can explain all that to him." Eloise steered the wombat away. "Lorch, if you'd be so kind."

"Yes, Princess." He took out his purse and counted the coins.

The skink scooped them up and dropped them in a metal box with "Admissions" on it. "Enjoy your visit to the Whacking Great Hole, the hugest hole in the realms. Please don't die while you are here."

The path to the Whacking Great Hole was snow-covered and undisturbed. The Nameless One snorted twice and pointed with his head.

"What'd he say?" asked Jerome.

Hector looked around and nodded. "He said that last time, the place was packed, but today there are no carriages."

"We must be the first ones here today," said Lorch.

They trudged the two strong lengths toward the hole and reached the viewing area. The convenient, yet overpriced refreshment stand was shuttered, and not another soul was taking in the snow-laden magnificence of the Whacking Great Hole.

"Çalaht be bluffing a bloviating, blinkered, blister-covered, blaspheming, blatherer! This. Be. Amazing!" RoyLee danced with the joy of discovery. "I be being right back!" The wombat shot for the edge of the Whacking Great Hole.

"Careful of the edge!" called Lorch. "It really is a whacking great hole."

The wombat stopped, called, "Got it!", then carefully walked to the edge of the hole and poked his head over so he could look directly down into it. "Hello!" he yelled.

"Hello-o-o-o," replied the echo.

"Wow! Wow, wow, wow! I can no be waiting to tell Master Shovelhovel about this! Can you be imagining how many wombats it be taking to make a hole like this? All of them! It be taking all of them!"

RoyLee crawled along the edge, squinting to see as far as he could, and calling out "Hello!" after "Hello!" to test the echo from different angles.

Jerome scanned the area. "The place really is deserted. I don't even see any of the drawing pad vendors."

"The skink said it was the off-season," said Eloise. "I guess visiting the Whacking Great Hole is not considered much of a winter sport. Can you imagine sitting in that booth the way she does, waiting for no one to show up? And she's a reptile. In winter."

The two horses, two humans, and the chipmunk stood in a cluster, silently taking in the view and watching the wombat's utter joy for a quarter hour, and then another.

"I might go for a closer look," said Jerome. "Coming, El?"

"Not just yet."

"I'll come," said Hector, and the Nameless One nodded agreement.

The three of them wandered closer for a final look. Eloise could hear Jerome say, "It could still do with a guardrail. Or at least a piece of string showing where the edge is, plus some warning signs."

"More than just, 'Please don't die here?'" agreed Hector.

"Yes, maybe something more specific. Like, 'Deathly dangerous hole just five lengths ahead.' Then another that says, 'Certain death three lengths ahead.' Then one saying, 'OK, now you're just being stupid.' Something like that."

Eloise and Lorch watched the others. "What do you think, Princess? Do you feel like you've gathered your good fortune?"

"I think so, yes."

"Shall we go?" prompted Lorch.

"Yes, I think so. But maybe I can have a few moments alone."

"Princess, I don't know."

"Lorch, please. This journey has been... Well, you've been here, you know how it's been: non-stop stress and strain. And you know that when I get home, there won't be a second to spare. I just need a tiny bit of alone time to get myself in the right frame of mind for stepping back into Court life."

"Princess, it worries me."

"Look around. See any footprints? Signs of carts? Skis? We have this wonderful spot to ourselves for now. Maybe you could gather RoyLee and the others and start heading back. I won't be long."

"As you wish, Princess."

"Thank you, Lorch. I need it."

❧ 69 ☙

SEVEN-WORD PLAN

Eloise observed Lorch gathering the others, who one by one looked over at her, then nodded their assent to the guard. She watched Jerome crack a joke, RoyLee going dutifully, if sadly, with one last, longing look at the Whacking Great Hole, and the Nameless One and Hector shooting into a gallop, racing each other to the skink's shack.

Once they were gone, she allowed herself the extravagance of sauntering down to the Whacking Great Hole (but not too close). She found a park bench with a good view, brushed off the snow, tucked her travel cloak beneath her and sat.

All by herself.

Eloise inhaled long and slow, held it, and exhaled tension and worry. She did it again, and then a third time.

Closing her eyes, Eloise felt the touch of a faint breeze on her skin. She listened to the silence, noticed how much noise there was in that stillness—from her own breathing to a clump of snow falling from a branch, causing a small cascade, to a distant cough, perhaps a fox or a horse.

She had to admit that she was nervous about going home.

Her mother would be livid, that was a given. The trip had stretched to months. Eloise had failed to bring back Johanna—the sole reason she'd left in the first place. She'd communicated sparsely and poorly. She'd bumbled her way across three-and-a-half of the four-and-a-half realms, coming close to triggering diplomatic crises in all of them.

Queen Eloise Hydra Gumball II wasn't usually one for corporal punishment, but maybe she'd make an exception this time. Or perhaps she'd blow the dust off the pillory, set it up in the Culpability Court-yard where they'd been used in generations past, and give Eloise a "time out" with her head and wrists stuck through its holes and the public invited to provide "feedback." Or maybe the queen would be feeling magnanimous, and only put Eloise in the stocks.

Eloise was clear about one thing: to expect a hug and a "nice to have your home" was to invite disappointment. Better to have her expecta-tions suitably calibrated to the upbraiding end of the spectrum.

Well, so be it. If Eloise was really going to be honest, she knew she deserved whatever was coming.

In spades.

Best be ready for it and accept it with dignity.

Another long, slow breath.

There was another cough. Closer this time. Much closer.

Eloise calmly opened her eyes, stood, and turned around.

For the love of Çalaht, it was Turpy.

She stood there looking at him. *Stupid me*, she thought. She'd sent the others two strong lengths away so she could have a little privacy.

"Turpy." A nice neutral statement.

He staggered forward, favoring the foot she'd stomped on. He had a bandage over the eye she'd injured, and traces of blood flecked his upper lip from the nosebleed he got from the Lower Glenth housewarming. His face was flushed and fevered, his eyes grim and tinged with madness, and his manner determined.

Then there was the knife—much bigger and sharper than the one he'd had before. He moved toward her like an injured hunter.

Start friendly. "Turpentine Snotearrow McCcoonnch. What a nice surprise." Eloise gestured toward the view. "It is, indeed, a whacking great hole, is it not?"

"You ruined everything," he growled. "Everything." He moved forward, and Eloise tried to circle in response, keeping the bench between them. But even limping, he was longwalker fast, and Turpy maneuvered her away from it.

"Everything, huh? Well, my apologies, Your Jesterness. I'd offer to get you an overpriced cuppa at the refreshment stand and talk it through, but unfortunately it's closed."

If he heard her, he didn't show it.

"I'd even have sprung for an overpriced biscuit, if you'd have fancied it."

"You. Killed. My. King." Each word a spitting condemnation. And with each word, he stepped closer. Eloise realized he'd maneuvered her so her back was to the hole.

Not good.

Then he laughed. More a bark, and devoid of humor. "You know, the plan was simple. A simple seven-word plan. Even that idiot Doncaster should have been able to pull it off. But no."

Eloise gauged the distance to the hole and figured she still had a little time to bargain with him before something more drastic had to be done. "What simple plan was that?"

"Seven words," he said. "Seven simple words. 'Marry the sister. Fog the heir. Wait.' It was a perfect plan."

"Marry the sister. Fog the heir. Wait," Eloise repeated. She tried to move so that she was sideways to the hole, but the knife said otherwise. "I don't get it. 'Fog the Heir.' Well, that bit is pretty clear. That means kill me. 'Marry the sister.' Clearly that has to do with Johanna. But she wouldn't marry you, would she? You're a jester—not that there's anything wrong with that—but our mother would never agree to it, if nothing else."

"Not me, you idiot," he snarled. "Çalaht driving daggers into a donut, are you really this stupid? Doncaster! Doncaster was supposed marry her. And he would have, except you ruined it."

Eloise tried to make run for it.

Fueled with anger and frustration and still faster than the panther he'd sent after her, he blocked her way before she'd taken three steps.

"If your mind is so feeble you can't make the jump from one to the next, let me help you. Phase one: Doncaster marries that brainless bint, your sister. Phase two: get rid of you. Phase three: Wait."

"Wait for what?"

"Wait for your mother to cark it. Maybe help that along if the opportunity presents itself. The bint inherits the Western Lands, since you're out of the picture, and Doncaster takes control."

"There are so many holes in that plan you could drive one of Lurid Eddie's carriages through it. But let's start with the most basic one. How is that supposed to help you?"

"I controlled the idiot king. I controlled your brain-dead sister. It would have been nothing for me to control the Western Lands and the Half Kingdom, both. They were mine!" On the last word, he lunged at her with the knife. It caught Eloise's sleeve, but she backed away before he could do anything worse.

"But you ruined it. You, with your quirks and your tics and all the strangenesses you try so hard to hide. You cleared up her head and it all fell apart."

"You seem to be leaving out a few bits. Like the part where you tried to have us killed. And the part where you were, indeed, sitting on the throne. And then you just let it slip through your fingers. Gee, I wonder if, maybe, you weren't supposed to actually be there, and things just worked out like they were supposed to."

"Shut up!" snarled Turpy. "Shut up! Shut up! Shut up!" He waved the knife at her, forcing her further back.

"You know, if you are going to kill me, you could at least be polite about it."

"Shut. Up."

Eloise snatched up a handful of snow, balled it, and hurled it at him. Turpy let it hit him on the side of his head, not flinching.

"Give me the Star of Whatever." He slipped back to an almost-reasonable tone. "That's really the only way you're going to get out of this alive."

"Why would I possibly give you the Star of Whatever? What are you going to do with it?"

"Because I know what it is. I know what it did. I know what it *does*. With the Star of Whatever, I'll be able to have what should have been mine before it all turned to nothing."

"That's perhaps the funniest thing you've said so far, which is pretty sad, since you're supposed to be a jester." Eloise felt her anger gathering. She took a step toward him. "It didn't turn to nothing, it was always nothing. At best, it was a fever dream. A mirage you convinced yourself was tangible. A bedtime story you told yourself over and over, with about as much basis in reality. Get a grip on your haggleberries and wake up and smell the tea!"

"I said give it to me. Now!"

"I would rather die than let you anywhere near the Star of Whatever."

"So be it," he whispered.

Turpy used every bit of his longwalker weak magic and flung himself at Eloise. The former royally appointed jester to His Highness, Doncaster Worsted Halva de Chëёёkflïïïnt, slammed into the Heir and Future Ruler to the Western Lands and All That Really Matters.

They both went over the edge of the Whacking Great Hole.

❦ 70 ❦

MORE PLUMMETING

oly Çalaht suffering salacious sacerdotal sacraments, thought Eloise as she flew backwards over the lip of the hole. *Not bloody again.*

There were immediate and eerie similarities to the tumble she took at Mortimer Falls, as well as several key differences.

First, there was the same sense of time flowing very slowly, allowing her mind to cover a lot of territory as she plunged into the unknown depths. There was the same screaming *Ahhhhh!* that may have been in her head and may have actually been coming from her throat (she was too busy trying not to die to be sure). There was the same flapping of her travel cloak above and behind her, like it was being blown by a hurricane. There was the same worrying about how she should land at the other end.

Aaaahhh!

But there were differences as well. For one, while it was possible that there would be enough water at the bottom to break her fall—this was hole, after all, the hugest in the realm—it didn't seem likely. It could be strong lengths deep or a few weak lengths. Who knew?

Also, it was darker. The light rapidly receded into a shrinking oval above that left only a small amount of emerald green light coming through.

The biggest difference, of course, was the presence of Turpy, who had successfully extended his streak of making questionable life choices. He had knocked her into the biggest hole in the realm and followed along. Who does that? Was it a miscalculation? A whoopsie? A deliberate move based in spite? (That's what it looked like.) It certainly seemed counter-productive to his goal of ruling the realms.

What a jester.

And what did he think she'd say when he demanded the Star of Whatever? Did he really think she'd go, "Sure thing, Turpster. Here you go!" and hand over the most dangerous magical object in all the realms?

Eloise really didn't get him. Not at all.

But he didn't seem to get her, either. So maybe she should call that one even.

Aaaaahhhhhh!

Turpy had flung himself at her mid-section, tackling her like a hockey sacking defensive girder. As they fell, he grabbed at her. No, that was wrong. Not at her, but at the box with the Star. Even as they fell toward certain death, he was still trying to get the thing.

Bonus points to Turpy for focus, thought a particularly detached part of Eloise's mind.

Aaaaaaahhhhhhh! screamed the bulk it.

Not a Çalaht-cursed chance! took up the remainder. She'd keep the Star of Whatever from him with every ounce of her strength and will, even if she died doing it.

Eloise fought off Turpy with everything she had. Their struggle took their plummet into the unknown and turned it into a tumble, both of them grunting and grappling. Eloise twisted to keep the box out of reach.

"?" sent the spark of something in the Star of Whatever.

"Bit busy right now, Sparky," Eloise sent back. He really did pick the oddest times to perk up.

"Loulou?" he insisted.

Aaaaaaaaahhhhhhhhh! The scream in her head blended with her "!" response, which was all the explanation she had time for. She had to hope that Sparky would interpret that as, "I'm falling to my death and fighting off a demented jester to keep him from getting you."

There was the faintest "??." from Sparky. It was a combination Eloise had not experienced from him before.

She felt more than heard a "snick" from the box.

It opened.

How many times had she tried to get it open? How much fiddling, poking, puzzling, and attempting to communicate her intention? All yielding no result at all.

And Sparky chooses this moment to open up? She understood him even less than she understood Turpy.

The Star of Whatever glowed a bright emerald green. In the pitch blackness of the Whacking Great Hole, it was like a lamp, illuminating the wall as it rushed by, uncomfortably close. The Star was larger than she remembered. Somehow it had shrunk in her memory from the size of a big grapefruit to more of an over-enthusiastic orange.

The emerald glow illuminated a lunatic gleam in Turpy's eyes. He gasped, realizing what had just happened. For a moment, the three of them—Turpy, Eloise, and the Star of Whatever—formed a tableau of shocked stillness as they rushed toward a certain crushing at the bottom of the Whacking Great Hole. The main sense of movement was from the Star of Whatever, which appeared to be floating slowly down and away from them.

The jester pushed away from Eloise, shoving them apart, leaving him two lengths below her and closer to the glowing stone. He extended his arm, stretching toward the Star of Whatever, just a few weak lengths from being able to grasp it. The sight of Turpy with his arm outstretched reminded Eloise of all the skeletons she and Johanna had found in the Purple Haze. They, too, had one arm reaching forward. She knew now that they, too, had been reaching for the Star of Whatever—they just didn't know it.

Aaaaaaaaaaaahhhhhhhhhhh!

Turpy kicked the air like he was swimming, fingers splayed wide, stretching his whole being toward the gleaming light.

He snatched the stone. A cry of triumph ripped from his throat.

Suddenly, someone said, "No."

The voice came from Sparky. Eloise heard it as clear and as loud as she had under the influence of the dream wife's vision herbs.

"This is not part of our accord."

Turpy's victorious exaltation twisted into a screech of agony. His muscles spasmed like he'd hugged a thousand shockfish. Tremors ripped through his body, and his limbs straightened and strained, uncontrolled.

Aaaaaaaaaaaaaahhhhhhhhhhhhhh!

The Star of Whatever did exactly what it had spent more than two centuries doing to every living being who came within its reach, with exactly three exceptions—Melveeta, who'd created the destructive spell, and Eloise and Johanna, because they were of Melveeta's blood. Eloise thought she'd ended the spell, but it was like the spell's imprint was so strong it lingered, its echoes still active.

If Turpy had been far away from the Star of Whatever—say, the same distance as the edge of the Purple Haze at Stained Rock had been from where Melveeta had lain in torment for 232 years—then Turpy would have convulsed into a palsied fit the way his brother had, died within a few minutes, and then turned to bones and dust over an hour or two, like every other formerly living thing in the Purple Haze.

But that's not what happened.

For Turpy, grabbing the Star of Whatever was like grasping the sun. Eloise watched the Star of Whatever and the spark of something within it (it didn't seem like a "Sparky" in that moment) latch onto Turpy's body and drain every morsel of life from it. It stripped away Turpy's flesh, starting at his hand and zipping in a line up his arm, across his body, and out to his extremities. Skin, tissue, muscle, viscera, and blood all sizzled away in a flash of green light that ended in a flare at his toes. All that remained plummeting alongside Eloise was a parched, seared, skeleton, the tattered remains of a jester's harlequin, a flimsy bandage around the skull, a jester's scepter that dully reflected the Star of Whatever's green light, and a fine, residual powder of no-longer-Turpy littering the air, which Eloise fell through, gagging.

What remained of Turpy crashed into a jutting outcrop. His brittle bones shattered, pulverized into nothingness, and burst into a cloud of no-longer-Turpy particles. Eloise whooshed through that as well, snapping her mouth shut and trying not to breathe him in.

The Star of Whatever flared for a heartbeat with a dazzling light, and the spark of something sent Eloise a ".".

It was done.

And it was gone again.

That moment of brightness confirmed something for Eloise: the Whacking Great Hole was not, in fact, bottomless. There was most certainly a bottom, and she was seconds from hitting it.

Aaaaaaaaaaaaaaaaaaaahhhhhhhhhhhhhhhhhhh!

※ 71 ※

BADE TO BE SILENT

From the way the light from the Star of Whatever illuminated the hole's floor, it was hard to tell what the bottom consisted of. Eloise couldn't tell if she was about to dash herself onto rocks, drown in a deep pool, or die from some other horror.

Aaaaaaaaaaaaaaaaaahhhhhhhhhhhhhhhhh!

The spark of something roused again. "?" it sent.

Aaaaaaaaaaaaaaaaaaahhhhhhhhhhhhhhhhhh!

"??"

Aaaaaaaaaaaaaaaaaaaahhhhhhhhhhhhhhhhhhh!

"What's up, Loulou?"

Aaaaaaaaaaaaaaaaaaaaaahhhhhhhhhhhhhhhhhhhhh!!!!!

There was another sudden glow from the Star. As it had at Mortimer Falls, a pulse of light enveloped Eloise at the very instant she reached the bottom of the Whacking Great Hole.

It wasn't stone.

It definitely wasn't water.

What Eloise slammed into at full force was more like thick soup. She hit it with a kind of splattering, splooshing, sucking "splorch," and sank into the viscous muck. She lay submerged for a few heartbeats, absorbing the pain of the impact, and registering the thought that she was still registering thoughts.

Then she scrambled to find the surface, so she didn't drown in whatever it was. Her knees hit something solid.

Eloise stood up and gasped air.

The gunk she was in was only thigh high.

A quick assessment. No sharp pains indicating broken bones. No obvious bleeding or damage to her internal organs. She felt clobbered all over from the impact, and wondered if it was possible for one's entire skin to turn purple with bruising. Her body throbbed, like a posse of carpenter's apprentices had used her to practice their competitive hammer swinging techniques.

She'd be feeling it for a while. But she was alive.

The Star of Whatever had saved her life. *Sparky* had saved her life. Again. Despite falling for what felt like a thousand strong lengths, somehow, Sparky had intervened enough for Çalaht to allow her soul to remain in her body for a while longer.

Incredible. Absolutely incredible.

Eloise realized she was standing in the dark. The glow from the Star of Whatever was gone. She had no idea where it was. It was gone in a place where it would be impossible to find.

She felt the missing of it.

She took a steadying breath.

The smell of the place assaulted her. It was like someone had scraped the morning mouth of every snorer in all the realms, and flicked the scrapings into the hole, then added a dozen bouquets of corpse flowers in full blossom, mixed in with the changing-room odor of every hockey sacking team that ever played, poured on a garnish of evil, bad intentions, corruption, and ennui, then added vinegar, sulfur, bat guano, the output of a skunk battalion, several strong weights of rotted eggplants, and a hint of paprika.

And it was all over her clothes, her skin, her hair.

Eloise's habits screamed. They screamed like they had never screamed before. Yelled like they had been asleep for a while, then woken up to find themselves in a cesspit.

Which was exactly what had happened.

Eloise threw up, retched dozens more dry heaves, then screamed right along with her habits. This was far worse than having Melveeta's blood on her. At least the blood had been a single, known substance that could be understood and dealt with. This goo was some mystery mix of the dead, the decaying, and the Çalaht-cursed. Frantically, she tried to squeegee it off her face and arms, flicking wet globs of it back to the pool of filth. She felt around with her foot see if there was somewhere she could stand that was a bit higher and out of the stuff, but the surface below her seemed to slope down in all directions, not up.

She resorted to more frantic screaming, which soon turned to sobbing. But even through her wailing, it was obvious that no amount of yelling, crying, pleading, or praying could possibly change the fact that she'd landed in filth, had filth all over her, and was surrounded by an infinite supply of darkness-shrouded filth. If she had spent a month trying to conjure a scenario that would aggravate her habits as much as possible, she could not have dreamed anything up that would outdo this.

For five, ten, fifteen minutes, Eloise oscillated from gut-wrenching weeping to throat-tearing screams, as she continued to wipe, scrape, and claw at her skin, clothes, and hair. But the foul, stinking slush was more than her match. It clung. It dripped. It stained. It soaked through her clothes and oozed into her shoes. It snuck into her mouth and soaked into her pores.

It was everywhere. And in the dark at the bottom of the deepest known hole in all the realms, there was absolutely nothing that Eloise could do about it.

Nothing.

That's when it happened—something broke inside Eloise. Something fundamental. Something deep and profound.

What broke were her habits.

Faced with a situation Eloise could not escape, could not control, and could not tolerate, she could either let her habits shatter her mind or stop giving them heed.

She chose the latter.

For the first time in more than a dozen years, when her habits had first started whispering and niggling, Eloise bade them to be silent. Insisted. Adjured. Ordered. In that moment, she could do nothing to adequately meet their tuggings, the cravings they insisted to be assuaged through ritual and patterned behavior. No amount of counting or arranging of things would work here.

So she stopped. She stopped being their slave. She detached herself from them and their demands. She stood, panting from her exertions, and accepted that this feculence was on her and would stay on her for the foreseeable future.

She forced her habits to be silent.

They would be silent, for now anyway. She commanded it.

And she felt a relief like she'd never felt in her life. A freedom. An emancipation.

Tears flowed again, but they were different this time. They were the tears of a millstone being removed.

Eloise adjusted her weight and took a step to steady herself. Her toes landed on a largish rock that slid along beneath the pressure of her foot.

"?"

She stopped, careful to keep her foot where it was, and sent a "?".

"?" replied the spark of something in the Star of Whatever. "Is that you, Loulou?"

"Hey, Sparky. Thanks for saving me."

"No problem." He paused. "Loulou, is it possible that I'm in a huge hole?"

"Yes."

"Would you say this breaks our accord? I believe one of my terms was, 'You don't just get rid of me. You don't just bury me in a hole or chuck me in a ravine, never to be seen again.' I seem to have been thrown into a rather substantial hole."

"No."

"No, I'm not in a hole?"

"No, this doesn't break our accord. I've neither buried you nor chucked you in a ravine. The person you demolished caused the sequence of events that led you to being here. Also, I'm here. I've not tried to get rid of you."

"Point taken," said Sparky. "Our accord holds."

"Good."

"Now, are you going to leave me here?"

"No," said Eloise. "I remain the Light Bearer. I shall bear you."

"Good."

But...

To pick up the Star of Whatever would require either squatting down or reaching into the slimy nastiness and getting filth on parts of her that she'd wiped off as best she could. Her habits would hate it.

No, they would have hated it.

But they were gone.

Eloise lowered herself slowly into the lagoon of malicious, abominable fetor, careful to maintain contact with the stone at her foot. She grabbed it and hauled it above the surface.

The Star of Whatever still glowed, casting a green light on the cavernous space around her.

"." sent Sparky.

"..." replied Eloise.

She turned her attention to getting out of there.

72

DETRITUS SOUP

B eing able to see her surroundings gave Eloise a bit more information.

This was not necessarily a good thing.

The unknown filth she stood in became a known filth. It turned out to be a kind of detritus soup—a potage that was part garbage dump, part boneyard, part sludge pond, part grease trap, part storage facility for very long snake corpses, and part lucky dip for every kind of nastiness that existed in the world. Clearly, people of all species had thrown just about anything that could be flung into the Whacking Great Hole, including themselves, if the number of skeletons in the muck was any measure. She guessed some of it was accidental, but that the bulk was deliberate. At some level, Eloise could understand this. There was a curiosity about the hole that could only be answered by chucking something into it—a torch, a stone, a just-purchased drawing pad—and seeing how far down it went before you could no longer see or hear it. She also guessed that plenty of people leaned just a little too far, flown a little too low, or crawled a little too deep and found themselves either dead or stuck (which was, she guessed, the same thing).

How in the name of Çalaht's belligerent, beatified belching am I supposed to get out of here? thought Eloise. She had no intention of staying there. And no intention of dying there. There had to be something she could do.

Presumably the others would have noticed she was missing by now. Would they know where she was? Would they have heard her screaming? She couldn't hear anything from them. Perhaps they could read her fate in the marks she and Turpy had left in the snow. But what were they supposed to do, come after her? She was a very, very long way down. They'd have to assume she had died. What other conclusion could they come to?

No, this one was on her.

Right, then. Resources. What did she have that might be usable? An immeasurable amount of slimy awfulness. Her clothes, including her travel cloak, all horribly dirty. The Star of Whatever. Herself.

Maybe she could free climb her way out. That was unlikely. It was a long, long, long way up. Fatigue would be an issue if nothing else. Her clothes were heavy, which would make climbing harder, at least until they dried out. The walls were probably slippery. Unless there was a way to secure the Star of Whatever as a kind of torch, she'd be climbing in the dark and by feel. That would take forever. Plus, there were a thousand mistakes that could cause her to fall and die. Sparky had just saved her from a fall, and had done the same at Mortimer Falls. But she didn't think unexpected magical intervention was likely to be a reliable safety net.

Free climbing remained an option, in theory at least, but it was definitely at the bottom of the list—a list that so far had only one item on it.

She held the Star closer to the muck and used its glow to see if anything there might be useful. Skulls. Bones. Bits of food in various stages of decay. Bits of bodies, mainly non-human, also in various stages of decay. All those snake corpses.

She looked closer at one of those.

It wasn't a snake carcass. It was a length of rope.

Rope! That made sense. If people (probably humans) tried to climb down into the hole using ropes, then it was certainly possible that some of them (the ropes, not the humans—although probably the humans as well) fell into the depths. In fact, it was a certainty. Otherwise, the Whacking Great Hole wouldn't need the motto, "Please don't die while you're here." If trying to get to the bottom was something people did reasonably often, then it made sense that there might be a lot of rope down there.

Possibly useful.

Eloise tucked the Star of Whatever under her chin so she had both hands free and drew the nearest tangle of rope toward her. She tugged on a section of it to test its strength. It disintegrated like pasta that had been cooked for a week.

She gritted her teeth, trudged forward through the slime, found another bit, and gave it a yank. Once again, overcooked pasta, but slightly less so. So, progress.

It took what felt like hours of sloshing through awfulness, but Eloise eventually found two dozen usable, non-pasta-ish stretches of rope. Only a few had skeletal remains wound into them, and she was grateful none of them were recent violators of the park motto. When tied together, they formed a relatively sturdy coil that would reach maybe 150 lengths—a bit longer than a couple of standard climbing ropes. The Whacking Great Hole was much deeper than that, but the rope might help get her at least part of the way out.

Maybe.

There were a number of problems with this line of thinking. For one, the rope was not just covered with the Whacking Great Hole's special version of slimed grotesqueness, it was soaked through with it. This made it both incredibly heavy and slippery to handle. For another, it wasn't clear exactly how the rope would help solve her problem. What was she supposed to attach it to? There wouldn't be hooks or rings or anything. Maybe closer to the rim, but not down here. She wished she had a top rope or more equipment, so she could rig some sort of self-belay setup to make the climb safer. But no. She might as well wish for a nice cup of haggleberry tea.

She could try tossing the rope to see if she could loop it over something.

Hold it, Eloise thought. There was another resource she hadn't considered—her weak magic for throwing. Could that help?

Eloise fastened a lasso at one end of the coil, did a wind-up swing that sent flecks of yuck spinning away, and let fly. The heavy loop blorped into the muck no more than five lengths away.

Not very impressive.

She reeled the rope back in and tried again, this time giving it more intent.

Ten lengths distance.

She sloshed over to the wall of the Whacking Great Hole and held the Star of Whatever up to see if it was climbable, or if there was anything to loop the rope onto. The wall was wet, as she'd expected. As for looping the rope onto anything, it would be luck if she did. The green light only reached a dozen lengths above her. She'd be throwing it up with a guess and a hope.

Well, that's all she had right now. It was worth trying.

She wound up and flung the rope.

It came down and hit her on the head, covering her with even more filth. Eloise gritted her teeth and refused to give in to the habit of her now-banished habits.

She tried another four dozen times, varying the height, the angle, and the direction of her throw. The closest she got was a temporary snag that came away with the smallest tug. With every try, Eloise went further into herself, trying to call on her weak magic for throwing. She focused her intent. She visualized the coil unspooling, rising higher, hooking onto something. Then she pushed her imagining further, seeing it unspooling upward, cresting the rim and, improbably, wrapping itself around the park bench at the top.

The more she threw, the more desperate she became. Despite herself, tears came.

"This isn't working," she yelled at the hole. "This is never going to work."

The Whacking Great Hole didn't answer, but it seemed to agree.

What else did she have that might help her? She went through her list again: an immeasurable amount of slimy awfulness, her clothes, her travel cloak and whatever was still in her pockets, the Star of Whatever, herself, and a coil of scavenged rope.

Wait! The Star of Whatever. Could it help? Melveeta had used it to amplify a spell that ruined half a realm. Could Eloise use it to amplify something as simple as her throwing?

She held the Star of Whatever in front of her face and said, "Sparky, are you there?"

"Hey, Loulou. What's up?"

It was the first time he'd directly responded to a query from her since she first met the mole-rat. Other times, he'd initiated the communication, or had been a bit vague. Here he was, clear in her mind in all his pink, near-hairless, weird-toothed glory.

"We're in a predicament."

"Thought that might be the case."

"Sparky, you gotta help me out or we're both going to be down here forever."

"What am I supposed to do? I'm just a dumb rock."

"Come on. Don't give me that." The naked mole-rat looked falsely modest. "I'm barely keeping it together here, and that's a finite thing. I only have so much sanity in me."

The naked mole-rat scratched the back of his head with a hind leg. "And?"

"Can you help me amplify the weak magic of my throwing?"

"Probably."

"What do I do?"

Sparky tilted his head to the side. "You really don't know how this magic thing works, do you?"

"No one does. It's passed from common use since Melveeta's spell drained it from the realms," said Eloise. "So tell me. What do I do?"

He gave a mole-rat shrug. "You focus your intent. You picture what you're trying to achieve. You apply your will. You draw on me for assistance. You execute to the action. Magic's pretty simple, when you spell it out like that." Sparky chuckled. "See what I did there?"

"Hilarious." Eloise organized herself to fling the rope again, but it was awkward trying to throw while holding the Star. She could put it into its box, but she worried that might dull the Star's ability to work with magic or communicate with her. Instead, she slipped it into her travel cloak in the same pocket as Odmilla's Çalahtist prayer beads. She took a breath, steadied herself, and said, "Right. OK, here goes."

Eloise gripped the lasso, positioned the coil, and attempted what Sparky had said. She focused her intent and pictured the rope flying upward and coiling around the park bench. She set her will on the task, began a circling wind-up above her head, sent, "OK, Sparky, help me," and let it fly.

The rope unspooled more than it had on any other throw, and went higher than before, but it still fell back down.

She tried again. And again. And another score of times.

Exasperated, Eloise looked into her pocket at the green glow. "This isn't working."

"Of course it isn't," said Sparky. "You're forgetting something."

"What?" she asked. "What am I forgetting?"

Eloise tidied the rope, adjusted the lasso loop, and slid her arms through opposite sides of the coil so it rested on her forearms. She lifted it out of the wet filth so some of the slime could drip off.

"You need the magic word," said Sparky.

"Sorry, what?" Eloise knit her brow. "Magic words? You didn't say anything about magic words before. You mean like an incantation? I don't know any incantations."

"Not an incantation. Just the magic word."

"What are you talking about?"

"Think about it." Sparky produced a nondescript tuber from nowhere and chewed it, waiting.

Eloise stared at him, eyes narrowed. Then the coin dropped.

"You have got to be kidding."

"What?" said the mole-rat.

"Do you mean 'please?'"

"It's not called the 'magic word' for nothing."

"Really?"

"Try it."

"Please, Sparky, can you please help me do this?"

Without warning, Sparky grew from something that could fit in her hand to something twice her size. He towered over her with his pink, hairless body and his strange, protruding, independently moving teeth. "Throw it!" he boomed. "Throw it now! As hard and as far as you can! Go! Go! Go! Go! Go!"

The change to the mole-rat was so shocking that Eloise didn't think. On instinct, she dropped the coil down her forearms, grabbed it with both hands, and did what was second nature to her—spun into a hammer throw. The thigh-high muck made the complicated heel-and-toe foot movement difficult, and she couldn't do the initial spins over her head like a proper hammer. Instead, Eloise whirled her whole body, holding the coil with straight arms in front of her, keeping her hips, arms, chest, and face in a line. One, two, three, four turns—every muscle straining to give motion and momentum to the coil. Normally she let go on the fifth turn, but she kept spinning. Five, six, seven, eight, nine, ten turns. On the eleventh turn, she screamed, "Help me, Sparky!"

There was a pulse of dazzling emerald light through her pocket. A buzzing like a million bees filled her ears and a shock of energy and power crackled up and down her spine. In perfect hammer thrower style, Eloise howled as she gathered every weak weight of intent and will she could muster, and flung the loose coil up into the darkness.

It flew impossibly high and fast.

The dangling lasso end of the rope snagged itself around Eloise's wrist, tightening hard and fast. The flying coil of rope, propelled by the full force of strong magic channeled from the Star of Whatever, snatched her into the air. It was like being yanked upward by a careless giant.

Eloise felt bone and tendon crack and tear as the unexpected jerk broke her wrist and ripped her arm out of her shoulder socket.

Aaaaaaaaaahhhhhhhhhhh!!!

Eloise flew upward even faster than she had fallen as the rope rushed toward the mouth of the Whacking Great Hole, unspooling as it rose. It felt like the thing wanted to rip her arm off.

Aaaaaaaaaaaaaahhhhhhhhhhhhhh!!!!!

For length after length, Eloise soared toward the mouth of the Whacking Great Hole, which appeared first as a pinprick of light, then widened quickly to almost fill the sky.

She thought the rope would haul her out of the hole, but it didn't. The far end of it snaked over the edge, disappeared from sight, and suddenly the pull on her injured arm and wrist stopped.

Momentum kept Eloise flying upward, past lengths of rope that curved along below. With nothing lifting her, gravity kicked in and her rate of ascension slowed. She still came within 20 lengths of the hole's lip, but it might have been a thousand strong lengths away.

For a fraction of a second, gravity and momentum fought to a standstill, and she hung in midair. Eloise had a terrifying moment of exquisite clarity. She was about to drop to the full reach of the rope—easily 50 lengths down. She'd jerk at the bottom with her full body weight, and one of two things would happen. Scenario A: the bodged-together rope would snap and she'd plummet back to the bottom. Scenario B: the rope would hold and she'd jerk to a stop with her entire body weight straining against her dislocated arm and broken wrist.

Gravity did what gravity was wont to do, and began pulling her downward.

Aaaaaaaaaaaaaaaaahhhhhhhhhhhhhhhhh!!!!!

There wasn't much she could do about Scenario A. The thing would hold or it wouldn't. She'd have to deal with the consequences if that happened.

Scenario B, however, she could maybe do something about. If she could grab the rope with her other hand, maybe she could take the drop on her left arm instead of her right.

Aaaaaaaaaaaaaaaaaaaahhhhhhhhhhhhhhhhhhhh!!!!!

Two options: grab the rope she was whizzing past on the far side of the rope curve or grab the slack bit on her side of it. The former option would probably give her a serious rope burn, but was more likely to slow her descent. The latter would avoid the burn, but would maximize the jolt at the bottom.

Eloise decided to risk the burn.

She flung her left arm out and scrabbled for the rope. She grabbed it, clutched it to her body, tangled her legs into it, and squeezed. Length after length slithered past, and Eloise realized the soaked-in bottom slime was acting as a lubricant. She wasn't getting the horrid burn she'd expected, so she was able to apply more pressure for longer.

Hooray for Whacking Great Hole bottom slime, thought a detached part of her mind. It was a set of words she had never expected to think.

Aaaaaaaaaaaaaaaaaaaaaaaahhhhhhhhhhhhhhhhhhhhhhhhh!!!!!

Eloise jerked to a halt like a dropped puppet tied to a string. She caught most of it across her legs, but the bounce spun her, she lost her grip, and came to a dangling stop hanging from her dislocated arm.

Aaaaaaaaaaaaaaaaaaaaaaaaaaaahhhhhhhhhhhhhhhhhhhhhhhhhh!!!!!!!!

It hurt like a torture.

But she was alive. Scenario A had not come to pass. Not yet, anyway. She hoped that was a better result, but given the pain, she wasn't certain.

Plus, how in Çalaht's holy name was she supposed to get herself up the final 150 lengths with a ruined arm?

Aaaaaaaaaaaaaaaaaaaaaaaaaaaaaaaahhhhhhhhhhhhhhhhhhhhhhhhhhhhh!!!!!!!!!!!!

Eloise gave in to her pain with delirious crying and screaming, her throat raw, her voice spent, her howls ragged.

Through it, something niggled. Something seemed to want attention.

A voice.

"El!"

73

ACROBATIC PYTHON

Jerome saw it first.

He was sitting on a park bench near the rim of the Whacking Great Hole, staring at the marks in the snow and grieving. There was no other way to interpret the evidence. Princess Eloise Hydra Gumball III, his "El," had come all this way, only to leave the mortal realm this close to home. He'd failed her yet again as champion. Lorch was scrambling around trying to figure out where she had gone, but Jerome knew in his gut that his best friend was at the bottom of the hugest hole in the realm.

He wiped the back of his paw against his eye, holding back sniffles as best he could.

Suddenly, without warning, the longest, skinniest, most acrobatic black python Jerome had ever seen came screaming out of the hole and sped toward him. The chipmunk had only just flung himself out of the way when it wrapped itself around the bench in a complicated knot. A second slower or three weak lengths closer, and the python would have crushed Jerome in its coils.

The snake lay still, looking very dead for something that had been so active a moment before.

"Hello?" said Jerome. "Hey, mate. Are you OK?"

The snake seemed to have truly expired.

Jerome looked down its length. It was an impressive former python, with its tail stretching into the hole.

Except it couldn't have expired. It was still screaming.

Not a snake. A rope. And someone else screaming.

"El!" Jerome cupped his hands around his snout and shouted for Lorch. "The princess! It's the princess!"

Lorch, Hector, the Nameless One, and RoyLee rushed over to where Jerome was looking over the edge of the Whacking Great Hole. The princess dangled from the end of the rope, crying and yelling.

"Princess!" yelled Lorch. "Princess Eloise!"

No response.

"Come on!" Lorch, Jerome, and RoyLee grabbed the slippery rope "Ready?"

Hector grabbed on with his teeth, but immediately spat it out, gagging. "Çalaht haranguing hackneyed haymakers! That's... That's disgusting." Then he and the Nameless One bit down on the rope again.

"Pull!" commanded Lorch.

Eloise screamed as they yanked the rope up ten lengths.

"Hold on, hold on," said Hector, spitting out the rope again. He walked to the edge and poked his head over the rim. "Princess Eloise, what's the matter?"

She replied with more pained blubbering.

"Let's just get her out of there," said Jerome. "We'll figure it out when she's up."

"Agreed," said Lorch. "But if she's injured, then we should do this as smoothly as possible. On three. One, two..."

"The rope!" cried RoyLee. "It be fraying at the edge." Strands popped, one by one, as the rope rubbed on the edge of the hole.

Lorch leapt forward and grabbed the rope below the fray.

"Pull!" called Jerome.

There was more hysterical screaming from the princess as two horses, a wombat, a chipmunk, and a human hauled her up from the hugest hole in the realm. Lorch grabbed her under the arms and lifted her the final length.

Eloise was delirious, crying uncontrollably, and covered in filth.

"Goodness," said Hector. "She smells just like the rope tasted."

With one hand still supporting her, Lorch took off his cloak, spread it on the snow a safe distance from the hole's edge, and gently laid her on it.

Like he had when they'd found her after falling down Mortimer Falls, the guard began a practiced first-aid damage assessment, honed to speed and accuracy through years of practice on campaign. "No obvious head or spine damage. Substantial, widespread bruising from what looks like impact trauma. Legs appear normal. Shoulder issue. Wrist issue. No external bleeding. Internal bleeding unknown." Lorch pointed at the rope around Eloise's wrist. "I need to cut that off. It's acting like a tourniquet and I don't like the swelling, or the color of her hand. Jerome, can I please borrow your champion's sword?"

"Of course." The chipmunk slipped it from its scabbard, flipped it around, and handed Lorch the hilt.

"RoyLee, I need you to hold down her arm while I do this. I need her still while I cut away the rope. But be careful, I think her shoulder is dislocated. Nameless One, if you can keep a hoof on her chest, that'll help keep her from thrashing. Hector, I'm going to need a blanket, if you and Jerome can unpack one, please. And one of my tunics, preferably one of the less dirty ones."

The Nameless One stepped to Eloise's side and gently put a hoof on her sternum. RoyLee straddled her right arm so he could apply his full weight as an anchor. Hector and Jerome rushed to get a blanket and a tunic.

Lorch narrated what he was doing for Eloise, not seeming to care if she listened or not. "I'm going to brace your hand below the wrist to help RoyLee hold it in place. Now, I'm going to slide Jerome's sword blade between the rope loop and your wrist. I'm going to cut through it slowly so your blood flow eases back gently. You're doing fine, Princess Eloise. Doing fine." Lorch let a full minute pass between starting the cut and making it through the loop. "That should be feeling a bit worse now, as feeling returns. That's to be expected." He gently probed her wrist, which Eloise tried to pull away. "Princess, I think you've had a fracture. We're going to need to stabilize it until we get the healers to set it properly. RoyLee, please continue to help the princess keep her arm still. And talk to her."

"What about?"

"Anything. Just keep it soft and soothing."

As RoyLee began chatting about his favorite mosses to eat, Lorch handed the champion's sword back to Jerome, who set down a blanket and tunic and took it back. "I need you to put a pile of snow on her shoulder to contain the swelling," said the guard. "And talk to her as well."

"Got it." Jerome hurried to heap snow onto Eloise's shoulder.

Lorch looked around like he was trying to find something. He stood, walked the few steps to the park bench, drew his own sword, and with two quick, sharp cuts, hacked through its seat. The result was a loose board forty weak lengths long. He then tore the tunic Jerome had found in half at the side seams, folded the back bit neatly, tore the front part into strips, and rolled two of them. "Princess, I'm going to splint your wrist. This might be a little uncomfortable." He held one of the rolled bandages where she could see it. "This is for you to bite down onto. Would you like that?"

Eloise looked at him, nodded, opened her mouth, and clamped down on the cloth. It was the first response she'd given any of them that wasn't some form of wailing.

As gently and quickly as he could, Lorch placed the second roll in her palm, put the board against the underside of her forearm, and used the remaining tunic strips to wrap from fingers to elbow. When he was done, he checked her immobilized wrist. "I think that will do. What do you think, Princess?"

Eloise nodded.

"Now, Princess, unfortunately, this next bit won't be quite as fun."

The princess whimpered and shook her head. "Huh-uh," she said through the tunic roll in her mouth.

"I'm afraid we have to, Princess." Lorch's tone was soft but commanding. "You've dislocated your shoulder. I'm going to need to slide it back into place."

"Huh-uh. Huh-uh. Hurts too much." Eloise tried to squirm away, but the Nameless One's hoof kept her in place, as did RoyLee, her injured back, and the injured arm.

"Princess, that's a very reasonable position for you to take. I completely understand it. But I've seen this on campaign."

"Whuh?"

"It hurts a lot, right?"

"Uh-huh."

"When it's back in place, it'll hurt less. A lot less. I promise."

Lorch reached over and gave the princess's uninjured hand a small, comforting squeeze. It was so out of character that Eloise's eyes shot open. She furrowed her brow. "Thud suhruhs?" she mumbled through the tunic roll.

"Yes, Princess, it's that serious."

Eloise sniffed. "K. Duh uht."

"Do it. Right." Lorch nodded at RoyLee and the Nameless One. "Thank you, but I'll need her free now." When the wombat and horse were clear, Lorch sat down next to her, slipped one hand under her elbow, grabbed the splinted forearm with his other hand, and carefully moved her arm so it was at a 90-degree angle from her body. "Apologies, Princess, but..." Lorch swallowed and a light tinge of red flushed his face. "I'm sorry, I'm going to need to brace against your side. It will help with the leverage."

Eloise nodded. "Guh ahud."

He placed his feet against her torso, and slowly, steadily pulled the arm away from her body.

"Guuuuuuuh!" cried Eloise.

There was a "clunk" as the head of her humerus slid under the bone of her shoulder. Both Lorch and Eloise exhaled with relief. She tested her shoulder, winced, but nodded. Eloise took the rolled bit of tunic from her mouth and rasped, "Thank you, Guard Lacksneck of Lower Glenth."

"Princess, if you can sit up, please, I'll fashion a sling," said Lorch. He folded the front part of his tunic into a rough triangle, put it under her forearm, and tied it around her neck. "That will help with both the wrist and the shoulder. Can you stand?"

"Th-think so."

Lorch helped her up and wrapped the blanket around her. "You're shivering, Princess."

"W-winter?" she chattered.

"That, plus shock." Lorch turned to the others. "We need to go. The princess needs to be somewhere she can get warm, get clean, and get a healer's attention."

"Where?" asked Jerome. "Do you want to try to reach Castle de Brague?"

"No. Too far and too hard a ride. But I think I know exactly what the princess needs. Nameless One, can you carry both of us? I don't think the princess should try to ride on her own."

"S- S'okay," said Eloise, sniffling a yawn that pushed past her shivering.

"Princess, if you fall asleep or lose balance and fall off, you'll damage an already bad situation." Again, Lorch's cheeks reddened. "Please allow me to ride behind you and attend to your wellbeing."

Eloise, barely able to move, shrugged with one shoulder and trudged to the Nameless One's side. Lorch removed his pannier, tied it to Hector, helped RoyLee into it, and then lifted the princess onto the Nameless One's back, making sure her blanket was secure.

Through her pain and exhaustion, Eloise instinctively felt for the Star of Whatever. The lid of the box was flapped open, and the stone was gone. She gasped, looking, and swallowed back a panic. Quickly, she patted herself down. With a sigh of relief, she found it where she'd last put it—in the pocket with Odmilla's prayer beads. "Hey, Sparky," she whispered.

There was no reply.

Moments later, they were cantering away from the Whacking Great Hole. Eloise glanced around one last time, and hoped she'd never see the Çalaht-blighted hole ever again. She'd been twice, and perhaps if she squinted at the situation from the correct angle and ignored everything that had happened, she could consider it good fortune that she was still alive. No need to go again. That would be a "thrice" visit, which the not-very-good old saying said would be a curse.

It had certainly turned out that way for Turpy. She didn't think she'd ever shake the memory of the Star of Whatever turning him into dust.

"You should have listened to the stupid old saying," Eloise muttered to herself.

"What was that, Princess?" asked Lorch.

But Eloise was asleep.

They settled into the ride, and it was Jerome who finally asked the question that hung between them. "Does anyone have any idea what exactly happened back there?"

No one said a thing.

❧ 74 ☙

A HOT BATH AND A COOL HEALER

They reached the town of For The Love of Çalaht Cut It Out You Two, which was shrouded in winter and distinctly lacking in its previous grapefruitery. Lorch led them directly to a half-timbered five-story building a block off the town's main square.

"N-not here," said Eloise.

"Here," said Lorch.

"R-resources. Not enough for this place."

"Princess, the proper allocation of resources is the least of my concerns at the moment." With that, he helped her down from the Nameless One, supported her uninjured arm, and walked her into the Legs Not Arms.

There was a tasteful "ting" as the opening door rang a bell, a sound that evoked the giggles of the most cultured butterflies in the realm. That hadn't been there before, but otherwise, the reception area was the same—dark wood paneling, oak furniture, silver ornaments, and exquisite artwork. Also the same was the centipede at reception, with his red head, black body segments, cliff-sheer pompadour, and the silver rings on each of his legs. "Welcome to the—" he started.

"Master Lëëëäääfääännïïïhïïïlääätööör," said Lorch. It was the first time he'd gotten the centipede's name right. "Princess Eloise Hydra Gumball III requires a room."

"One does not just barge into the Legs Not Arms demanding—"

"She'll need the room immediately. Im-me-di-ate-ly. She'll need a hand-maid to draw a hot bath. And I need for you to fetch a healer who can attend to a wrist fracture."

Elgin Lëëëäääfääännïïïhïïïlääätööör looked at the filth-covered figure in rags wrapped in a blanket at Lorch's side. "I've met Princess Eloise, and I can assure you this is not she."

"Hello again, Master Lëëëäääfääännïïïhïïïlääätööör," croaked Eloise. "Lovely to be here again. I would be most grateful—"

"Princess! What in Çalaht's great garden of greenery has happened to you?" Without waiting for a reply, the centipede raised his body and brought his full weight down on a desk bell. Its clang was a klaxon compared to the delightful tinkle of the door. Before it finished rever-berating, a dozen grasshoppers in bellhop uniforms flooded into Reception. "You!" he said to the closest. "See Princess Eloise to the Suite En Low."

"But, sir—"

"Just do it. She needs to be on the ground floor. We can adjust the furnishings to something more appropriate later. You!" he said to the next. "Go into town and tell Goodwoman Íïîméëèldáää that her healing talents are required *tout de suite*. See if one of the llamas is avail-able to take you. It'll be faster."

"A llama, sir? But—"

"Do it. Now. Just go."

"Yes, sir."

"You! Tell my wife of our guest's arrival."

"Yes, sir!"

"You! Inform the kitchen that an impromptu menu is going to be required and that they should consult with me about it."

"Yes, sir."

"You!" This one was at Lorch. "Will you be seeing to the princess's change of attire or shall I?"

"I will see to that," said Lorch. "With regard to coin—"

"We do not need to address that just now. There will be time."

"Thank you. That's—"

"That, too, can wait. Now let's bring her to her room."

Within half an hour, Eloise was sitting on the edge of a bathtub of water that was deliciously just a little too hot against her legs. She wasn't sure if she should undo the bandages around her torso to wash the burns on her back, or if she should leave them in place until she got home, despite their filth.

A brusque, ample woman barged into the room without knocking, dismissing the handmaid who'd undressed Eloise with a wave and a stern look. The woman carried a bag that looked like it was sewn together from cut up tapestries, and wore a brown crofter's smock, and an impressive pair of incongruously fancy shoes, a pinched expression, and hair pulled back in a severe trio of braids that were, in turn, braided together and hung down to her waist.

"My name is Íïìméëèldáäà Cóöòsmáäàr. I'm the healer hereabouts."

"Pleased to meet you, I'm—"

"I've been informed who you are."

The herbwoman circled the tub three times, assessing Eloise grimly. "You are, simply put, a disturbing mess. Your back. Your hand. Your shoulder. Bruises from top to bottom, and you smell like you'll need three baths before you're actually clean."

"Things have been... Well, they've been eventful."

"Many people undergo eventful times and manage to not pass for orphaned urchins cast out from their devotional houses and left to rummage the garbage middens of the Sclerotic Wold."

A scolding wasn't what Eloise needed—there would be plenty of that when she got home. But she was too tired and too sore, so she let the healer have her say with nothing more than a "Yes, mistress" in reply.

Íïméëèldáää opened the tapestry bag, which was full of gallipots, bottles, and implements of her trade, and pulled out a small, brown, stoppered vial. She sprinkled precisely ten drops into the tub water. "Horsetail oil. Reduces pain and swelling around broken bones." Next, she produced a thin, sharp blade. "Now, let me take off the bandages so I can see what disasters await me there."

She sliced away the dream wife's poultices, sucking air through her teeth as commentary. "Slide into the tub, and I'll look at this hand."

Eloise did as she was told, and tried to enjoy the bath as much as she could with the healer fussing with her wrist. There was another sucking of air when the wrist was fully exposed.

"That would have hurt," said Íïméëèldáää. "And you say that this..." She gently felt the swelling at Eloise's shoulder, "...happened at the same time?"

"Yes, mistress."

"Whatever you were playing at, I suggest you don't do it again."

"Yes, mistress."

The healer drew out a bundle of neatly rolled, beautifully white bandages and a bowl. Into that she began mixing together a white paste, like she was starting some kind of arts and crafts project. "If I were you, I'd stop by a devotional house and make an offering. You were lucky."

"Was I, mistress?" Eloise wasn't feeling particularly lucky at that moment, and she certainly had no intention of darkening the door of a devotional house.

"Yes, you were. Whoever was the first to attend the burns on your back was not a complete incompetent. You've no fever, nor pus running everywhere. I mean, there's plenty of infection and pus—you can smell it now that the rest of your odors are not dominating the air. But it is certainly not as bad as what it ought to be. I would rate your chances of healing with only horrific scarring, and not atrocious disfigurement, as highly likely."

"Horrific scarring is good?"

"In your case, yes, it is, given how this could have gone. I've seen much less do much worse to people."

"Well, thank Çalaht then."

"Yes, blessed be the Divine One." Íïîméëèldáäà poked her head out the door and bellowed, "I need the handmaid back. Tell her to bring a loofah."

Two hours later, Eloise had been scrubbed like a kitchen floor supervised by a military commandant, smelled like a florist's guessing game, and was chewing a fat wad of willow bark shreds. Her hand was bound in a plaster cast that prevented any movement. Her back was smeared with a new variety of ointments, unctions, and oils, and the ample poultice was bound to her with fresh bandages around her torso. Her shoulder ached, but was tolerable, and she could move it a little again.

"Put this on," said Íïîméëèldáäà, handing her a fresh linen shift. "Drink the tea. Say your prayers to Çalaht. Get some sleep. Eat when you wake. Understood?"

"Yes, mistress. And thank you for your ministrations. I'll ask my companion to bring his coin purse."

The healer waved that away. "I have an arrangement with Master Lëëëääfääännïïîhïïîlääätööör. You need not worry about that. I would ask one thing."

"What would that be, Goodwoman Íïïméëèldáäà?"

"Dedicate yourself to the Divine One. Live a holy life following the word of Çalaht. You've been given a second, if not a third or fourth chance. Don't waste it."

"I'll do what I can, mistress. I won't take vows, but I'll be guided by her goodness."

The herbwoman looked at her, waiting for more. When nothing else came, she sniffed. "I guess that will have to do. May Çalaht guide your days and light your ways. Goodbye."

And she was gone.

Eloise closed the door and latched it to ensure her privacy. She touched her travel cloak, newly cleaned. Through it, hanging by its sash on the same peg, she felt the box for the Star of Whatever. The stone was back in it, the box had snicked shut, and Sparky was silent. She lifted the cloak and saw the slim line of emerald light that escaped through the crack.

Bed. She was going to become very comfortable, and sleep as long as she could. Eloise slipped between sheets that were as good as anything she'd find at Castle de Brague, fluffed a buckwheat-stuffed pillow that was a magical balance of firmness and softness, and closed her eyes.

There was a sharp knock.

She ignored it. Whatever it was, it could wait. Probably the handmaid returning her tunic and breeks.

Another knock, louder this time. "Princess? Princess Eloise?"

Lorch.

"Guard Lacksneck, I'm just fine. Trying to sleep. Can we talk in an hour or two or 100?"

"Princess, I'm sorry. I must speak with you now."

"What? Wait. Hold on."

Eloise hauled herself out of bed, draped a blanket over herself to cover the immodesty of the shift, and unlatched the door. "What's going on?"

Lorch was cleaned, shaved, and dressed ready to ride. "Princess, we must leave immediately."

Eloise yawned. "Sorry, it just sounded like you said we have to leave immediately. Whatever for? What could possibly be going on that can't wait until after we've all slept and had a decent, overpriced meal?"

"I don't know, Princess. I'm sorry. A pair of horses from Hector's Horse Guards have just arrived from Castle de Brague at full gallop. Their message to him and to you is clear: we must leave at once for the castle. Don't pack. Don't dawdle. Just go."

"Why?"

"I don't think they know. But it's a direct order from Queen Eloise. I've brought garments." He held out a small bundle of warm winter clothes, including a new pair of serviceable riding breeks and a new tunic.

"Right. I'll be ready in five."

❈   75   ❈

IT'S MOTHER

Lorch was right. Hector's two horse guards had been given exactly one instruction: get to Eloise as fast as possible and bring her home without delay.

Not good, thought Eloise. *Very not good.*

Hector, with Eloise and Jerome on his back, charged down the Queen's Roadway at full gallop. Beside him raced Lorch, RoyLee, and the Nameless One. Despite having rushed to For The Love of Çalaht Cut It Out You Two, the horse guards—a bay stock horse mare named Twellton and a black one named Ëëëniïïïd—ran back with them as escorts.

It would normally take two days to get from For The Love of Çalaht Cut It Out You Two to Brague, but Hector set a blistering pace, cutting hours off the journey. Instead of the better road to Itchy (recently renamed Pustule), they took the shorter, more steeply curved, less maintained route back to Itchier (now called Ulcerated Carbuncle). Charging along the more difficult path, they reached the village, stopped just long enough to let the horses catch their breaths and grab a quick bite at the inn they'd stopped at before, I Still Think "Dangly Dale" Was Just Fine. Then it was down Cleanest Facilities

Anywhere Street, across the Children Eat Free fields, and up Mount Try Our Lovely Scones.

Eloise's mind worked overtime as Hector bolted along the road beneath the moonlight. It wasn't like before. There were no habits niggling and no recoiling from Hector's sweat as it soaked through her breeks. Now, her full focus was on why they'd been recalled to the castle so urgently. She couldn't think of a reason that wasn't unpleasant. A war declared? A crisis of Court? Some sort of diplomatic fracas? Only a war would seem urgent enough for Eloise to need to return with such haste. But there were no signs of war, and the tightlipped horse guards didn't seem to know anything about anything.

So she brooded and kept her focus on making the ride as easy for Hector as she could. There was no chatter among the party. Everyone seemed lost in the same kinds of thoughts, full of speculation but with no answers.

When they reached the First Night Inn (formerly the First Knight Inn), the moon was well past halfway through its night's journey across the sky. The horses were lathered and exhausted.

"It's up to you, Princess, but I suggest we rest here," said Lorch. "Grab four hours of sleep and be gone again at dawn."

"Agreed?" asked Eloise.

"Agreed," said the others.

Mistress Spleenfluke greeted them in the courtyard, served them the inn's famous three bean soup—this time spiced with curry, cumin, and chillies—then led Eloise to a small spare room where she was grateful to topple onto the bed, and fell instantly asleep.

Dawn arrived rudely soon and before Eloise knew it, they were gathering in the inn's courtyard, ready to set out for the day's ride to Brague.

"Princess," said Hector. "Horse Guard Twellton and Horse Guard Ëëëniïïd have offered to carry you and Lorch, and give the Nameless One and me a bit of a break today. Would that be acceptable?"

"That's very kind of them. Is it OK with you?"

"It has been a long, hard run, and we have a full day ahead. I think we'll go faster if we make the change at least for a few hours."

"Then, fine. Of course."

Mere minutes later, the horses were galloping through a thick cover of old snow, new frost, and a dull red early morning light.

The closer they got to Brague, the tighter Eloise's stomach got. Her sense of foreboding grew, not based on any facts or observations, but just a gut knowing. Exactly what her guts knew, she had no idea.

I'll find out soon enough.

After a few hours of riding, Jerome wrapped his claws in Twellton's mane and turned around to check on Eloise. "You OK, El?"

"I think so," she said. "I mean, physically, I'm handling it, although my wrist, shoulder, and back are all throbbing. But this race to the castle has me worried. Very, very worried."

"Yeah, I know," said the chipmunk. "Another few hours and we'll find out."

Eloise, Jerome, Lorch, and RoyLee changed to Hector and the Nameless One and back several times during the day. Lorch insisted on real quarter-hour breaks every two finger's width of sun across the clear winter sky. It let them reach Brague by mid-afternoon instead of at night. They rushed ahead of other traffic to the grand, main entrance, the monolithic William Gates, where the guards, obviously expecting them, waved them through without a word. Hector led the way, rushing through the streets of Brague until they reached the castle gates, which stood open, waiting, then clanged shut behind them.

By the time Hector, the Nameless One, and their escorts stopped at the main entrance to Castle de Brague, their chests heaved like bellows.

Eloise slid off, said, "Thank you," and sprinted for the door.

Someone opened it before she reached it.

Johanna.

"What?" said Eloise, stopping short.

"Where have you been?" Johanna waved her forward, and gave her a short, hard hug. "What happened to you?"

"Why are you here?" said Eloise, wincing at the pressure on her back and shoulder and trying to keep her broken wrist out of the way. "Why aren't you at Stained Rock?"

"What took you so long?" Johanna gave her a last squeeze, then held her at arm's length. "I didn't think you'd make it."

"What do you mean, 'make it?'"

"It's Mother."

❧ 76 ☙

SOME MEASURE OF DISTRESS

Eloise and Johanna burst into the Salle de la Famille and found King Chafed sitting on a chair outside his and the queen's bedchamber with his face in his hands. He looked up when he heard them, his bloodshot eyes brimming with tears. "Your mother wants to see Eloise alone for a few moments." He sniffed. "I'm... I'm glad you made it. Now go."

"What—"

"Go."

Eloise stepped past him and pushed open the door.

The queen lay on her bed propped up by pillows. She looked impossibly thin, like she'd been fasting for months.

"Mother! Mother, what's wrong?"

"I fear you have returned with most excellent timing." Queen Eloise placed a claw-like hand on her daughter's cheek, stroking it. It was the most familiar thing she'd done since Eloise had stopped carrying dollies around. "I'd planned to rule a bit longer, despite everything." She waved vaguely, indicating her body. "If nothing else, I wanted to give you a fraction more time to grow up. Plus, there were things I still wanted to do. Wrongs to right. Projects to carry out." She put her hand back down to the cover, like holding it up was too much effort. "It is not to be."

"Mother, what are you saying?"

"I'm saying that the queendom will need you soon. Very soon, I suspect." She coughed into a handkerchief and tried to hide the spot of blood. "Look at you. Your hair. Your hand. Your..." She waved vaguely again, this time at her daughter. "Your everything. There's a story there. Perhaps I'll hear it."

"What happened? You were fine when I left."

"A blueberry pie."

"I don't understand."

"Not a week after you left, we had blueberry pie for dessert. You like blueberry pie, don't you?"

"Yes. Yes, I do. Maybe not as much as key lime pie, but blueberry will do. What does that—"

"You're going to have to hush and let me speak. This is harder than it looks."

"Yes, Mother." Eloise sat on a chair next to the bed and slid it closer. She took her mother's hand and laced her fingers into it. Eloise hadn't done that in a decade at least, and didn't know if the queen would allow it. Her mother gave a weak squeeze. Permission. Eloise squeezed back, and whispered, "Go ahead."

"Not much to say, really. It was a delicious blueberry pie. A tasty tribute to all of Chef's culinary prowess. There were a couple of crunchy bits, but nothing really to worry about."

Dread crept up from Eloise's stomach to her throat. "Except there was."

"Except there was," agreed the queen. "It soon became clear that someone had hidden two raw haggleberries in my portion. It was not long before I was experiencing, let's say, some degree of digestive distress. But by then, the damage was done. And here we are."

"How is that possible? Chef guards the kitchen and all it touches like a mother Komodo dragon with a tooth abscess. Unless she..."

"Chef was not responsible. Not as far as anyone can tell. We're pretty certain someone placed the haggleberries in my dessert between the kitchen and the table. One of the servers, a goanna who'd not been in service as long as some of the others, went missing shortly thereafter. They found her hanging by the neck in the woodshed just outside the kitchen. There were signs of struggle, and her legs were bound. The end of her life was, let's say, assisted."

"This is terrible."

"Yes. There's no question that terrible things have happened while you were gone. I've had the matter of the young goanna looked into. She had no affiliations to any known groups who wished me ill, and had no personal grudges that we could identify. There were some gambling debts in her family, and a cousin with a rare ague that needed expensive treatment. Perhaps those made her vulnerable to blackmail. But the connections are tenuous, and the source herself is unavailable for questioning. What's clear, though, is that someone wanted me dead, or at least significantly damaged."

"For the love of Çalaht, Mother. That's, that's... That's unthinkable."

"Sadly, you're wrong there. It was thought. It was acted upon. Not everyone favors the throne."

"How's Chef handling it?"

"Chef took her own life."

The five words hit Eloise like a fist to the stomach. She was already reeling from what she was seeing in front of her, but somehow, Chef's act of self-harm and all its implications were somehow more fathomable than her mother's grave illness and all that might mean. Chef was gone. And gone by her own hand.

The queen continued. "I didn't want her to do anything like that. I spoke to her directly, trying to assuage her. I truly did not think the incident was her fault. I still don't. But she was deeply distraught, as you can imagine. It happened on her watch. In her food. In her domain. It was all too much for her, and a week after it happened, when the full extent of the damage to my digestive system was becoming clear, she barred herself in her room, ate a last scone, and downed a substantial number of dead cap mushrooms. When the kitchen wenches and scullery maids finally got enough nerve to have a guard break in, she was gone."

The queen reached for a goblet of water, but had trouble lifting it. Talking was exhausting her. Eloise picked up the goblet with her good hand and held it to the queen's mouth at a careful angle so her mother could sip.

"We can fight this, Mother," said Eloise. "We can get you better. Someone will have an answer."

"I thought that for a while, too. Called in all the healers, bleeders, apothecaries, chirurgeons, spiritualists, and whoever else might have helped, whether certified by a guild or not. I've swallowed every nostrum, herb, potion, and tonic that anyone thought might do some good. When those didn't work, I then turned to all manner of quackery, hoping that some random element in their fakery might be efficacious." Her voice dropped to a whisper. "Yet, here we are."

"I'll find—"

"Eloise, dear, let's use this time some other way. There are things to speak of."

"Where did the raw haggleberries come from? You've always had such strict controls on them. It's not like they grow around here."

The queen lifted her shoulders. Barely a shrug. "They are small. Perhaps someone had a weak magic for concealment. Plus, there is a haggleberry bush nearby. Very nearby, it turns out."

"Oh."

"The old apothecary reminded me of it. It came from one of his seeds."

"You don't mean..."

"Your sister's garden. Her first plant in there. It was a haggleberry bush. Don't you remember? You and I visited it once when it was just a seedling, before the garden became verboten to us all."

"You think that the haggleberries came from Johanna's bush?"

Queen Eloise moved her hands in the slightest "who knows?" motion.

"I'm sorry, Mother, but that's not possible," said Eloise.

"Of course it's possible."

"No, Mother, it's not."

"And why not? She has the plant. It bears fruit. It's not exactly a stretch."

"Because Johanna grew that plant using her weak magic," said Eloise. "Its fruit can't harm you because you can't use magic against blood."

"Ah. 'Knackknick, chili stick, periwinkle, spud...'" quoted the queen.

Eloise finished the nursery rhyme. "'No kiss for my sweetheart, no magic against blood.' That's right, Mother. You ought to be able to swallow a dozen raw haggleberries from Johanna's plant and they shouldn't hurt you. Not that I'd be game to test it."

Eloise watched her mother's face as she considered this new idea. The queen hadn't lost any of her sharpness of mind. It was just her body giving out.

Queen Eloise raised the back of her hand and dabbed at the corner of her eye. "That's... That's a weight off my mind." She sighed, relaxing. "Make sure you mention it to your sister and father. It will help."

"I will." Eloise blinked back her own tears. "What can I do for you? What do you need?"

"I need you to listen. And then I need to rest." The queen gave Eloise's hand another small squeeze, then let go. She extended her index finger like she was going to count. "First, don't refer to your father as 'the dowager king' or the 'queen father.' I don't care what Protocol says, he won't like either of those, and he's going to feel displaced enough as it is."

"Of course not." Eloise stood. "Mother, please, don't go yet. I'm only just back. I have so much to tell you. And if I'm going to be queen, which trust me, I don't want to be—not yet—I need you to tell me how to do it."

"Shhhh... You've been watching me for years. You'll know more than you think. Now, sit. Second, the First Advisor is smart and loyal. He knows where the bodies are buried, much better than your father, who doesn't have the mind or temperament for that kind of thing. Most of the bodies will be metaphorical, but not all. I suggest you keep the First Advisor in his role, at least for a while. That is, unless untoward evidence comes to light, in which case, he's best dealt with swiftly. And permanently. Do you understand what I'm saying?"

"I think so."

"Third..." Without warning, Queen Eloise dropped off into an unexpected nap. It was like her body was rationing the amount of advice she could dispense or the amount of wakefulness she had left.

This is a nightmare, thought Eloise. She stared at her mother, petrified. *This really can't be happening.* As the moments dragged into minutes, Eloise counted the queen's shallow breaths, wondering how long she should sit alone, waiting. Would she sleep for hours?

Her becoming queen was supposed to be a "someday out there maybe later" kind of thing.

Not this. Not a matter of a finite number of breaths measured in, what? Low thousands? Hundreds? Dozens?

With an unflattering snort, the queen jerked back to awareness. She licked her lips, turned her head, and looked toward a makeshift desk next to her bed. "Oh, by the way. It's a little late, but happy birthday. There's a present for you over there. Johanna's already had hers."

Eloise reached for the desk but her mother stopped her. "Later."

"Yes, Mother."

"You know what's silly?"

"What?"

"I have a craving for blueberry pie."

"I'll call for some."

The queen closed her eyes, slowly shaking her head. "It would be wasted. Nice, but wasted."

Eloise sniffed, sniffed again, and looked for a handkerchief. She ended up using the filthy hem of her travel cloak. "I'll have a blueberry pie brought in. You can smell it. That might be nice—the odor of blueberry pie wafting around the room. It might give you strength. You're going to need your strength if you're going to fight this."

"Shhhhh." The queen made a slight wave. "Too much."

"Sorry, Mother. We can sit here and imagine the smell of blueberry pie."

"Nice." She smiled and opened one eye, looking at Eloise. "Good to see you again."

"Would you like to hear about my journey? I—"

"Shhh."

"Mother, please. I really want to talk to you."

"Shh."

Eloise took her mother's hand again. It was colder than it had been before. Eloise cried openly as she raised it to her lips and kissed it.

The queen opened her eyes, her pupils much too wide for the amount of light in the room. She looked at Eloise. Looked through her. Looked through to an infinity that only she could see. Slowly, like a morning glory seeking the dawn, the queen's head turned, then eased gently backward, pressing into her pillows. There was an almost imperceptible tightening on Eloise's hand, and the tiniest shudder through her body. A shallow inhale. A bare exhale.

Nothing followed.

"Mother, no," whispered Eloise. "Not now. Not yet." Her tears blurred the death dance.

There were small, almost-breathing motions, but they were echoes only, habits of a body that no longer needed them. Another tiny idea of a shudder. Then an even smaller one.

Gouache had headed toward death with violence and confusion, and was lucky to have dodged it. Death came to Melveeta with the weight of centuries dropping on her like a boulder. Doncaster, felled by the Purple Haze, did death the kindness of meeting it halfway. Turpy unwittingly invited death to him, and it consumed him like a ravenous ghost.

But death found Queen Eloise quiet, ready, and waiting. It took her by the hand and whispered, "Come, beloved. I will guide you to stand at Çalaht's side."

The hand Eloise held went limp. She clasped it her cheek, unable to accept what had just happened.

The door cracked opened. It was Johanna. "El? Is everything..."

Eloise shook her head.

Johanna hurried in, calling over her shoulder, "Father! Father, now!"

The king banged through the door, rushed to the far side of the bed and grabbed his wife's hand. "Elsie. Elsie, sweetheart. Elsie, my love." Chafed dropped to his knees and sobbed. "Don't. Don't, don't, don't. Just don't."

But she had.

"I'm sorry, Father," said Eloise.

She placed her mother's hand on top of the covers, stood, and took a step back to give her father space. Johanna put an arm around Eloise's shoulder and gently squeezed. Eloise leaned into her.

A healer in a black robe bustled into the room carrying a tray of teas and medicaments. She stopped short when she saw the grieving family and the queen's slackness. The healer masked her face in professionalism, set the tray down on a side table, and strode forward. "Excuse me," she said to the twins, going past them to the bed.

"Pardon me, your Highness." It wasn't clear if she was speaking to Chafed or the departed. The woman felt for a pulse at the wrist, lifted an eyelid, then felt for a pulse at the neck. She took a step back and curtsied to the body. "The queen is dead," said the healer in a voice soft enough to be respectful, but loud enough to be definitive.

Then she turned and faced Eloise, curtsied again, and in the exact same tone, said, "Long live the queen."

EPILOGUE

Jerome looked over Eloise's gown. "I didn't know Lurid Eddie designed dresses as well as carriages," he said.

Eloise glanced in the full-length mirror and smoothed down the front of her outfit, a jaw-clenchingly ornate explosion of brocade, embroidery, gussets, crinoline, chiffon, taffeta, and two dozen other mismatched dressmaking miscreants who shouted for the onlooker's attention. "I know, right?" she said. "It's like Lurid Eddie took all his worst impulses, went to a fabric monger, said, 'Some of each,' and then sewed them all together under the influence of a raging fever."

"Hold still," said Johanna. "There are still about a thousand buttons to go."

"Odmilla was happy to do it," said Eloise.

"Your handmaid has very kindly given me permission to do it. She allowed that it was not every day one might help one's sister dress for becoming queen." Johanna gave Eloise a small squeeze on the shoulder.

"You know, that collar makes you look like a frilled neck lizard," said Jerome. "Not that having a lizard neck is necessarily a problem."

"This thing is a monstrosity," said Eloise.

"The Raiment of the Queens is a tradition," said Johanna. "But it definitely wasn't designed to fit someone wearing a cast on their forearm and with bandages plastered to their back."

"Sorry," said Eloise, waggling her cast.

"Really, El, hold still. The buttons are hard enough as it is."

Jerome pointed at the dress with his tail. "Couldn't you get Seamstress Linttrap to whip you up something a little less likely to induce a diabetic coma?"

"Apparently not. She'll be doing all my other outfits—the coronation gown, the reception gown, the Queen's Ball gown, and about three score others. Those are all going to be fabulous. But for the Crown Plonking itself? It's this abomination. My mother wore it, and her mother, and hers, all the way back to Agnes Delion Frostbite Gumball herself."

"One just wishes tradition wasn't so ugly," said Jerome.

"Seamstress Linttrap assures me that two centuries ago it was about as chic as it got."

"Agnes Delion Frostbite Gumball did not wear this dress," said Johanna, buttoning the upper arm of a sleeve.

"What do you mean?" said Eloise. "That's what everyone says. Even she said it."

"Agnes Delion Frostbite Gumball would have worn the oldest parts. I bet if we found a record, it would describe the tiniest bit of what's here. It might even have been elegant."

"Okay, good point." Eloise tugged on the collar. "Each queen adds to the thing somehow. I think Mother had these lacy cuffs put on. Grandmother probably had all this red embroidery of cherubs holding apples added. Apparently, she liked that kind of thing."

"Have you added to it?" asked Jerome.

"You mean, besides slitting the sleeve so my cast will fit, having laces fitted to the back to accommodate my bandages, and having a 'matching' sling made?" Eloise smoothed down the front of it again. "I feel kind of bad for the dress. The poor thing has had to put up with so much. So I kept my creative contribution simple." She lifted the frill of her collar to reveal new embroidery—bright green stitching just above the heart. It depicted a particular glowing stone radiating emerald light in all directions. "It's all I could think of, and they were rushing me."

"I kind of like it," said Jerome. "It'll give your successors something to wonder about."

"Successors? We haven't even had the Crown Plonking yet, and you're thinking about successors?"

"Sorry, that's the way these things work." Jerome nodded and Eloise lowered the frill. "I don't get the point of this Crown Plonking procedure anyway. Why don't they just do one thing, the coronation, instead of two?"

"I know," said Eloise. "I mean, Mother is still lying in state. It seems rushing it to declare a new queen. Unseemly, even."

"Protocol is very clear about this," said Johanna. "In fact, it eats this kind of thing for breakfast. The issue is the awareness Protocol has of the need to organize properly for a coronation. It takes months. Months! All that planning. All that catering. The invitations. The need for people to travel. The entertainment. The pomp, the circumstance, and the negotiations and haggling over niggling details that no one in their right mind would find important, but that some pedant somewhere will stake his life on. It all takes time." She moved to Eloise's other side and started working on the buttons of her sleeve. "Look at it this way. The Crown Plonking is a bit like eloping before you get married. Protocol wants to make sure there is no question that someone's running the realm. So they dress the new queen in this bit of history, plonk a crown on her head, let her go ahead and start queening, and then give everyone plenty of time to create a coronation that people can be proud of, which reflects the tastes and preferences of the new monarch."

Jerome shrugged. "Makes sense."

"You know, it was nice to live without Protocol for a while," said Eloise. "But, well, so it goes." She wriggled inside the dress a little, adjusting it on her body. "How are those buttons going, Jo? Are your fingers reduced to bone yet?"

"There are rather a lot of them."

"Well, thanks for your help."

"When I have my coronation in a couple of months, you can come to the Half Kingdom and button my dress for me."

"I'd... I'd like that."

"We have a deal then."

Eloise gave a vague wave. "This is so much your kind of thing, Jo. The Protocol and planning and everything. You'll be good at it."

"Yeah, Protocols and Procedures wasn't exactly your favorite class."

"No."

Jerome stepped in front of Eloise so he could see himself in the bottom bit of the mirror and adjusted the angle of the strap on his ceremonial sword. "So, are you nervous?"

"Of course she's nervous," said Johanna. "Who wouldn't be nervous becoming queen?" Johanna looked at her sister. "Sorry, didn't mean to jump in. Are you nervous?"

"Of course I'm nervous. Who wouldn't be nervous becoming queen? I'm too young for this."

"So was Mother. She did OK."

"I'm younger than Mother was. And Grandmother was most certainly not OK at being queen. What if I'm more Grandmother than Mother?"

There was a soft knock at the door.

"Come in," called Eloise.

Lorch poked his head inside. "Princess Eloise, they're ready for you. Shall I let them know you're coming?"

"Oh, gosh. Already."

"Yes, Princess Eloise."

"Jo, is the button nightmare almost done here?"

"Just about. Two minutes more, then yes."

"I'll tell them," said Lorch, and he closed the door.

Eloise, Johanna, and Jerome were silent as Johanna made the last adjustments to the gown. She slipped the sling over the front of the dress and helped Eloise put her arm in, then stepped back and nodded. "Stunning."

"With this dress, that's probably literally true," said Eloise. She swallowed. "Well, this is it, I guess."

Jerome waved her toward the door. "After you, Queen Eloise," said Jerome.

"Don't call me that. I'm not queen yet."

"Get used to it, El. In about 20 minutes that crown's going to be sitting on your queenly pate."

Eloise blanched.

Johanna saw her expression and reached out her with left hand. With her right, she flashed a word in the now-disused sign language they'd made up as girls. *Ready?*

Most of me thinks 'no,' Eloise signed back. *But the small, calm part of me says, 'As ready as I'm going to be.' That might have to do.*

Good. Johanna smiled. *Go show them what a queen looks like.*

Right. I think I'll do that.

490

✦

Thank you for reading *The Light Bearer*!

Next up is *The Crown Plonked Queen*. You'll definitely want to find out what happens to Eloise now that her mother's passed on and she's going to be queen. To say she's in over her head would be a total under-statement.

✦

Want to read more about Eloise and Jerome? Six months before the start of *The Purple Haze*, they
played hooky from Court and headed out for a stolen adventure. It goes well. And then it really doesn't.
Claim your copy of The Wombanditos today to find out what happened!

✦

And if you're wondering just what exactly happened at their Thorning Ceremony that caused Eloise and Johanna to go from being as close as twins can be to as estranged, then you'll definitely want to check out the standalone prequel novel, *The Thorning Ceremony*. I promise you, you'll never guess what caused the rift.

THANK YOU

Thank you for reading *The Light Bearer*. Reviews are crucial for helping other readers discover new books to enjoy. If you want to share your love for Eloise, Jerome, and all the gang, please consider please leave a review. I'd really appreciated it.

Recommending my work to others is also a huge help. Feel free to give this book and the whole series a shout-out in your favourite book recommendation group to spread the word.

ACKNOWLEDGMENTS

It is a joy to get to say thank you to those who have helped me bring this book to the world.

Tamsin Dean Einspruch, our daughter, has been with this story the whole way. When I'm not sure of an idea, she's the one I got to first for perspective and thoughts on words. She is my first reader and helped me talk through the story when I got stuck.

Many, many thanks to my alpha and beta readers Cheryl Hannah, Olivia Martinez, Brian Busby, and Jacqueline Chambo. Cheryl was, again, the first person outside my family to read the manuscript, and her encouragement continues to give me the heart needed to keep going. Olivia, Brian, and Jacqueline brought keen eyes to the words, and provided very different perspectives to what they read. Valuable and valued input all.

Thank you as always to my editor, Vanessa Lanaway, and my proofreader, Abigail Nathan. Y'all continue to rock, and I'm so grateful for what you do.

Thank you to Maria Spada for the fantastic cover.

Finally, a huge, massive thank you to my wife and partner, Billie Dean. As with the previous books, her knowledge and teachings of shamanism and magic have shaped my understanding and given rise to many of the words and ideas within these pages. I love you and I thank you. L^3.

Andrew Einspruch

July 2019

ABOUT THE AUTHOR

Andrew Einspruch is fond of the wordy, the nerdy, and the funny, which means that if you arranged for him to have lunch with Weird Al Yankovic, Tom Lehrer, William Gibson, and any of the Monty Python guys, he'd be your friend forever. Visit his web site for a complete list of his books at andreweinspruch.com.

Andrew is an ex-pat Texan living in Australia, and is the co-founder of the not-for-profit charity the Deep Peace Trust, which fosters deep peace and non-violence for all species. With his wife and daughter, he runs the Trust's farm animal and wild horse sanctuary. (You can see why there's the odd animal or two in his books.)

If pressed, he'll deny he ever coded in COBOL for a bank.

If you haven't done so yet, use the QR code below to claim your copy of the standalone prequel, *The Wombanditos*.

www.ingramcontent.com/pod-product-compliance
Lightning Source LLC
Chambersburg PA
CBHW020001120726
47903CB00004B/1077